Sophie Pembroke has bee[n] and writing romance ever [since] Mills & Boon as part of he[r] degree at Lancaster University, so getting to write romantic fiction for a living really is a dream come true! Born in Abu Dhabi, Sophie grew up in Wales and now lives in a little Hertfordshire market town with her scientist husband, her incredibly imaginative and creative daughter and her adventurous, adorable little boy. In Sophie's world, happy *is* for ever after, everything stops for tea, and there's always time for one more page...

Cara Colter shares her home in beautiful British Columbia, Canada, with her husband of more than thirty years, an ancient crabby cat and several horses. She has three grown children and two grandsons.

COPENHAGEN ESCAPE WITH THE BILLIONAIRE

SOPHIE PEMBROKE

THEIR HAWAIIAN MARRIAGE REUNION

CARA COLTER

MILLS & BOON

First published in Great Britain 2025
by Mills & Boon, an imprint of HarperCollins*Publishers* Ltd,
1 London Bridge Street, London, SE1 9GF

www.harpercollins.co.uk

HarperCollins*Publishers*, Macken House, 39/40 Mayor Street Upper,
Dublin 1, D01 C9W8, Ireland

Copenhagen Escape with the Billionaire © 2025 Sophie Pembroke

Their Hawaiian Marriage Reunion © 2025 Cara Colter

ISBN: 978-0-263-39670-6

01/25

This book contains FSC™ certified paper
and other controlled sources to ensure responsible forest management.

For more information visit www.harpercollins.co.uk/green.

Printed and Bound in the UK using 100% Renewable Electricity
at CPI Group (UK) Ltd, Croydon, CR0 4YY

COPENHAGEN ESCAPE WITH THE BILLIONAIRE

SOPHIE PEMBROKE

MILLS & BOON

For Laurie, for everything.

CHAPTER ONE

ELLIE PETERS TUCKED her hair behind her ears, pushed her glasses up her nose, straightened her spine and… reached for her cup of tea, instead of focusing on the screen in front of her. The accusatory *blank* screen. The one that should have been filled with chapters and chapters of witty, wise and warm observations on happiness by now—but wasn't.

Oh, she'd started the book. She'd written a whole proposal and sample chapters for her editor before they'd paid her the advance that made the whole thing possible. There was a detailed outline, plans and joyous suggestions for research trips and adventures, seeking out happiness here in Denmark, one of the happiest countries in the world. And normally that would be enough to ensure the work got done. When Ellie committed to doing something—for someone else, at least—it got done, no ifs or buts. Keeping that kind of commitment to things she promised *herself* was a little more hit and miss. But she prided herself on being someone that others could rely on to keep her word. She'd said she'd write a book on happiness, so she would write a book on happiness.

The only problem was, she'd written that book proposal back when she *was* happy. When her marriage seemed solid, her day-to-day work as a features editor for a glossy women's magazine proving both fun and satisfactorily lucrative. When her London townhouse felt like home, and she had friends and family she could rely on. When a research trip to Denmark—where, not coincidentally, her best friend Lily had moved after marrying her Viking true love, Anders—seemed like an adventure. A chance to make her life even more fulfilling, happy and enviable.

Now? Now things were different.

Now, Denmark was an escape. As evidenced by the fact that it was New Year's Eve in Copenhagen and she was sitting in semi-darkness, one solitary candle—a present from Lily—burning beside her on the desk, staring at a still blank page.

She'd escaped her life by running away to spend four whole months searching for happiness hacks in Denmark. But she couldn't escape her deadline.

And Ellie just would not let down her editor, or her readers. Especially not when she was already letting down her mother and her half-sister, for perhaps the first time in her life.

Who even am I, these days?

Ellie wasn't sure she recognised herself any longer. And she knew her family were baffled by her sudden inability to go along with everything they asked of her.

Maybe if I'd ever said no to them before, this wouldn't be such a shock. Or if I'd ever admitted to being anything other than happy about how my life has turned out.

With a sigh, she clicked out of the empty document and back onto her web browser. Immediately, her own face—beaming, happy—filled square after square of the screen. Photos of her in London, arms around friends or dressed to the nines. Photos of her boarding her plane to Denmark, passport in hand, looking excited and only a little nervous. Selfies from around Copenhagen, filtered to look brighter and happier than the Danish city ever could in winter.

All of them a tiny fake moment in time, captured for observers rather than herself.

Ellie had built up quite a following online—first as someone 'in the know' in London, and now as a happiness adventurer or influencer abroad. Her publisher was thrilled she had so much interaction from her fans. Which was fine for her publisher—nobody there had to keep up with answering all the messages and comments in her peppiest, happiest tone.

Checking her notifications, she sent fast, emoji-heavy replies to some of her most faithful followers.

One of them read:

So exciting to see you growing out your natural grey hair! I grew mine out two years ago and haven't looked back!

Ellie winced. There was no way she could admit that the grey regrowth since her last colour and cut was due to her not having the courage to find a Danish hairdresser that could replicate it—even though Lily had recommended hers. She'd looked at the box dyes on the shelf, but hadn't trusted herself either. What if the instructions were only in Danish? Besides, she'd been wearing a woolly hat pretty much permanently since she arrived, so it wasn't as if her roots were often on display.

After a moment's thought, she replied.

I'm learning that happiness requires authenticity. I'm forty-four—I have some grey hairs. That's who I am and I'm happy with it!

That sounded on brand, right? And freed her from having to find a hairdresser before she headed back to London in another six weeks. Although she might have to see it through, now she'd commented about authenticity. Would it be inauthentic to dye it again now? Probably. Maybe there was some sort of blended look she could get her regular hairdresser to implement—half highlights, half grey or something. She should research that.

Before she could open the search browser though, she shut herself down. No distractions. She was supposed to be *working*. Deadline, remember?

Ellie clicked back to the blank document again. She couldn't face being the sort of authentic her followers expected from her right now—which was, of course, about as inauthentic as it got.

Her phone buzzed and she picked it up, pretending to herself that she wasn't eager for the distraction. It could be important, right?

Hey, El! Getting this message in now in case the lines are jammed at midnight. Just wanted to say how proud I am of my little sis and this huge adventure you're on. You haven't let the world get you down, even when nobody would have blamed you for it. It makes me so happy to see how well you're doing over there in Denmark! Can't wait to hear all about it properly when you're back home at the end of Feb. Until then, stay happy, keep having fun...and find a hot guy to kiss at midnight for me! Sarah xxx

Ellie's jaw tightened as she read through the message from her older sister. At least this sojourn in Denmark was making *somebody* happy. If even Sarah, who knew everything, believed she'd genuinely come here for work and self-growth, rather than to run away from everything she'd left behind in Britain, she had to be doing something right.

Her phone buzzed again—another message from Sarah.

I know, I know, you're not going to rely on a man for happiness ever again. Just have fun though, yeah?!

Well, that much was true, at least. Ellie was *definitely* never finding her happiness in a guy again. She'd learned that lesson too well from her now ex-husband.

Ellie's gaze flicked up towards the clock. The afternoon had disappeared without her noticing. It was hard, sometimes, to tell the passing of time when there was so little daylight to judge it by. In Copenhagen in December, the sun didn't rise until long after breakfast, and it was down again by mid-afternoon. Lily claimed that the day wasn't *much* shorter than it would be in London at this time of year, being on a similar latitude, but it still *felt* it.

Just one reason that Ellie was glad Lily had moved to Denmark rather than, say, Northern Finland. The Finns might have claimed the happiest country crown recently, but with less than three hours of daylight in December,

Ellie wasn't sure she could have faked happiness there if she'd tried.

And Copenhagen *was* lovely. She'd explored a lot of it on foot, alone, and found it charming. She just wasn't sure what there was about the place to make the Danes so much *happier* than other nations. And at this point, halfway through her Danish stay, she wasn't sure she was ever going to figure it out. She'd read all the studies and the articles about work-life balance, family support and high taxes providing high levels of care. She just couldn't quite see what that had to offer *her*—a self-employed, newly single woman who was child-free by choice.

She sighed, and pushed her desk chair away from her computer. If anyone was going to teach her about happiness in Denmark, it would surely be the sickeningly loved up newlyweds, Lily and Anders. They'd invited her to spend New Year's Eve with them and a few friends, and Ellie hadn't been able to find a polite way to refuse. Plus, she was hoping that those Danish friends might have some happiness insights that would kickstart her book writing. Besides, there was no way Lily was going to allow her to 'stay in her little rented flat and moulder away as the clock ticked midnight'—to quote Lily herself.

So Ellie would go and see in the new year with her friends—which, honestly, was about as close to true happiness as she could imagine getting here in Copenhagen.

But what did she know? Maybe tonight would be the night that the secrets to happiness revealed themselves to her.

As long as they didn't come attached to a man, she'd welcome them in.

* * *

Jesper Mikkelsen drummed his fingertips along the arm of the perfectly designed visitor's chair in his brother-in-law's office. Or ex-brother-in-law, he supposed. Did a man lose his relatives by marriage after the death of his wife? Jesper wasn't sure. Maybe he'd ask Will.

Or maybe not. His sister's death was still a painful open wound for both of them. No need to bring it up tonight, when the new year beckoned, full of promise.

Besides, Will would still be his financial advisor, even if he wasn't technically a brother any more. That was something. Maybe he'd even still be a friend.

Jesper had lost a lot of people over the last few years. Most of them, he was fine without. But he'd hate to lose Will, too.

He gazed around the empty office, taking in all the touches that made it special. The beautiful Danish furniture—all costing a fortune, but worth every krone, in Jesper's opinion. The building deserved it—the way it caught the last of the disappearing daylight, but at an angle that didn't blind him, the graceful lines of the exterior that always felt as if they were welcoming him in. Yes, Will had done well with this office.

But eventually, Jesper had to look at the desk. There wasn't much on it: Will's laptop, a small potted plant and a single photo frame containing the last photo ever taken of the three of them together—Jesper, Will and Agnes.

She was pregnant when that was taken, Jesper realised with a start. *Did she know it?*

He hadn't. He hadn't known until the doctor at the American hospital where she succumbed to her injuries after the car crash let it slip. If she had known, she hadn't told him. But then, she hadn't told him much of anything, towards the end.

Jesper shook the thought away and got to his feet, pacing towards the window even as the office door opened and Will reappeared.

'Sorry about that,' he said with a smile. 'Just something I wanted to get tidied up before the holiday.' New Year's Eve wasn't a public holiday, but New Year's Day was. Jesper wondered how many people in Will's office were actually working today, and how many had taken it off to prepare for the celebrating ahead. At the least, most of them would have finished early—or earlier than Jesper was used to after years running his own business in America.

Another new year to enjoy. Sometimes it still seemed impossible that the world kept spinning.

'I'm surprised you were even in the office today,' Jesper said as Will took his seat behind his desk. 'Don't you and Matthew have your usual New Year's Eve dinner party tonight?'

'We do—as you'd know if you'd let us invite you.' Will gave him a stern look. 'You know, I was really hoping that now you're back from the wilderness and around people again, you might be ready to, well, actually be around people again.'

'I am!' Jesper protested. 'Many people. Well, some.' More than he had been in the years immediately following Agnes's death, anyway. The years he'd spent avoiding society, after his move back from the States, when he'd been trying to find a new way to exist in a world he barely recognised.

He'd done it, though. Those wilderness years, as Will called them, had saved him, in lots of ways.

It was just learning to live in the regular world again that was hard.

'So, what are you doing this New Year's Eve?' Will rested his forearms on the desk and leaned towards him. 'Other than deciding to hold this meeting to check on your financial health and wellbeing—a meeting which, I feel, really could have waited until after the holiday.'

'I just asked if you were in!' Jesper protested. 'You were working anyway. Don't blame me for that. And, actually, I only asked because I needed to be in Copenhagen today anyway—because I have New Year plans.'

Will raised his eyebrows. '*Actual* plans, or moping alone watching other peoples' fireworks from a hotel room plans? Because I can still call home and have Matthew set an extra place for dinner...'

'As lovely as that would be, I really do have plans.' It wasn't that Jesper didn't want to spend the evening with his ex-brother-in-law and his husband, it was just that... Will and Matthew's New Year's Eve dinners were legendary. The sort of event that took much longer than the single public holiday that followed to recover from. And Jesper didn't do that sort of extreme any more.

Time was, he'd have worked all day on the thirty-first of December, cramming as many last-minute meetings and actions as possible into the old year, before changing into his tuxedo, grabbing a car to pick up Agnes, who would be stunning in something expensive and revealing, but probably mad at him for being late, then heading out across Manhattan to at least one but often more parties that they just had to be seen at.

If they'd been home in Denmark for the holidays, he'd still have worked—just in the hotel suite they'd have booked, instead of his own office. Then they'd have made their way to Will and Matthew's for the party of the year. They'd eat and drink and laugh and talk all night, before heading up to their roof garden to watch the fireworks from across the city.

And he'd have been back at his desk by seven the next morning, hangover and holiday bedamned. That was the sort of life he'd lived, for too long.

'Really?' Will looked pleasantly surprised at the idea that Jesper really was re-entering society. 'What plans?'

'My friend Anders and his wife Lily have invited me to join them for a low-key supper,' Jesper said. 'Just a few friends, apparently. Nothing too overwhelming. Then a trip to the Tivoli Gardens for midnight itself.' Which probably would be overwhelming in a 'lots of people' way, but at least not a 'lots of people he had to talk to' way. At least at Lily and Anders' cosy flat he could fade into the background in a small group.

'A few friends?' Will smirked. 'Sounds like they're setting you up with someone. That's exactly what Matthew says when he wants to introduce a couple he thinks will hit it off without letting on that's what he's doing.'

'Anders wouldn't do that.' Jesper was almost certain about that. Lily, however… Anders *had* mentioned something about a friend of Lily's visiting from London last time they'd talked. Would that friend be there too, or had they gone home already? At least there would be other people around as a buffer.

'Well, we'll see,' Will said with a smirk. 'Maybe it would do you good to meet someone to kiss at midnight. Part of rejoining the real world.'

Jesper shot him a look. 'I'd have thought you, of all

people, wouldn't be encouraging me to get out there and fall in love again.'

Will's smile turned slightly pitying. 'It's been three years since Agnes…left us. You don't have to live in perpetual mourning your whole life, you know. You still get to live.'

Jesper wasn't really all so sure about that. The mistakes he'd made… He wasn't sure he deserved that kind of happiness. Love was too much of a risk.

'And kissing some random woman at midnight isn't the same as falling in love, anyway,' Will went on. 'It doesn't have to be all or nothing, Jes. It can just be fun. A moment of happiness. You deserve that.'

'I am happy,' Jesper said automatically. He'd spent nearly three years, mostly alone in the wilderness, finding that even keel of existence that brought him out of the pit of grief and guilt after Agnes' death and back up to the contentment he now enjoyed. He was happy. He'd fought hard for it.

'Are you?' Will asked softly. 'I hope so. I really do.'

Lily and Anders' flat was everything Ellie had imagined a Danish home would be, before she came to Copenhagen. Beautiful Scandi design, zero clutter but perfectly placed cosy touches everywhere—candles that gave the space a warm glow, knitted and fluffy throw blankets for when the night grew cool, and everything in calming tones of neutral colours.

Ellie loved it, but it was basically the exact opposite of anywhere she had ever lived before.

'It's all about the hygge,' Lily had told her, the first time she'd visited. 'It's cold here in the winter, and dark.

People spend a lot of time in their houses, so they want them to be warm, comforting places to be.'

Settled on Lily's white couch with a glass of white wine on New Year's Eve, Ellie had to admit, it did feel comforting, and comfortable. At least here she was with friends—people who knew her, understood her and what she'd been through, and loved her all the same. She didn't have to put on a facade of happiness for Lily, and she'd never appreciated that as much as she did right now.

Until she asked, 'When is everyone else getting here?' and Anders replied, 'Well, Jesper should be here soon. He had a meeting, but he promised he wouldn't be late.'

Ellie's whole body stiffened, and she even pulled back from reaching for one of the delicious delicacies on the charcuterie plate Lily had set out on the wooden tray that topped the cushioned surface of the multi-purpose foot rest and coffee table. 'Jesper? Just Jesper? I thought...'

She'd thought there'd be a group of them. Now she was starting to sniff a set-up.

'Oh, well, we invited a whole gang, of course, but sadly no one else could make it.' Lily's breezy excuses were completely unconvincing to anyone who'd known her as long as Ellie had—and that was before she spotted Anders looking utterly baffled by his wife's statement.

'We did?' he asked. 'I thought the idea was—' He broke off as Lily elbowed him in the ribs on her way past.

Definitely a set-up. Ellie sighed. She should have guessed.

But it was too late to back out now. She'd just have to make the best of it.

'So, who is Jesper?' Maybe he'd be good for Danish

happiness research, anyway—although she was certain that wasn't what Lily had in mind.

'He's an old friend of Anders',' Lily explained. 'He happens to be in the city for the weekend and, well, it's been a while since we saw him, so we thought it would be nice to invite him along tonight. You'll like him!'

Ellie gave her oldest friend a look that said very clearly that she knew exactly what Lily was doing and she did not approve. Lily winced and looked away. Oh, this was going to be a disaster. No amount of book research was worth an unexpected blind date on New Year's Eve. What if it was an utter disaster and set the tone for the whole year ahead? Okay, that was probably taking superstition too far, but really, given everything that had happened in her life lately, Ellie wasn't taking any chances.

Before she could come up with any even half convincing excuses to leave, there was a knock at the door and Lily skipped away to answer it. Ellie sat, tensed on the sofa, waiting to see what this Jesper looked like. She'd met a few of Anders's friends already, and they all looked a lot like him—big and blond and Viking-like. She imagined Jesper would be the same.

But the man who handed Lily a small potted plant and a bottle of red wine wasn't much like Anders at all. He was dark where Anders was fair, although his hair was greying significantly at the temples and there was white in his short beard, too. He had lines around his eyes that creased up when he smiled at the joke Anders made—in Danish, and too fast for Ellie to try and translate, so presumably not for her ears. His eyes were a bright, sharp blue that she could distinguish even from across the room, which made her strangely uncomfortable. Still, she got to her feet and smoothed down the wool of her knit skirt over her thermal tights—too hot for the flat, but she'd need them later, Lily had assured her.

'Jesper, this is Lily's friend Ellie, from London,' Anders said, gesturing towards her. 'And Ellie, this is one of my very oldest friends, Jesper.'

'It's a pleasure to meet you.' Jesper stepped towards her with a warm smile and an outstretched hand. His voice was lower than she'd expected, the rumbling, gravelly sort of voice that she could feel in her chest. It unsettled her almost as much as his eyes which, up close, were even more striking. Worse, she couldn't shake the feeling that he saw far deeper than most people—into the heart of her. Somehow, she sensed that this man wouldn't buy the fake versions of happiness she'd been peddling online.

'And you.' Her throat felt scratchy as she spoke, and she swallowed as she took his hand, looking up into those too blue eyes. Her palm brushed against his and she felt honest-to-God sparks flash between them.

Probably the thermal tights. Static electricity, that's all.

Except it wasn't. And if the slightly stunned look in Jesper's eyes was anything to go by, she wasn't the only one feeling it.

Ellie wasn't sure what unsettled her most. The fact that he was gorgeous and made her skin spark when she touched him, or the way that she knew, without quite knowing how, that this man would see the real her, far more than anyone else did, if she let him.

She'd just have to make sure she didn't let him, then.

Ellie dropped his hand and stepped away again, reaching for her wine.

'Jesper was living in the States until a few years ago,' Lily said, obviously keen to make conversation and find common ground—and perhaps convince Ellie that her obvious set-up wasn't a terrible, impulsive idea. 'New York. You lived there once, too, didn't you, Ellie?'

'I did.' It had been just after they were married, and she and Dave had still been madly in love. When his job offered a secondment to the Big Apple for two years, they'd jumped at it. It had been an adventure—a real one, not like this manufactured one she was currently undertaking. Every day had brought new experiences, new discoveries about the city around them—and about each other. It was hard to remember being that young, that happy, that optimistic, now. 'It was a long time ago.'

'And now you are in Denmark.' Jesper's voice held traces of American and Danish accents, mingled together—although his English was clearly perfect. And it would have been a damn sight better than her Danish even if it hadn't been. And his voice… Ellie forced herself to ignore the way it seemed to vibrate inside her chest when he spoke and concentrated on what he was saying. 'What brings you here now?'

'Ellie is researching why we Danes are so happy!' Anders answered for her before Ellie could even open her mouth. 'I told her, it is because we are lucky enough to be born Danish, in this magical part of the world, but apparently that's not enough to write a book about.'

'I see.' There was something of a shadow behind Jesper's eyes as he answered, and Ellie got the strange impression that he *did* see. That he understood something of a desperate search for happiness in the face of unsurmountable odds. It made her want to know him better, which was annoying. She hated it when Lily was right about these things. 'And have you had much luck? Have many of my other countrymen and women been able to share better insights than our friend Anders, here?'

Ellie glanced away, towards the darkened windows. Lily hadn't pulled the shades yet, and outside the night seemed to press in, smothering them.

'To be honest, it has been difficult to find many people to talk to about it,' she admitted. 'The city is busy, but even in the after-work hours most of the people I find to talk to are tourists.' She didn't add that she hadn't tried *very* hard. A few half-hearted attempts in the cafés had sapped her hope of the answer to true happiness falling into her lap, and after that she'd sort of lost the energy to keep looking.

'It is the wrong time of year,' Jesper said knowledgeably—even though Ellie had no earthly idea what he meant.

'That's what I said!' Anders pointed a finger at Lily. 'And you told me not to get involved.' Lily rolled her eyes.

'The wrong time of year how, exactly?' Ellie asked.

'In the winter, we Danes tend to hunker down—to embrace the hygge,' Jesper explained. He'd sat down on the sofa beside her, and Ellie could feel the warmth from him spreading out towards her. She hoped Lily was right about the tights; right now, she felt as if she might overheat. Danes kept their homes so *warm*. That was obviously the only reason her cheeks felt so hot. Nothing to do with how close Jesper was sitting.

'The hygge,' Ellie repeated, trying to focus. 'Even us

Brits know about that. It's all cushions and candles and stuff, right?'

He gave her a patient smile. 'That's part of it. But more than that, it's about being cosy at home, with your family or loved ones. Like tonight. Later, we might venture out into the city to celebrate the New Year, I think. But right now, we are here, enjoying each other's company, some good food and drink, the candlelight and the companionship.' His mouth twisted a little, until his smile looked somehow sad. 'This is what I missed when I was away.'

'I suppose life in the States must have been a very different pace,' Ellie said. The Danes valued their work-life balance very highly—and she knew from experience that wasn't always the case in America.

'Uh, yes. Very different.' Jesper sounded surprised, as if he hadn't been thinking about America at all, which was curious.

He gave her another tight smile, then turned his attention to the platters of food Lily had prepared for them. Ellie followed suit, but she couldn't help wondering what he *had* been thinking about when he talked about being away.

Jesper was an interesting man. And she knew her sister, if she were there, would point out that he was an incredibly good-looking one, too.

Two things Ellie knew she'd do better to avoid, given what had happened last time she'd allowed herself to be beguiled by an interesting and gorgeous man.

But still, she had to admit she was intrigued. Intrigued and incredibly attracted.

Across the room, Lily gave her a knowing look and a small waggle of the eyebrows, and Ellie looked away—

fast. The last thing she needed was her best friend getting ideas about her thinking this set-up was a good idea.

Especially since only Lily understood the real reason she was in Denmark in the dead of winter to begin with.

CHAPTER TWO

JESPER LEANED BACK into the soft welcome of Anders and Lily's sofa, side plate in hand, and watched the woman beside him with covert glances when she wasn't looking.

He had to admit, he was intrigued. Intrigued and attracted. And while the attraction was unexpected, it wasn't so surprising—Ellie was gorgeous, with her warm hazel eyes and wide smile. Something about her sparked a physical reaction in him he hadn't anticipated feeling that evening, or any time soon. But it wasn't even the most interesting thing about her.

There was something deeper inside her, something soul-deep about her that he wanted to know, to understand. And that surprised him more than anything.

It had been a very long while since a woman had intrigued him.

He wondered if that was why Anders had invited him along, knowing she'd be there. His best friend had always had an unerring sense of what would pique Jesper's curiosity, what would draw him out of his shell. It was how he'd lured him away from his studies at university, and later persuaded him to leave work for the occasional fishing trip when he'd visited them in the States, or even convinced him to come back to Denmark for high days and holidays like today.

It had been Anders who had introduced him to Agnes in the first place, of course.

Or perhaps it had been Lily. And perhaps this set-up—it hadn't escaped his notice that the other promised guests were entirely absent—was more to do with Ellie than him. Something else to wonder about.

Beside him, Ellie had turned slightly to chat with Lily, sitting on the armchair beside her, her face lit up by the candlelight. Anders' wife was a beautiful woman, made more beautiful by the way she responded to his friend's love and care. Jesper had been honestly delighted when he heard they'd married—even if he suspected that their sudden elopement and tiny wedding had been at least partially because the obvious best man hadn't been available.

In fact, Jesper had been so completely off-the-grid he hadn't heard about their wedding until three months after the fact.

Had Ellie been there? Yes, she must have been. He could see her beaming in a photo with Lily in a wedding dress, set out on one of the shelves beside the fire.

If he'd been at the wedding, they would have met there. Maybe shared a drink, flirted a little. If he still even remembered how to do that. In another world, one where he hadn't been grieving his wife, hadn't been married at all, perhaps, anything might have happened. Who knew where a little flirting might lead…

He could try tonight, he realised. Will had been right. He needed to get used to being around people again. He couldn't live the rest of his hopefully long life alone in the backwoods, like some story of a man made up to frighten school kids.

Well, he *could*. And if he was totally honest with himself—something he'd been working hard on being for the last few years—a lot of days he wanted to. But the world would still be out there, and sometimes he had to interact with it.

Maybe it was time to dip his toe back in the water of social interaction. He was certain that was what Anders and Lily had decided, which was why they'd invited him tonight at all. Unless…yes, more and more, he was convinced that this cosy double date wasn't solely for his benefit.

He gazed again at Ellie's profile in the candlelight. Lily would have told her that winter was the wrong time for her project, if she wanted to meet other Danes out in the wild. Or she'd have been able to introduce her to more people even in the coldest, darkest season, if that was the real reason Ellie was here, and there had been no other time she could visit. No, he suspected there was another reason for Ellie's sudden Danish odyssey.

Maybe she was hiding, just like he had been.

But what from?

Jesper looked away. He was not in the business of getting involved in other people's lives and problems—he never had been, but certainly not since his own life had imploded. He knew only too well that there was little you could do for others when their world fell apart. Many friends and family had reached out to help him, even those whose friendships he'd sorely neglected over the years he was consumed with building his business.

But in the end, there was nothing they could do for the grief and the regrets.

All he'd been able to combat them with was time and solitude.

Well, that and a complete upheaval of everything in his life that had gone before.

He suspected that wasn't what Ellie needed. Few people ever wanted or needed the extremes he seemed to be programmed to go for. It certainly wasn't the Danish way. He was an outlier.

Or he had been. These days, he worked hard to walk that middle line. To find that balance so craved by his countrymen.

He'd learned a lot, out in the wilderness the last few years, with nothing to keep him company but his own thoughts and regrets. But, in the end, what it had taught him most was that either extreme—workaholism or dropping out and checking out—wasn't going to make him happy.

For that, he'd come back to the Danish lifestyle he'd always eschewed before as too easy, not ambitious enough.

He found it faintly ironic that it turned out his mother had been right all along. He wished she was still alive, so he could tell her so.

Maybe that was the same lesson Ellie needed to learn—not that he expected to be the person to teach her. Happiness was a personal thing. Every person needed to find out for themselves what made them happy. Yes, there were some broad tenets that could be applied, but Jesper had never been a believer in one size fits all.

'Well, if you want to meet more Danes, there'll probably be some at the Tivoli Gardens tonight,' Anders told

Ellie, excitement clear in his voice. 'I mean, many of them will still be tourists, but maybe from Denmark? Who knows? You could perform some informal interviews, perhaps?'

Ellie curled her legs under her on the sofa. It made her look curiously young—even though if she was of an age with Lily, Jesper knew she couldn't be many years younger than his own forty-eight. 'What do Danes usually do for New Year?' she asked.

'It depends,' Jesper said. 'My brother-in-law Will and his husband Matthew always throw a lavish party for their many, many friends—ending with watching the fireworks from the roof garden at midnight.'

Ellie gave him a curious look. 'And you didn't want to be there tonight?'

Jesper winced. 'Will is more my...ex-brother-in-law. Or something. I'm not really sure. Although he did invite me when I saw him earlier today. But, uh, no. I chose to be here instead.'

He wasn't sure any of that made sense, but he didn't really want to get into the issue of his widower status right now. He assumed Lily and Anders hadn't mentioned it, or Ellie wouldn't have asked the question. Indeed, Lily was giving him an awkwardly apologetic smile even now. She was British, of course. She felt a social faux pas acutely. Jesper suspected it was bred into the Brits, even now.

Her husband, meanwhile, had no sense of embarrassment or shame—something Jesper suspected he'd only become quite so sensitive to since his years in the States. He clapped Jesper on the back with a broad, firm hand. 'And that was the right decision! Or else you wouldn't have had the company of the lovely Ellie for our visit to the Tivoli Gardens winter wonderland, would you?'

'This is true.' Jesper turned to offer Ellie a friendly smile and found her already watching him, her hazel eyes wide under her fringe. She had brown hair, something Jesper would have thought fairly nondescript until now, watching all the colours hidden in it—from red to gold to umber, with silver threads coming through—shining in the candlelight.

She dipped her gaze and tucked her hair behind her ear, and Jesper took a moment to catch his breath.

Yes, there was definitely more to Ellie than he'd imagined when he'd arrived. And suddenly he knew he wouldn't sleep unless he found out what it was, and why he felt so captivated by her hazel eyes.

The Tivoli Gardens were a highlight of Copenhagen life. Lily told her that in the summer they were swarming with tourists from the moment they opened in spring to when they closed in the autumn, everyone eager to experience the rides and shows, music and spectacle. They'd been closed for the winter when Ellie had been planning her last-minute trip, but opened for a winter spectacular all over the Christmas period. This, however, was her first visit to the Copenhagen landmark.

And she had to admit it was pretty magical.

The whole place had been lit up with thousands upon thousands of tiny lights, every tree, every building, every structure, railing against the dark of a winter night. Music played—she wasn't sure from where, except that maybe it was everywhere—and children, up way past their usual bedtime, she assumed, raced around enjoying the sights and begging to go on the different rides.

Anders and Lily walked hand in hand in front of her, Lily resting her head against her new husband's upper arm as they soaked in the magic.

Ellie hung back and stuck close to Jesper, who seemed to be doing the same thing, just in case she got lost.

'It's quite something, isn't it?' Jesper said. Somehow, his voice carried through all the noise and hustle—or maybe she was just standing closer to him than she'd realised. Yes, now she checked, she was practically pressed up against his side, in her attempt not to get lost in the crowd.

She took a step to the side. 'It really is. What do you think? Does it rival the Rockefeller Center for Christmas merriment?'

Jesper rumbled a low laugh. 'I think it probably does. Although I have to admit, I never went ice-skating or whatever it is you're supposed to do there when I was in New York.'

Ellie gasped in mock horror. 'You didn't? Well, what *were* you doing there?'

'Wasting my time, clearly,' he joked back. But then, as he looked at her, his expression turned more serious, pensive even. 'Mostly I was working. All of the time.'

'Not very Danish of you.' The words popped out before Ellie could stop them, and she winced. 'Sorry. It's all this Danish happiness research I've been doing.'

'It's okay. You're right.' He gave a small shake of the head. 'I...wasn't very Danish for a long time. Not all Danes are, you realise. I mean, as a country we have a certain reputation, and most of us live up to it, but...we're all individuals as well. We need to find out for ourselves what makes us happy.'

'I *do* realise that,' Ellie replied. 'I think that's part of what makes understanding the Scandinavian happiness phenomenon so hard. I mean, I know so much has already been written about it, for years now. But I was hoping that, now the initial hype of hygge and Swedish death cleaning and everything has passed, I could find something new to say. Something real.'

'But you haven't?'

'Not yet.' Ellie sighed. 'But I still have two months. And, I mean, everyone here looks pretty happy, so there are worse places to be on New Year's Eve.'

'You're still working now, then,' Jesper pointed out. 'On New Year's Eve. Not very Danish of *you*.'

'Ah, but I'm a writer,' Ellie countered. 'We're never not working. Inspiration doesn't work to a schedule.'

'And your inspiration—your muse, perhaps?—have they been good to you in Copenhagen?' he asked.

It was only a polite question, she knew that. Just a half-interested enquiry from a new acquaintance. People were always interested in her writing process, in her experience—either baffled by the very idea of wanting to get words down on paper in the first place, or because they believed they had a book in them that they'd write one day, if only they found the time.

That was what *she'd* believed. After years of writing articles and essays and posts online, she'd thought it was finally time to pull it all together in a book. But here she was in Denmark, with all the time in the world and nothing to do but write, and still the words wouldn't come.

'Perhaps not as good as I had been hoping,' she offered with a small smile.

A group of young twenty-somethings approaching from the opposite direction almost barrelled into them with shouted apologies after the fact, and Jesper pulled her out of their way, tucking her against his body with her arm slotted through the bend in his. She should object, she thought, to such a casual ownership of her space, her arm. But at the same time…he had protected her. Somehow, his arm around her felt…right. And the slow, low buzz of attraction that filled her at his touch was certainly keeping her warm.

'So now you're back from the States do you find you work less, here in Denmark?' Time to turn the conversation back onto him, she'd decided. Her own woeful writing work was *not* what she wanted to be focusing on this New Year's Eve.

'Far less.' Jesper huffed a small laugh, sending a cloud of steam into the night air. 'If I'm honest, I've hardly thought about business since I returned.'

Ellie frowned. She'd been expecting a line about settling back into the balanced way of working and living the Danes seemed to have sussed, but this sounded like something else. More like he'd gone from one extreme to another.

'I don't understand,' she said slowly. 'I'm sure Anders said that you had a business meeting before you came to the flat.'

'That is true.' He didn't elaborate.

Maybe she was asking the wrong questions. Or he was deliberately offering unhelpful answers.

Perhaps both.

'Why *did* you return to Denmark?'

That was clearly the right question, but she was almost sorry she'd asked it. Jesper's arm tightened around hers, and for a moment a flash of something an awful lot like pain filled his features.

'My wife died,' he said softly. 'In a car accident. I was... I was at work, of course, so she had taken a cab back from our penthouse apartment to the airport for a visit home to her family here in Denmark. And there was an accident and she died. And suddenly I didn't want to work any longer.'

Ellie squeezed his arm in reply, sudden guilt filling her for thinking that the attraction she felt in his presence might have been reciprocated. Maybe she'd been wrong about this being a set-up at all. 'I'm so sorry. I shouldn't have asked. It's the journalist in me—I'm always asking questions that people would rather I didn't.'

He shrugged. 'No, it's fine. I've got to get used to saying it. People will ask.'

'Was it very recent?' It certainly sounded that way— raw, and as if he hadn't grown accustomed yet to sharing the awful news with others.

To a lesser extent, Ellie knew how that felt. For months after she and Dave first split up, she'd find herself forgetting that they weren't still together, especially when making plans with friends. Telling everyone had been by far the hardest part, and it seemed to go on for ever, as if there was always someone for whom it was news. And of course that just made it ache all over again.

'Agnes died three years ago now,' Jesper replied.

So, not very recent, but obviously not anywhere close to enough time to have got over the tragedy at all. He must miss her enormously, still. Perhaps they'd been together a long time—since school, or whatever. To be heading into the second half of his life without the person he'd expected to spend it with must be very hard to come to terms with.

Actually, she knew it was. Because while Dave was still very much alive, her future—the one she'd expected to live—had vanished.

'You must have loved her very much,' she said finally. 'I'm so sorry for your loss.'

God, what a New Year's Eve this was turning out to be. Two middle-aged people who couldn't seem to get over the lives they'd lost. This probably wasn't what Lily had planned for them when she'd brought them together for the evening.

Maybe it was time to call it, and head back to Britain, book or no book.

Except she couldn't. Not until after January was over, anyway.

There was no way in hell she was going to be in London until after then. Whatever her mother or half-sister said.

If she was, she knew she'd only end up going along with what they wanted her to do once again, like always. And this time, this one time… Ellie knew she couldn't do it. However unhappy it made people.

After a lifetime of people pleasing, she knew that this time she needed to stay far away. And being in Denmark gave her the perfect excuse to *not* do what her family wanted, without having to tell them how much she hated that they were asking it of her in the first place, and ruining their relationship for ever.

She couldn't leave yet.

* * *

Jesper had visited the Tivoli Gardens many times in his life, although never before at New Year. He'd seen the fireworks though, from his brother-in-law's roof garden.

Before, he'd always resented the time taken away from more important things. Tonight, however, he felt certain that there was nothing more important that he could be doing than talking to Ellie.

She fascinated him—far more now they'd started talking than when he was merely watching her back at the apartment. It wasn't just the hum of instant attraction that he felt between them. This was something more.

The way she asked questions. The line that formed between her eyebrows when she tried to figure out his answers and what they meant. He knew, instinctively, that this was a woman who had lived a full life to this point—she was brimming with it. And yet, all that enthusiasm and life seemed to be tucked neatly away inside her winter coat, as if she were afraid to let it out again.

No wonder she was having trouble finding enough happiness to write about. The woman was clearly *un*-happy, even if she didn't seem willing to admit it—to him, or to her friends. She plastered on a smile over the cracks of her misery, and everyone seemed willing to accept that as reality.

Everyone except him.

Why?

Maybe they genuinely didn't see it. Or perhaps they already knew what she was covering and understood that was what she needed to do right now. He didn't feel he could ask Lily: announcing that her friend was miserable and how could she not have noticed, wasn't exactly the best vibe for a New Year's Eve celebration.

And yet…he couldn't help thinking about it. Why would a woman so patently unhappy be writing a book about happiness?

They paused beside the ice rink, watching the skaters glide in circles around the ice, under the sparkling lights and the branches of the nearby trees. Lily and Anders had disappeared to explore the many food stalls, promising to bring back delights to supplement the nibbles they'd had back at the apartment. Jesper had been tempted by the aromas drifting from some of the nearest wooden stalls, but in the end elected to stay with Ellie and watch the skating.

She rested her forearms on the white metal railing that surrounded the rink and Jesper followed suit, carefully avoiding the garland spotted with fairy lights that hung from it.

'They look happy, don't they?' Ellie observed, staring out at the skaters.

'Going round and round in circles and getting nowhere? I suppose they do.' Jesper had meant it as a joke, something to lighten the mood, but the more he thought about it, the more true it felt.

'That was me, before, I suppose,' she said thoughtfully, almost as if she hadn't meant to speak out loud at all. When he looked at her, waiting for more, she gave a small, embarrassed smile and looked back out over the rink again. 'I mean, I think it's very easy to live your life and think you have everything sorted, but then something happens that means you look at it all differently…'

'And realise that you were just treading water,' Jesper finished, when she trailed off. 'Or skating in circles.'

'Exactly.' She gripped the edge of the railing tight, then leaned back, her feet anchoring her on the step at the bottom of the railing, her body stretching out to form a triangle. She reminded him of a child, swinging off the bars in a playground, perhaps. For the first time since he'd met her earlier that evening, she seemed...free.

But then the moment was over and Ellie stood straight against the railing again, a wistful look in her eye.

'Would you like to try?' Jesper suggested, motioning out towards the skaters.

For a moment, he thought she might be considering it. But then she bit her lip and shook her head. 'We should go and find Lily and Anders. Besides, I'd probably just fall over. It's years since I've been ice-skating.'

'All the more reason to do it, then,' he said. 'Not the falling part, obviously. I'll go with you, if you want.'

She glanced up at him in surprise, and for a moment he could see worlds in her eyes. A life lived where just wanting to do something wasn't enough reason to do it, and where no one ever offered to just go along for the ride.

He got the impression that Ellie had spent far more of her life so far doing what others wanted or expected her to do than chasing after her own wishes and dreams.

'Sometimes skating in circles can be fun,' he said softly. 'We don't always have to be trying to get somewhere.'

'I suppose.' She held his gaze for a long moment, those expressive hazel eyes telling whole novels he could only read snippets of. Then she looked away and smiled—not the real one he'd been hoping to surprise from her though, but another of those fake plastered-over smiles—and he knew the moment was over. 'Lily, Anders!' She waved their friends over as they approached with trays of food, then she hopped down from the step by the ice rink to approach them.

Jesper followed more slowly behind. Ellie had wanted to go skating, but she'd stopped herself. He wondered who had told her she couldn't do the things she wanted to do. Wondered how she ever expected to be happy if she didn't.

Wondered if maybe, maybe, he could be the person to change that belief.

The night darkened and deepened as midnight approached, it seemed, even though the sun had been down for hours. Full of street food from the stalls—including some delicious desserts Jesper hadn't been able to resist, and had been totally worth it for the sight of Ellie licking chocolate sauce from the corner of her mouth—they wandered the busy paths of the gardens to find the best spot to watch the fireworks from. Obviously, they weren't the only people trying to do that so competition was fierce.

'They'll be up in the sky, you realise,' Anders pointed out as Lily rejected yet another site as not quite right. 'We'll be able to see them wherever we are.'

'I know. It's just—ooh! Let's try over there!' And Lily was off again, chasing another spot that might be perfect, tugging Ellie along behind her.

Jesper shared a fondly exasperated look with his friend as they followed.

Finally, Lily was satisfied, and the four of them settled in with moments to spare to watch the iconic firework display, which fired at eleven so as not to conflict with the other firework displays around town at midnight. This suited Jesper perfectly; it meant they could be back in the safety of Anders and Lily's flat before the midnight madness started and *everyone* in Copenhagen seemed to want to set off fireworks.

Of course, they weren't the only ones to find this area around the open-air stage the perfect place to view from, so they found themselves surrounded by others, oohing and ahhing as the first fireworks split the skies.

Ellie was jostled towards him again and Jesper put an arm around her, holding her against his side. He glanced down to check that she was okay and she gave him a shy smile, before jumping as another loud firework exploded. Her attention was drawn quickly back to the sky, and Jesper knew he should be watching the fireworks, too. But somehow, he found himself watching *her* watching them instead. Seeing the wonder and joy in her eyes as golds and reds and greens and whites cascaded across the night sky.

This, he felt certain, was a woman capable of great happiness.

And part of him really wanted to be the one to show her how to find it.

Just for a little while.

CHAPTER THREE

THE FIREWORKS WERE, Ellie had to admit, spectacular. Still, part of her was secretly glad when they were over and it was time to head back to Anders and Lily's flat to ring in the New Year with champagne and toasts. She tried to convince herself that it was just because she was cold and the crowds were growing a little oppressive, but she knew the truth was that she wasn't sure how much longer she could spend pressed up against Jesper's side without starting to get ideas.

Find a hot guy to kiss at midnight for me! Sarah had said in her message. And suddenly, Ellie was beginning to think that her sister had the right idea.

Which was a clear sign that she should probably say no to another glass of champagne when they got home.

'Are you okay?' Lily asked, as they made their way out of the park and back to the flat. She had her arm through Ellie's like they'd used to do at university, walking home from pubs and clubs late at night, sharing secrets and gossip from their night out. It made Ellie feel twenty again, instead of more than double that. Where *had* the years gone? 'Ellie?' Lily asked again, and she realised she hadn't answered her friend's question.

'I'm fine,' she promised. 'Just thinking. About the new

year ahead, you know.' That sounded better than admitting she was growing maudlin about all the years gone by, lost to them for ever.

'And who you might *kiss* at New Year?' Lily whispered, giggling very close to Ellie's ear.

Ellie glared at her. 'Has Sarah been texting you too?'

'Maybe.' Lily tried to keep a poker face and failed. Miserably. 'But mostly I was just thinking how nice it was to see you and Jesper talking tonight...'

'He's a good conversationalist.' She resolutely did not elaborate on the way his bright blue eyes seemed to see past all of her defences, or how incredibly good his arm felt around her when they walked together. 'I'm glad I wasn't the third wheel for you and Anders tonight. You know, since everyone else *cancelled* on you.'

Lily beamed, looking utterly unrepentant about her set-up plans. 'Oh, good! I know you don't like it when we spring people on you, and I know things are...sensitive at the moment. But I had a feeling the two of you would get on. And besides, if you're looking for a Dane to talk about happiness... Jesper has been on both sides of that equation. He could be really good for your book, if you're still looking for more material.'

'Maybe,' Ellie allowed. She wasn't about to admit how little material she had—to Lily *or* to Jesper, for that matter. It was just too humiliating.

Back at the flat, Anders cracked open the champagne and they all stood at the tiny barred balcony outside the living room window and counted down to midnight, their glasses held ready.

'Ten!' Lily had jumped up onto the sofa to get a better view over their heads, and was in danger of spilling her champagne.

'Nine!' Anders wrapped an arm around her waist and steadied her.

'Eight!' Ellie looked up and shared a smile with Jesper at their friends' antics.

'Seven!' Her breath caught as her gaze met his.

'Six!' She was still counting. How was she still counting when all she could think about was his eyes?

'Five!' It must be muscle memory, her lips still moving as they knew they should, even as her brain started to short-circuit.

'Four!' This was all Sarah's fault. And Lily's. She'd never have even thought of kissing a virtual stranger at midnight if they hadn't suggested it.

'Three!' And now it was all that she could think about.

'Two!' She licked her lips between numbers, and saw Jesper's throat bob as he swallowed. He didn't look away though.

'One!' Maybe she wasn't the only one thinking about midnight kisses. Maybe...

'Happy New Year!' They all yelled it together as, outside, more fireworks boomed and crackled and exploded. Ellie didn't need to look back to see that Anders and Lily were wrapped around each other in a joyous embrace.

She couldn't look, anyway. She could only see Jesper's bright blue eyes.

'Happy New Year, Ellie,' he whispered, and she tried to smile, tried to respond in kind, but couldn't.

He leaned in, obviously aiming for her cheek to kiss, but then hesitated as he grew closer. One hand came up to cup her cheek and, as his gaze met hers again, she gave what she thought was probably an imperceptible nod.

Jesper saw it, though. And his kiss didn't land on her cheek.

As his lips met hers, Ellie tried to relax, to sink into the feeling, but she couldn't shake the thought that this was her first kiss since her divorce. Her first post-Dave kiss.

There had been so many firsts since they'd separated— first birthday alone, first night in her own place, first solo dinner out—but this one, oh, this one she could enjoy.

She leaned into it now, feeling his lips curve against hers in a smile as she kissed him back. And for the first time in a long time, Ellie Peters began to feel alive.

Two days into the new year, she was still thinking about that kiss.

No, not the kiss. Well, not *just* the kiss.

She was remembering what Jesper had murmured to her as they'd parted later that night, or in the early hours really—him heading back to his hotel and Ellie setting up camp on Lily and Anders' pull-out bed for what was left of the night.

'It's been most interesting to meet you, Ellie,' he'd said. 'And…if you ever want any help finding that path to happiness, give me a call.'

She'd raised an eyebrow at the obvious line and he'd chuckled, shaking his head.

'Not like that. I just mean…happiness and how to find it is something I've spent a lot of time thinking about and working on personally, since my wife died. I'd be happy to discuss it further, if you'd like.'

He'd nodded once more and walked away—leaving Ellie remembering the fact that she'd just kissed—quite passionately—an obviously still grieving widower, and feeling icky about the whole thing.

So she'd tried—unsuccessfully—to put it out of her mind.

But two days later, with three unanswered emails from her agent in her inbox, all asking how the book was going, Ellie was getting desperate.

Then, worse, the phone rang. Not just a message or an email, but an actual phone call. Ellie had almost forgotten that people even did that.

She checked the caller ID before answering, obviously, but she was certain it would be her agent—until she saw the name scrolling across her screen and groaned.

This was worse. Far worse.

The ringing stopped, then started up again mere moments later.

Ellie took a deep breath and answered.

'Hi, Mum. Sorry—it rang off just before I could get to it.'

'Hmm.' Her mother didn't sound convinced. 'Well, I've got you now—and it's just as well. There are a million things we need to talk about before the wedding!'

The wedding. The whole reason she'd run away to another country to begin with.

'Mum, I can't make the wedding. I told you that. I'm in Denmark for work, remember?' A trip that had been arranged almost entirely around the premise of being out of the country for the January wedding date, and the run-up to it.

'Oh, Ellie.' Her mother had that half pitying, half 'I

know you better than yourself' tone that Ellie hated, and she knew that this was not going to be a good phone call. 'I know you said you wouldn't be able to get back for it, but Tom and I are happy to help with the airfare if that's the problem.'

'That's not the problem, Mum.' And, quite frankly, if her mother couldn't see what the real problem was… Ellie had very little hope for the human race.

No, her mum knew full well why Ellie didn't want to be there. She was just trying to ignore it.

She was so used to barrelling through and expecting Ellie to toe the family line to keep the peace, to keep everyone happy, that she couldn't see that this demand was an ask too far. That what she wanted this time was so far over the line that nobody in their right mind would ask her to do it.

Well, unless they'd spent forty-four years with Ellie doing exactly what they asked, every time, because it was easier than having a fight, or dealing with her mum getting upset or throwing a tantrum.

Ellie *knew* she'd brought this situation on herself. But it didn't make it any easier to deal with.

'Ellie, I think you're being very oversensitive about this,' her mum said. 'We all do!'

Ellie wondered who 'all' were. She could guess though. Her older sister Sarah, for instance, didn't think she was being oversensitive. She'd come over to help her pack and made cocktails while they did it.

No, 'all' would be her mum, her stepfather Tom and her half-sister Maisie who, at twenty-two, was proving to be quite the Bridezilla.

And Ellie knew exactly *why* they all wanted her there

too. To stop the gossip. To prove they were one big, happy family and everything was fine. But they weren't, and everything wasn't.

'I'm not being oversensitive,' Ellie said, as calmly as she could manage. 'But I'm also not coming home for the wedding. I'm doing important work over here, and I'm going to keep doing it.'

Her mother scoffed. 'Important work? Writing about *happiness*, when you're ruining the happiest day of your sister's life?'

'Half-sister,' Ellie replied. Normally, she'd have left it there. But she was feeling…different since New Year. As if maybe she could take a stand in her own life, for once. So she didn't keep her next words confined to her own internal monologue. 'And, in fairness, she ruined my marriage first.'

For one blissful moment her mother was shocked into silence. Sadly, it didn't last. 'Ellie, you know that's not true. Maisie and Dave only got together after you two had split up. Everything was totally above board. But you not showing up at the wedding gives the wrong message about that. Maisie's very upset at the idea that people might think you don't give them your blessing.'

I don't, Ellie's mind screamed. *I don't give them my blessing. My ex-husband is marrying my half-sister— who is also half my age—and I am not okay with that. I don't see why I should be.*

But she couldn't say any of that to her mum. Not even now, not even when she knew she should.

Keeping the peace in her family was far too ingrained in her to go that far.

'I'm not getting any younger you know, love,' her mum

said, despite the fact that, at sixty-seven, Tracey Peters had more energy than Ellie had possessed in years. 'I just want to see all my girls together and happy. Is that so wrong?'

Ellie sighed. There was no way she was going to win this argument, anyway. She never had. Why start a fight now when she knew she'd never win? 'No, Mum.'

'So you'll come?'

No. Not in a million years.

'I'll…see what I can do.' Ellie hated herself for even saying it, but she knew she'd never get off the phone otherwise.

'That's all I ask.' Her mum managed to sound suitably martyred, even though Ellie knew full well that was *not* all she asked, and anything less than doing things exactly her way would never be tolerated.

She'd hoped that putting significant air miles between them would help her escape the guilt trips. Apparently, she'd been wrong.

But maybe it would at least help Ellie to avoid caving in.

Mum mollified, she managed to get off the phone after only another fifteen minutes of unwanted updates on what every single one of Tracey's acquaintances was up to. As she pressed the end call button, Ellie lowered her head to her arms on her desk and focused on just breathing in the quiet for a moment or two.

Then her email pinged with another message from her agent.

This was ridiculous. She had to do *something*. About the book, about the wedding, about her *life*.

And right now, she could only think of one thing she *could* do.

So she picked up her phone and messaged Lily to ask for Jesper's phone number.

Jesper hadn't been expecting to hear from Ellie again. Hoping, sure. But not expecting.

These days, he tried not to expect too much from other people. He knew that the only person who could shape his reality was himself, and so he relied only on himself, as far as possible.

And Will, he supposed, when it came to financial matters.

And Anders, and by extension Lily, to keep him anchored to the wider world.

And now maybe, maybe, Ellie, just a little bit. To feel useful. As if what he'd learned in the last few years could be of service to more people than just himself.

It had been a strange impulse that led him to invite her to get in touch to discuss happiness, if she wanted, for her book. He'd been a little shaken by the kiss, if he was honest with himself—and he did try to be, these days. He hadn't kissed a woman since Agnes' death, and he hadn't expected to that night, for all of Will's teasing and the strange draw he felt towards Ellie. At most, he'd have imagined a peck on the cheek—or maybe lips, if he was feeling daring.

But instead…instead he'd found himself drawn in by her, until the planned brush of his lips against hers turned into something far deeper. A lingering kiss that had stirred something inside him he'd thought lost. A kiss that he just had to deepen, that called for him to wrap his arms tighter around Ellie's waist and hold her against him.

A kiss he knew he wouldn't forget in a hurry.

So maybe that was why he'd told her to call, if she wanted. He didn't have her number, and wouldn't ask Lily or Anders for it without Ellie's permission, so the ball was in her court. She could find him, through their mutual friends, if she wanted to—and she had the excuse of it being for work. It was all up to her.

He hadn't really expected to hear from her again, though. Certainly not a mere two days later.

Jesper had to admit, seeing her text message had lifted his spirits rather, though.

Fortunately, he was still in Copenhagen when she messaged, having spent the holiday catching up on some reading and walking around the quiet city, before a more in-depth meeting with Will on the first working day of the year.

And now, the day after Ellie's message, he was sitting in one of his favourite Copenhagen cafés, waiting for her to join him for pastries and coffee.

He was early—he usually was—so he had the luxury of watching for her, and seeing her pause outside the café window, checking her phone, presumably to confirm that she was in the right place. Then, with a small nod to herself, she pushed the door open and stepped inside, scanning the tables for him.

She looked much as she had on New Year's Eve, as they'd toured the Tivoli Gardens, her sunny yellow bobble hat pulled down over her still mostly dark hair. He'd seen strands of silver glinting in the fairy lights when she'd taken it off that night, although not nearly so many as peppered his temples and beard. He liked them. They gave her a faintly ethereal air, somehow.

Or maybe he just liked that she wasn't trying to stay—or at least look—forever young. Agnes had spent a fortune—in time, money and energy—keeping time at bay, but in the end, all of that time she'd keep fending off came for her at once. Nowadays, Jesper appreciated the signs of ageing, of still being in the world, all the more.

Jesper half stood, waved, and smiled when she caught sight of him and her shoulders visibly relaxed as she hurried over to his table. They did the awkward greeting of two people who had only met once—but had already kissed—before she took the seat opposite him.

'Hi,' she said again, looking faintly embarrassed for reasons he didn't fully understand. 'Thanks for doing this.'

'Of course. Let me go get you some coffee and pastries, and we can start.' Even if he wasn't entirely sure what they were starting.

Ellie started to get up, reaching for her purse. 'I can get them! I mean, you're here helping me...'

Jesper waved her away. 'Think of it as a welcome to Copenhagen.' Even if she'd been there two months already, she looked so ill at ease, he thought she still counted as a newcomer.

It didn't take long to procure a plate piled high with various specialities and return to the table. Ellie's eyes widened at the sight of all the pastries and sweet treats.

'I wasn't sure what you'd already tried and what you haven't,' he explained. 'So I got one of everything. Plus, this bakery is my *favourite*, and I'll be leaving Copenhagen to head home again tomorrow, so I need to get my fill while I'm here.'

'You don't live in Copenhagen?' Ellie reached tentatively for a *kanelsnegle*—a cinnamon swirl—and he gave her an encouraging nod.

'Not any more, no. I grew up here, though I lived in other parts of the country at different times. Then I moved to the States after my marriage, and back to Denmark again after—' He broke off. They were here to talk about happiness. He didn't want to frighten her off too soon by mentioning his wife's death again. Even if it *had* been the thing that set him back on the right path.

Ellie didn't miss a beat. 'But not to Copenhagen. So where?'

'I have a house out on the coast, up in North Jutland. About four hours' drive away from here.' And a world away from everywhere, it always seemed, when he was there. Which was why he loved it so much, of course.

She nodded, obviously computing as she chewed. 'That's about how long it used to take us to get to visit my grandparents from London as a kid. It seemed like for ever then, but now… I suppose it's not so far. These pastries are amazing, by the way.'

'Try the jam *spandauer*,' he suggested, pointing to the jam-filled pastry with icing sugar sprinkled over it. 'They were always my favourite when I was small.'

'If you insist.' She didn't sound as if he was twisting her arm. 'So, now you only come to Copenhagen for business? Or to visit friends?'

'Yes, I suppose. I hadn't been back much before this trip, I must confess.' He smiled at the sight of her face as she took her first bite, icing sugar powdering her top lip. 'I'm glad I did, though.'

'So am I.' Ellie licked away the sugar, and Jesper felt a new warmth rise up in him as his mind filled with memories of their kiss.

It was possible he was in more trouble here than he'd anticipated.

For a moment, Ellie forgot how incredible the Danish pastries tasted and lost herself in Jesper's bright blue eyes once more, just as she had on New Year's Eve.

Oh, this was a bad idea. She'd known it when she'd asked Lily for his number, been certain when he'd responded to her text with the suggestion that they meet here at the café, and had almost turned back twice on her way there.

She needed to get this situation back on track. She needed his professional help, that was all. This was business, not pleasure.

Well, except for the pastries. *They* were pure pleasure.

Ellie looked away, swallowed the last mouthful of her jam-filled pastry—good, but not as incredible as the cinnamon swirl—and gathered her thoughts. She was here to ask him about happiness.

'So, moving back to Denmark, the house up in Jutland…they were part of your…um…happiness quest, after your loss?' She'd done a little research before their meeting—she was a reporter after all, and if he was going to be her source, she needed to know he was the real deal.

She'd started with a quick internet search, which had told her all about his high-flying business career in the States, and the tragic death of his wife three years earlier.

Ellie had jotted down all the facts and figures—and then she'd called Lily again for the real story. Like where Jesper had been for the three years since then, and why he suddenly believed he was some sort of guru of happiness.

Lily had been reluctant to say much, insisting that if Jesper wanted to work with her on her project then it would be better for him to share the story with Ellie directly. But she had managed to get some fundamentals out of her friend.

Like the fact that, after his wife's death, Jesper had gone basically off-grid for years on some sort of personal happiness quest. Not massively unlike the one Ellie herself was *supposed* to be undertaking for her book, except that Jesper seemed to have actually done it properly.

'After Agnes died, I needed to get away from everything for a while.' Jesper spoke slowly, his broad fingers systematically shredding a cinnamon swirl onto the plate in front of him. It was a chronic waste of a pastry, but Ellie didn't interrupt him. This was what she'd come here to hear. 'I needed to…reset, perhaps. To reevaluate…everything.'

Ellie took a sip of her coffee before murmuring, 'I can understand that.'

Hadn't she needed to do the same? Wasn't that what she was *supposed* to be doing here in Copenhagen?

She just hadn't been very good at it so far.

Jesper's gaze turned sharp as he looked at her. 'Why did you really come to Denmark, Ellie?'

She blinked. 'I told you. The book. And this was the only time that fit with my schedule. Why? Did…did Lily say something?'

Lily, of course, knew all about the wedding. But if she

suspected the timing of her trip had more to do with her ex marrying again, she hadn't mentioned it. And Ellie didn't want to talk about it either—especially not to Jesper, who seemed to genuinely enjoy her company. If he knew what a pathetic, people-pleasing runaway she was, that might change.

Better that, though, than admitting how her husband had cast her aside for her half-sister, who was bright and perky and twenty-two—all the things Ellie could never be again.

'Lily didn't say anything,' Jesper assured her. 'It just seemed to me… You came all this way, to Denmark, for four whole months. But you don't really seem to be doing anything different here than you would at home in London. Am I wrong?'

Ellie swallowed, and looked away. 'Not…wrong. I just…' She broke off with a sigh.

After a long pause, Jesper said, 'You don't have to tell me your reasons, Ellie. But I will listen if you want to. Perhaps…perhaps we might be able to help each other.'

'What do *you* need help with?' she blurted out. 'I thought you had this happiness thing all sorted. That you were some kind of guru or something.'

He laughed at that. 'Not a guru. But I have managed to find some…contentment in my life, of a sort I don't think I had before. Happiness, maybe. The problem *I* have is bringing that new mindset back into the real world again, and holding onto it once normality resumes.'

'Lily said you went off-grid,' Ellie offered. 'Is that true?'

'Essentially.' Jesper popped a segment of his destroyed cinnamon swirl into his mouth.

'Like…no people, no news, no internet kind of off-grid?' she pressed. 'Is that what you think *I* need to do to find happiness? Because while the no people bit sounds good, I kind of need the internet for my job…'

'No, no. That was what I needed. It might not be right for you. And now I need to find my way back, so…no. I don't think you need to go completely off-grid to find happiness. Nor does anyone.'

'Well, that's a relief.' Ellie tilted her head as she studied him. 'So, what *do* you think I need to do? I mean, if it's not what you did, why do you think you can show me how to find the famous Danish happiness?'

'I don't know if I can,' Jesper admitted. 'But I can show you the places that brought me joy in my darkest moments. The ones that made me think about the world in a different light. The ones that brought me back to the self I thought I'd lost when Agnes died—before, even, when I was giving everything I had to my job and neglecting the people who made life worthwhile. People, you see, are everything.'

'Says the man who lived away from them for, what—two, three years?' Ellie shook her head. 'Not a ringing endorsement of people, is it? Besides, the one promise I made to myself when I came here was that any happiness I found wouldn't be dependent on other people. I've been burnt trying to find happiness in others before, and I'm never doing it again.'

He raised an eyebrow. 'Never? There's a story there, I assume?'

'There is. But not one I'm ready to share with you just yet.' God, who was she right now? She barely recognised herself, being so open and yet also setting her boundaries.

This was everything all those motivational podcasts Lily kept recommending told her to do—and everything she'd never managed before in her life. Before, she'd worked hard at saying what other people wanted to hear, winning them over to her with give and take—although mostly giving, if she was honest with herself.

Which was why, of course, her mother still believed she might actually attend her half-sister's wedding to her own ex-husband. She'd never said no before, for fear of ruining those always fraught relationships with her loved ones.

But she and Jesper didn't *have* a relationship. They barely even knew each other, and once she left Denmark it was probable that she'd never see him again. Maybe that was why it was easier with him.

He must have felt that too, because he gave a small nod and said, 'That's fair. Maybe one day you'll want to tell me—but if you don't, I respect that, too.'

'Good answer.' The words popped out without her meaning to say them.

He smiled. 'I try to respond to people the way I wish they'd respond to me, these days. And I know all about not having the capacity to share terrible things, sometimes.'

They exchanged a small smile, and Ellie realised that, unlike most people in her life, this was someone she *could* imagine sharing her feelings about Dave's upcoming wedding with. Her suspicions that, whatever everybody said, the relationship between him and Maisie had started long before their marriage had officially ended. The experience of being cut loose in her forties and just not knowing where to go.

She could talk to him about that, perhaps. One day. But not yet.

'So,' Jesper said. 'If your happiness quest isn't about other people, what *is* it going to be about? Because, I have to admit, the Danes put a lot of focus on community and family. If you don't want to write about that, you're going to need something else, right?'

'Right.' Her brain whirred as she tried to order her thoughts, all the possibilities and ideas that were flying at her. For the first time, she felt excited about this project again. Maybe this wasn't *quite* the direction that she'd promised her publisher in her proposal, but she knew it was what she needed right now—and maybe other people, readers, would need it too.

It wasn't as if anything else was working, anyway. So what would it hurt to try?

'I think what I need,' she said slowly, choosing her words with care, 'is to experience a little of what you did over the past few years. I need to go…not off-grid exactly, but, well, *out there*. I need to see what you saw. What helped you find contentment and peace—and made you want to reconnect with people when you came out the other side.'

He raised both eyebrows. 'Is your book about me now?'

'Not exactly. But maybe a bit?' She could use his story to frame certain chapters, perhaps. And, if nothing else, the Denmark he showed her could make for some good descriptive prose. Make it more of a journey of discovery than just a story of her sitting around in Copenhagen's cafés failing to talk to people.

The whole idea was crazy, she knew that. But she also

knew in her bones that she had to try, or she'd regret it for ever.

Ellie *couldn't* go back to London with her tail between her legs—no book, no plans, no money. And even her mother couldn't expect her to attend the damn wedding if she was semi off the grid in the most remote parts of Denmark, could she?

She took a breath, and then took her chance. 'So, what do you say? Are you willing to show me *your* Denmark—and how you found happiness in it?'

CHAPTER FOUR

Jesper's head was screaming at him just how bad an idea this was.

But his gut was telling him it could be interesting. Important, even.

And these days, Jesper made a point of listening to his gut.

He took a long sip of his cooling coffee to consider his options. Oh, he was going to do it, that much was certain. But he knew himself. He needed rules—guidelines, at least—to make sure this didn't pull him under again. His even keel existence was hard won, and he knew that anything that made him list too far to one side or another would destroy him.

Happiness was a step further than what he'd found for himself. Jesper had chosen contentment, which was an altogether more managcable level of joy. Would that be enough for Ellie and her book? He didn't know.

On the other end of the spectrum, while he knew how important other people were to long-lasting wellbeing, he hadn't managed to work up to letting himself get too close to anyone again just yet. Even with Will or Anders, he knew he was holding back, not going into too many details about how he was really coping, or every emotion that had almost pulled him under over the past few years.

If he expected, or even wanted, Ellie to share her secrets with him, he knew she'd want him to do the same in return, and he wasn't sure that was something he could offer.

The basics, those were easy.

I had a wife. I loved her. She died, tragically. I grieved, and I took time away to cope with my grief. In the process, I found a joy in life I hadn't expected.

Maybe that *would* be enough. The people reading these kinds of books and articles seldom wanted the messy details. They wanted the soundbites, the easily actionable items to bring them the same results.

He didn't have to share anything he didn't want to, just like Ellie.

Especially not the details on how he'd failed his marriage, long before it was over. Or how guilty he felt, every single day, for the way Agnes had died. She didn't need to know about the screaming fights or the nights he'd just stayed at the office rather than facing what was waiting for him at home. Or how he'd spent every year of their marriage knowing what she wanted from him but also realising how impossible it was for him to give.

He had never been enough for Agnes. Never been able to live up to her expectations.

Why on earth would he think he could live up to anyone else's?

But Ellie wasn't looking for a happy-ever-after from him. Hell, she wasn't even looking for a relationship.

She just needed someone to help her with her research.

And Jesper had to admit it would be good to have a sense of purpose again, even if only for a little while.

'Okay,' he said after a pause he knew had been too long, but hopefully convinced her he was taking this seriously. 'I'll do it. But we need to do it my way.'

Ellie huffed what might have been a laugh. If it was, Jesper was certain she was laughing at herself. 'Has to be better than my way, given my current progress.'

'The book isn't going well, then?' That didn't surprise him.

She reached out for another pastry. 'Honestly? It's not going at all. I've been able to keep up my social media presence and convince everyone that I'm out here uncovering the secrets of a great life, but in reality… I've got nothing.'

'Nothing?'

'Not a single page.' She looked lighter just for saying it, as if the admission was freeing somehow. 'I haven't written a word of the book since the original proposal I wrote two years ago, before everything went to hell.'

'Hell?'

She looked up sharply, her eyes hunted. 'One of those things we're not talking about yet.'

'All right.' A picture was forming, even without her telling the story. *Something* had blown her life up recently—maybe not as comprehensively as his, but enough. Given the way her right hand was fiddling with the empty ring finger of her left, he suspected it had something to do with a husband—or, more likely, ex-husband.

'So, what are your rules?' she asked.

'Guidelines,' he replied. 'Not rules.'

'Fine, guidelines. What are they?'

Yes, that was a good question. What *were* they? He'd decided that he needed them, but trying to put them into words was another thing altogether.

Maybe he really had been out of society for too long. He'd forgotten how to communicate effectively.

'I can't promise that I'll find you happiness,' he said slowly. 'That's the first thing you have to understand. I can show you the places I went, tell you what I found there—what I discovered about myself. But happiness—contentment, really—is a personal thing.'

She nodded. 'I get that. And honestly… I'm not really expecting to find joy, or contentment, or happiness on this trip. I just need something to write about.'

That made it easier, he supposed. Less pressure. But it still made him a little sad to hear.

'What else?' she pressed.

'That's the main one, I guess. A disclaimer, really. Other than that… I'll need a few days here to get everything in order before we can go. And once we're on the road… I might need time alone sometimes. I'm not really used to socialising on a daily basis yet.'

She smirked. 'That one is definitely not a problem. I'm kind of an introvert these days, too.'

Something occurred to him. 'Last one,' he promised. 'You have to go along with the places I want to take you to, and the things I suggest you try. Otherwise, what's the point of all this?'

'That's fair.' She pulled a face as she said it, though, and he knew it would be a struggle for her not to argue with him about some of them. Already he was forming a mental list of the destinations and activities for their road trip of joy.

He found himself strangely looking forward to it. Far more than he'd expected to.

'I have one rule—sorry, guideline—too,' Ellie blurted out suddenly, and he wondered how long she'd been thinking it over while he spoke.

'Of course. What is it?'

'On New Year's Eve…we…well… What happened on New Year's Eve…' She trailed off again, and Jesper took pity on her.

'You mean the kiss we shared?'

'Yes.' There was the faintest pink flush to her cheeks that made Jesper want to kiss her again, just to see if he could get it to deepen. Had she been thinking about it as much as he had? If so, their adventures together might be even more fun than he'd hoped…

'That can't happen again,' she said, shattering his growing optimism. 'It was…just a New Year thing. A midnight kiss, right? But even if it were anything more, if we're going to do this happiness trip, we can only be friends. Because, like I told you—'

'You can't have your happiness rely on another person,' he finished, to show he'd been listening. 'I understand. Really, I do.' Which wasn't the same as *liking* it, but he had to admit she was probably right. Neither of them was in a good enough place for getting tangled up in something *more* than friends to be a good idea. 'Just friends.'

Even if another kiss might have convinced him of the value of being back in the world far more than all the fairy lights and fireworks of New Year's Eve had managed. He couldn't give any more than he'd already agreed to—so it wasn't fair to ask for any more from her.

'So, we're going to do this?' There was a hint of excitement in her voice that made him smile. 'We're going to go hunt down happiness together?'

He raised another pastry—this one filled with custard and icing—and held it up to her in a toast until she met it with her own chocolate laden one.

'We are,' he said, and smiled.

Deciding to go on some sort of Danish epic quest for joy was one thing. Actually doing it, Ellie was rapidly discovering, was something else.

For instance, what was she even supposed to pack? She didn't know exactly where they were going still, despite the map Jesper had pulled up on his phone in the café to demonstrate his proposed route.

'Just take everything,' Lily said when she called to strategize with her best friend. 'Jesper's car is a decent size. It's not like you're flying.'

In a way, it would be easier if they were. But apparently everywhere Jesper wanted to go in Denmark—which seemed to be almost everywhere—was drivable. Which, Ellie was realising now, meant a lot of hours trapped in a car together, with nothing to do but talk.

Somehow, she suspected she wasn't going to have many secrets left by the end of this trip.

That was only fair, really. She wanted him to spill his guts and give her everything she needed about his years in the wild to add to her book on happiness. It only made sense that he'd want a little openness and truth from her in return.

Even if she wasn't looking forward to sharing the humiliating part about her ex's wedding, and how she ran away to another country to avoid it.

Eventually, she took Lily's advice and shoved almost everything she'd brought from Britain for her four months stay back into her large suitcase and called it good, just in time to grab her coat and layer up to lug it down the stairs to where Jesper's car was waiting outside.

'Got everything?' he asked as he hefted the suitcase into the boot without breaking a sweat.

'This country of yours requires a lot of layers,' she replied, earning a laugh.

Ellie settled into the comfortable passenger seat, familiarising herself with the layout of the car she assumed she was going to be calling home for most of the next three weeks.

That was how long Jesper had estimated it would take them to cover all the ground he wanted to show her. It meant she'd be back in Copenhagen just before the wedding in London, but she was hoping she could fudge the timings on that when she made her next round of excuses to her mother.

'No satnav?' she asked as he pulled away from the kerb and she realised he had no guidance for where they were going.

'Don't need it,' he replied. 'I'm going home. How could I lose my way?'

Since Ellie had once managed to get lost between the tube station and the office she walked to every day, just because one tiny stretch of pavement had been closed and she'd had to take a slight detour, she wasn't sure she had his faith in a person's ability to unerringly find their way home. But as Jesper took turns and roads confidently on his way out of the city, it became clear that he, at least, could do it.

He had some music playing—something light, unobtrusive, something that would allow for as much conversation as they wanted, but Ellie found herself listening to it too deeply, perhaps to avoid talking at all.

Or perhaps because she was in a strange car with a strange man going to a strange place and, really, wasn't that a little bit extreme to avoid telling her mother she wouldn't go to her half-sister's wedding?

'Are you having second thoughts?' Jesper asked after a while. Ellie wasn't sure when he'd learned to read her mind, but she didn't like it. Or was she just that much of an open book?

'Not second thoughts,' she lied. 'Just thoughts.'

'Such as?'

'Where exactly are we going first?' She'd text Lily the details, just in case. Oh, she trusted Jesper—and so did Anders and Lily, or she wouldn't be going in the first place. But if something happened, something went wrong, someone should know where she was.

And she definitely wasn't telling her mother. She wouldn't put it past Tracey Peters to be on the first flight out there to haul her home again if she thought she was running away again.

'I'm going to take you to my home, in Jutland,' Jesper said. 'It's where I went first when…when I returned to this country.'

When his wife died, Ellie's mind filled in for her.

Was it strange that she was relying on someone in such a different situation to help her find happiness? Jesper had experienced true, total loss, and had to rebuild his life knowing he'd never see Agnes again.

Dave wasn't dead. And Ellie was more afraid of having to see him again than not.

'We'll pass some interesting places on the way though,' he promised. 'Just watch.'

And she did. Maybe she was just too tired to object, or perhaps it was a convenient way to avoid more awkward conversation—Ellie honestly wasn't sure. All she knew was that her brain took the instruction and ran with it.

She leaned back in the comfortable padded seat of Jesper's car and rested her aching head as she stared out of the window. Yes, maybe this was craziness, but there was something calming about watching the snowy Danish countryside speed by outside, while the thrum of the engine and the warmth of the car lulled her into a sort of peace. For once, she didn't even feel the need to think— to plan, to strategize, to figure out what was next or what she was going to say to her mother or her agent next time they called.

She just…was.

After a long while of travelling in silence, Jesper's rumbling voice filled the car. 'If you're sleeping, you might want to wake up and open your eyes for the next bit.'

'I'm not sleeping,' Ellie said automatically, even though, actually, she wasn't sure. Her eyes felt heavy and gritty, and her mouth was dry. Maybe she'd dropped off. She hoped she hadn't been snoring.

She blinked a few times, then focused in on the view out of the window. 'What is *that*?'

'That is the Great Belt Bridge. Fourth longest suspension bridge in the world.' Jesper sounded personally proud of this Danish achievement. 'It means we can cross from Zealand—the island Copenhagen sits on—to Fyn and then on to the Danish mainland in practically no time at all.'

Ellie wasn't sure that bridges automatically led to national happiness, but she was willing to concede that it was quite the sight. And actually, now she thought about it, being able to get around a country easily and quickly had to be a plus, right? She still had occasional nightmares about being stuck in Crewe station in the freezing cold, having missed a connecting train back to London on her way home from university.

This bridge had the high concrete pylons and massive cables that spoke of solid and reliable engineering and, from what she could see, it was in heavy use.

'Is that a lighthouse?' Ellie peered out of the window at a small island that seemed to link one part of the bridge with another.

'That's the island of Sprogø,' Jesper replied without looking. 'There's a rail link as well as the road bridge from there, in the tunnels.'

'So, good transport infrastructure,' Ellie said. 'Road to happiness?'

He laughed. 'Could be. You're writing a social media post in your head already, aren't you?'

Rather than deny it, Ellie just opened the camera on her phone and snapped a few photos of the bridge and the lighthouse to post as a sort of immediate travel log with minimal commentary. She'd do a fuller, more reflective post later.

'You really are desperate to find the deep truth of

happiness to share with your followers.' Jesper sounded slightly pitying, which instantly put her hackles up.

'I'm desperate not to have to pay back my advance to my publisher,' she countered. 'We can't all afford to go off-grid and search for our bliss for a couple of years. Some of us are on a budget and a timetable.'

He glanced across at her for just a second, before fixing his gaze firmly back on the road again. 'That's fair enough.'

They crossed the rest of the bridge in silence.

They arrived at his home in north Jutland late in the afternoon, just as the sun was slipping down over the horizon again. Ellie had slept for much of the drive, reducing the need for conversation, and Jesper had found himself strangely grateful for the solitude.

Or maybe not strangely. He was more used to being alone than in company these days, anyway.

And he didn't *understand* Ellie. He'd thought he did, when he'd offered to help her. He'd assumed she was a happiness tourist, fresh from a divorce, looking for life hacks to find her joy. He'd thought that he could show her a bit of Denmark and help her realise that true happiness went deeper than that. He'd believed this could be a fun, friendly jaunt to give his vague wanderings some purpose for the next few weeks, while he figured out what he was going to do next in his life. Something between the all and the nothing of his workaholic days and his stint in the wilderness.

Then, last night, he'd pulled out his laptop and searched for Ellie Peters online.

He'd found her social media instantly, before her website even, and been sucked in against his will. He wasn't a social media addict—avoided it like the plague if he could. Partly because he was certain that he was a happier person without it, but mostly because it was full of people who'd known him and Agnes before, and expected him to be the same person.

He couldn't be that person any longer. Couldn't fake it, even online to people he'd gone to primary school with. And he didn't feel comfortable showing them who he was now either.

Ellie, however, didn't seem to have any problem with being a completely different person online.

It had taken him a few moments to be sure he was even looking at the right person. Yes, there was the same hair, same eyes, same smile—except the smile looked less guarded in photos than in real life, and her eyes sparkled in a way he'd never seen.

There were shots and selfies from the night they'd met, taken at the Tivoli Gardens—fireworks and hot, greasy food and crowds and smiles. None of him, he noticed gratefully, but one of Ellie and Lily with their heads pressed together, smiling broadly.

Intrigued, he'd read the caption below, where Ellie had waxed lyrical about the power of a new year, the opportunities ahead, how she was excited to see where it led her. How her happiness quest had brought her experiences she'd never dreamed of, and so on.

None of which gelled with the frustrated author with writer's block—and happiness block—he'd shared pastries with in the café and promised to try to help.

Now, as he pulled his car to a stop in front of his seafront home, he looked over at the sleeping Ellie and wondered which was really the true woman, and which was the fake. He *thought* that the woman he'd been getting to know was the real thing—and, in truth, it seemed far more likely than the beaming, happy woman in the photos online.

Maybe nobody was really who they said they were any more.

But he found that he wanted to know more. To understand why and how she preserved this fake persona. What it gave her. What it achieved.

Who she really was underneath it all. Because if that Ellie wasn't real, maybe the one he'd met wasn't either. Maybe the truth was a different woman altogether.

Would he get to meet her during this happiness experiment? He hoped so.

As the engine cut out, Ellie stirred in the seat beside him. 'We're here?' Her voice was fuzzy with sleep and she blinked up at him adorably as she tried to focus. Here, again, was that different Ellie. Neither the beaming social media presence or the focused journalist he'd made his deal with. Just a woman waking up.

How long had it been since he'd watched a woman waking? Had he *ever?* He'd always been an early riser, and Agnes had liked to sleep in. He'd usually been in the office before she awoke, when they were married. Her days had been rather more…relaxed than his own, despite all the committees and boards she'd sat on.

'We're here,' he confirmed, his own voice a little gruff from misuse. 'Come on; I'll show you around and then we can bring the bags in.'

She nodded and fumbled for her seatbelt release. Jesper gritted his teeth to stop himself reaching to do it for her, and got out of the car.

She was his guest, not his lover. They'd agreed to be friends and nothing more. He was a teacher in this situation even—anything else would be a gross abuse of power.

But knowing that didn't seem to stop him wanting to know her better as a person. To lean in and help her with her seatbelt. To tuck her hair behind her ears and smile at her, maybe even steal another kiss.

Which was going to be a problem if he couldn't push those thoughts aside. Ellie had made it very clear that wasn't what she wanted from him, and he intended to make sure she never suspected he'd wanted it in the first place, in case it made her uncomfortable.

He just wasn't entirely sure how he was going to do that yet.

His housekeeper had been by that afternoon to air the place out, change the sheets and stock the fridge; her message to say that all was ready for them had buzzed through on his phone while he'd been driving. She'd left the lights on, too, so his home looked bright and welcoming against the darkening sky and the dramatic coastline beyond.

Jesper was surprised to feel a warmth of homecoming as he stepped up the path to the front door. He hadn't owned this place for more than a few years, and he'd spent most of his time there dragging himself out of the deepest despair. He'd always planned to sell it once he had himself back together again and move back to the city, or at least somewhere with another house within shouting distance.

But he hadn't. And now he wasn't even sure if he would. This place was his refuge, and he found himself reluctant to part with that.

'When you said you had a little place by the beach… this isn't exactly what I was expecting.' Ellie's tone was dry, but not disapproving.

He tried to look at the place through her eyes. He supposed it was a little larger than a beach house—he'd certainly found himself rattling around in there when he'd first moved in, unsure how to use all that space for one person. After a while, when he was feeling a little more stable, he'd got an interior designer in to sort the place out, while he was off somewhere else on a retreat. He'd left an empty shell and returned to a home, which had been a blessing he'd felt utterly unworthy of at the time, but now appreciated beyond measure.

'Come and take a look inside.' He held a hand out to her automatically, a misplaced reflex he couldn't bring himself to regret when she actually took it, her smooth palm and fingers cool in his. 'Welcome to my home,' he said, and meant it.

CHAPTER FIVE

WHEN JESPER HAD talked about his beach house, Ellie had imagined something like a small summer home, cabin-like even, perhaps. Instead, he'd brought her to a Scandi mansion by the sea.

The place was huge, that was a given. But it was also beautiful. Clean lines and pale, natural materials outside, blending in while also, somehow, standing out against the rugged coastline of northern Jutland. Its black roof spoke of stormy skies, while the pale wood walls echoed the sand she couldn't quite see over the green hills.

The lights were on inside, a beacon welcoming them home. Jesper led her through the dark front door, only dropping her hand once the door had shut behind them. She wasn't even sure why she'd taken his hand—or why he'd offered it. She wasn't a child, needing to be led. And she wasn't a date either—they'd both made that very clear.

But it had felt right. And now he'd let go…she missed the comforting warmth of his hand in hers.

Ellie shoved her hands in her pockets and looked around.

Inside, an open-plan living space spread all the way from the door to the huge windows that filled almost entire walls, looking out over the darkened beach, out to the sea. Any walls that weren't made of glass were either a soothing off-white colour or natural brick, and there was a wood-burning stove in the fireplace that kept the whole huge space toasty warm.

The living space was split into a large sitting area with a comfortable-looking dark grey corner sofa and a coffee table loaded with oversized books and magazines; a high-end kitchen with soft grey cabinets and wooden surfaces, with a long counter with stools that looked out over the dining area next door. A huge dining table filled that space, near one of the window walls, and it was fully set with eight places.

'Are we expecting company?' Ellie gestured to the dining table with its leafy green centrepiece in a wooden vase and the stacked plates on each of the woven willow placemats.

Jesper laughed. 'My housekeeper lives in hope. She's probably stocked the fridge with enough food for an army.'

At the very mention of food, Ellie's stomach rumbled—and she realised what a long time ago the sandwiches they'd stopped for on the road had been.

He gave her a grin and a knowing look. 'Come on. Let me show you to your room, then I'll grab our stuff and make us some dinner.'

Her room—one of four guest rooms, as far as Ellie could tell—was beautiful. Simply but expensively furnished, with a huge bed covered with white linen and a soft sage-coloured headrest and a small wooden bedside table. The wooden floors were warm—underfloor heating, she supposed—and a floor-to-ceiling window on one side of the bed gave her what she was sure would be a magnificent view in the daytime.

She poked her head into the en suite bathroom while Jesper fetched her bag from the car and saw the most luxurious bathtub she could have ever imagined, as well as a large walk-in shower.

Yes, if she was looking for a place to find true happiness, she could have done a lot worse. Even the company was pretty good, she thought as Jesper dropped off her bags with another one of those enigmatic smiles that warmed her middle more than the underfloor heating did her toes.

Leaving unpacking for later, Ellie wandered through to the main living area again in time to see Jesper pulling out some wonderfully fresh-looking vegetables and other food from the fridge.

'Is pasta okay?' he asked without looking up. 'I figure it's quick and easy and we're both hungry.'

'Sounds perfect.'

He glanced up and smiled. 'Then take a seat, and I'll let you know when it's ready.'

Ellie nodded then moved away, towards the living area. But then she spotted the window seat—a long, cushioned bench set against one of those huge windows looking out over the beach. Grabbing a magazine from the coffee table, she curled herself up on it and made herself at home.

The magazine was in Danish, but that didn't matter since she only really wanted to look at the pictures. It was some sort of home and lifestyle glossy mag, with photos of perfect-looking Danish homes much like Jesper's, and perfectly styled dishes that made her stomach rumble again. Just leafing through it reminded her of the career and the life she'd left behind in London and, after a few minutes, she closed it again and stared out of the window instead.

She could hear the sea, she realised. The dull roar of the waves as they rushed forward and then pulled back, the rattle of the stones and sand as they were tossed in the water. The winter wind, as it whipped by them. The beach house was so well constructed and insulated that she hadn't noticed it at all anywhere else. But here, even by the obviously thick and double-glazed window, she could just make it out.

It awakened a sort of longing in her that she hadn't expected. She just couldn't quite identify what it was a longing *for*.

What did the sea tend to signify? Escape? Change? She wasn't sure.

She still hadn't figured it out by the time that Jesper called her over for dinner, but she was still pondering the question as she blew across the pasta and sauce before taking her first mouthful.

'This is delicious,' she told him, after she'd tasted it. 'Do you enjoy cooking, then?' Simple, easy, getting-to-know-each-other questions. That was what she needed to feel more on an even keel here. The problem was she'd gone too far, too fast—in fact she'd done almost every-thing so far in the wrong order.

She'd kissed him, then had deep conversations about happiness, and only *now* was she learning about his hob-bies.

'I never used to,' Jesper admitted. 'Agnes and I...in New York we mostly survived on takeout, restaurant meals and leftovers. But when I moved back here…it's not so easy to find someone willing to deliver a pizza to the middle of nowhere. And, besides, I didn't want to see anyone, not even delivery drivers, for a while. So I taught myself to make some healthy, simple dishes, mostly so I wouldn't starve.'

'Well, it worked out well for me,' Ellie said with a smile, before taking another mouthful of the creamy pasta and sauce.

They ate the rest of the meal in a silence that started out comfortably but grew more awkward as it stretched out, filling the huge open-plan room. It lasted through the loading of the dishwasher, interrupted only by polite commentary and instructions. Ellie was about to yawn pointedly, maybe even with a little stretch, and make an excuse to disappear for an early night—even though she'd slept in the car—before Jesper cleared his throat and said, 'Would you like to take a walk on the beach before we turn in for the night? I always think the moon on the sea is the most beautiful thing about this place.'

And how could she possibly say no to that?

Jesper hadn't intended his suggestion to be romantic— in fact, he'd been trying to find anything that distracted him from the fact that he was staying in his remote beach house with a woman he found both attractive and in- triguing, with no hope of doing anything at all roman- tic about it.

Which he knew, objectively, was for the best—he wasn't in a place to be pursuing romantic interests still, and he'd promised himself he'd keep things on an even, safe keel. Lust was the opposite of even.

Still, now they were strolling along the winter beachscape, wrapped up in warm coats and scarves wrapped around their necks, Jesper had to admit that there was at least a romantic edge to the outing.

From the way Ellie was keeping a careful one metre distance between them, he suspected that she had noticed it too. He tried to think of a way to explain what he'd really been thinking, bringing her out there. The last thing he wanted was for her to regret coming with him because she thought he was going to spend the whole time hitting on her.

He wasn't. No matter how tempting that idea was—because it was only really tempting if she reciprocated, and she'd already told him she wouldn't.

'Winter swimming is a big thing here in Denmark,' he said eventually. 'Going from the cold water to the sauna and vice versa especially.'

'You think I should go swimming in this sea?' Ellie sounded sceptical. He didn't blame her. The night was so black it was hard to tell where the beach ended and the water began.

'Well, not now,' he allowed. 'But before you leave, perhaps.'

'Maybe.' She eyed the waterline uncertainly. 'I know wild swimming has really taken off in the UK too, but I haven't tried it. Yet. But people say it does incredible things for their wellbeing in all sorts of ways.'

Jesper shrugged, hands safely in his pockets. 'Water has always been said to have healing properties, I suppose. And we're, what—eighty per cent water? Makes sense that we'd want to go back to it.'

'Hmm.' This time, she sounded rather more like she

was considering the idea, which Jesper decided meant his work was done for the evening. All he'd promised to do was introduce her to things that might spark happiness. The sea, for him, was one of them.

He made a mental note of a few other water-based places they could visit as he continued walking—which meant it took a moment or two for him to realise that she wasn't following.

When he turned back, he found her standing a little closer to the shoreline, phone in hand as she photographed the moon's reflection shimmering on the waves.

'Sorry,' she said sheepishly when she was done. 'I realised I'd need a new image for tomorrow's social media posts and, well, this looked perfect. I might use a few of your house while I'm here too, if that's okay? I'll make sure they're all just glimpses and don't give away where we are—or show you at all. I know you value your privacy.'

'I do,' he replied. 'But I'm sure some carefully curated photos will be fine.'

They turned to continue their walk, but the interlude had given him exactly the opening he'd been looking for since he'd stumbled over her online presence the night before.

'I have to admit, I checked out your social media accounts last night. You have a lot of followers.'

Ellie looked momentarily taken aback, but recovered quickly. 'I suppose that makes sense. I mean, you've invited a stranger into your home. Of course you'd want to know a little more about her. Me, I mean.'

'That was part of it, yes. But also… I wanted to know more about your quest for happiness.' He didn't mention that he'd felt like he knew her *less* after reading her online posts than he had after they'd spent New Year's Eve together.

'And what did you think?' Ellie asked. 'Like you said, I have a lot of followers. They expect a certain kind of content from me, so I try to live up to that.'

'It was all very well written, and the photos were beautiful.'

He could have left it there. He didn't have to say any more really, did he?

But Ellie gave him a knowing look and prompted, 'But?'

'It just didn't feel very like you, if I'm being honest.' He winced a little in anticipation of her response.

Luckily, Ellie didn't look offended at his observation. In fact, she laughed.

'Well, no. It's not me. It's the me that I'm comfortable putting out there for others to meet.'

'That makes sense, I suppose.' Jesper shrugged. 'I guess I was just…surprised. Social media always feels like a game for teenagers or terrifyingly confident young adults to me.'

'I think it still is, in lots of ways,' Ellie admitted. 'Certainly, I think they are the ones who are comfortable putting their whole selves on show, the way their audience demands. But there's a place for us *older* contributors too, you know.'

'I wasn't saying you were old,' he said quickly.

Her laugh seemed to carry and crash onto the waves, breaking into melodic shards of echoes. 'I know that. And I understand what you're saying. But these days? Online is one of the only ways we have left to reach a larger audience, assuming you don't have the megabucks of the big companies. It's much more targeted, too. It's the great equaliser in some ways—and it means I can reach women just like me, or ones who want to read about the things I'm writing about. I'm not on there giving make-up tips or what have you. I'm writing exactly the same way I write in my book, so that when it's published they'll already know if they like it or not.'

He nodded. 'I can understand that. Except...you're *not* writing the book, but you *are* writing your social media posts. Why is that, do you think?'

Ellie pulled a face—one he could only just make out in the moonlight but made him laugh all the same.

'Isn't that the million-dollar question?' She sighed. 'I don't know. It's easy enough to keep up the facade when I'm writing online, but the moment I try to create some-thing more...real, I suppose, it all dries up.'

Jesper considered the question. It seemed to him there was a fairly simple explanation, although he wasn't sure how well she'd take the suggestion. And really, what did he know of writing books? But if she could write one thing and not another...

'You might as well say it, you know,' Ellie said. 'What-ever it is you're thinking, I mean. We're stuck together now for the next few weeks. Might as well be honest with each other while we're at it. How am I supposed to learn about your happiness quest otherwise?'

He weighed up for a moment if she really meant it, and decided that she did. It was a question he'd had to ask himself often with his late wife, and one he'd regu-larly answered wrongly. But Ellie was watching him with wide, waiting eyes, as though she'd welcome whatever answer he had to give.

He supposed it didn't really matter what he thought anyway, which maybe made it easier to hear.

'I was just thinking that…maybe you find it harder to write the book because those pages are where you are truly yourself. Perhaps it is easier to put on a mask for others than to examine the truth in yourself. Being true to yourself, I have found, is an important part of happiness.'

Ellie's smile was somehow sad in the moonlight. 'You're probably right. But I'm not sure I've ever met anyone who is truly, completely themselves—and honest with themselves about it, too.'

'You've met me now,' he countered.

Her gaze turned speculative. 'Yes, I have. And do you honestly believe that you are true to yourself, and truthful *about* yourself, all the time?'

Did he? He'd thought that was what he'd been doing out here in the back of beyond all this time—finding his true core self and learning what made it tick, what he needed to survive and thrive in this world.

To be happy, but in a way that meant he'd dragged himself out of the pit of despair Agnes' death had put him in. The sense of his utter, utter failure that had led to it.

But now, with Ellie watching him so closely, waiting for his answer, he wondered if he'd really ever reached that level of truth.

I never told anyone about Agnes being pregnant when she died. Not even Will. And I never told them she was leaving me either.

Could he really claim to be truthful with himself, to

be his *true* self as he was accusing her of not being on-line, if he still held those secrets so close to his chest?

'Maybe it's a work in progress for all of us,' he said finally, and she nodded her agreement.

'Well, perhaps I can get better at it during our trip.' Ellie tucked a hand through the crook of his elbow, the same way they'd walked together at the Tivoli Gardens on New Year's Eve. 'Perhaps we both can.'

'Perhaps.' Jesper couldn't shake the discomfited feeling her words left inside him, though. He'd brought her here to help her, to teach her, to show her all he'd learned.

He hadn't considered that she might have anything to teach him, too.

Or that he might have even been wrong about how far he'd come.

She shivered, and he turned them around, spinning past the shining sea to head back the way they'd come.

'Come on,' he said. 'Let's get back to the house. I've got a big day planned for us tomorrow.'

He'd show her the first places that he'd visited on his happiness quest. That would help him feel more in control of this situation.

He hoped.

'So, where are we going?' Ellie asked as Jesper's car pulled away from the beach house.

To be honest, she'd been reluctant to get back into the car after yesterday's long drive, but Jesper had promised her it would be worth it. He'd filled her in on his plans for the day over a simple breakfast of fruit and pastries, and excellent coffee. But it was only now she realised that, while he'd told her how long it would take to get there, what sort of footwear and layers to wear and where they'd stop for lunch, he hadn't actually told her where they would be going.

Jesper flashed her a quick smile. He seemed much more playful than he had on their pensive moonlight walk the night before. At moments, she'd felt he was almost nervous around her, keeping a safe distance away in case she got any ideas about this being anything more than an educational trip—which she definitely wasn't. And after their rather deep conversation about truth and reality online, he'd been keen to call it a night early—leaving her to enjoy the delights of the huge bathtub in her en suite bathroom before bed.

The relaxing water and bubbles hadn't stopped her thinking, though. Reflecting on everything Jesper had said about authenticity and being her true self. Although, if she was honest, she was more interested in what *he'd* been thinking about when he'd gone all quiet and decided it was time to return to the house and their separate rooms. Was there something he wasn't being honest with himself about? She thought there might be.

And, if she was being totally honest with *her*self, she had to admit that the part she was lying about most, even in her head, right now, had nothing to do with the book she hadn't written, or who she was online.

No, she was mostly lying to herself about how much she wanted to kiss Jesper again. As in she kept telling herself she didn't.

But she really, really did.

She sneaked a sideways look at him as he headed back out onto the main road. He was still smiling, his face handsome and just a little bit rugged in the weak winter sunshine, the silver at his temples sparkling.

'No, really. Where are we going?' She wasn't good with ambiguity. She needed to know the plan—and she had a horrible feeling that part of Jesper's quest for joy and authenticity involved throwing out the map and the plan and taking life as it came.

She'd never been very good at that.

'We're going to visit a church,' he said finally, still smiling as if he knew something she didn't. Which he did.

'A church?' She wasn't exactly a religious person. High days and holidays, weddings and christenings, that had been about it in her family—and less after her grandma had died. If Jesper thought she was going to find her true, authentic happiness and write about it through finding religion, he—and her publisher—were going to be disappointed.

Lily would have mentioned if he was a religious nut, right? One of those people who cults sent out to lure new people in—lost, hopeless people like her? The sort of cult that had nothing to do with real religion, or the nice church down the road that held jumble sales once a season, and more to do with crazed obsessiveness and sometimes mass suicide?

'Are we going to be…meeting any other people at this church?' she asked carefully, suddenly apprehensive.

He rolled his eyes. 'Your distrust of other people, and your conviction that happiness is something you can only find solo, is only going to make things harder, you know.'

Well, Lily had said the Danes could be blunt.

So could she. 'Is that a yes?'

Jesper sighed. 'No, Lily, we will not be meeting any

church members or cult-like figures today—that's what you're worrying about, right? I can't promise that there won't be any other people there, though. This particular church is quite a popular tourist attraction around Skagen.'

Skagen. That was right up at the tip of Denmark, she thought she remembered from the map she'd studied before her visit. 'I've never been to Skagen.' She admitted it as sort of a peace offering—an apology for believing, even for a moment, that he was about to kidnap her into a cult.

'It was the first place I went, after I moved back to Denmark and bought the beach house.' Jesper didn't sound offended by her assumptions, so hopefully that meant he'd forgiven her. 'I just got in the car one morning and drove, heading to the edge of the world—well, the country—to see what I found there.'

'And you found a church.' Ellie knew she still sounded sceptical. She couldn't help it.

'I found a church,' he agreed. 'And now, so will you.'

The drive wasn't too far and, less than an hour later, Jesper pulled into a car park that was already populated by at least a few other cars.

'I don't see a church,' Ellie said.

'This way.' He tucked her hand through the crook of his arm, just as she had done last night, and led her the way he wanted to go.

Ellie blinked as the church came into sight, not entirely sure of what she was seeing. 'That's the church?'

'What's left of it.' Jesper was smiling far too broadly now, obviously enjoying his joke. 'Everything except the tower got buried under the sand by shifting dunes, over two hundred years ago.'

Ellie pulled away from him to explore closer. It was the strangest sight: a bright white church tower with a darker brown roof, poking out of the green grasses and purple heather of the dunes that had swallowed it.

'Back when it was built, in the fourteenth century, it was one of the largest churches in the area. Vastly wealthy, big congregation, you know. Important.' Jesper's voice was soft as he told her the history of the place. 'Then the sands came and in no time it was gone. Stripped of anything of value, and all that remained was this.'

'Oh.' The sound she made was involuntary, an exclamation of understanding more than anything.

Now she saw why he'd brought her here.

He was the church. She knew how rich and successful he'd been over in the States, before his wife's death. The event, like those shifting sands, that had changed his fortunes overnight.

But he'd dug himself out, hadn't he? He wasn't still buried in the sands like the church was.

Like she was, if she was honest with herself. Burying herself, or her head at least, in the sand and pretending that Dave and Maisie's wedding wasn't happening. That her career wasn't on the verge of collapsing.

'What does it make you think about?' Jesper's voice was suddenly very close, and she realised he was standing directly behind her. She wondered if she'd looked wobbly as her revelations had crashed over her, and he'd been making sure he was close enough to catch her if she fainted or fell.

She had to admit, her legs felt less stable than they had.

'It makes me think…that nothing stays the same,' she said slowly. 'That even strong, stable, eternal things can crumble or be swallowed up. That change always happens, and all we can do is work with it.'

He nodded. 'That's what it makes me think, too. And, you know, this church is now a popular tourist attraction—probably more popular than it would have been if it had stayed as a church. In the summer, you can even buy tickets to go inside the tower, and there's a kiosk selling ice cream and all sorts.'

Even after disaster had struck, after the church had been buried and could have just been left to decay and fade away...it had found a new life as something else.

Ellie smiled up at him. 'I like that idea.'

'Me too.' He reached over to squeeze her shoulder. 'Come on. I've got plenty more to show you.'

'Where are we going next?' she asked as they headed for the car.

'Somewhere else with another message for us.'

CHAPTER SIX

JESPER FELL BACK and watched as Ellie stood at the very tip of Jutland, watching the ever-changing line in the waves where two seas met and merged. He couldn't see her face, but he could imagine the look of wonder he was sure was there. Even from behind, he could make out her hands, held at her sides but with the fingers taut and stretched, as if she was holding herself back from touching the water.

If it had been summer, he was sure she'd have her shoes off and be ankle-deep in the waves already. The currents were too strong to allow for sea-bathing, but there was still something magical about being at the point where two worlds collided—and a person could see it happening.

He'd been pleased—and silently relieved—that she'd understood the message he'd found in the church, and his reasons for taking her there. None of the metaphors for change and growth he'd come across on his 'quest' as she called it had been particularly subtle, but then, in Jesper's experience, once he'd started looking, almost *everything* he came across had a message for him.

Maybe it was more about the recipient than the message. In which case, he hoped that Ellie was as open to receiving them as he had been.

What was she thinking right now? She'd been standing there, staring at the waves, for ages now.

Jesper had never claimed to be a particularly patient man.

'What do you think?' he asked, raising his voice a little so she could hear him over the waves.

Ellie didn't turn around as she responded. 'I think it's wonderful. Two worlds colliding.'

Hearing her echo his own thoughts only confirmed to him that he'd been right to bring her here. She needed this.

She hadn't confessed all her reasons for coming to Denmark, he was sure of it. But he sensed that she was at a crossroads, much as he had been when he'd first come to this spot. He hoped it would help her make sense of the world, the same way it had him.

'It's like…it's like a sliding doors moment somehow,' Ellie went on, almost as if she were talking to herself and not him. 'I'm at a place where two seas meet, and I have to decide which one I'm going to sail and leave the other sea, the other life, behind.' She shook her head. 'Listen to me, I sound ridiculous—like I'm about to take up a life of piracy.'

'No. You don't.' He stepped closer, until he stood almost beside her on that tip of land that marked the end of Denmark and the start of whatever came next, listening to the waves and watching the warring water where it met. 'I felt exactly the same when I came here for the first time. Like I was choosing which future I wanted. Which way to go next.'

He'd thought, back then, that he'd made the decision. That he knew where his life was going.

Coming back here with Ellie, though… Jesper found himself staring out at the waters, wondering if he was at another turning point. Another moment in his life when two possible paths were separating out in front of him and, sooner or later, he was going to have to decide which one to walk.

He'd let people back in. First Will, and Anders and Lily. Now Ellie.

Sure, none of them were Agnes. There wasn't the heavy responsibility of a marriage he couldn't make work, couldn't dedicate himself to. The expectations he couldn't live up to—because, God knew, Agnes had expected a lot, but that was what he'd signed up for, and in the end he'd been found wanting.

But they were people, all the same. People he cared about and, in Ellie's case, someone he found himself drawn to know better. To understand.

And however much he lied to himself about it, however careful he was to respect her space and keep his distance…in his heart he knew he wanted to kiss her again. Had wanted it ever since the moment their lips had separated on New Year's Eve.

Was that why he was doing this? Out of a misguided hope that it might get him into her bed?

He hoped not. He hoped he was a better person than that. He'd worked hard to be, these past few years.

No, he was doing this for her, to help her find happiness. And if it gave him a sense of purpose for a few weeks that was an added bonus. This was about her, not him.

But she was showing him a life where he didn't have to

be alone for ever. The one thing he hadn't contemplated after Agnes' death—the idea of finding, well, love again.

He didn't love Ellie. He barely knew her.

But he couldn't shake the feeling that he *could* love her, if he let himself. If she let him.

A cold, sharp wind blew across them and Ellie shivered, huddling back into her coat. Jesper moved instinctively closer, then stopped himself before he touched her. What was he going to do? Wrap his arms around her? Warm her with his body heat?

That didn't sound like something just friends did, and she'd been very clear that was all they ever could be.

Besides, on the wind he could hear his personal demons whispering, reminding him what happened when he felt too much, when he moved to the extremes—of work, of love, of life.

The extremes were where everything fell apart. Go too far one way, and everything else would be ripped away from him.

The extremes got people killed, and he couldn't lose another person.

Even if, in his more rational moments, he knew that the universe didn't really operate that way, that Agnes hadn't died because he'd worked too much, it didn't change the fundamentals.

If he hadn't been obsessed with his work, too busy to pay her the attention she'd needed, to love her the way she'd wanted, to live the life she'd married him for, then she would never have been on her way to the airport in the first place. She'd never have been in that car crash, and she wouldn't have died, taking their unborn child with her.

If he had been enough, Agnes would still be alive.

Jesper stepped back. 'We should get going.'

Ellie nodded and turned away from the waves, casting one last look over her shoulder at the place where two seas met as she headed for the car.

He followed more slowly, still thinking.

Yes. The extremes got people killed.

And love was about as extreme as life got, wasn't it?

It wasn't a risk he could take.

They headed into the town of Skagen proper, with its golden houses and red roofs, somehow sunshiny and hopeful even in the depth of winter. The seaside town was beautiful, the museum they toured fascinating and the harbour atmospheric. The café they stopped at for a late lunch was inviting and cosy and the freshly caught seafood delicious.

But Ellie knew she wasn't paying full attention to any of it. Whatever lesson Jesper thought that Skagen had to offer, she was missing it. Because she was still hung up on the last one.

That incredible sight of two seas meeting, washing up over each other, fighting for dominance and retreating again, away from the spit of land where they clashed. She'd never seen anything like it.

She wondered what Jesper had seen there, the first time he'd visited. The message it had for him. He'd said it was the same as hers, but she could sense that there was something he was holding back. But what? He'd already told her his story—the tragic death of his wife, and his retreat from the world until he'd found a way to exist in it again.

What more could there be?

But then, he probably thought she'd told him her whole story, too.

'Time to head back to the beach house?' she asked as he waved away her offer to split the bill. She'd feel worse about that if Lily hadn't told her he was richer than God. 'The sun will be going down soon.'

He flashed her a sudden smile. 'Exactly. Which means we've got one more thing to see.'

Ellie frowned as she tried to figure out what he was talking about, and quickly gave up. Jesper knew this place far better than she ever could and, given the wonders he'd shown her today—sights she'd never have thought to visit on her own—there was no point in even trying to guess.

It turned out to be another beach, of sorts, not too far away.

'This is Høgen—Old Skagen,' Jesper told her as they made their way towards what seemed to be a purpose-built viewing platform above the dunes. 'And this is Sunset Viewpoint. Come on.'

He reached out and took her hand, leading her towards a long, slatted wooden bench that undulated along its length like the sand dunes it sat beside. They took their seats, along with a few other couples—some older, some younger—and waited, and watched as the sun began to sink over the waves, turning the whole sky a fiery orange followed by a glowing pink.

She reached for her phone and snapped a couple of quick photos.

'It's beautiful,' Ellie admitted in a whisper. 'I assume there's another message here?'

'Of course,' he murmured, and she realised he was

closer than she'd thought, his head bent near to hers to hear her speak. 'Can you guess what it is?'

Ellie stared out at the changing sky, the disappearing sun, going out in a blaze of glory even in the dull winter sky. It would stay down for long hours tonight, she knew. But it would be back again in the morning, ready to do this all over again tomorrow night.

Just like her, she supposed.

'When the sun goes down on one day, there's another one waiting to dawn?' she guessed. 'Very musical theatre of you, really.'

'Well, yes,' he admitted. 'But it also has the magic of being true. There's never yet been a sunset that didn't see a sunrise, too.'

'Unless you live right up at the tip of Finland or one of those places that doesn't get light at all in the winter,' she mused, mostly to rile him.

He rolled his eyes, close enough that she could see the amusement in them. 'I suppose.'

She nudged his shoulder with her own. 'I take your point though. One ending is always a beginning of something new.'

'Exactly. Knowing that, believing that…it helped me a lot. I felt like my life had ended when Agnes died. The first thing I had to recognise was that it was the start of something new. Not something I wanted, or enjoyed, or looked forward to, not at first, and some days still not now. But it *was* new, and different. And that meant I could live it differently, too.'

Ellie nodded slowly, her mind turning his words over and over as she considered them. Moving on was hard at the best of times, and the death of a spouse was anything but that. She had to admire his ability to make that choice in the first place—and to share it with her, to help her do the same?

Jesper was a stronger man than she suspected he'd ever give himself credit for. And it stirred up all sorts of feelings inside her chest that she really wasn't ready for.

'You must still miss her terribly,' she said.

'I… I do,' he replied, but Ellie could sense a 'but' coming. 'We didn't…towards the end, we didn't spend much time together at all. I wasn't, well… I wasn't all she'd hoped for in a husband, I think. Know, really. I know I wasn't. So yes, I miss her. I miss what I thought our marriage could have been. I miss the woman I fell in love with. But some days…some days it feels like she's just in another room, another place, waiting for me to come home so she can tell me how I've let her down today.'

It wasn't what she'd expected. Without realising it, she'd painted a picture of the perfect marriage in her head, to explain the depth of his grief that had driven Jesper away from the world. But she knew herself that even the most perfect-seeming marriage had its cracks and fissures. Just look at her and Dave.

Her only failure, as far as she'd been able to ascertain, was not being twenty-two any longer.

She swallowed and looked away, eager to find a new subject. 'So, tomorrow's new dawn—what will that bring? What have you got planned for us next? Another message, I assume?'

'Of course.' Jesper sounded relieved to be back on topic, too. 'But I can't tell you what just yet.'

She jerked her head up to meet his gaze, only to discover that he was closer than ever. So close that, if she wanted, she could bring her lips to his with only the slightest movement.

If she wanted to.

Oh, God, she wanted to. However inappropriate it might be.

Her throat dry, she tried to swallow before she spoke. 'You can't tell me?'

He shook his head, bringing his face even closer to hers, the last of the sunlight shimmering off the silver in his beard. 'But I promise you it's magical.'

Magical.

That kiss at New Year had been magical—unexpected, with literal fireworks going off in the sky behind them. A gentle but all-encompassing kiss that had suddenly opened up a world or a future she hadn't even contemplated before. That kiss had been her sunken church finding a new lease of life, her oceans meeting and crashing, her sunset before the sunrise.

And she could have it again, if she just leant in one iota.

She couldn't breathe with wanting it.

Except...

Her new day couldn't be about some guy. Her joy, her future, had to be something she found in herself, not another person.

For too long, her husband had been her happiness— her marriage, her lifestyle, everything they had together had been what made her *her*. Ellie.

And she couldn't risk falling into that trap again.

She pulled away—but not fast enough to miss the spark of hurt in Jesper's eyes.

But then he gave her a small smile, got to his feet and held a hand out to pull her up.

'Come on. We should get back. Big plans tomorrow.'

'Right.'

Ellie followed him back to the car, still thinking.

She couldn't kiss him, and she'd told him why. But she hadn't told him everything.

If he knew about Dave and Maisie, if she told him the truth about why she was in Denmark, then he'd understand why she couldn't risk kissing him again.

She owed him that much.

She just needed to figure out how to do it.

'Thank you for this,' she said suddenly, before he could open the car door. 'Really. I think… I think today has given me at least part of what I was looking for. I think that maybe I can even start writing now.' She'd have to update her social media accounts before she looked at her manuscript, but for the first time in a long time she thought she could be honest there, too. Well, a *bit* more honest, anyway.

His smile was slow and warm and made her feel the same way the sunset had. 'I'm glad. But I promise you, we're only just getting started.'

He opened the door and climbed into the driver's seat, which meant he didn't see her shiver.

Or hear her murmur, 'That's what I'm worried about.'

Ellie had something she wasn't telling him—Jesper was almost certain of it.

She was quiet on their return from Skagen, retreating into her bedroom at the beach house immediately after they'd shared a light supper—during which she was almost silent.

The next day he took her to the Troll Museum, and

they laughed at the funny hair and odd expressions of the little creatures that were supposed to bring good luck, apparently.

'My dad used to have a whole collection of them,' Ellie said absently. But that was about the most she *did* say.

Oh, she took photos, of course, and uploaded them from her phone to her social media accounts while he watched, adding pithy commentary about their adventures. But he knew instinctively that those words didn't match her thoughts. She was being her online self again— just when he'd hoped she might have started being her real self a bit more.

'Did you like it?' he asked on their way back to the beach house.

'Well, you promised it would be magical,' Ellie replied. 'I suppose trolls count. Although when you said trolls I was sort of expecting, you know, full-sized monster ones.'

'These are cuter,' he said with a shrug. 'Did you get the message, though?'

He'd had to spend a little time thinking about what the message would actually be. He hadn't really planned out their itinerary for their time together, much as he might like to give the impression that he had. He was just retracing his steps from his own adventures. And the Troll Museum, while quirky, hadn't exactly been a planned stop for him. More somewhere he'd found himself unexpectedly while wandering. But he'd been charmed all the same.

He'd hoped Ellie would be, too.

She screwed up her nose as she thought about it.

'Um…that you have to lighten up and laugh at life

sometimes?' she guessed. 'I mean, that's what I'll probably use in my round-up post tomorrow.'

He grinned at her. 'Yeah, that works.'

She stared at him for a moment, her mouth slightly open. 'You're making this up as you go along, aren't you?'

'Not all of it,' he protested. 'I just thought you'd like to see the trolls.'

She gave him a soft smile—one of those ones that made his heart start to ache. 'I did. Thank you.'

Still, when they got home to the beach house that evening, she pulled out her laptop and worked while he cooked dinner, and then she went to bed as soon as they'd finished clearing up. No more moonlight walks on the beach, and no more almost kisses like there had been in Skagen.

Was that why she seemed more distant? Was she *trying* to put space between them after that moment—that glorious moment when he'd thought, hoped, that she might be about to kiss him?

She hadn't, and he'd respected that. She didn't need to put space between them on his account.

Which meant she had to be doing it on hers. Because maybe she had wanted that kiss as much as he had.

And whatever her true reason for not trusting in the thing that was building between them—chemistry, connection, whatever she wanted to call it—Jesper was certain it was the reason she was hiding in her room every evening.

That there was something she wasn't telling him.

He'd never been good with secrecy either.

Luckily, he had plenty of opportunities to try and tease the truth out of her.

* * *

'If you're not going to try wild swimming in the sea—'

'In January, in Denmark,' she interrupted. 'No.'

'Then we'll just have to find a suitable alternative,' Jesper finished, casting her a smile.

She'd been suspicious when he'd insisted on her packing her swimming things for their latest day out—he could tell by the way her eyes had narrowed as she'd studied him, searching for nefarious intent. But when he'd promised she wouldn't be swimming in the freezing ocean, she'd finally agreed. That didn't mean she'd stopped asking questions, though.

In fact, she was still asking them right up until the moment he pulled up outside the most exclusive spa hotel in the region.

There were other, more famous spas in the country, and he'd considered taking her to all of them, but many of the best-known ones would be rife with tourists even in January, and besides, this was the spa he'd visited in his own quest for a new, content life, so it seemed right to bring Ellie there too.

The hotel building stretched out along a bank of green grass, pale stone topped by a red-tiled roof, and small windows with copper-green canopies. Another time, he thought he might have brought her here to stay the night, or longer, but that sort of thing suggested a more romantic purpose than Jesper had in mind.

Something he had to remind himself of after they'd checked in and separated to change into their swimwear. And when they met again, outside the thermal baths, and he got his first look at her in her swimsuit.

It wasn't as if it was anything particularly revealing

or racy. Just a fairly standard-cut one-piece swimming costume in a dark forest-green. Perfectly ordinary. Except for one thing.

The zip that travelled up between her breasts to the V of the neckline. A zip that she could, at any time, just undo…but of course she didn't. Which didn't stop him from imagining it, all the same.

Ellie gave him a puzzled look. 'Everything okay?'

Jesper cleared his throat. 'Fine. Shall we…explore the spa?'

'Sounds like a plan.'

Together, they set off through the heated air, completing a full circuit of the facilities—from the thermal showers to the salt-water bath overlooking the forest, from the three different temperatures of sauna to the cold plunge pool just outside. They didn't have the spa to themselves, but at the same time it wasn't busy, which Jesper decided was probably the best combination. Alone, he might have been even more tempted by that bloody zip.

They completed their first circuit and decided to take a dip in the forest pool to acclimatise. Jesper hung back and watched as Ellie kicked off and covered the distance between the tiled steps and the far end of the pool in long, easy strokes.

When she paused, arms resting on the far edge, he followed.

'What do you think?' he asked as he drew level.

'It's amazing.' Ellie stared out at the wide, wide window surrounding the three sides of the pool that jutted out into the forest, almost as if they were swimming in a lake between the trees. Then she looked up at him with an impish smirk. 'Although I have to say I'm relieved that we're allowed to wear swimwear. I thought all your Danish spas and saunas required guests to be naked.'

He chuckled. 'Many of our saunas and spas *are* nude facilities, but I wasn't sure that would make you happy right now. And since that is the object of the exercise...'

'You're right.' She looked down at her body—lithe and lean with muscle, curving in absolutely all the right places, and with that damn zip hanging on by a thread. 'Maybe twenty years ago I'd have been game, but now... not so much.'

Jesper stared at her for a moment with a complete lack of comprehension.

'Clearly, you don't see what I see.' And it was probably only the heated air making his voice rough. Ellie looked up in surprise and he swallowed, forcing himself to look away. For him, she was far more gorgeous than any twenty-something. But he couldn't exactly say that when they had set their rules so carefully to ensure that they were only friends.

Something he perhaps should have thought more carefully about before planning to spend the day with her in nothing but that swimsuit.

Instead, he played a hunch and asked, 'What would you have done if it was a nude spa?'

Ellie laughed. 'I'd have been incredibly uncomfortable, I imagine.'

Jesper wasn't joking, though. 'But you'd have told me? You'd have refused to come in? I mean, if you were so uncomfortable, you wouldn't have stripped naked and come in anyway, just to avoid conflict?'

'No. I... I mean, I agreed to do whatever you suggested on this trip, to go where you wanted, so... I hope

I'd have at least *mentioned* that I wasn't entirely comfortable with the idea.' She didn't even sound fully convinced of that much.

'You hope,' he repeated flatly.

Ellie pulled a face and spun around in the water, leaning back against the tiles and staring into the spa itself instead of out into the woods. 'I suppose… I've always been one to go along with what others expect of me. To not let them down more than to avoid conflict, I think. I want people to think well of me.'

'I hope you know that if I ever ask for something you don't want to give, I'd always rather you say no than do something that makes you uncomfortable,' he said.

'I do,' she replied, her smile a little tight. 'Now, I'm going to take advantage of this beautiful pool for a while before you drag me into the sauna!'

She pushed away fast, her head in the water and her arms arcing out overhead as she sped away from him. Jesper watched her go, relieved that he wasn't going to be drawing her into anything she didn't want, but wishing he wasn't so sure that he was the only one in her life who wasn't.

The spa Jesper had chosen to bring her to was stunning, but Ellie had to admit that she wasn't entirely sure what the message was in it. When she asked him, over a delicious light lunch taken in fluffy white dressing gowns, he simply shrugged and said, 'Some days you need to let go and relax,' which Ellie wasn't sure was everything she was supposed to get from the experience.

Oh, but it felt good, though.

Just pushing her body through the water, feeling the

movement, her progress, felt like a shift. Like she was making something happen, instead of letting life happen to her.

Even this happiness quest was being guided by Jesper—he was choosing where she went and when, what lessons she learned. But her own body was something she still had control over. And that gave her control too, if the way Jesper's eyes kept darting down to the zip closure of her swimming costume was anything to go by.

Eventually, she couldn't put off the sauna any longer.

'If you really hate it, you don't have to stay in,' Jesper said prosaically. 'And we'll start with the coolest one. Then, when you get too hot, you go out there and jump in the cold plunge pool.'

She shuddered at the very idea. 'No, thanks.'

Jesper held the sauna door open for her, heat radiating out. 'Don't knock it until you've tried it.'

Even the coolest sauna felt like the hottest summer's day she could remember, surrounding every inch of her. Jesper climbed up the wooden slats to sit on the very highest bench, while Ellie stayed further down. When he tipped his head back and closed his eyes, she couldn't quite resist taking a good, long look at him in his own swimming trunks, though.

She knew he had to be older than her, nearly fifty if he was the same age as Anders, but she wouldn't have guessed it otherwise. Despite the traumas and isolation of the last few years, he'd kept himself in great shape, with only the silvering hair giving away his age.

She made herself look away. Sweat was starting to drip down between her breasts from the sauna alone.

She didn't need to make things worse by salivating over a man she'd already decided she couldn't have.

Still, by the time she'd stretched out and found a comfortable position on the lower, cooler bench, she was starting to wonder if he'd actually fallen asleep up there.

Until he said, 'So. Tell me about your husband.'

'Ex-husband,' she shot back, trying not to sound startled. 'Did Lily tell you I was divorced?'

'She did.' Jesper opened his eyes and peered down at her. 'But mostly I just learned about it from your social media. It seemed…amicable? Or was that just for the masses?'

'Why do you care?' She didn't mean it to come out as harsh as it sounded. It was probably the heat, going to her head.

He shrugged, and water droplets ran in rivulets down his torso. 'I care about helping you, about this quest we're on together. I'm trying to get a picture of the real you so I can help you best, but so far…it's hard to tell which is the real you and what's just a front you put on for your readers.'

That, as much as it pained her to admit it, was fair. 'It *was* amicable. We just…grew apart, I suppose. I mean… we were still teenagers when we met, at university. And nobody stays the same person their whole life, do they?'

'I suppose they don't.' The words sounded heavy in the thick, hot air. 'I know Agnes and I… I thought I knew who she wanted me to be, and I gave everything I had to be that person. But in the end, it wasn't enough to make her happy.'

Ellie's chest tightened at the sadness in his voice. This man who tried so hard—was trying so hard now, for her, just out of a new, budding feeling of friendship. It broke her heart that he felt he wasn't enough—and could never be now, for a wife who had died unsatisfied.

But then, she knew too how hard it was to know that there was nothing she could do or say to magically become what someone else wanted, no matter how hard she'd tried over the years to contort herself into the right shape, the perfect wife.

It wasn't as if she could wave a wand and become twenty years younger, after all.

'I know how that feels,' she said softly.

Jesper looked down, his gaze somehow hotter than the sauna air. 'He wanted you to be someone other than you are?' He shook his head. 'Then he's an idiot.'

Suddenly, the rising heat of the sauna was too much. 'I need to...' Ellie motioned vaguely towards the door and let herself out, and didn't even pause before sinking straight into the ice-cold plunge pool outside.

CHAPTER SEVEN

AFTER THEIR DAY at the spa, when he'd finally thought he was making some progress in getting Ellie to open up to him, Jesper was rather disappointed to discover that the next week progressed in much the same way as it had before. He'd make them breakfast—well, lay out whatever treats his housekeeper had left for them the previous day—and they'd drink coffee together, then they'd venture out into the wider world to see or experience something Danish and meaningful. Something he'd seen on his quest that had stuck with him.

Each evening, he'd check her social media to see what she'd had to say publicly about their adventures, and assess how it matched up with the experience as he'd lived it. He was pleased to see that at least the smiles in her selfies, and the comments underneath, were beginning to reflect the woman he was growing to know a little more every day.

He particularly liked the shot she'd taken from the spa pool, looking out at the forest from the water, with the caption, 'my new happy place'. It seemed his ill-thought-out and impulsive plan was working.

He never did manage to persuade her to try wild swimming, despite her sudden affinity for the icy plunge pool, and she laughed when he took her to Legoland, but was happy to find a message about play and creativity in there that he wasn't sure he'd have come up with on his own.

Every day they experienced something together and talked about it. Every day he felt a little bit closer to her, as if he understood her a little bit more, even if he knew there were still many things she didn't feel comfortable telling him, yet.

And every day he resisted the urge to kiss her when her eyes lit up and she talked about what she'd found in their day's adventures.

Then every evening they'd go back to the beach house and she'd curl up with her laptop, eat dinner and go to bed, without ever allowing that same closeness to penetrate the world they had in his home.

Was it because she was afraid they wouldn't be able to resist the attraction between them? It was a reasonable fear, he supposed. But all he knew was that, once the sun went down, he felt her pull away from him. And it stung a little bit more every day.

After a week, he decided it was time to move on.

'Move on to where?' Ellie asked, in between packing up those belongings of hers that seemed to have migrated over every inch of his home.

He picked up a fluffy cardigan that had been left hung on the back of a dining chair and tossed it to her. 'Aarhus. Denmark's second city. Known as the city of smiles.'

He punctuated that knowledge with a smile of his own, pleased and relieved when she returned it.

'Where will we stay?'

'Will and Matthew have a penthouse apartment there

that they rent out,' he explained. 'I asked them if we could use it for a few days.'

'A few days? Is there lots to see there?' She seemed intrigued at the idea.

'Plenty. And besides, I think…maybe you'll feel more comfortable in a city. Somewhere less remote.' Somewhere she could leave and get a hotel room if things started feeling too close, perhaps.

She gave him a puzzled look. 'Comfortable? I'm plenty comfortable here, you know. This place is like…extreme luxury to us mere mortals. You should have seen my flat in Copenhagen!'

'I didn't mean that kind of comfortable,' he said awkwardly. 'I just meant…it's only the two of us here, and don't think I haven't noticed the way you retreat to your room every time that's the case.'

She winced, and gave him an apologetic smile. 'That's not… I'm not uncomfortable. I just think it's for the best. I've got… I've got a lot on my mind.'

As if he hadn't noticed.

This was it, he realised. His best chance to ask her *what* exactly was on her mind. What she wasn't telling him.

So he took a breath, and said, 'Want to tell me about it?'

It was the perfect opportunity. The perfect moment to tell him everything—just like she'd been meaning to all week.

And yet, when she was presented with it…she bottled it.

'Nothing, really,' she said lightly. 'Um, things are just going really well with the book, finally. No more blank pages—I'm making real progress! And that's all thanks to you, so…thank you.'

It was true, all of it. The document on her laptop was filling out with anecdotes and mini essays on their adventures—a mixture of travel writing and personal reflections, descriptions of the places they'd visited and accounts of the conversations they'd been having about happiness and messages along the way.

She genuinely felt she was learning what she needed to on this trip. Jesper had lived up to his promise and then some.

So yes, it was all true.

It just wasn't The Truth, with the capital letters.

Because the truth was that every place they went, every sight they saw together, every meal spent discussing the Danish way of life and how hard it had been to adjust back after life in the States, and how he'd just had to go cold turkey and not do *anything* for a while…every moment she spent with Jesper, she fell harder for him.

It wasn't even just the way she wanted to kiss him any more.

That first walk on the beach, or that day watching the sunset together, or yes, the day at the spa, kissing had been the main thing on her mind. She'd experienced his lips once and she'd like to do it again, please.

But, worse than that, she was starting to have *feelings* to go along with the wanting to kiss him. The sort of crush-like feelings she hadn't felt since before she was married. Since the early days after she'd met Dave, actually.

Which was the part that was freaking her out the most, she knew.

Oh, it wasn't as if she was falling madly in love with him and would be heartbroken when she left or anything. She'd only known the guy for a week or two, and she liked to think that she had more sense than *that*.

It was just…she could feel the potential humming underneath their every interaction.

They could be *magnificent* together. But if they were, that meant giving up her quest to find happiness on her own terms, without relying on somebody else to give it to her.

And she just couldn't do that.

Which was why she hadn't told him about Dave and Maisie getting married. Oh, she'd meant to—even started to a couple of times. But she knew that once all her dirty laundry was aired, and he understood the real reasons she was in Denmark, there was no going back from that.

What if he looked at her with pity? She couldn't stand that.

But worse…what if he understood, and convinced her that she could move on, could have something with him, and she believed him?

What if he broke down all her defences, and she fell?

Right now, her secrets and her early bedtimes were the only thing protecting her from screwing up this happiness book project. And, okay, fine, yes, also protecting her heart. Because she'd never been good at casual and carefree, and she was fairly sure Jesper hadn't either. They were the sort of people who felt things deeply.

And she couldn't risk feeling that way again. Not after what happened last time she fell.

Jesper watched her for a few more moments then, when it became clear she wasn't going to say anything more, gave a small nod. 'I'm really glad it's going well. The book, I mean.'

'Me too.' Ellie nodded and smiled and knew he was seeing right through it. He knew she wasn't saying something.

And she suspected he also knew that she couldn't keep silent for ever.

I'm going to have to tell him. But I'm going to have to protect my heart when I do.

Ellie was sad to leave the beach house; it had been a happy place for her, in a way that the apartment in Copenhagen never had been. But she was excited to explore Aarhus, too. On the drive, she used her phone to look up facts about Denmark's second city, relating them all to Jesper, who just nodded and said, 'I know,' to every one.

After he'd failed to be surprised by the information that the city had been founded by the Vikings in the eighth century, that the cathedral was the longest *and* tallest in Denmark, or that the Danish women's handball team had their headquarters in Aarhus, Ellie took to making up facts to see if she could catch him out.

'Oh, and the world's largest emerald was found there in 1789,' she said casually.

'I know.' Jesper's reply was automatic. Then he frowned. 'Wait. You made that one up.'

Ellie laughed. 'I wouldn't have to if you weren't such a know-it-all.'

'I lived in Aarhus once, when I was younger,' he said with a shrug. 'I know the place pretty well.'

She stared at him. 'You realise that if you'd told me

that sooner I wouldn't have spent the last half an hour trying to tell you about the place?'

'I liked listening to you,' he replied simply. 'It's nice to hear you excited about something.'

'Hmm.' Ellie returned to learning about Aarhus in silence. At least she might get some ideas about where he was likely to take her while they were there.

Knowledge was power, after all.

He'd really thought she was going to tell him the truth.

Instead, she'd prattled on about the book, then spent the whole drive to Aarhus telling him facts he already knew. Which, actually, he'd quite enjoyed, but that wasn't the point.

She wasn't telling him something. And the longer she went not telling him…the worse whatever the secret was became in his imagination.

He'd considered calling Lily and just begging for information, but just about managed to resist. Partly because it was a gross violation of Ellie's privacy, and mostly because she wouldn't tell him anyway.

She'd tell Ellie he'd been asking, though. Maybe that would prompt her to talk…

But not if it was really bad. Still, he was fairly sure that whatever she was keeping from him couldn't be as awful as the things he hadn't told her about his wife's death.

So maybe they would have to call it even.

Will and Matthew's flat in Aarhus was as splendid as he remembered, and Ellie's face lit up when she took in the luxurious accommodations. He knew she'd been sad to leave the beach house, but it seemed that a penthouse apartment looking out over Aarhus harbour made up for it.

They spent the first evening wandering around the city, stopping for drinks and dinner at bars and a restaurant that appealed to them from the street. It was still too cold to be outside for too long at night, but they'd wrapped up warm and besides, the chill gave him an excuse to take her arm and pull her close against him.

He kept her out late deliberately, so she couldn't escape to her room away from him too early. As a result, they talked and talked until way past her customary bedtime and, when they did make it back to the flat, Jesper fell into bed with a smile on his face.

Then he sat up again, and scrubbed a hand through his hair to bring him to his senses.

What was he doing?

He was grinning like a schoolboy after a first date with his high school crush, and they hadn't even *kissed* yet. Well, they hadn't kissed again, anyway. The closest they'd got that night was when she'd given him a hug goodnight, still wrapped up in jumpers and scarves and her coat, and pressed her cold lips against his cheek.

Was he really this happy at a kiss on the cheek?

Well, it seemed, yes, he was.

God, he was in trouble.

But he was still smiling when he fell asleep.

The next day, he took Ellie to the ARoS Art Museum.

'The place with the rainbow panorama?' she asked, bouncing on her toes a little as they walked.

'That's the one.' Of course, she'd seen all about it during her Aarhus research session in the car. It was a shame, in a way. He'd had no idea about the installation when he'd returned to Aarhus for the first time in twenty years, and had been blown away by the sight of it—a glass walkway, one hundred and fifty metres long, in all colours of the rainbow.

'Can we walk inside it?' Ellie asked excitedly.

'Of course,' Jesper promised.

It was as spectacular as he remembered. From inside the rainbow panorama they could see out over the city, all tinted with whichever colour they were currently standing inside. Ellie insisted on doing the walk in full rainbow order, so they started with red and made their way around.

Given her excitement about visiting the glass walkway, he'd expected her to be bubbly and full of more facts and information as they walked. But instead, she seemed to grow quieter and quieter as they made their way from red to orange to yellow to green to blue, stopping to look out at each colour change. By the time they reached indigo and violet, she'd been silent for long minutes.

Jesper stood at her side and looked out over the purple-tinted city. 'So, what do you think?'

She started at his words, as if she'd been in a world of her own. 'Um, about the rainbow? Or the message?'

'Either,' he said easily.

'I think the rainbow panorama is amazing and every city should have one,' she said. 'And as for the message… After the rain comes the rainbow? No, that's too easy. What about… Life comes in many shades, and we need them all. Without darkness, there is no light, no colour, right?'

'That works.' He'd long since given up pretending that

he had any trite messages to share about happiness from each of the places they visited, although he knew she liked to drill down to them to find the essence of each place to include in her book, or her social media captions, so that was what he tried to give her.

But for him, each of the places they went had simply given him hope at a time when he had none, and that was enough for him.

They stared out at violet Aarhus a moment longer.

Then Ellie said, 'I've been trying for more than a week to figure out how to explain the real reason I came to Denmark.'

Relief whooshed through him like a sigh and Jesper took a breath to try and figure out how to respond. 'I… I noticed. Well, I noticed that there was something you seemed to feel afraid to tell me. But I hope I'm not that scary to talk to.'

She glanced up at him over her shoulder and gave him a quick smile. 'No, not scary. And I'm not scared to tell you, exactly. More…embarrassed?'

That was something he hadn't considered—that her secret might be more of a personal humiliation than something truly terrible. He'd probably have slept better a lot of nights if he had.

'And ashamed,' Ellie went on. 'Because I know I'm being a coward about it.'

'About telling me?' Jesper asked. 'Or being in Denmark in the first place?'

'Both.' She sighed. 'The truth is…after my husband asked for a divorce, it seems he went and fell in love with my twenty-something half-sister, and now they're getting married and everyone wants me to be there to show that

I give my blessing or something, but I don't think I can and so I ran away to Denmark to give myself an excuse to avoid being at their wedding.'

Jesper blinked. Whatever he'd been expecting, it really hadn't been that.

And he knew how he responded to it would shape whatever happened next between them.

Except surely there was only one way to respond to that information?

'Your ex-husband is marrying your sister?' Jesper spoke slowly, as if he was still processing the information.

'Half-sister,' Ellie corrected miserably. 'Much younger half-sister.'

He was going to pity her, she could tell. Poor, cast aside, old maid Ellie, who had not just had to watch the love of her life replace her with a younger model, but still had to see them at family gatherings.

'And your family expect you to show up at their wedding and *give your blessing?*' His voice got louder at the end, loud enough that people walking the rainbow panorama behind them stopped to look.

She really should have chosen a better place for this conversation. But something about all the colours, seeing the city in so many different ways…it had made her wonder if there was a different way to see *this*, and she'd wanted to hear Jesper's thoughts.

'Are they delusional?' Jesper asked. 'Or do they hate you for some reason?'

Ellie turned and blinked up at him, and the fury in his expression made her laugh helplessly.

'I… I don't know,' she admitted, between gasps of

laughter. 'I...they just all acted like it was perfectly normal, and Mum just wants everyone to be happy, and my stepdad hates a fuss, and Maisie has always been the golden girl and they always loved Dave and they were so angry when we got divorced—with me, even though he was the one who left. I think Mum thought I should have done more to keep him happy, that I'd concentrated on my career instead of my marriage, or that it was because we'd never had kids, and... I don't know. It just all felt like my fault, and now I'm avoiding Mum's calls because she just makes me feel awful and guilty for not wanting to be there.'

The words had just tumbled out of her in a rush, like a waterfall, and all that was left behind when they were done was an overwhelming sense of relief. It was all out there now, for him to think what he wanted about it.

But she'd been honest about how she felt for the first time. And that felt amazing.

'Guilty,' Jesper repeated incredulously. Well, she'd told him she was a people pleaser. Now he got to see how far that ridiculous trait had taken her.

'Even when Lily asked, I told her I was fine with it all,' she said, trying not to laugh at herself. How ridiculous she'd been, and not even realised. Of course she wasn't fine with it. Who would be? 'I don't think she believed me, but, well. Dave and I were already over when he and Maisie got together, so...what could I do?'

'Are you sure about that?' Jesper asked sharply. 'That they only got together after your divorce, I mean?'

'They said so,' Ellie replied. 'They were adamant about it. And honestly? If they were together when we were still married... I'm not sure I want to know.'

She would have, back then, though. Back when she still loved him. And it would have broken her.

Now? Now the idea just left her with a vaguely sick feeling in her stomach.

'You're ready to move on,' Jesper said softly. 'That's why you don't want to know.'

She stopped, and considered. 'I guess... I am. You're right.'

That was good news, right? She'd kind of thought she *had* moved on—physically, at least. She'd left her job, gone freelance, moved to Denmark for four months... Moving had been taking place. But she realised that, inside, she was still back where she had been the day Dave had told her he was leaving, and still reliving the day when her mum had told her about Maisie marrying him.

It was nice to think that, finally, she might be able to move past all that to whatever happened next. Like this rainbow marked the end of that storm, and the promise of something better to follow. Wasn't that what rainbows meant? That God would never send another flood, or something. Or, in this context, that the universe would never let her half-sister marry her ex-husband again. Which, she had to admit, was pretty niche.

Maybe just that if she moved past this storm it was all sunshine and rainbows from here on in.

She'd take that.

Ellie smiled up at Jesper, but his expression was still serious, as though he had something more to say, so she waited to hear what it was. She'd not regretted listening to him yet, and she didn't imagine she was about to start now.

'I understand a little better now, I think, about you

not wanting to make your happiness contingent on another person,' he said slowly. 'It was different for me. But here…it's like your ex-husband took your happy life and gave it to another person. Your sister.'

'I… I hadn't thought about it that way,' Ellie admitted. 'But yes, I guess so.'

'But has it occurred to you…in your determination to not attach your happiness to another person, you're attaching your *unhappiness* to one? Well, two really.'

She stared up at him, his words sinking slowly through the protective layers of hardened emotions she'd surrounded herself with since the divorce.

She'd been so focused on finding happiness, she hadn't even considered the act of discarding unhappiness. She'd buried it deep instead, and tried to cover it over with rainbows and trolls and sunsets and the like. But Jesper was right. It was dragging her down, keeping her from ever finding true happiness, because she couldn't move past that moment when she'd realised that she wasn't enough.

That Dave had chosen younger, prettier, perkier Maisie over her, and cast Ellie on the scrapheap.

'She's pregnant, you know.' She blurted the words out, that last bit of pain stabbing her. 'He and I, we never did. We didn't want kids, we knew that from the start. But she… I'm not supposed to know, but my other sister let it slip. Maisie is pregnant and that's why they're getting married so fast.'

Ellie had never wavered in her decision not to have children. It wasn't the right path for her. But now…was her mother right? Was Maisie giving him everything she couldn't?

Had she failed?

And, if so, how could she ever hope to succeed at anything again?

Jesper reached out and grabbed her forearms, pulling her square with him so she had no real choice but to look up into his eyes. The way they held each other's arms felt like some sort of Viking promise or oath, and normally she'd have laughed at the very idea, but now didn't feel like a time for laughing.

It felt like a time for revelation.

'Your life, your future, your happiness, it's not about them any more,' he said, his voice soft but firm. 'Let them live their lives—you don't owe them anything more than that, no blessings, whatever anyone says. But let them get on and do whatever they want. Because *your* life, your future, your happiness… Ellie, it's going to be so much better than anything you had before.'

His words seemed to settle over her before being absorbed by her mind, her body, the truth of them sinking into every inch of her.

She *was* going to have a happier, better life than before. Because she wasn't twenty-two any longer, like she'd been when she'd said yes to Dave's proposal, shackling her whole life to his. She wasn't a twenty-something newbie journalist desperate to learn the ropes and live the city life. She wasn't the submissive daughter who had to do whatever it took to keep the peace, the same way her mum always had. She wasn't the woman who worked so hard not to let anyone down, even if it meant letting *herself* down.

She wasn't any of the women she'd been before in her life.

She was Ellie. A forty-four-year-old divorcee, living

her own life on her own terms for the first time in decades, maybe ever. She was carving a new career writing about things that mattered to her, influencing other
women finding themselves after years lost in marriage
or motherhood or careers that didn't appreciate them or
parents or spouses or friends who tried to control them...

She was Ellie. And she was going to be happy.

However she saw fit.

'I really want to kiss you right now,' she whispered.

Jesper smiled. 'I've been waiting for you to say that
for days.'

Then he dipped his head, pausing at the last moment
to give her a chance to pull away, in case this wasn't really what she wanted.

But she didn't.

And kissing a gorgeous man under a glass rainbow
felt more spectacular than anything the old Ellie had ever
experienced.

CHAPTER EIGHT

JESPER HAD REMEMBERED that kissing Ellie felt wonderful. But this…this was something else.

He knew her now. Understood her, perhaps. Felt a part of her life.

When he'd kissed her on New Year's Eve, it had been sweet and nice and had woken up parts of him long dormant. But he could still have walked away without harm.

This time when their lips met, he knew that one kiss was never going to be enough.

He'd told himself, over and over, that he was only doing this, this quest, for Ellie. To help her. But now, kissing her, he had to admit it had been for him, too. To make the last few years of his introspection and isolation mean something for someone other than him.

And to be near her, just a little while longer. To have the chance to maybe, maybe hold her again like this.

Finally, though, he had to pull away. 'We should…we need to get out of here.'

Ellie looked around, her eyes dazed, then nodded. 'Back to the apartment. Now.'

Heat surged through him as he realised what she was suggesting. 'Are you sure?'

She met his gaze with her own direct one. 'Very.'

* * *

They made it back to the apartment in record time. Jesper didn't think he'd let go of Ellie's hand the whole way.

'There are all sorts of things we're missing seeing at the art gallery, you know,' he said as they hurried across the street.

She gave him an incredulous look. 'Do you really care about that right now?'

'Hell, no.'

And he didn't. This, her, in his arms, wanting him the way he wanted her, it was all he'd been dreaming about for days.

But that didn't seem to stop his head from interrupting the bliss his body was chasing.

She doesn't want anything serious. That's good. Neither do I. She hasn't been with anyone since her husband, I'm guessing. And I haven't been with anyone since Agnes. But that was a lot longer ago than her divorce... What if she has been with people since then? I mean... Good for her, I guess. But it means I'm really out of practice.

He shook away the running commentary in his head. It wasn't as if making love was something he could forget how to do. And besides, he'd been imagining all the ways he'd kiss and touch her—and hating himself for it—every night after she went to bed. He knew what to do.

As long as she was sure this was what she wanted.

The apartment door slammed shut behind them and her lips were on his in an instant, the pair of them walking—her backwards, him forwards—towards his room as they kissed. After the last couple of weeks of not kissing, it seemed impossible to stop now, even for a moment.

But he had to.

He tore his lips away as the back of her knees hit his bed, and refused to be swayed by her needy, desperate look.

'Are you sure you want to do this?' He tried to sound serious but, given the way he was panting, he wasn't sure he pulled it off.

'Are you kidding me?' She reached up and grabbed the back of his neck, trying to pull him down for another kiss.

But Jesper held firm. 'I need to hear the words. Because you told me...you were adamant that we couldn't do this, that it would ruin your whole quest, your project. And if you want it now because we talked about your ex and you need to feel desired or something...trust me, I desire you. I want you so badly it hurts. But if it isn't what *you* want, then we need to stop now. Because the worst thing for me would be you regretting it afterwards.'

Ellie's grip on the back of his neck softened, and she dropped down from her tiptoes so she was even shorter than him than she had been before. But she kept her gaze fixed on his, searching his face for something.

'You really mean that, don't you?' she whispered, and he realised she was going to take the out. She was going to put the brakes on and think about this some more.

And however much it felt like parts of him might actually fall off from frustration, if that was what she wanted then it was the right thing.

'I really do,' he promised.

She swallowed, and glanced down for just a moment, before looking up and meeting his eyes again with a fiery certainty.

'Then trust me when I tell you, I've never wanted anything as much as I want you inside me right now.'

That was all the reassurance Jesper needed.

Ellie hadn't given much thought to what it might be like to have sex with a Viking. She had, however, given considerable thought to the question of what it would be like to have sex with Jesper. Now she'd experienced the latter, she knew that they were in no way the same thing.

A Viking pillaged and plundered, right? Took what they wanted and then left.

Jesper, on the other hand, gave far, far more than he took. Even if she did feel rather plundered the morning after.

Also, he hadn't gone anywhere.

Ellie stretched carefully against his sheets, checking in with her body for every sign of the night—and afternoon, if she was honest—they'd spent together. The ache in her thigh muscles, and the beard burn on the skin over them. The reddened skin of her breasts where he'd lavished her nipples with attention with his tongue until her toes curled. The deep-seated contentment in her chest, and the heavy, relaxed feeling in her whole body from just too many orgasms.

All right, not *too* many. Just a lot more than she'd had in one go in a really long time.

She'd been nervous at first—well, at first, she'd just been desperate to kiss him, to feel him, to *have* him. But after his last attempt at chivalry, when he'd suggested they hold back if she wasn't sure…after she'd convinced him she was *very* sure, all bets had been off. It had been a while since she'd had any man's focused attention on her, and Jesper had certainly been very focused.

It was hardly surprising he was still passed out cold on the bed next to her. The man had put in a shift and a half since they'd landed on his bed the afternoon before.

She twisted on her side to watch him sleeping, the silver in his hair and beard glinting in the morning light, but the crow's feet around his eyes smoothed out by sleep so that he looked younger than she'd seen him before. It amazed her that this man, who'd suffered such loss, could still talk so freely of happiness. Could show her the path to her own joy.

'Your life, your future, your happiness, it's not about them any more,' he'd said. *'Let them get on and do whatever they want. Because your life, your future, your happiness... Ellie, it's going to be so much better than anything you had before.'*

Was he right? She hoped so. And in that moment when he'd said it…she'd believed it with her whole heart.

That was why she'd given in and kissed him. Not because he spoke a lot of pretty words, but because he made her believe them—made her believe in herself.

Something she was going to have to learn to do on her own, she knew. But just for now…it was nice to have the help.

And this morning? She felt more powerful, more desired, more in control of her own destiny than she had in for ever.

This wasn't about making her happiness contingent on another person. And it certainly wasn't about doing whatever someone else wanted to keep the peace, or keep their love. This was something else.

She wasn't quite sure what to call it yet, but she knew it felt real.

Beside her, Jesper stirred, his bright blue eyes blinking open. He smiled when he saw her still naked beside him. Ellie considered pulling the sheets up to cover her more, but didn't.

God bless Danish housing and its overactive heating systems.

'Good morning,' he said, his voice raspy. 'Sleep well?'

'Wonderfully,' she assured him.

She only noticed the tension in his shoulders as it disappeared at her words.

'You thought I was going to regret this?' she asked.

'I really hoped not,' he joked. 'Because if you did, we wouldn't get to do it again, and that would be a crying shame.'

'It would,' she agreed as his arm snaked out to wrap around her middle and pull her body flush against his again. 'You know, I thought I'd feel self-conscious, being naked with a strange man for the first time since my divorce, but I don't.'

'I object to the term *strange* in that sentence,' Jesper replied. 'But I'm glad you don't feel self-conscious. It would also be a travesty for you to cover up that wonderful body again.'

Ellie felt a flush of pink to her cheeks that might have been to do with his words, or the Danish heating system, or maybe the way he was pressing his hardness against her stomach, showing her how much he wanted her again. And probably again, if last night was anything to go by.

She knew that men's recovery time lengthened the

older they got, but it seemed to her that Jesper had some brilliant ideas on how to pass the time in between...

Her body wasn't the same as it had been at twenty-two, she knew that. She'd lived half her life since then, and long since waved farewell to the perfectly smooth skin, vibrant chestnut hair and flat stomach she'd had back then. Maybe she could have retained it all with a celebrity's skincare, diet and exercise routine, not to mention their hairdresser on call, but Ellie had always felt that there were more important things in life than how she looked.

Besides, she *liked* that her face and body showed that she'd lived. Experienced. Grown and thought and learned and *been*. She looked like who she was.

And while she might have doubted her value as a forty-something woman post-divorce for a little while, one night with Jesper had definitely reminded her of everything she loved about her body.

'What are you thinking?' he asked in a ticklish whisper by her ear, before he lowered his lips to kiss her neck. 'You have the most *devilish* smile on your face.'

'Just how glad I am we are here,' she replied. 'I think... I needed this. I didn't realise it—tried to resist it, even. But I needed something to remind me of who I am, and what this body is capable of.'

'Glad to be of service.' He placed one last kiss on her collarbone then pulled back, sitting up against the headboard. 'Does this mean sex with me is just a part of your happiness quest? Is last night going in your book?'

She laughed. 'Definitely not.' Experiencing great sex was one thing. Writing about it for thousands of people to read was another. 'I'm sure I can find some discreet euphemisms to use.'

'You're the writer.' He wasn't meeting her eye any more, and Ellie realised she'd said something wrong.

Sitting up beside him, one leg folded under her as she looked at him, she ran back through the conversation to figure out what it was.

'I didn't sleep with you because it was a step on my happiness quest,' she said bluntly.

He raised an eyebrow. 'Are you sure? It's the only reason you're here with me. It would make sense. And I'm not exactly complaining.'

Maybe not, but she could tell he didn't like it all the same.

Ellie reached over and grabbed his hand, toying with his fingers. 'This, us...this was just for me. Not for the blog or the book. Or for revenge against Dave and Maisie. Or any other reason except that I really, really wanted it. Wanted you.'

His fingers tightened around hers. 'I'm glad.'

'You were right, yesterday,' she went on. 'My happiness is up to me now. And whatever I choose to do with it isn't contingent on another person any more. And right now I'm choosing this. Us. You.'

He gave her a small one-sided smile. 'I'm sensing a *but* there.'

She hadn't known she had a caveat to that until he'd pointed it out. The moment she considered it, there it was, waiting for her to realise.

'But I'm leaving next month.'

'As soon as the wedding is over, right?'

She nodded. 'Not because...not because this is just

about running away any more. But because I've been hiding out long enough, and it's time to find my real future.'

'Somewhere else.' There was a strange, sad look on his face, one she couldn't quite read.

But she understood it, all the same. It was the knowledge that anything between them was over before it had really even started. Because she couldn't just throw herself into another relationship. She needed to finish finding who she was, the new woman in her new life, first.

She shifted closer to him, folding herself in against his side so his arm came around her and she could feel his heartbeat under the hand she placed on his chest.

'Remember at the rainbow yesterday, we talked about the contrasts of happiness? Light after dark. The sunshine after the rain.'

'I remember.' His chest reverberated with his words. She got the feeling that Jesper would remember every moment of that trip for a long time.

She knew she would. It had changed her whole view of the world.

'I realised that I can remember the happy times I had with Dave, the person I was then and how I grew, without the memories being ruined by how it ended.' That sounded very fully visualised and grown woman, didn't it? 'Well, I hope I will be able to, one day soon, anyway,' she added, needing to be honest with herself as well as him.

'That's good,' Jesper said. 'That's a really good thing. I want that for you.'

Did he have it for himself? Was he able to think about his wife without remembering the sickening moment when he knew she was dead? Or regretting so many things that came before? Ellie didn't know.

She hoped so. But given the few things he'd said about the state of his marriage before her death, she wasn't sure.

And if he couldn't…maybe she could help him find a way to being able to.

'I want to enjoy this while we can have it.' She pressed herself firmly against his side so he knew exactly what she was talking about. 'Like the fairytale romance while it lasts.'

'And when it's over?' he asked.

'Then I might miss it—I *will* miss it. But I can look back on it fondly, too.' She smiled up at him a little sadly. 'Maybe making a bank of happy memories is a part of finding happiness. Good, happy thoughts to get you through the harder times.'

'Maybe it is,' he agreed.

Ellie bit her lip before asking, 'Is that how you feel about your wife now?' Because if he had managed it, surely she could too.

But Jesper's muscles stiffened underneath her touch, the room suddenly cooler and darker, even though the winter sky outside hadn't changed.

'I'm sure I will,' he said shortly. He pulled away, swinging his legs out of the bed. 'Come on. We should pack.'

Ellie blinked up at him, thrown by the sudden change of topic and tone. 'I thought we were staying in Aarhus a few days?'

'We were.' Jesper already had a towel around his waist and was heading for the en suite bathroom. 'But you mentioned a fairytale. I know what I want to show you next. And I happen to know a fantastic hotel in Odense.'

And then he was gone, into the bathroom, leaving Ellie still naked on the bed, confused and concerned about what had just happened.

Odense sat on the central Danish island of Fyn, between the mainland and Zealand, where Copenhagen was. It was another city Jesper knew relatively well, and it didn't have the same connotations with Agnes and her family that Aarhus did.

And right then, he really needed to not think about his dead wife.

Besides, the First Grand Hotel really was a fantastic place to stay, and he couldn't let Ellie leave Denmark without experiencing Hans Christian Andersen's home village, nearby.

That was what this was about. Ellie's quest, and her book—everything she needed to discover and achieve here in Denmark before it was time for her to leave. And as they drove back across the bridge to Fyn, Jesper clasped his hands tight on the wheel and reminded himself of that again and again.

Because he'd got too close to forgetting, lying in bed with her that morning.

He'd known, going into this, what Ellie could offer him. And he'd known how much he could take, too. But for a moment there he'd been truly happy, wrapped up around her naked body.

Until she'd asked about Agnes.

It wasn't guilt that had filled him, or grief. He'd made

his peace with her death as well as he could reasonably expect to.

No, it was the realisation that Ellie had already reached the point where she could think back fondly on her marriage—maybe not all the time, he wasn't imagining that one night with him had performed that kind of miracle—but he hadn't.

Three years of solitude and inner work and still, when he thought of Agnes, he remembered all the ways that he had failed, and everything he should have done differently.

Maybe Ellie didn't feel that way because she hadn't done anything wrong. It seemed to him that her ex-husband was the failure in that marriage, not that he imagined *he* was feeling the kind of guilt that Jesper himself carried.

But he'd realised in that moment that even if he couldn't move past the wrongs he'd committed in his past, Ellie was on the right path. And it was his job to keep her walking it.

He couldn't pull her down with him.

Their next destination on the happiness quest had suddenly been clear in his head, and he'd started moving, keen to keep her on track. Why waste what little time they had together? And as much as he liked Aarhus…it held a lot of memories for him, and he'd wanted a little distance between him and them, too.

It was only later, when he saw the puzzled frown line between her brows, that he'd realised she might have taken his sudden burst of movement the wrong way. But it was too late to do much about that now.

Better to keep moving.

'Are you…is everything okay?' Ellie's voice was tentative and she sat in his passenger seat looking uncertain if she was even supposed to be there.

Damn. He'd screwed this up. Already.

It might be a new record.

'It's fine.' A lie, and they both knew it.

'Only you're gripping that steering wheel rather tight. Your knuckles are white.' She gave a tiny laugh, as if it might a joke, but the humour evaporated in the thick air of tension in the car.

Jesper sucked in a breath, trying to remember some of the mindful breathing exercises he'd done on a breathwork retreat a couple of years before.

This wasn't fair to Ellie. He wasn't being fair.

She'd told him her truth. He owed her more of his, too.

She'd be gone soon. And he was wasting this time with her.

He sighed, and tried to hold the steering wheel a little more loosely. 'I'm sorry. I just…when you asked about Agnes, I realised you've made more progress moving on from your marriage over the past couple of weeks than I have in the last three years.'

He sneaked a glance over at her and saw her blink three times in rapid succession.

'I'm not sure that's true,' she said slowly. 'But even if it were…my circumstances are rather different.'

'I know.' He sighed again. 'I'm being ridiculous. I just… There are things I haven't told you about my marriage.'

'Would you like to?' she asked carefully. 'Tell me, I mean?'

Jesper swallowed. 'I think I might.'

It was easier to talk while driving, somehow. Maybe because he didn't have to look at Ellie as he spoke, and only caught glimpses of her reactions out of the corner of his eye.

'Agnes and I, we met in Aarhus, where her family lived at the time. I told you that, yes?' He checked to see if she remembered, and continued when she nodded. 'Her family had money, far more money than anyone I'd ever met before, and it was as if she lived in a different world. But she wasn't spoilt or entitled particularly—her family liked to use their wealth to help people. And it made me want to do the same. I wanted to be rich and successful so that I could help people too.'

'That's…admirable?' Ellie sounded as if she wasn't sure, as if she was waiting for the other shoe to drop.

She wouldn't have to wait long.

'I was offered a job over in America, and we moved there together. To start with, it was wonderful. Agnes made new friends, went new places. We both got used to living the high life. I branched out and started my own firm, and had even more success than I'd had before—and more money too. We used it for philanthropic projects, as well as our own comfort and fun, just as I'd always planned. We were living the life we'd dreamed of.'

He paused for a moment, the memories stinging inside his chest, his eyes raw with remembering.

Ellie didn't interrupt, didn't try to guess the ending, even though she knew exactly where it was heading. Maybe she guessed that there was another twist to come before the tragic conclusion.

'I became… Agnes said obsessed. I wanted to do better. Make more, give more. I was working all the hours

God sent, leaving her to represent us at galas and charity events. I made the money, she gave it away. I thought it was the right thing to do, but…she resented the time it took. I was too busy earning the money to hang off her arm at the galas and charity balls. I wasn't interested in that part and, honestly, I didn't have the time.' Now he knew why his eyes hurt. It wasn't the memories. It was the tears he'd been holding back for so long.

He couldn't let them fall now. He had to get through this.

Still, in the interest of safety, he pulled over at the next opportunity. Even if it meant having to look at Ellie while he spoke.

'Sounds like she wanted to have her cake and eat it.' She said it mildly, as if she was afraid to speak ill of the dead. 'She wanted you to earn a lot of money but resented the time it took. She didn't like the trade-off.'

Jesper shook his head. 'I just wasn't good enough. I couldn't give her what she needed.'

'I don't think anybody could.' Ellie's hand rested on his thigh, rubbing small circles on his leg.

'Maybe.' He wasn't sure he could believe it, though. 'I always knew I had something of an addictive personality. My parents…neither of them ever did anything by half measures. My father used to say you had to be all-in or all-out, nothing in between was worth anything. You might not be surprised to learn that he was not your typical Dane.'

'No, I can see that. As a nation, you've got more of a reputation for balance.'

Balance. Exactly what he'd been looking for the past

few years—and thought that he'd found, until Ellie came along.

'I lost any sense of it when we were over in the States. All I could think about was work, but I was so *happy* there, living that life. And Agnes…she grew to hate it.' He took a breath. 'She tried to talk to me, I think. But I couldn't listen. No, I *wouldn't* listen. So she left me. She was on her way to the airport by the time I came home and found the note. But she never got there because… there was a car crash. She was killed instantly.'

'Jesper, I'm so sorry.' Her hand tightened on his leg.

'That's not the end of the story.' This was the hardest part—the part he'd never told anybody. That only he and one doctor at the New York hospital where Agnes had been treated knew. God, he was glad he wasn't driving right now. 'She was pregnant when she died. She… it wasn't something we'd been trying for, and she didn't tell me before she went. I don't even know for sure that she knew herself. But I think she did. I think that was why she was leaving. Because she knew that I couldn't be what a child needed. I couldn't be what anyone needed.'

'You were what I needed.' Ellie's voice was small, quiet, and he almost missed her words. 'When you agreed to take me on this happiness quest…you were exactly what I needed.'

He gave her a small, sad smile. 'For now.'

It wouldn't last—couldn't last. She would leave as planned soon enough and he'd be alone again.

And that, Jesper realised, was only for the best.

'I'm so sorry.' She sounded almost as broken as he felt.

With an incredible force of will, Jesper pushed it all

aside. He didn't want Agnes to hang like a spectre over what little time he had left with Ellie.

'It just threw me off-balance,' he said. 'I'll be fine when we get to Odense.' He'd never visited Odense with Agnes, he wasn't sure why. But there were no memories lurking there for him.

'If you want to get separate rooms at the hotel there— I mean, maybe you were planning that anyway, I don't want to presume,' Ellie said. 'But if you want me to stay away, I'll understand. Last night…it doesn't have to mean anything.'

But it did. It meant an awful lot and Jesper wasn't willing to give that up, even if maybe he should.

'I don't want that.' He tried to give her a smile but from her pained expression, he wasn't very successful. 'Agnes…she's been gone a long time. I know I need to move on, and I have in lots of ways. It just still surprises me sometimes.'

'I can understand that,' Ellie said softly.

'But that doesn't mean I don't value being here with you, right now,' he went on. 'Because I do, very much. This…this adventure with you has made me feel more like myself than I have in years. And the connection between us—I know it can't last, but I don't want to give it up a moment before we have to.'

Ellie blew out a breath he guessed was relief. 'That's… that's good. Because neither do I, really. Being with you—I mean our travels as well as last night—it's been helping me find my way back to myself, too. But I think I have a little further to go still, you know? And I hope we can still help each other get there, until I have to go home to London.'

'Then that's what we'll do,' Jesper promised. 'Together.'

He felt lighter for telling her the truth. He wondered if this was how she had felt after confessing about her ex in the rainbow panorama the day before. If so, he could understand better what had happened next.

It was exhilarating, opening up to another person— and being understood. He felt closer to Ellie than he had to anyone in such a long time. This shared journey had connected them in ways he'd never expected.

He just needed to remember what would happen when she left. Once this was over, he still needed to be able to keep himself on an even keel. He knew now that the temptation to throw himself into work, or another project, would be overwhelming.

Maybe that was what his first attempt at going off-grid, seeking happiness, had been too, at its heart. Something to replace the work he'd left behind.

But now he knew better. Life wasn't all extremes—it couldn't be. He needed to find balance.

Perhaps he needed this happiness quest as much as Ellie did.

Either way, they were in this together. And he wasn't going to lose that before he had to.

He just needed to hold on and not let himself fall in too deep.

How hard could that be?

CHAPTER NINE

THE FIRST GRAND HOTEL, right in the centre of Odense, was very grand indeed—from its red brick facade to the elegant luxury of its reception lobby, the smooth and re-assuring presence of the staff and the gold trimmed lift that took them up to the best suite the hotel had to offer, the moment Jesper handed over his credit card.

Ellie hadn't really stopped to think all that much about exactly how rich Jesper was, but she supposed that a person couldn't afford to go off-grid and not work for two or three years unless they were sitting on a significant nest egg.

Still, she didn't think today was the day to ask about it.

After his confession in the car, at least some of the tension that had been pulled taut between them since they'd left the apartment in Aarhus had dissipated. She felt she understood him better now. And despite the fact they'd spent so much of the journey discussing his late wife, the same way they'd talked about her ex-husband the day before, somehow, talking it through seemed to diminish Agnes' shadow rather than deepen it.

She hoped that Jesper felt the same. That by putting it all out in the open between them it had brought them closer together, rather than pushing them apart.

All the same, when he'd asked for the suite—a suite which came with two bedrooms, she noted—Ellie had fully expected him to retreat into one of them for some time alone before they began whatever his next outing was. The Hans Christian Andersen Museum, she thought he'd said, although at the time she'd been too busy obsessing over what she'd done wrong to really listen.

But she *hadn't* done anything wrong. And neither had he, really. It was just that they both had their past lives hanging over them whether they liked it or not, and that wasn't ever going to change. A consequence of living, she supposed. When you had that flush of first love in your teens and twenties, you only had all the ways your parents or childhood had screwed you up to contend with. By the time you were in your forties, you had to add another twenty years of your own mess-ups and other people's idiocy to the mix. It wasn't a thing you could simply overlook.

So Ellie was prepared for a quiet evening working on the book, maybe taking a bubble bath and ordering some room service, if Jesper deigned to come out and join her. But, to her surprise, the moment the bellboy had left their baggage and shut the door to the suite behind him, Jesper darted across the room and wrapped his arms around her middle from behind, his lips already on her neck.

Her blood grew warmer with every kiss. 'Are you sure you—' He pressed himself more firmly against her backside. 'Oh. Very sure, then.'

And if he wanted this, who was she to argue? Especially since she wanted it just as much.

Needed it too, she thought as she turned in his arms to kiss his lips. Needed the connection between them that had been strained by his unexpected behaviour that morning. A physical connection to match the emotional one they'd forged through their conversations.

Maybe Jesper knew that was what she needed, too. Because after he led her to the largest of the two bedrooms the suite had to offer, he laid her out over the silken, embroidered bedspread and took the time to remind every single inch of her how much he wanted her. As if he was memorising her, she realised. So he couldn't forget.

She surged up underneath him, wrapping an arm around his neck as she kissed him, deeply. 'My turn,' she murmured, and promptly manoeuvred him onto his back—not an easy feat given the height and weight advantage he had over her. But luckily, he didn't seem to object enough to try and stop her.

Certainly, he seemed to have no problem at all with the way she kissed a trail down his chest, her hands running over his skin as she went, memorising him the way he had her.

After all, if they only had this time together, hadn't she vowed to make the most of every second?

Later—quite a lot later, if Ellie was honest—she realised they still hadn't eaten.

'Did you want to get some dinner?' She propped herself up on one elbow to look at him as she asked the question. His eyes were closed, but she was pretty sure he wasn't asleep. He was breathing quite heavily, though, which was fair enough.

It had been a very energetic afternoon.

'Did you want to go out?' he asked, without opening his eyes. 'I know some great restaurants in Odense.'

That sounded nice; she loved sitting across from him in restaurants, getting to know each other a little more with every mouthful. And she wasn't above enjoying the way that other women—and more than a few men—looked at them together with a shade of envy.

But going out involved getting showered. And dressed. And probably putting on make-up and nice shoes for the sort of restaurants Jesper likely knew in the city.

And the bed really was very comfortable…

'We could get room service?' she suggested.

Jesper groaned in what she quickly realised was relief. 'Oh, thank God, yes, please. I don't think I can leave this room for at least a day. Maybe more. You've broken me, woman.'

She snickered, and placed a kiss against his temple as she went to find the room service menu. 'Oh, dear,' she said with false sympathy. 'I guess we'd better not do that again, then.'

He sat up with alarming alacrity. 'Now, hang on, I didn't say that…' He reached for her, and Ellie dodged out of the way, giggling as she held the room service menu out of reach.

And she realised, as he caught her around the waist and pulled her back down to the bed and into his arms, that she was happy. Truly happy.

Was that what exorcising ghosts and secrets could give them? Happiness?

Maybe. Either way, just for this moment, she could let herself be happy. It wasn't a quest or a challenge or a puzzle to solve, it just *was*.

She knew it couldn't last. Even if she wasn't going back to London soon, happiness with another person never did. They'd become entrenched and bored and have all the problems couples faced. She could only be this happy right now because she knew it was fleeting.

But maybe she could hold onto it a little bit longer.

'You know, I think I like Odense,' she said, snuggling back into her pillow.

Jesper brushed her hair away from her face with a smile. 'You haven't seen anything of it yet.'

'I don't need to,' she replied. 'I'm happy, just here.'

For a moment his eyes widened, and then darkened as his pupils grew. 'Me too.'

'Maybe…maybe we could stay here, just for a little while,' she suggested. 'Before we head back to Copenhagen.'

The wedding was in two weeks, and she'd booked her return ticket for nine days after, in the hope it made it less obvious she was only there to avoid the wedding. She'd have no reason to stay beyond that, and she knew that once they were back in the city she'd be counting down the days until she left.

But here? Time sort of disappeared. And she liked that.

'I think we can manage that,' Jesper said, and leaned in to kiss her again. 'I'm sure we'll manage to fill the time somehow…'

It was rather a lot later *again* before they got around to ordering room service.

It took them a while to make it to the Hans Christian Andersen Museum that Jesper had promised Ellie they'd visit. In fairness, he didn't think it was entirely his fault. Neither of them had wanted to stray too far from the hotel room—or from each other—for a while. The café down the road and the hotel restaurant was about as far as they'd made it from the bed for the best part of a week.

Ellie's social media posts had relied heavily on photos taken from the rainbow panorama, the morning or evening light from their hotel window, and arty shots of coffees and pastries for the last few days. The captions though, to Jesper's mind, had seemed more authentically her than any he'd read before. Even if she hadn't mentioned him at all—which he understood. Ellie's journey here was about *her*, not him.

But last night, as they'd lain in each other's arms in the darkness, Ellie had said, 'I think it's time to go back to Copenhagen, isn't it?'

He'd wanted to say no, wanted to keep them in this private bubble of bliss for just a little longer. But he knew she was right. Her stay in Denmark was finite after all, and it wasn't all about him. She'd want to spend time with Lily. She would need to pack up her apartment before she left. And it wasn't as if she'd spent a lot of the last week writing either.

Of course she needed to get back to reality. And he probably should too, as much as he hated the idea.

'We'll leave tomorrow,' he'd said with a heavy heart. 'We can stop at the Hans Christian Andersen Museum on our way.'

He'd felt her smile against his skin, where her cheek rested on his chest. 'You're determined we're going to get there, aren't you?'

'I think you have to indulge in the fairytale before we leave, don't you?'

'I think I already have,' she'd replied.

And now they were here.

The place was more of an art installation than a museum, an immersive experience that pulled them into the fairytale world Andersen had created, using light and sound and texture and possibly magic, Jesper wasn't sure. Ellie certainly looked captivated, enthralled even, and he couldn't help but think about the day in the rainbow panorama, and how it had changed their entire relationship.

He couldn't shake the feeling that this experience might, too. And not in such a good way.

If the rainbow walkway over Aarhus had given Ellie the courage to open up to him, and to risk kissing him again, he could feel the fairytale experience drawing her away from him. She was already picturing her next life— he could see the hope and the excitement in her expression.

She was getting ready to move on. To write her own fairytale. To take the world and the happiness he'd shown her, and apply it to her real life back in London.

Without him.

He should be happy for her. He *was* happy for her—he wanted her to live the life that brought her joy. He was glad he'd been able to help her move on from her ex-husband, to see that her family's expectations of her blessing his remarriage were unreasonable and that she didn't have to give in to them. He was especially glad that he'd been the one to help her appreciate that physical pleasure and connection with another didn't mean you were putting all of your faith and happiness in that one person. That you could stay your own self, even when you were with others—and you didn't have to sacrifice what you wanted to make that other person stay.

Except that last was exactly why he *couldn't* ask her to

stay longer. Ellie was ready to go home—or she would be, when the time came—and he couldn't, wouldn't stop her.

Not least because he knew he had nothing to offer beyond what they'd enjoyed these last few weeks.

He couldn't fall in love with her, couldn't give over his life to her the way he had to his work before. He knew that he wasn't capable of being what someone else needed—he'd tried with Agnes, and look how that had ended up. He couldn't promise her anything more than a casual, friendly arrangement with great sex. And Ellie wanted the fairytale—he could see it in her face now. She might have been adamant that she wouldn't hang her happiness on another person, but he knew that once she had that happiness as a bedrock of her soul she'd want to share it.

She would find someone who could love her the way she deserved to be loved. Someone who wasn't him.

And he was happy he'd helped her get to the point where she was ready for that.

Really, he was.

Even if part of him wanted to beg her to stay longer. Not for ever, just…longer.

He swallowed back the impulse when she bounded towards him, beaming. He wasn't going to ruin this moment for her, or bring down their last days together.

'Isn't this place amazing?' Ellie grabbed his hand and swung back around, still trying to drink in every inch of the place. 'I'm so glad you brought me here.'

'I'm glad too.' His voice was raspy; he'd been thinking too long, not talking with her. He should have been experiencing this with her instead of standing back and watching.

'We can visit Hans Christian Andersen's childhood home too, while we're here. If you want?' Ellie looked up at him with wide eyes, and he couldn't say anything but yes, of course.

But he regretted it when he saw the humble home where Andersen had grown up. The poverty and hardship he'd been raised in. The terrible, tragic life that had perhaps inspired some aspects of his tales, like the bed where his father had died, while Andersen lay shivering on the floor, believing the ice maiden had taken him.

Jesper had never lived that life. But he had made his own fortune; his parents had no money to spare, especially after his father had finished spending it, gambling or drinking or just 'treating' them. Money had flowed out of his hands faster than it came in, because his father had always felt that life was for living and money was for spending.

Jesper had never had to look too far to see where his tendency for extremes came from. Remembering his childhood with his parents was like looking in a mirror. For them, it had been life and fun. For him, it had turned out to be work. But it was all the same in the end.

Agnes has been born into money, had always had it so never wanted for or worried about it.

Had that been the difference between them? He couldn't help dwelling on the idea as Ellie moved around the small cottage, learning about Andersen's life.

He'd always known that money mattered, that he had to sacrifice to get it, that he needed to make it to keep her, to keep them in the way she'd expected and he'd come to appreciate. She hadn't been materialistic or grasping or anything like that. But she'd always had enough and wouldn't understand *not* having it. She'd have gone to her family to ask for more, and Jesper...he could never have done that.

So he'd worked for it instead. He'd worked and worked and thrown himself into the business and been a success and he'd never known when to stop. Never realised that she was waiting for him to finish, to come home to her.

That was when the problems had started. It wasn't money, he knew that really. It was his obsessions, his tendency to go to extremes. That was what had ruined his life, had killed Agnes in the end.

He couldn't risk that again.

Ellie was still absorbed in the museum so Jesper leaned on the nearest doorframe and watched her, struck by the difference between the fairytale experience and this house. It felt like the contrast between his time with Ellie—the fairytale—and what would come next, the moment she was gone.

He'd be alone again. He needed to...he needed to figure out how he was going to do that.

Because he'd done what he always did—what he'd sworn he'd never do again.

He'd gone too far, too fast. Taken things to extremes. Gone off the deep end to the exclusion of everything else.

He'd made his whole world about Ellie and her quest.

He'd fallen in love with her.

And now he had to make damn sure he fell out of love before she left, or it was going to break him.

Love was too risky an emotion for the likes of him.

'Are you ready?' He blinked, and realised that Ellie was right in front of him, speaking to him, and looking up at him with concern in her eyes.

'Ready?' he asked, knowing he sounded confused.

'To go, I mean. Back to Copenhagen. I think I'm done here if you are,' she said. 'Or we can grab a coffee from the café before we leave?'

'No. No, let's get on the road. We can stop for coffee on the way.' The car was all packed up, and it was time to head back to reality.

Before he fell so hard for the fairytale he might never recover.

It was good to be back in Copenhagen.

Ellie felt as if she was seeing the city through whole new eyes in Jesper's company. After the week they'd spent mostly in bed in Odense, she'd sort of expected the same once they were back in the city, but life in Copenhagen was very different.

In fact, Jesper had left her at her short-term rental apartment the first night they'd returned, excusing himself to deal with some personal admin. The searing kiss he'd given her on departure, and the fact he'd spent every night since in her bed, meant she hadn't taken it at all personally. And honestly, it had been good to have a little time and space to catch up with herself and her feelings.

It had meant another awkward conversation with her mother, though. This time, at least she'd been rather more confident in her answers.

'Mum, I'm not coming home for the wedding. I'm doing something that is important to me here in Denmark, and I'm not willing to give it up just so Maisie can feel better about marrying my ex-husband.' There had been a sharp intake of breath from her mother there, but Ellie had ploughed on. 'In fact, I can't think of anything more awful for everyone than for them to have the ex-wife there haunting the proceedings at the back of the church. They've moved on and are starting a new life together. Please, let me do the same.'

She'd hung up the phone before her mum could respond, and had poured herself a large glass of white wine to celebrate.

Since then, she'd focused on really making the most of her remaining time in Denmark—and with Jesper. And if she'd expected to be doing that mostly in bed, she'd been wrong. It turned out that Jesper had a long list of places to take her and things to show her and he was determined to get through all of them before she left.

'I made you a promise,' he told her when she questioned the manic schedule. 'I promised to show you exactly why the Danes are so happy, and I intend to fulfil that. I showed you the places that saved me, when I was at my worst. Now I'm showing you all the everyday things that affect the Danish sense of wellbeing. We lost time in Odense, but I think we can still make it up.'

'Or I could always change my flight, I suppose.' The idea wasn't as unattractive as it would have been before New Year. Then, she was just waiting for the wedding to be over so she could go back home. Now…a few more weeks in Denmark with Jesper definitely wouldn't be the worst outcome. Especially since the book was actually coming together, and she wasn't panicking about having to pay back her advance.

But Jesper just gave her a small smile and said, 'Don't worry. We'll get through everywhere on my list in time.'

And so the days passed in a whirlwind of galleries and museums and restaurants and open spaces. Jesper talked to her about the power of architecture and design to affect people's moods, even introducing her to his ex-brother-in-law's husband, who was a designer and spoke about the magic of design with such alacrity that Ellie couldn't help but be inspired. She scribbled notes as fast as she could, and ignored Jesper all evening while she added a new section to the book afterwards.

He took her to a local ceramics centre, where he'd arranged for her to try her hand at pottery-making. As she fashioned an almost serviceable bowl on the wheel—after a few failed early attempts that required Jesper to leave the room so he didn't laugh in her face—they talked about the importance of making things that lasted. How it provided a satisfaction that lasted much longer than fleeting happiness.

'Legacy,' Jesper said, as she focused on her bowl spinning slowly under her hands. 'Like your book. You're creating something that will outlive you, be read by people you'll never meet, live in the world completely apart from you. That's amazing.'

'Unlike this bowl.' Ellie squinted at it. 'I don't think anyone but me will ever want this thing.'

He smiled. 'I would.'

'Then it's yours,' she promised. 'Something to remember me by.'

'I'd like that,' Jesper replied.

But long after the clay had—finally—been cleaned from her hands, and Jesper had arranged to come and collect the bowl after it had been fired, she was still thinking about his words. Was that really what she was trying to do with her book? Outlive herself? She supposed that maybe it was. A way to leave a mark on the world.

She liked that. Almost as much as the thought that Jesper would remember her when she was gone too, every time he looked at that ridiculous, lopsided bowl on his shelf.

After a week of exploring Copenhagen with Jesper, they caught up with Lily and Anders for dinner at Lily's favourite restaurant.

'How are we supposed to act in front of them?' Ellie asked Jesper in the car on their way over. 'I mean, are we just friends, or do we let them know about…'

'All the sex?' Jesper answered, in his usual, blunt way. 'It's up to you.'

She considered. 'If we tell Lily we're sleeping together, she's going to make it into some personal victory—especially after New Year. Worse, she might decide we're madly in love and I'm moving to Denmark permanently, because that's what she did with Anders. Which is obviously ridiculous.'

The idea of it, though, prickled under her skin. She *wasn't* in love, because that wasn't what she was here in Denmark for. It wasn't the deal. And she definitely wasn't falling in love with a man who had been very clear about not being able to love her back. That way disappointment lay, and she'd had enough of that already lately, thank you.

Jesper shrugged. 'So we just act like friends. How hard can that be?'

It turned out, rather harder than Ellie had anticipated.

She'd thought they were doing a good job of just being friends, until Lily dragged her to the bathroom after the first course and demanded to know what was going on between her and Jesper.

158   COPENHAGEN ESCAPE WITH THE BILLIONAIRE

Ellie blinked, and caught her reflection in the mirror, looking like a deer in the headlights. 'I...what do you mean?'

Lily rolled her eyes. 'The pair of you are ridiculous. I mean, the way he smiles at you, the way he handed you your menu, the way he guessed your wine order...not to mention the way he kept brushing his arm against yours. You're clearly sleeping together, and I want to know all the juicy details!'

Ellie glanced down at the bathroom tiles to hide her smile. 'Okay, fine. But later, okay? I want to get back out there before the main course arrives and Jesper starts stealing my sides. He's terrible for sharing food.'

She brushed a hand against the back of Jesper's shoulders as she went to sit down, and let him take her hand and kiss it, and that was the cat completely out of the bag.

They went back to Lily and Anders' flat after dinner, to the scene of their first kiss, and Ellie couldn't help but lose herself in reminiscences as she sank into the squashy sofa. Anders and Jesper were out on the tiny balcony, looking at something in the night sky—Ellie wasn't sure what—so it was just her and Lily now.

Her friend, sitting on the other end of the sofa, studied her carefully, a small frown line forming between her eyebrows.

'You look different.'

Ellie looked up in surprise. 'I stopped dyeing my hair weeks and weeks ago. Last year even, technically. Has it really taken you this long to notice?'

'It's not your hair.' Lily waved a dismissive hand. 'It's your...you. You look, well, happy. Sort of.'

Sort of?

'I *am* happy,' Ellie said. 'Or content, at least.'

'Because of Jesper?' There was a hint of concern in Lily's voice now, and Ellie realised what the problem was. Her friend thought she'd fallen in love with Jesper and was going to get her heart broken.

She shook her head. 'Not the way you mean. He's been…it's all been great. He's been such a huge help with the book, with helping me to see the world, and my future, differently. And now… I finally feel like I'm ready to get back to my real life again, back in London. You know?'

'That's great.' Despite her words, Lily still sounded doubtful. 'But are you sure—'

'You do realise that you're the one who set the two of us up for New Year, right?' Ellie interrupted.

Lily flushed pink. 'I know. And you haven't even said thank you for that yet, you realise? But I only did it because…'

'Because?' Ellie prompted when she trailed off, genuinely unsure where her best friend was going with this.

'Because I wanted you to have a little fun, and God knows Jesper needed some too, and I thought the two of you would get along well,' Lily said. 'But I didn't imagine… I see the way you look at him, El. And the way he looks at you, for that matter. It's just been so fast! And it's not just a bit of fun any more, is it? And I don't want you to get hurt, is all. You're both—'

She broke off as the door to the balcony opened and Jesper and Anders came back inside. Ellie thought it was probably for the best. She wasn't sure she wanted to hear what Lily had been about to say. It certainly wasn't the reaction she'd expected from her best friend.

'So, where are you two off to next on your Danish magical mystery tour?' Anders was asking.

Jesper shot Ellie an amused look. 'I'm taking her to Hamlet's castle.'

'Kronborg Castle? Brilliant!' Anders grinned at Ellie. 'You'll love it.'

Ellie wasn't so sure. 'I studied Hamlet at A Level. Seems to me there was a lot of waffling and then everybody died.'

'That's pretty much it,' Anders agreed happily. 'But the castle is spectacular.'

'So, "to be or not to be" happy. That's tomorrow's question, then?' Lily got up and tucked herself into Anders' arms as Jesper came and joined Ellie on the sofa in her place.

'Something like that,' he said softly. But there was something in his gaze Ellie couldn't quite place.

She blinked, and it was gone. Probably she'd imagined the strange look.

She hoped so. Because she didn't think she'd ever seen him look so sad. And she couldn't for the life of her figure out why.

CHAPTER TEN

ELLIE HADN'T TOLD him exactly when the wedding day was, only that she was avoiding it by being in Denmark. But she didn't have to. Jesper knew from the moment he woke up in bed alone on the thirty-first of January, the day after they'd visited Hamlet's castle, that it was the day that Ellie's ex-husband would be marrying her half-sister.

Every other morning they'd woken up together, Ellie had been curled up against his side, warm and soft and wonderful. Today, he could hear the clatter of her keyboard in the next room as she wrote.

Normally, she was a late at night writer, often writing until he coaxed her into joining him in bed. He didn't mind; he was happy to read while she worked, and it meant she tended to sleep in with him too, which provided all sorts of opportunities, in his experience.

He'd never seen her get up early to write before. Which was how he knew something must be wrong.

Tugging on some pants and a T-shirt, he checked his phone on the bedside table and saw a text from Lily, warning him that Ellie might need a little extra care and attention that day.

I don't know how much she's told you, but there's something happening in London today that's going to be pretty hard for her. Just look after her for me, okay?

Jesper thought he could do that.

He padded through to the living area of the tiny apartment Ellie had rented in Copenhagen. When they'd returned, he'd considered moving them both to one of his preferred hotels, or even renting a better apartment. He needed to buy somewhere eventually, but there wasn't time for that before she left, no matter how much money he threw at the problem.

But then it had occurred to him that it might be good for them to have their own space in the city. The time when Ellie would have to leave was drawing ever closer, and he knew he needed to start putting some distance between them, to protect himself when the time came. So, their first night back he'd checked into a hotel and forced himself to stay there all night, under the guise of catching up on some admin stuff. In truth, he'd spent the whole night watching bad movies and wishing he was with Ellie.

The next night he'd ended up staying with her in that tiny apartment, and somehow he'd never left again since.

Now, he was glad of it. It meant he was there today, when she needed him.

This day, her ex's wedding day, was the whole reason she'd come to Denmark in the first place. The reason for her happiness quest.

The least he could do was live through it with her, and be there for support.

Jesper leaned against the small kitchen island that separated the living space from the cooking, and watched her. Ellie sat at the small bistro table in the window, still wearing her pyjamas, looking out over the street below, her laptop in front of her, a frown on her face as she typed. A small piece of hair, shining in the weak winter sunlight, kept falling into her eyes. Every few moments she'd brush it away but it would fall straight back again.

God, he loved her. He didn't want her to leave. He wanted to spare her the pain of this day.

But all of that was about him, and none of it was about her.

So he didn't say any of it.

Instead, he eased himself into the chair opposite her, and waited for her to finish her train of thought. After a few more moments of frantic typing, she looked up and smiled.

It looked fragile, he thought. The sort of smile a person put on when they were trying to convince someone else—or themselves—that everything was fine. The sort of smile it made his heart hurt to see on Ellie's beautiful face.

'Hey. Sorry, I just woke up and… I couldn't sleep any more, and then I had an idea about something I needed to include in the book, so I thought I'd get some work done,' she said.

'Makes sense,' he replied. 'You must be hungry by now though. Can you take a break for some breakfast? I could go out and get something, or we could head down to the bakery for pastries.'

She tilted her head to one side, considering. 'You know what? Pastries would be good. Just let me get showered and dressed and we'll go.'

* * *

They'd visited a lot of cafés, bakeries and restaurants since they'd been back in Copenhagen, but as they left the apartment Jesper had a hankering for the one where they'd met, back at the start of January, to discuss the trip that became their happiness quest. Ellie looked amused when she realised where they were heading.

'Finally, the truth comes out. The true reason Danes are happier is because of the pastries. You could have just told me that the first day we met here and saved me a lot of time, you know.' She pushed the door open and stepped inside ahead of him, leaving a waft of sugary scent to hit him in the face.

He inhaled, and followed. 'Would you really have wanted that?'

She turned back to face him, a soft smile on her face. 'Not for a moment.'

'Good.'

They ordered a selection of pastries and large coffees before settling in at their table. Jesper tried to keep the conversation light and inconsequential, not wanting to demand too much of her on a day when her mind was clearly elsewhere. But when the coffee was done, neither of them was quite ready to return to the apartment yet.

'We should take a walk,' Jesper suggested. Walking always helped him stay in the moment, rather than ob-sessing about things he couldn't change, and he suspected that was what she needed today. 'It's a lovely day out there. Well, for January.'

She laughed, and it gladdened his heart to hear it. 'It is. Bright and cold and crisp.' Her face started to fall, and he knew without asking that she was wondering if the weather was the same in London.

He took her arm and got them moving. 'I haven't even taken you to see the Little Mermaid statue yet. I think that might be an actual crime, to come to Copenhagen and not see it.'

She gave him a wan smile. 'Didn't you check out my social media? I walked up the river to see it my first week in Denmark.'

Of course she had. If the Little Mermaid had any message at all, it had to be about fighting for happiness whatever the odds.

'Well, you haven't seen it with me,' he pointed out. 'And maybe you'll see it differently after our visit to the Hans Christian Andersen Museum.'

'Perhaps.' She didn't sound convinced, but she went along with him all the same.

They made their way through the city, past the green domed roof of the marble church, past the familiar buildings of the city, and Jesper realised he wasn't even paying attention to his surroundings because there was a question he needed to ask—one that had been bothering him since before they'd left the apartment.

'So, what was the idea for the book that couldn't wait? What were you working on this morning?'

Ellie stared out into the distance, at the Kastellet, the star fortress, and the river up ahead. They'd walked further than he'd thought already, both lost in their own thoughts. 'I was thinking about something else you need for happiness. Trust.'

'Trust?' Jesper frowned. He hadn't known what to expect, but it hadn't been that.

'Yeah. I figured that happiness is all about trust, really. You have to trust that life will be good, or that things will get better. You have to have faith in life, I suppose. And...and you have to trust other people, too. Or want to trust them at least. Because if you walk around expecting the worst of people all the time, how can you ever be happy?'

'That makes sense, I guess.' And it did. Too much sense. Her words were cascading around his head like a waterfall, and he hated it.

'It's like marriage,' she went on. 'When you get married, you put your whole heart in someone else's hands and trust them not to squeeze too hard.'

Was that what he'd done to Agnes? Taken her heart and squeezed the life out of it?

Was that why she'd left?

Maybe.

But he couldn't think about that now. He had to keep listening, trying to understand what Ellie was saying. 'And once someone has crushed your heart like that... it's hard to imagine trusting anyone that way again. But you have to—you have to trust the world, and you have to trust other people, or how can you be happy? Does that make sense?'

'I... I think so.' It was hard to get the words out. Because right now it felt as if it was *his* heart being crushed. He knew it wasn't because he couldn't trust her, though. But because he couldn't let her trust *him*.

Not when he couldn't trust himself.

Ellie's heart was beating too fast, and she knew it wasn't the cold, bracing air or the leisurely speed of their walk past the red walls of the Kastellet towards the river. She'd done this walk before, and while the sights still enchanted her, they weren't enough to distract her from her own thoughts. Not today.

Up ahead, she saw a small crowd around where she knew the statue of the Little Mermaid sat in the water. Everyone always said it was smaller than they'd imagined, but Ellie liked that about it. Liked the idea of this one, small mermaid taking on forces greater than herself in the pursuit of a life that would make her truly happy.

Of course, she had to admit to preferring Disney's ending to the fairytale than Andersen's.

The crowds parted and she came into view, a small bronze mermaid perched on a rock, staring out into the distance, imagining the life she could have. Did she know even then that she'd give up her voice for human legs, one freedom for another?

Ellie didn't want to give up anything. She wanted it all.

That was the problem.

She knew what she needed to say, but right until the last moment she knew she wouldn't be sure that she'd have the confidence. Instead, she stared at the statue for long seconds, until another crowd of winter tourists came along, and she stepped back to let them see.

Jesper tugged her arm and led her to a nearby bench, where they could still see the statue in between the waxing and waning crowds.

'It's Dave and Maisie's wedding today,' she said after a moment. It was the first time she'd acknowledged it out loud, even though the fact had been at the front of her mind all day.

'I know,' Jesper said.

'How? Did Lily tell you?' Had he known all morning and not said anything? Why?

He sighed. 'She texted me, yes. But I didn't need her to tell me. I knew the moment I woke up and you weren't in bed with me. But I wasn't sure if you *wanted* me to know, so...'

'So you took me for pastries instead.'

'Basically.' He gave her a small smile and a shrug. 'Was that the wrong thing to do?'

'No. It was...pastries are always good.'

'That was what I thought.' He settled back onto the bench, arms folded over his chest, a pleased smile on his face.

She hoped the smile would stay past what she had to say next.

'It got me thinking, though. The wedding, not the pastries,' she clarified. 'About trust, like I said. But also... about wanting what you can't have, or wanting something and regretting it when you get it. For the longest time, all I wanted was my old life back—my marriage, my friends, the future I'd imagined for us. But now... I wouldn't have it all back as a gift, and I wonder if Maisie will feel that way some day. If she'll realise that my life wasn't what she really wanted at all, and leave Dave in the same state I was in.'

'It's not your responsibility to worry about that for them,' Jesper said softly.

'I know. I know that, I do.' She searched for the right words to explain. 'It's just... I look back at the woman—girl, practically—I was then, when I got married, and I realise that she knew nothing about who she really was, who she could be. I'm not sure I ever did, before now. I just went along doing the next thing and the next thing and never stopping to think if they were really the things that I wanted to be doing in the first place. And then, when it all fell apart, I just ran away. All the way to Denmark.'

'And I, for one, am glad that you did.' He nudged her with his shoulder and she looked up at him and tried to smile.

Because this was the scariest part of all. The part that came next.

'I thought I was running away.' Her throat was dry, and she forced herself to swallow, to keep the words coming. 'But now I wonder if I wasn't running towards something. Towards trusting in happiness again. Towards love. Towards you.'

She wished she wasn't looking at him as she said it. Wished she'd kept her gaze fixed on that hopeful bronze mermaid out in the water, looking towards a better life.

Because if she had been, she wouldn't have had to watch the horror settle over Jesper's face as he realised she'd said the word 'love'.

Love.

She hadn't really said it. Or if she had, she didn't mean it.

This was all because her ex was getting married today. She was maudlin or wistful or something. She was romanticising the life she'd had, and imagining the life she wanted—fantasising that maybe he could give it to her. But he knew that he couldn't—and any other day, he was sure she'd know that too. She wouldn't want him if she wasn't feeling the way she was because of her ex-husband getting remarried.

He'd *told* her—explained how he couldn't be a good enough husband to make Agnes stay. How he always went too far, wanted too much, and couldn't live up to the man people wanted him to be.

She was a people pleaser, keeping the peace and giving others what they needed. If he let her love him, how long would she go along with what he wanted, pretending it was what she wanted too, before it became too much?

Before she left him, the same way Agnes had, because he'd let her down?

So, no. She couldn't mean it.

Because if she meant it, then he would have to be the strong one and walk away. To save them both.

He needed to show her that she couldn't love him. Remind her of everything she'd told him about the importance of her own happiness, and how she didn't want to be dependent on someone else for it.

She hadn't really said the words yet, she hadn't said 'I love you,' even though her eyes were screaming it.

Even though every part of him wanted to say it back.

He broke away to look out across the water. He just needed a moment. He needed to think. He needed to convince her that this was the wrong thing for them. That in the end he'd only ruin it, ruin her. That everything he'd given her the last four weeks was all he could *ever* give her.

And then he needed to walk away.

'You were right, back at the start, when you told me you couldn't let your happiness be dependent on another person.'

'That's not what I'm doing!' Ellie shot back. 'I lo—'

He couldn't let her say it, so he broke in before she could finish.

'You know... I told you about my marriage. About why I can't do that again. And I'm sorry if I gave you the impression...' Jesper shook his head, words beginning to fail him as the hope started to drain from her face. 'For a short time, I made you my new project, my new obsession. That's what I do, you see? I fall in too deep, too fast, and I obsess and then...it all falls apart.' He looked away, unable to bear the pain in her eyes any more. Instead, he stared out at the river, the ever-changing water, and tried to find some of the peace he'd felt in his three years away from society. 'It took me such a long time to move past Agnes' death. I gave it all up—the business, the New York penthouse, the lifestyle. I handed all my money and investments over to Will, had him sell the company, and trusted him to keep me solvent. I bought the beach house and I just...retreated. I thought I was returning to the way of life Agnes wanted me to have, by being the polar opposite of how I'd been the last few years of our marriage. But I realise now that I'd just taken things to another extreme. Because that's what I do. And I can't... I can't live that way any more. I have to find a way to have that balance everyone talks about.'

I can't love you. I'll fail again and you'll leave me, and I won't survive that a second time.

'Balance.' Ellie huffed a small laugh. 'That perfect Danish way of living I'm supposed to be writing about. The happy hygge life. *That's* what you're searching for?'

'I don't know. Maybe?' He ran a hand through his hair. 'I just know I can't go on the way I have been. It's too much. It…it doesn't matter how I feel about you, Ellie. Because I'm not ready for it, not yet. I thought I'd moved on, but being with you has only shown me how much I'm still the same man I was back then. Because you're going to leave—if not now, one day, because I can't be what you need. And if I let myself think about what we could have, and what I'll lose, it'll break me again.'

He risked a look back at her face to see if she understood, and was only slightly surprised to find her eyes blazing with anger.

'You've already played our whole story out to the end without me, haven't you?' she said. 'It's not that you don't care about me, it's that you don't trust yourself, let alone happiness. You won't take the risk that this could be wonderful. Happiness is trust and it's risk too. You have to take a leap of faith, and you won't.'

'I *can't*.' Not again. Not when he'd only so narrowly survived the last time.

Maybe she heard the pain in his voice, or maybe she'd just given up on him, Jesper wasn't sure. But the anger faded from her expression and her shoulders sagged against the back of the bench. 'You were supposed to be my teacher. The one who showed me how to be happy. And you *did*. It just turned out that, in the end, I know more about happiness than you do. Or I'm more willing to take a chance on it, anyway. I'll be happy with or without you, Jesper. I would just rather it was with you.'

'I'm sorry, Ellie.' He wanted to hold her, to kiss her, to do anything to make this better.

Anything except open his whole heart to her and admit how much he loved her.

Because if he did that, he knew he'd never be able

to walk away, and the whole terrible cycle would begin again.

So instead, he got to his feet, cast one last look back at her beautiful face, then turned and walked away, his heart breaking a little more with every step.

CHAPTER ELEVEN

ELLIE STAYED WITH the Little Mermaid, thinking about everything that had happened since she'd arrived in Denmark, or since New Year at least, for a long time. How could it have only been one month since that midnight kiss with Jesper with the fireworks in the background? She felt like a completely different person to the woman who'd gone to the Tivoli Gardens that night.

But at the same time she felt more herself than she had in decades, and she knew that was thanks to Jesper. And while her heart was aching now, she also knew that he'd given her the tools she needed to recover from that heartbreak. To make her new life, shape it the way she wanted.

First, though, she had a book to finish.

She wiped the freezing tears from her face, stood up to say a silent goodbye to the Little Mermaid and headed back to her flat, a new determination in her step.

It took a steely resolve to ignore all the signs of Jesper still lingering in the flat—from the rumpled sheets to an abandoned jumper on the arm of the sofa to other, more personal memories of what they'd done together there—but Ellie was focused. She settled back down in front of her laptop at the bistro table she'd been working at that morning and started reading through everything she'd already written.

By the time she got to the end the sun was going down, and she had a notebook full of scrawled thoughts and observations about the book so far—and how she now knew she needed to write it.

She turned to the next blank page in her notebook and started a new list, mumbling to herself as she worked.

'The structure needs to change, that's obvious. And I want to make more of the vignettes from the places we went, the importance of light and shade, balance…and then the ending…'

Oh, she had big ideas for the ending.

Because, finally, she knew how her Danish adventure ended. With heartbreak, yes, but also with hope.

And that was the story she was going to write.

Starting now.

The beach house seemed empty without Ellie.

It had never seemed empty before. It had always *been* empty, he supposed, apart from him. But it had never *felt* that way until now. Before, it had always been a retreat, a place to rest and restore and regroup. It didn't need anyone else in it.

Now…

Well. Lots of things were different now.

Or maybe that was just the vodka talking.

He took another sip as he stared out of the window, watching the moon reflecting on the water, breaking and reforming with every wave. This was the same window seat Ellie had sat in so often during her visit, reading, writing notes in her notebook or even typing away, while he cooked in the kitchen, usually.

He felt closer to her here. Which was ridiculous because she was still miles away in Copenhagen.

If she hadn't gone back to London already. She was supposed to leave in two days' time, but what if she'd changed her ticket? Would Lily have told him if she had?

Lily and Anders hadn't been in touch at all since he'd left Ellie at the Little Mermaid a week before, so he didn't know. Didn't even know if Ellie had told them about their…was it a breakup? He wasn't even sure what to call it if they'd never really been a couple. Just two people travelling the same path for a while. And now they weren't.

And now Jesper couldn't sleep.

Partly it was because he missed her warmth at his side, burrowing in to keep warm, or just stay close.

And partly it was because every time he closed his eyes he relived every moment of his life where he'd screwed up. Where he could have done better. Where he didn't see the problems until it was too late. It wasn't even just Agnes and Ellie. It was every single mistake he'd made since his memories started, before he'd even gone to school.

Maybe his brain was trying to make him learn something from them. But if so, he had no idea what.

With a sigh, he sank down onto the window seat, pretending to himself for a moment that he could still smell Ellie's perfume there. He rested his head against the window and watched the waves for a moment, glass of vodka still in hand.

He supposed that every mistake he'd made had led him here. And so had every right choice, too. For all the things that had gone wrong, it was hard to regret many of the things that he'd done or chosen in his life. Despite how it ended, his marriage to Agnes had been a blessing, and so had his work in New York. Would he do things differently now, knowing what he knew?

He'd try to. He'd try harder. He supposed that would have to be enough.

Or would it? Ellie's words floated back to him.

'She wanted you to earn a lot of money but resented the time it took. She didn't like the trade-off.'

Jesper remembered his own response, repeated it to the empty room. 'I just wasn't good enough. I couldn't give her what she needed.'

I don't think anybody could.

Was she right?

Maybe there had been a way to save their marriage, to find a life they were both satisfied with, happy even. But maybe, just maybe, it wouldn't have only been him who had to change. In another world, perhaps they could have found a compromise. If the car hadn't crashed...

He'd never know for sure. But suddenly it seemed possible that he wasn't the only person in that marriage who'd been at fault. And while he'd always mourn the death of his wife, he couldn't change it. Nothing he did now would change the facts of that terrible afternoon.

He was living in a different world now. A post-Agnes world.

And that was where he'd met Ellie. He wouldn't change that either, now.

But he'd made his choices, and they'd brought him here. Alone, with his vodka and the moon.

And this was where he'd always be, he realised suddenly. Because if he wanted that perfect balance, to maintain a cool, calm life with no space for the extremes that had led him into trouble so often before…well, there was no room for other people in that life. On the periphery, perhaps, looking on and checking in, before they went back to their own fuller, happier lives.

He'd thought he could work past what had happened with Agnes, but being with Ellie had only shown him that he was still the same person he'd always been.

Perhaps he always would be.

So maybe he just needed to accept that person and find a way to live with him. To make it work.

And he had to decide now if he really wanted to do that alone, for ever.

He stood up suddenly, his mind racing to keep up with his thoughts, and dislodged a cushion from the window seat, sending a piece of paper fluttering to the ground. With a frown he picked it up and read it.

Ellie's looping writing filled the page.

Happy Things she'd titled it. And below was a list of things that must have been making her happy in that moment. And they were all…tiny. Inconsequential.

Jesper's coffee machine.
The birds on the water outside the window.
The quiet here.
The way he looks at me sometimes.
Pastries for breakfast.
Knowing it's almost time for our next adventure.
The troll Jesper bought me at the museum, and its ridiculous red hair.

None of them were earth-changing. But as he read them, Jesper found himself smiling.

And suddenly something clicked inside his head, almost like a switch, a lightbulb turning on.

Happiness didn't have to be that extreme he'd always thought. It wasn't all or nothing, burn out or checking out, New York City or three years in the wilderness.

It could be those small moments in a long day. An appreciation of the world around him—and the people around him, too. The comforting presence of someone he loved, even when they weren't saying anything...

And he did love Ellie. He'd accepted that much, and it was far too late to stop the feeling now. He'd thought it would lead him—or worse, her—to another ruin.

But maybe...maybe he could just love her in small, everyday ways. And he could do that well enough that they could find happiness, a future together.

If he could even convince her to give him another chance to try.

Jesper put down his drink, folded Ellie's happiness list and tucked it in his pocket and headed to his room to pull out his suitcase.

He had things to arrange.

It was done. The book was done, and Ellie could hardly believe it.

She wasn't sure she'd left the chair for the last week, except to pass out in bed, use the bathroom or acquire food, but the book was done.

And it was good.

She stretched her arms high above her head, feeling something pop in a strangely pleasurable way, then read back over her last few paragraphs one last time before sending it to her agent for her thoughts.

Happiness can be so many things to so many people. We think the Danes have it nailed, and they do, in their own way. So many things about their lifestyle are conducive to also having the time, freedom, space and money to seek out joy in the world.

But one thing I discovered in the long Danish winter was that happiness can so often only be really seen in the contrasts. When night falls before we're ready, we have to trust that the sun will rise again in the morning. That when life seems dark, the brightness of happiness may be only just around the corner, if we can keep our faith in it long enough to find it.

In the end, permanent joy, the 'happiness' I think so many of us are seeking, is an impossibility— simply because, without the contrasts, we soon fail to appreciate what we have. Better, I've found, to strive instead for a resilient sense of personal joy. One that finds bright moments in dark days—but also acknowledges and works through that darkness, ready to step back into the light when we're ready.

The world is full of happy, joyous things—and also sad and humbling, hurtful ones. We have to learn to live a life between the two, finding our balance on life's tightrope, and turning our face towards the sun whenever we get the chance.

In short: happiness is made, not found. We just have to look for it, recognise and enjoy it when it comes, and trust that, when it seems far away, it will return, just like the sun.

Ellie sat back with a satisfied sigh. She'd need to edit it more, she knew—and she was certain that both her agent and her editor would have changes they wanted made, clarifications and explanations, not to mention tidying up her writing.

But she thought that she'd finally found what she'd come to Denmark to write. She'd never expected to write it so fast, but a looming deadline and a little heartbreak did wonders for her writing process, it seemed.

She quickly attached the manuscript to an email before she could have any second thoughts, and sent it off to her agent before closing her laptop down.

She was done. And that meant it was time to go home.

Her flight was booked for late the following afternoon, but tonight she had one last night in Copenhagen with Lily and Anders to enjoy.

She spent an hour or so packing up her belongings, wondering how she had so many more than she'd arrived in the country with—from hygge candles and blankets from Lily when she'd seen the bare furniture of the flat she'd rented, to the troll with the red hair that she still couldn't look at too long without crying. When she'd done as much as she could for now, she hopped in the shower and made herself look presentable for her last night on the town.

The book was done, her trip was over.

It was time to go home and start her new life.

'You're here!' Lily greeted Ellie with a huge hug when she arrived at their apartment later that evening. 'Did you see the lights on the way? They're even better in the city centre. Come on in!'

They'd made plans, early in Ellie's visit, to do a tour of the Copenhagen Light Festival on her last night in Denmark. And however much Ellie hadn't felt like it a week ago when Lily had reminded her about the date, there was no way she was going to be allowed to get out of it. Now the day had arrived, Ellie was glad that Lily hadn't let her cancel. It was good to mark the end of this period of her life with something tangible. Plus, she hoped it would give her one last happy memory of Denmark for the road.

They shared a delicious dinner at the apartment before venturing out, during which nobody mentioned Jesper, which Ellie appreciated. She'd given her friend a bare bones account of what had happened, but hadn't mentioned the part about love. She knew Lily wouldn't let her leave if she thought there was a chance that Jesper could be persuaded to rethink—but Lily hadn't seen his face before he'd walked away.

This was the right decision, for both of them. Ellie had no plans to chase after a man who had made it so clear he didn't want what she had to offer.

Lily *did* ask about the wedding, however.

'Have you spoken to your mum? How did it all go? Was the church struck by lightning when Dave said his vows?'

Ellie chuckled. 'Nothing so dramatic, I'm afraid. Apparently, it all went off without a hitch. I haven't spoken to Mum, but I had a call with Sarah the other day and she filled me in on it all. In fact, she had a message for me from Dave.'

Lily's eyebrows shot up. '*Really?* And what did the devil incarnate have to say?'

'Just that he was sorry Mum and Maisie had been pressuring me to be there—seems he didn't know about it until Sarah mentioned it,' Ellie explained. 'He agreed that it was best I wasn't present, I think. It would have all been just too weird.'

Lily raised her glass. 'Amen to that.'

Once dinner was over, they ventured out onto the streets of Copenhagen to enjoy the light festival. It was, Ellie had to admit, pretty spectacular. Denmark knew how to do light, she reflected, and how to make the most of the light it had. Here, whole buildings were lit up, or had pictures or patterns projected on them, some looking like water, others like rustling leaves. The lights weren't static; they kept moving, illuminating new pockets of the city she'd never seen before, as well as highlighting some of its most famous features. Even the river was lit, with lights strung over boats and beams shooting into the sky. Ellie wondered if they'd make it as far as the Little Mermaid, and what lights she'd have around her tonight.

The streets were crowded with tourists and locals alike, all taking in the spectacle. For a moment, Ellie felt a pang of sadness; it was so like New Year's Eve it was hard not to compare how each event had ended in her head. One with a kiss, and a new adventure in this country she'd come to love, the other with her leaving for good, alone.

But no. She wasn't going to think about it that way. Because tomorrow was another fresh start, and how lucky was she to have that?

'Oh, look!' Lily grabbed her arm and dragged her across a street. 'The Tivoli Gardens are all lit up too! Let's get closer and see…'

But before they even reached the gates of the Tivoli

Gardens, Lily took a sudden turn, down a darkened street. 'Maybe there's something down here.'

Ellie frowned at the map in her hand and glanced back at Anders, who was standing at the entrance to the street, effectively blocking the route. 'There's nothing on the map, Lily. Let's head back to the main street.'

But Lily kept pulling her forward. 'No, I really think there's going to be something to see this way.'

They turned one last corner, into a courtyard Ellie hadn't even known was there. Lily swung her arm so Ellie moved ahead, taking a few small steps to catch her balance. 'What are you—'

She broke off as the lights ahead dazzled her.

This display hadn't been on her official light festival map, she was sure of it. A circle of rainbow lights shone down from the sides of the surrounding buildings, filling the entire courtyard. Red ran into orange then yellow and all the way through to violet, spinning and shifting, like a river of light, always moving. It was huge and bright— and far away from any of the tourists who'd come for the festival. Because this display was only for her.

It was the rainbow panorama at Aarhus recreated just for her. A never-ending circle of light that changed and adapted but kept going all the same.

And standing right in the middle of it, beside a bistro table laden with Danish pastries and a bottle of champagne, was the man who'd first kissed her in that same rainbow.

Ellie glanced behind her and realised Lily had gone— back to join Anders, she assumed. Because, of course, it wasn't the lights Lily had wanted her to see.

Clearly, this was another set-up, just like Lily's plans on New Year's Eve.

Ellie wondered how this one would end.

'Jesper.' His bright blue eyes shone in the lights that scattered across the courtyard. She had no idea how he'd been able to set up such a display, but she knew that he had—just for her.

When she hesitated about whether to step closer or not, Jesper took the decision for her, moving towards her with swift steps, but staying a respectful distance away, just within the rainbow circle. If she wanted to join him, she'd have to cross the swirling colours, turning slowly in from one shade to the next. He wasn't assuming anything. That was good.

Even if every inch of her body was fighting against her head to jump into his arms.

She needed to know what this was, first.

'I'm sorry,' he said. 'For surprising you, and for everything else. I needed to talk to you but I knew you'd have no reason to listen, so I wanted to *do* something, something more than words, and this was my best idea. Lily said... I think she thought this would be romantic.'

'I thought romantic was the last thing you wanted to be with me any more,' she snapped back.

He winced. 'I'm definitely sorry for letting you think that. I just... Can I have a few moments of your time, before you leave for London? I've got champagne. And pastries. And if, when I'm done talking, you never want to see me again, I promise I'll stay away.'

Ellie nodded, ignoring the shudder that went through her middle at the idea of never seeing him again. 'Okay. We can talk.'

She took a breath, waiting for Jesper to move back towards the table in the centre of the courtyard before she approached the rainbow lights shining down. She needed a moment to recalibrate. To try and figure out if this was another ending—or perhaps the fresh start she'd never imagined she could have.

Despite herself, something an awful lot like hope was blooming in her chest.

After all, hadn't she just written that people needed to look out for joy, in order to find it? Something like that anyway.

After a moment, she stepped forward, bracing herself as she reached the light barrier—even though she knew that was ridiculous. The colours were nothing but beams of light, they couldn't stop her, couldn't hurt her. Even if the man in the centre of them could—and already had.

Jesper pulled out a chair for her and she sat, tensed, and stared at the pastries as he took his own seat, then poured her a glass of champagne.

'You know, when we met in that café, back at the start of January, I really did believe that I could teach you about happiness,' Jesper said eventually. 'I thought I'd got it all sorted out. I'd come back from the brink, from the darkest moment, and I thought I was happy. I believed I could share that with you. But instead...' He shook his head. 'Instead, you taught me.'

Her breath caught in her throat. She wanted to say something, but the words seemed trapped. Her heart, though, was beating loudly enough to speak for her anyway.

Jesper put down his glass and reached across the table to rest his open palm on it, ready for her to take, if she chose. But she couldn't, not yet. She needed to hear something more.

'I love you too. That's what I should have said that day, by the Little Mermaid. I love you, and I didn't believe I could ever have that again. But falling in love with you showed me how the life I'd carved out for myself after Agnes' death wasn't happiness. It was existing, simply existing within these strict parameters I'd given myself to keep me in check. To stop me feeling *anything* too much or too fully, in case I lost it or screwed up again and fell back down into that pit. I thought I could protect myself from having someone else leave me by choosing to leave first, but I was wrong. You taught me what happiness looks like for me now, and I only realised it when I walked away and felt the pain and the darkness that was left in my life without you.' He took a deep breath, and Ellie realised she was leaning in so close now that she could see the smallest spark of hope in his eyes, and his breath on the air as he spoke again. Her fingers inched towards his. 'So, if you can trust me with your happiness, I'd like to spend the rest of my life loving you, and making you as happy as you make me. If that's still what you want.'

Was it? She'd just got used to the idea of moving on alone, of starting over, taking what she'd learned here and starting again.

But what if she could start again *with him?*

You have to recognise happiness when you see it.

And she was pretty damn sure the tight, bright feeling of joy in her chest was nothing but pure happiness.

Ellie folded her fingers with his on the table, then reached up with her other hand to cup his cheek. Then, in the middle of a rainbow, she leaned across and pressed her frozen lips against his.

* * *

Jesper sank into Ellie's kiss with an overwhelming feeling of relief. He hadn't got a plan B, didn't know what he'd have done if she'd walked away. But he'd had to take the leap of faith, anyway.

Had to trust it would be worth it, if he got to be with her again.

And it was.

Keeping her hand in his, he guided them to their feet and moved around the table to kiss her again—deeper this time. He wrapped his arms around her middle, holding her close and, as she held him back, he vowed to himself that this time, this time he'd never let her go.

Not now he knew what real happiness felt like.

When they finally broke the kiss, Ellie fell back on her heels and looked up at him, a little breathless, he was pleased to note. Maybe she'd even missed him half as much as he'd missed her. The lights from his rainbow circle flickered over her pale skin, highlighting her soft smile, and he felt his chest tighten just to be near her again.

'What changed your mind?' she asked.

Jesper pulled the *Happy Things* list he'd found at the beach house from his pocket and handed it to her. 'I realised that happiness wasn't what I thought it was. And that if I clung onto my old ideas I'd be alone for the rest of my life—worse, I'd be without *you*. I realised you were right—I had to take a risk and trust in happiness. So I came back to see if I could persuade you to give me another chance—a chance for us to be happy together.'

'I'm very glad you did,' she murmured, looking down at her list. Then, with a quick smile, she pulled a pen from the pocket of her coat and added something to the bottom. She turned it around to show him; it read: *Kissing Jesper.*

He laughed, and wrapped his arms tight around her to pull her close again. 'So does that mean you'll stay here in Denmark with me?'

She shook her head. 'I have to go back to London.'

'Right. Of course you do.' Jesper tried not to feel too disappointed. He'd known it wouldn't be that easy.

'But I'll come back.' Ellie grabbed his hand and ducked closer so he was looking into her eyes. 'I'll come back, and you'll come and visit and I'll show you all the things in London that make me believe in happiness, too. And we can decide what happens next, together.'

'Together.' He liked the sound of that.

In fact…maybe *that* was the balance he really needed. Not to stop caring or doing or wanting or loving so much. Just someone else to do it with him. To keep him balanced.

They'd taken the biggest leap of faith together, and now, as the rainbow flickered around them, constantly changing but never ending, Jesper knew one thing for certain.

They'd never stop looking for happiness together.

* * * * *

THEIR HAWAIIAN MARRIAGE REUNION

CARA COLTER

MILLS & BOON

CHAPTER ONE

KAUAI.

Finally.

The Garden Isle was said to be one of the most beautiful places on the planet. And at any other time, Megan Hart, with her artist's eye and soul, would have taken in all the competing sensations eagerly: the warmth of exotically scented air, sensual on her skin; the vibrant jungle greens, threaded through with such an abundance of brilliant, colored flowers that she hardly knew where to look; the startling black of the lava rock in the construction of a low wall, whispering to her of things ancient and mystical.

But it was two in the morning. She was sitting on an uncomfortable wooden bench just outside the main doors of the Lihue Airport. Inside was chaos, as frustrated passengers felt the ripple effect of travel disruptions on the mainland. They were dealing with changing schedules and canceled flights as planes that were supposed to have arrived here were stuck somewhere else in a giant chain reaction.

The driver, Keona, who had been sent for Meg from the Hale Iwa Kai Resort, had taken one look at her face and, despite looking exhausted himself, had gently removed her luggage tags from her hand and shooed her outside.

Any eagerness she had felt about her first ever trip to Hawaii had been tempered two days ago when sudden winter storms in the East had sent North American air travel into a state of absolute meltdown.

Rerouted for the third time, Meg had found herself stranded at a medium-sized Midwestern airport, staring out at where a runway had been totally erased by the blizzard unfolding outside the huge windows.

It had occurred to her, looking out into the impenetrable white of the storm, that she was going to miss the wedding.

And the awful truth of that?

She had been relieved.

The truth was her trepidation had always outweighed her eagerness to see Hawaii.

It wasn't that she didn't want to be with her best friend, Caylee Van Houtte, as she exchanged vows with billionaire Jonathon Winston, at a wedding luau at the exclusive and very private Hale Iwa Kai boutique resort on Kauai.

How could Meg not want that, when she had never seen her best friend so deliriously happy? The wedding had been over eighteen months in the making—even if you had access to unlimited funds, which Jonathon Winston did, you didn't book all the beach cottages at Hale Iwa Kai on a whim.

No, it wasn't that she didn't want to share those moments with Caylee and Jonathon.

It wasn't that at all.

And it wasn't that she had a travel curse—a broken foot in Paris, food poisoning in Thailand, hypothermia in Switzerland—that could raise its ugly head at any time.

It was that Meg didn't want to see her nearly ex-husband, Morgan Hart. They'd been separated eight months now, and every time she contemplated the failure of her marriage it felt as if she was being swallowed by a darkness so suffocating Meg did not know how it was possible to survive.

And, of course, she was going to see Morgan.

For the first time. After the split, she had quietly packed

her bags and moved half a country away from him, from the Canadian city of Vancouver, British Columbia, to Ottawa, Ontario.

It had been best. A clean cut. Absolutely no chance of running into him.

But now, he was the best man to Meg's maid of honor. She thought maybe he was seeing someone. She hadn't been able to bring herself to ask Caylee if he was bringing someone to the wedding with him. But surely Caylee would have mentioned it?

Morgan and Jonathon had been best friends—as had she and Caylee—since they were children.

It was Meg who had introduced Caylee to Jonathon.

But how could she possibly see Morgan again without her heart breaking in two? Without falling at his feet and begging for a different finish? For a happy ending?

Particularly against the backdrop of a wedding? Even though it would be totally different than their own quiet, private nuptials had been, how could the romantically charged event not fill Meg with memories of that moment when she and Morgan had exchanged their own vows?

Believing, naively as it turned out, in forever.

Stop it, Meg ordered herself.

She'd had only a few winks of sleep in the last forty-eight hours. It was just the utter bone-melting exhaustion that was making her feel as if she couldn't do this. Hadn't she been rehearsing for the fact she could not possibly avoid seeing Morgan at the wedding every single day since she had left him?

Meg was positive she had the cool look down pat, the tilt of her chin, the proud set of her shoulders.

He would never, ever know she still loved him, would always love him.

Morgan would never ever know that she still woke in the

night reaching for him, that when she realized he was not there she would cry herself back to sleep.

He would never know how, in moments of utter weakness, she would go through her phone, looking at the photos, touching his face, recalling every detail of him, including how his skin felt under her fingertips, or how the memory of his scent haunted her and filled her with a longing, a hunger, that could never be satiated.

And he would never ever know the reason she had left him.

Meg snapped out of her thoughts when Keona, in his bright Hawaiian shirt, came out through the airport doors and gave her a sympathetic look.

For a moment, Meg thought her travel curse might manifest itself as no luggage. How could her bags have possibly followed her through all the changes in flight plans? Added to the travel delays, that should cover her travel curse for Hawaii, shouldn't it? What a relief it would be, if the curse played out early, so as not to disrupt the wedding.

But, no, her luggage was trundling obediently along behind Keona.

The reason for his sympathetic look must be that her tormented thoughts about Morgan were written all over her.

Though even without the thoughts, Meg was pretty sure she cut a pathetic picture, well deserving of pity. She had caught a glimpse of herself in a restroom mirror, and it wasn't good. She was white with exhaustion, her clothes were crumpled, there was a coffee stain on her pale pink shirt, her blond hair had long since escaped any attempts to tame it, what was left of her makeup was worthy of a horror film and she was pretty sure she smelled.

She sighed and followed Keona to the sleek, black limousine that waited. He held open the rear door for her, then stowed her luggage in the trunk. Meg settled into the back seat. It was, of course, pure luxury with deep leather, cool, fragrant air, a sound system, a bar.

It was a reminder of the life she'd had, ever so briefly, then turned her back on.

The car's powerful engine purred as it pulled smoothly away from the curb. Even though it was night, Meg wanted so badly to catch glimpses of this mystical island she found herself on. She peered out the tinted window, but all she could see was a star-studded sky and palm trees swaying gently in silhouette against it.

Soon, lulled by the lack of view, by the night, by the soft, soothing tones of the ukulele music, by the cool embrace from the vehicle's air-conditioning, Meg gave in to her utter and complete weariness. Her eyes fluttered shut.

And did not open again until a soft voice pulled her from the astonishing deepness of her sleep.

"Mrs. Hart."

For a moment, her eyes stayed closed. Maybe it was the most delicious of dreams and she still was Mrs. Hart.

But no, she opened her eyes and Keona was leaning in the back door, regarding her with soft brown eyes. She should really tell him that she wasn't Mrs. Hart anymore.

But technically, she still was. No divorce papers had been signed. In fact, she couldn't even make herself look at the thick separation agreement that had arrived from a well-known Vancouver law firm.

Still, it seemed as if correcting Keona about her marital status presented complexities she didn't really want to get into with strangers, kind as their eyes might be!

"We are very tired," he said, and she realized he was referring not only to her, but also to himself.

Meg did her best to shake herself awake and then scrambled sleepily out of the car. Keona assembled her luggage, carry case expertly fastened to roller suitcase, and it rattled along behind him as he entered a softly lit and completely empty open-air lobby.

Even though she had been Mrs. Hart for two years, Meg had never really become accustomed to the tastefully luxurious spaces of the world that welcomed the very wealthy.

The lobby of Hale Iwa Kai was such a place.

She was too tired to totally appreciate the powerful pillars that supported the soaring architecture of an impossibly high ceiling. The space contained a scattering of deep, inviting couches; oil paintings depicting Hawaiian historic events; huge wooden carved bowls; an entire wooden outrigger canoe.

"It's been a crazy day," Keona told her, quietly, conversationally, as they walked out of the lobby, past a lava-rock wall with water trickling melodically and soothingly down its rough face. "So many flights canceled. We have guests who were supposed to leave today and couldn't. Thankfully, some incoming flights have also been delayed, so we've been able to accommodate everyone. But we are tired."

She followed him through a passageway, over a bridge that spanned a lit pond constructed of the same dark, rich lava rock of the water wall they had gone by. She caught a glimpse of fish darting through turquoise waters.

The passageway opened to a wide path, as black as a lava flow, flanked on both sides by burning tiki torches and hibiscus, the pink blossoms the size of dessert plates. An exotic scent tickled her nose, a combination of the gases being burned by the torches and the perfumes from the flowers.

Curving walkways meandered off the main sidewalk, and at the end of each of those walkways she caught glimpses of nearly hidden cottages.

They weren't, of course, what most people would think of as a cottage, but people like Jonathon Winston and Morgan Hart were not most people. The white stand-alone buildings were spacious and whispered of opulence, with their steep, pitched beam roofs, lush landscaping and oversize stone urn fountains bubbling quiet welcome at each exquisitely carved wooden door.

The resort was slumbering. Except for the insistent call of a night bird, the slap of waves on a yet unseen shoreline, the whisper of Keona's sandals and the sound of her suitcase wheels rumbling along the walkway, it was completely silent.

Finally, Keona chose one of the pathways and followed its winding route through exotic shrubbery to a front door that was as much a work of art as an entryway.

A large stone urn fountain bubbled there. It had a word subtly engraved on it.

Huipu.

"Welcome to Huipu," he said, and quietly opened the door. Meg noticed it was not locked as Keona set her suitcase inside, then bowed slightly to her.

"What does the name mean?" she asked, curious despite how tired she was.

"Unite. Together. We are delighted to host many, many weddings here. We sometimes use this cottage for honeymoons if the main one is already in use."

Meg and Morgan had honeymooned in Paris. After she had broken her foot, on their second day there, he had promised a redo one day. It was possible they could have ended up in a place very like this one.

Keona nodded toward a fierce-looking carved wooden tiki that was nestled in the greenery beside the fountain.

"Lono, ancient god of fertility," he said, and then added, teasingly, "Don't touch, unless you want a baby."

Her fingers started itching. She had to anchor them on her pocketbook to keep from reaching out.

"May your stay be blessed with much *aloha*," he said.

"Aloha?" she asked, faintly confused. "Isn't that hello?"

"So many things," he said, his tired eyes twinkling. "Hello. Goodbye. And so much more. You'll see." And then he left her.

Alone, Meg hesitated for a moment, and then gave in to the desire to reach out. She rested her hand against Lono's wooden chest. The surface was surprisingly warm, as if it held the heat of the day within it.

"Where were you when I needed you?" she asked, then drew her hand away. It was too late and she could not afford to indulge what-ifs. Not when she would be seeing Morgan tomorrow.

Meg stepped inside the door and felt for a light switch. Instead of an overhead light coming on, two floor lamps blinked to life and bathed the space in a golden glow.

The room was soothing and sumptuous, with dark beams on the high ceiling and wide-plank wooden floors that seemed to glow from within. A huge ceiling fan turned lazily. The furnishings were exquisitely Hawaiian—beautiful wood tables, and rattan couches and chairs, their deep cushions upholstered in subtle tropical prints.

Meg could see a wall-to-wall, floor-to-ceiling bank of windows, opened, at the back of the room. The open windows, like the unlocked door, gave her a sense of being in an utterly safe space. The scent of the sea poured in on the gentle breeze that lifted white gauzy curtains.

Her whole apartment—with its three locks on the door—would have fit into one corner of this "cottage."

While it was unmistakably high-end, Huipu was unlike some of the expensive accommodations she had enjoyed as Mrs. Hart. This space was cozy and comfortable, a place where one could relax with a good book.

While she was trying to hide out from Morgan and recovering from whatever disaster struck this time!

Stop being superstitious, Meg chided herself, the woman

who had just longingly touched Lono's chest. She promised herself tomorrow she would give this gracious, inviting space the appreciation it deserved.

Tonight, she wanted only to return to the deep sleep she'd had a tantalizing taste of in the luxurious back seat of the limousine.

CHAPTER TWO

MEG NOTICED THERE was only one door, slightly ajar, off the living room, and she tugged her suitcase along behind her and went through it.

It opened into a spa-like bathroom, and through a door on the other side of it, she caught a glimpse of the foot of a bed.

Tired as she was, she could not resist the shower.

She tore off her rumpled, stained clothing, adjusted the tap, and stepped under it. Water fell on her from the ceiling and sprayed out from the walls. It was like being drenched in a sudden tropical cloudburst. The soap and the shampoo were as wonderfully fragrant and as subtly sensual as the Hawaiian air.

Feeling deliciously clean, she stepped out, regarded her suitcase for a moment and decided she simply did not have the energy to rummage through it in search of pajamas. Tonight, she would live boldly, and sleep naked, the cool, ocean-fresh breeze playing across her clean skin.

Meg wrung the water out of her hair with a thick white towel, and then wrapped another one around herself.

She stepped into the darkness of the bedroom. The bed, ever so faintly illuminated from the large open patio doors beside it, looked to be an antique piece, its pineapple-engraved posters reaching toward the dark beams of a high, open ceiling identical to the one in the living area.

The bed was huge and inviting, and she stepped over to it, dropped the towel and turned back the sheet.

And then froze as her tired mind tried to grapple with the complete shock of her discovery.

Her Hawaii disaster had struck!

There was someone in her bed!

Meg bit back her first inclination, which was to scream. Instead, she swallowed hard and tried to force her tired mind to fit the available information together, like a clumsy child trying to make sense of the scrambled pieces of a jigsaw puzzle.

It was not, she reasoned with herself, placing her hand over the hard beating of her heart, as if she'd encountered a stranger with a knife, intent on evil things, in a back alley in a bad neighborhood.

It's better to be naked in a remote tropical cottage with a stranger? another part of her mind chided.

Meg forced herself to be rational, which was not easy at nearly three in morning, in a place that, for all its enchantment, seemed as foreign to her as the face of the moon.

But, obviously, a mistake had been made. That was all. It wasn't a disaster. It was a human error. So far, no harm done.

Trying to be as quiet as possible, she hooked the dropped towel with her toe, crossed her arms over herself and scuttled a few steps backward toward the bathroom, her suitcase and the exit of Huipu.

But then she froze. A familiar scent tickled at her nose.

Clean.

Delicious.

Sensual.

It was, of course, the scent of the very same shampoo and soap she had just used.

But there were other notes to it. Deeper.

Masculine.

Unmistakable.

Morgan.

And her relief that he was alone in that bed was abject.

Her sleep-deprived mind fumbled to the conclusion that *now* disaster was imminent. Still, it could be averted if Meg backed out of the room as quickly and quietly as possible.

But as her eyes adjusted to the dark and she drank in the familiar lines of him, her husband, Morgan Hart, she was utterly paralyzed with longings as exotic, as mystical, as powerful as the land she found herself in.

Instead of doing the rational thing and making her escape, she drank him in. Her sense of safety, of just a few moments ago, abandoned her. She was aware of danger snapping in the air. And still, she could not make herself back away.

Morgan was sleeping on his belly, his head resting on a crisp, white pillow, his face turned toward her. His elbow was bent, one hand resting up beside his cheek on the linen of the pillowcase. He looked as if he was as naked as she was, though a sheet—that could have been mistaken for a stripe of moonlight—was draped over a narrow band of his hip and bottom.

She felt her mouth go dry as she took in the familiar wideness of his shoulders and the broadness of his back. Her eyes followed the graceful line of his spine, took in the jut of ribs, drifted down the beautiful narrowing of his back to where there were two identical impressions—dimples—just before the sheet-covered curve of his buttocks. His skin was flawless and it glowed like alabaster in the faint light.

The sight of him caused her to remember the heated silk feel of Morgan's body beneath her fingertips with such raw wanting that it jarred her.

There was a sound. The faintest of sighs, and her eyes flew to his face. It was framed in a tumble of sleep-tousled curls. His hair was the color of the golden sand they had once seen on a beach in New Zealand—where she had been so bitten by sand flies she'd had to see a doctor for prescription antihistamine.

His eyelashes, thick as sooty chimney brushes, swept down over the high cut of perfect cheekbones. His nose was ever so slightly crooked from where it had been broken during a rugby match in his youth.

Meg remembered running her fingertips over that thin white line of a scar the night they had first kissed, fascinated, sensing how the scar told of the warrior in Morgan. And, of course, she found out he was just that, a man who had faced incredible battles in his life with formidable courage.

Don't look at his lips, she ordered herself, but it was too late for orders. Her senses had been in full mutiny since she had realized it was him in that bed.

Now, she surrendered to taking in the line of his lips, full, faintly parted, the bottom one puffy, with that little line down the middle of it…

The taste of his mouth was as sharp in her memory as if the last time she had kissed him was yesterday, not months ago.

It seemed like a cruel jest of the universe—a terrible twist on her travel curse—that she had arrived in a paradise, at a place called Huipu, to find the man she still loved, naked in bed.

It seemed even more cruel that the cottage was guarded by the god of fertility when she had been unable to make a baby with this man.

Meg stopped herself from going down that road. She needed to solve the problem of the here and now.

It was probably the most natural of mistakes on the part of the resort.

He was Mr. Hart.

The staff, as Keona had told her, thought she was Mrs. Hart, which technically, she still was. They had paired them together, assuming they were husband and wife, and put them in the same cottage. Why wouldn't they?

But Morgan never even had to know about the error.

Meg could still avert disaster if she did the right thing. She took another tiny step backward, practically holding her breath so as not to make a sound and wake him.

Except at that moment, his eyes flicked open. And he looked at her with a look she remembered so well. That she longed for in her dreams.

When Morgan looked at Meg, those brown eyes—the color of exotic coffee, no cream, sprinkled through with gold flecks of stardust—were drowsy with welcome, as if he could not believe his good luck in waking to her.

The look she had seen every single day of their married life.

But then, abruptly, the sleepy welcome left his face, and his brows lowered down over eyes that darkened to a shade beyond black. His eyes suddenly flashed with anything but tenderness. His beautiful mouth turned down in an angry slash.

"What the—" he demanded. He used a word she had only heard him use twice, and one of those times had been when her travel curse had been a purse snatching—her purse that is—in a busy San Francisco coffee shop.

Meg suddenly became aware of the warm air of the tropical night on her body, and realized she was standing before Morgan, dressed in only moonlight!

Now was not the time to remember how comfortable they had once been with these kind of married-couple intimacies.

Meg reached out and yanked the sheet off of him, pulling it to cover herself. Unfortunately, that left Morgan as naked as she had just been. The gorgeous, chiseled lines of his bare buttocks were something artists tried to capture in stone.

And while she was no Michelangelo, she was, after all, an artist.

Morgan didn't know what had awoken him. A scent maybe.

More likely an instinct.

Still, opening his eyes to see Meg standing by the bed, as unclothed as Eve in the garden, her damp hair falling over the swell of her breasts, just like a statue they had seen on their honeymoon in Paris, was one of the shocks of his life.

It felt as if an earthquake—not unheard of here in the Hawaiian Islands—magnitude at least seven point zero, was rocking his world.

Though for one blissful millisecond, he thought he had awoken from the nightmare of the last eight months.

He hoped he had dreamed *them*, those months, and that she'd really been here, all along, looking at him with *that* light softening her eyes.

That light. The one he had waited for his entire life.

The one that said, despite it all, life could be good again.

The one that said, You are loved. You are cherished. I am yours. And you are mine. Forever.

But that feeling lasted only a second, and then he came fully awake, and fully aware *forever* was the biggest lie of all, a lesson a man should take seriously the first time, after tragedy had stripped everything from him.

He felt a surge of anger that he found himself in a tug-of-war over a sheet with the woman who had never loved him at all, no matter what he thought he saw in her face.

The woman who had destroyed him, already torn asunder by tragedy, all over again, by making him think she was something she wasn't. Meg had had made Morgan believe, however briefly, that in each other, they had found what every single person on the planet searched for.

The sanctuary of love.

A sanctuary he had once had, and longed for so completely, that it had made him vulnerable to what he thought Meg had offered.

Well, he would be vulnerable no more.

Morgan conceded the sheet to her and leaped out of the bed from the other side. With his back to her, he found a damp towel he had left on the floor the night before. He wrapped it around his waist and then spun around and glared at his soon-to-be ex-wife across the width of the bed.

Because it was over, even if the separation agreement remained unsigned by both of them.

"What the hell are you doing in here?" he snapped.

Meg flinched from his tone, but he steeled himself to her wounded look. She had done this, not him.

"I... I... I think the resort made a mistake," she stammered. "Because of the last names..."

Her voice drifted away.

Hotel errors seemed ridiculously small in the face of the larger question, which had haunted him for months.

Why?

Morgan wanted to demand to know *why* and not just about the lack of final signatures on divorce documents either.

Why, when they had experienced what he would have called two blissful years of marriage had Meg suddenly pulled the plug? She hadn't even had the courtesy to tell him in person.

An apartment that he had felt the emptiness of even before he found her note.

Couldn't adjust to the lifestyle.

It was useless to wonder what it was beyond her ridiculously short explanation. Hadn't he gone over it a million times in the past eight months? No answers from his silent, absent wife.

Maybe it was just that simple. She couldn't handle the lifestyle.

How lucky did a man have to be to find the one woman on the earth who could not adjust to being wealthy beyond her wildest dreams?

CHAPTER THREE

HOW LUCKY DID a man have to be, Morgan asked himself, to find the one woman who couldn't adjust to a honeymoon in Paris, a week in Thailand on business, a spontaneous trip to New Zealand, a weekend shopping trip to San Francisco?

How lucky did a man have to be to find the one woman who couldn't adjust to a penthouse in Vancouver's tony English Bay? Couldn't adjust to exquisite meals, fine jewelry, great cars, use of a private jet, backstage passes to some of the most coveted events in the world?

Fresh anger was clawing at his throat as he regarded Meg, tucking that sheet around her as if she was a model waiting to be painted.

She looked like a goddess, standing there in the faint light, draped in swaths of the sheet and moonlight. She was so beautiful. Her eyes were her most arresting feature, even now, when she was freshly scrubbed of makeup.

Maybe especially now, her beauty so natural. Her eyes were wide, fringed in a natural abundance of thick lashes, the color a deep, mossy green that was ever changing, one minute dark, the next sparking with light. Intelligence. Inquisitiveness. Mischief.

Desire.

Morgan could not think of that right now, with only a towel and a sheet between their total nakedness. Instead, he completed his inventory of her, trying to be dispassionate.

But it was hard to be that when he had tasted every inch of her from her high cheekbones, to the sweet little lobes of her ears, to the button of her nose and to the full sensual swell of her lips, the hollows of her collarbone.

Her breasts, her belly button, her toes...

The weakness—and heat—of those memories crumpled his defenses as much as being woken in the middle of the night by his unclothed ex had.

The slight lowering of his barriers allowed Morgan to see how tired Meg was, swaying with exhaustion, her skin frighteningly pale.

She was thinner, he noted, her cheeks more hollow and her collarbones sticking out, her shoulders fragile. Her eyes—those glorious eyes—looked bigger in her thinner face, and had dark circles under them.

They were a green that had always felt to him as if they held the calm of a deep pool on a summer day, but tonight they were shadowed.

With some secret sorrow.

He shook off his intense *need* to know what that was, and what part it had played in the demise of their marriage. She'd had eight months to confide in him, but no, not a word from her. Just packed her bag and disappeared from his life as if what they had shared had meant nothing and been nothing.

"Where's your girlfriend?" she asked stiffly, as if a man abandoned by his wife had somehow betrayed *her* by seeking comfort elsewhere.

And while there had not been a word from Meg about anything, she knew about that? Of course she would know. She and his best friend's fiancée, Caylee, were also best friends.

And yet Caylee had not shed any light on Megan's sudden abandonment of the marriage. If anything, she seemed as distressed and shocked by it as he himself was.

"None of your business," he snapped at Meg, but felt no

satisfaction at all when his arrow landed and she flinched from it.

Why not protect himself by letting Meg believe he had moved on?

The truth was the relationship with Marjorie had been as brief and disastrous as might be expected of a rebound. It had never progressed beyond a few casual dates, though he might have led Caylee to believe otherwise.

There had never been anything approaching intimacy, and not because Marjorie had been unwilling.

The truth was, he couldn't be intimate with someone else when he still felt intensely connected to the woman who had left him.

He had probably only accepted Marjorie's invitation to go out because Morgan had known word would get back to Meg that he had moved on, and swiftly, too.

It had been childish. It had reminded him of a group of boys in middle school, the tough kids who had played a game where one held a match and the other held his palm above it.

Unflinching, looking directly in the other person's eyes.

Giving a message. *No matter what you do, you can't hurt me.*

"She's not coming to the wedding?" Meg asked, even though he couldn't have been any clearer than *none of your business.*

"No," he snapped.

"Does she like children?" Meg asked.

"What?" He was not sure this middle-of-the-night conversation could get any crazier.

"Marjorie. Does she like children?"

"For God's sake, Meg, how do I know? Why would I care?"

She got a pinched look about her, apparently unwilling

to accept that this also fell solidly into the none-of-her-business category.

"Our immediate problem is accommodation. I'll go sort it out at the front desk," he told Meg coolly, moving toward the door.

"No, no. I can go. You were here first. I mean, there is no one at the desk. I just came by there, but I'll figure out something."

He turned and looked back at her.

"It's my curse," she said, "not yours."

She was trying, even above her weariness, to insert a bit of levity. Instead, it reminded him of her propensity for calamity, which he had to admit he had found mostly adorable.

It had always made him feel protective of her. And it did that now, too.

His wife. His forever.

He was not sure he could trust himself with the sudden surge of anger he felt, but still, just like those boys in the schoolyard, he wasn't going to flinch from holding his hand over the flame.

Morgan wasn't giving Meg the satisfaction of knowing how destroyed he was. He'd hold his hand above her flame until it blistered before he would let her know how badly she was hurting him.

"I'll take care of it," he said firmly, and when she went to protest, he held up his hand with all the authority of someone who ran a billion-dollar company. "We'll sort it out in the morning. You take the bed. I'll take the couch."

Not once, in their entire marriage, had they gone to bed so angry with each other that one of them slept on the couch.

"I can take the couch," she said, chewing her lip, apparently not getting it that he was the boss—of course, when had she ever?

Hadn't that been one of the things that delighted him? How

she didn't seem impressed by what he was? How, instead, she had seen *who* he was.

But in the end, *what* he was was apparently more than she could handle.

Besides which, he did not want to be thinking of one single thing about his wife that had delighted him.

"I can sleep in a lounge chair by the pool," she suggested, always creative. "Or go find Caylee."

He shot her a look. "Whatever our differences are, we are not going to let them ruin this for Cay and Jon."

Her mouth fell open and her eyes darkened. "As if I would!"

"Once," he said, and heard the weariness in his own voice, "I would have believed that. Back when I thought I knew who you were."

He saw the arrow had landed, again, and again Morgan took no satisfaction from the wounded look it provoked.

"This is their time," he said sternly.

"You don't have to tell me that!"

"Then let's not begin with an argument," Morgan said smoothly.

"It's not an argument. It's a discussion."

"Whatever it is, it's the middle of the night and I don't want to have it. You take the bed."

Before she could press further, he went out the door that led to the bathroom and shut it behind him. He walked past her unopened suitcase. He went through the door that adjoined the living room and closed it with a little more snap than was strictly necessary.

He might have thought he got in the last word.

However, a moment later that adjoining door whispered open. Meg had divvied up the bedding and she dumped a pile outside the door. She did it so quickly that he hardly caught a glimpse of her, except to see she was still swaddled in the sheet.

Then he heard her, on the other side of that door, deciding—too late, really—to dig through her luggage and presumably come up with some pajamas.

He gathered up the bedding she had tossed him—a thin blanket and a pillow. He folded the blanket in half lengthwise and put it on the couch. He let the damp towel drop and climbed between the rough fold of his makeshift bed.

He was still naked and didn't have a single piece of clothing out here with him. It was all in the bedroom, which he heard Meg make her way back into.

But he'd be damned if he was begging her for a pair of undershorts to wear to protect his modesty in the morning. Because once you started begging a woman like her, there was really no telling where it was going, or where it would end.

Morgan set the alarm on his watch, since his phone was still on the bedside table beside Meg.

He would not think of her lying in that bed. He just wouldn't. He had practical matters to turn his mind to.

For instance, what time would the lobby open? Six? It looked as if Meg needed to sleep for a week—Caylee had been reporting on her travel adventures—so he could sneak in the bedroom in the morning, get some clothes and get the accommodation kerfuffle sorted out before she was even awake.

He needn't have worried about setting his alarm though, because an entire army of Kauai's roosters began to raucously welcome the day before first light had even stained the sky.

Not that it mattered.

Morgan had not slept a wink since he had laid eyes on his beautiful wife and recognized from the ache in his heart that, despite it all, he loved her still.

A secret he was never, ever sharing with her. He would

not be foolish enough, weak enough to hand Megan Hart, his wife, the weapons to wound him again.

Not even if, in that first unguarded moment, when they had looked at each other for the first time in eight months, he felt as if he had seen some truth in her eyes, too.

The kind of truth that could make a man beg.

If he let himself be weak. Which Morgan Hart had absolutely no intention of being. Ever. Again.

CHAPTER FOUR

MEG OPENED HER EYES.

It sounded as if a thousand roosters were crowing right outside her window with joyous enthusiasm. Other birds joined in—*ooh-hoo*, *ooh-hoo*—a contest for superiority in the decibel department.

Though Meg had never actually been to a jungle, the exotic cacophony of sound seemed identical to movies she had seen with that setting.

As she woke up more, she became aware of the sensation of the sheets against her skin, a luxurious feel that only fabrics with impossibly high thread counts had. Sunlight, filtered through swaying pond fronds, poured through the windows and dappled the bed. A warm, scented breeze caressed her skin. She felt something she had not felt for a very long time.

Sensuous.

As if she'd been sleeping and something about this enchanted place was coaxing her back to life.

Beneath *that* feeling was one equally as astonishing. Could it really be?

Happiness.

Meg had not woken up feeling happy for eight full months. In fact, she had woken each and every morning since she had left Morgan with the same sense of crushing despondency.

Morgan.

Was her close encounter of the unexpected kind with her nearly ex-husband the reason for the happiness that was unfurling in her like a sail catching the wind?

The fact that he'd been alone in the bed?

Of course it wasn't!

Their encounter had been tense. Awkward. He had been angry.

No, who wouldn't be happy to wake up in paradise?

The sensuality was not so easily attributed to the enchantment of Hawaii. She stretched, aware of her body, breath and muscle, strength and grace.

Sensual. And maybe not happiness, precisely. Contentment. Which had a steadiness to it that made it seem even better than happiness, that elusive force that came and went with every shift in the wind.

But, no, it wasn't anything quite as staid as contentment. It was happiness, and there was no lying to herself. It was sharing a world with Morgan—even if he was angry—that caused it. His scent still lingered on the sheets, for heaven's sake. It would be pathetic to draw the bedding in close to her nose and inhale as if it was a drug, but she did that anyway.

She closed her eyes. Breathed deeply. Then frowned. Of course, there was the problem of him not knowing if his new lady friend liked children. Acting as if it didn't matter.

What was all this for, if he got involved with a woman who wasn't going to give him a family?

She had tried to ask Caylee, subtly, if Morgan seemed serious about Marjorie. How dysfunctional was this? Being worried about the quality of your ex's new relationship?

Caylee didn't know. She and Jonathon had only met Marjorie once, by chance. There had been no couples activities.

Was that good or bad? What right did she have to feel relieved that Morgan was not sharing *their* friends with his new woman?

She breathed in the scent on the sheet again.

Morgan.

"What are you doing?"

Meg's eyes snapped open. And there he was, in the flesh, her husband. Not that she wanted to be thinking about his flesh. And the way it had looked last night, turned to silvered, sensual marble by moonlight.

There was that word again. *Sensual.* There could not be a doubt left where *that* association was coming from. Meg felt heat rise in her cheeks.

She dropped the sheet from her nose, but only to her chin. Even though she was in perfectly decent pajamas.

Too decent. Unsuited for the tropics. It occurred to her she didn't want Morgan to see her rather frumpy choice of nightwear: light blue trousers, a button-up shirt top.

Meg didn't want him to know how far she had fallen from the woman who had, as his wife, explored an exquisitely feminine side of herself that had been hidden until he had drawn it out. She had given herself over to the delights of her husband finding her sexy. Her nightwear had been as bold and as beautiful as he had made her believe she was.

He moved on, thank goodness, from her sniffing the sheets.

"I have some bad news."

Of course he did! When didn't she have bad news when she traveled?

And yet it felt to Meg as if it didn't matter what he said.

Her husband was in the same room with her. He looked tired after spending the night on the couch and she could see every loss he had ever experienced in the dark shadows of his eyes.

Losses he had trusted her with.

Losses she had thought her love could heal him from.

Until she had discovered that she would be adding another loss to the layers that already existed in those eyes.

Mrs. Hart, the doctor had said, *I'm so sorry to tell you this.*

The secret she had never shared with him, the reason she had made herself say goodbye and put a world between them.

That world between them painfully evident now in the set of his broad shoulders under the bright, tropically patterned shirt he had on, in the way his hands were shoved deep into the pockets of his crisp khaki shorts. Had he come in here while she was sleeping and gathered some clothes? He must have. Had he paused and looked at her, the way she had looked at him last night?

The sun was dancing in the sun-on-sand gold of his curls, and she noticed faint stubble on his chin and cheeks that made her want to run her hand across them, to feel that sensuous roughness under her fingertips.

That scent—that was so purely him, that she had recognized last night and that he had left on the sheets—tickled her nose.

She closed her eyes for a moment. She could tear down his barriers with a single confession about why she had moved away. The temptation to tell him, to feel his arms fold around her and his tears touch her hair, had to be fought.

"There are no other rooms," Morgan told her, grimly.

"Wh-what?" she stammered.

"From the sound of it, not on the entire island. Air travel is in chaos all over the country. People who were scheduled to leave Kauai haven't been able to get out. I'm shocked that your plane arrived."

Keona had told her this last night, but even when Meg had found Morgan already occupying their cottage, she hadn't linked what he had told her to the consequences.

"We're just going to have to suck it up and figure it out," he told her.

"Figure it out how?" Meg squeaked.

"Look—" Morgan gestured expansively "—it's a suite. It's not like it's a studio. I can take the couch."

There it was again. The most inappropriate reaction to Morgan's bad news.

Happiness.

Of course, it was going to be absolute torment to share a space with him, to be in such close quarters, to not tell him the truth.

Torment, like someone who had developed a deathly allergy to chocolate finding themselves at an exquisite buffet with one of those chocolate fountains.

You could still enjoy the sight of it.

You could still enjoy the fragrance of it.

Couldn't you?

You just couldn't taste it.

"You're right," she told him, trying to strip every trace of happiness from her voice, trying to sound stoic and resigned, "we'll have to suck it up."

"I don't even know if we should tell Caylee," Morgan said, raking a hand through those tousled curls. "You've arrived now, but her parents aren't here yet. The wedding party clothes were shipped separately and haven't turned up either."

"Her gown?" Meg whispered. Caylee's wedding gown was like something out of a fairy tale. It had been custom made specifically for her by up-and-coming designer Dianne Lawrence. Dianne had taken her inspiration from the dress then–Princess Elizabeth had worn for her wedding to Lieutenant Philip Mountbatten. Each of the thousands of tiny seed pearls had been painstakingly hand stitched.

"That dress cost more than most people's cars," she said, stricken for her friend.

"Oh, yeah," he said, bitterly, "the world you don't want."

That was the lie she had told him. Though not quite a

lie. This was what people from humble backgrounds like hers did not know about marrying into extreme wealth: you never quite felt like you belonged. You always felt like the outsider looking in. Meg had felt like a child who had accidentally been seated at the adult table, an imposter waiting to be found out.

Though, not everyone felt that way. Caylee, from the very same wrong-side-of-the-tracks Vancouver neighborhood as Meg, had taken to Jonathon's lifestyle and wealth like the proverbial duck to water, delighting in every moment of it.

Still, practical Meg wondered if the dress was insured. Good grief, could you insure wedding dresses?

"What about everything else?" she whispered.

"All of it."

"The whole wedding party's clothes?" She thought of how she and Caylee had chosen the colors for the bridesmaid dresses, a green so dark it was almost black, so that it wouldn't compete in photos with the amazing colors and beauty of the location.

She thought of the painstaking custom tailoring that had gone into each of the men's lightweight summer suits. You did not just replace that!

"But the wedding is in three days!" she exclaimed.

Morgan lifted a shoulder, reminding her he was a man who had been battered relentlessly by life. On the scale of catastrophe, missing clothing, even for the wedding of the century, would barely register with him.

But the distress her best friend must be feeling pushed Meg's own chaotic emotions—thankfully—into the background.

"I'll go see her right away." Of course, she didn't move, still unwilling to let Morgan see her in the I've-given-up-on-life pajamas.

"Good idea. There is a breakfast buffet set up by the main pool for the wedding party."

"The main pool? How many pools are there?"

"That creek that meanders through the property joins half a dozen or so pools together. It's quite amazing. They're all so unique." For a moment, he looked wistful, and Meg wondered if Morgan was thinking of the days when they would have delighted in exploring such a space as Hale Iwa Kai Resort together.

But then the handsome features of his face hardened.

"Go left out the front door to the main pool. There's one you probably don't want to end up at. It's—"

He hesitated.

"It's what?"

He looked pained. "Not where breakfast is," he said gruffly. And then he was gone.

And even though everything was the same, including the sunbeam that danced across her bed, it felt as if he had taken the light from the room with him.

Meg was aware, as she chose an outfit and dressed, that she had prepared her tropical wardrobe with Morgan in mind. The choices had seemed unbelievably difficult. She was the one who had walked out on the marriage, so it would have seemed like the worst kind of mixed message to wear things that made it seem as if she was trying to attract him.

Or compete with his new friend.

So she had selected fade-into-the-background knee-length shorts and practical cotton blouses. Looking at herself in the mirror, she swept her hair back, clipped it into a messy bun and then sighed heavily.

In her beige shorts and paisley-patterned shirt, she looked as if she'd been inspired by the fashion sense of women who showed dogs and had only one desire—and that was for the dog to be the star of the show! Just like the pajamas, she suddenly didn't want Morgan to see her in an unflattering light. Particularly since his new friend wasn't here.

She reminded herself, firmly, this wasn't about her. Or Morgan.

It was about Caylee and Jonathon, and building toward a perfect wedding day for them. That focus was even more necessary now that there were some obstacles to overcome.

Meg noticed the blouse, which she had never worn because it had been purchased for this occasion, still had the price tag on it. She went into the kitchen area, marveling at the beauty and finishes of Huipu. The stocked wine cooler and the coffee bar with its barista-worthy machine she understood, but who on earth used a stand mixer whilst on vacation? In Hawaii?

A quick perusal of the drawers, and she found scissors and dispensed with the tag. And then, unable to stop herself, she took the scissors into the bathroom, took off the shorts and cut three inches off of the legs on both sides. She unraveled the fabric to give the hem a frayed look.

When she put the shorts back on, she was pleased. Her impromptu alteration had resulted in a bohemian look. Meg accentuated that look by undoing the bottom buttons of the shirt and tying it in a knot, exposing her midriff.

She eyed herself critically.

Too much?

Oh, no. So much better! As she walked out of the cottage, she was aware of the feeling of the warm air on her bare midriff, and also of a lightness in her step that she had not had in it for eight months.

She was not at all sure how wise it was, but she was definitely stepping away from the dowdy, heartbroken, nearly divorced image she had been wallowing in!

It felt as if Meg took in the resort, in daylight, with that same lightness of spirit her change of outfit had given her.

Her senses felt wide open as she breathed in the utter enchantment of a resort where every single detail had been designed to showcase Hawaii's incredible beauty.

CHAPTER FIVE

"MEG!"

As her best friend folded her arms around her, Meg felt a deep sense of homecoming. Caylee stepped back, her hands still resting on Meg's shoulders.

They took each other in with deep appreciation, sisters of the heart, reunited. Though almost identical in height and stature, in every other way their appearances were opposite. Caylee was as dark as Meg was blonde; she kept her hair short, in a pixie style that few could pull off but that she did.

Meg was so pleased to see how relaxed Caylee looked, radiating the well-being of a woman loved.

For a moment, Meg thought her friend was going to comment on her weight loss, the shadows under her eyes, but she didn't. Cay sighed happily.

"I am so glad you made it. I was so worried about you getting here. I couldn't do this without you."

"I think you should be more worried about your parents not being here. And the lost wedding clothes. Especially your dress!"

"How do you know about that?"

"Oh." Meg hoped her voice didn't sound strangled. "I, um, ran into Morgan."

"You did?" Caylee breathed hopefully. "How did that go?"

Cay's wish—that they had thrown themselves into each

other's arms, and that they were magically and completely reconciled—was naked in her voice.

Her wedding was in three days! She had other things to worry about.

"It was okay," Meg said.

"Oh."

"You must be sick about the entire wedding party wardrobe being missing," Meg said to change the subject.

"Oh." Caylee waved her hand as if at a bothersome fly. "It'll turn up."

"Caylee! A little panic might be in order." She held out a finger. "You have today. You have tomorrow. Then, the following day, you have *I do.* Not to mention your missing dress is worth enough to buy a small country."

"It's just a dress."

Just a dress?

"Tell that to someone who didn't get sent twelve hundred and sixty-two photos of wedding dresses. Who didn't meet you in Montreal—twice—to meet the designer. Who didn't field midnight calls—"

"I forgot the time difference," Caylee wailed.

"Six times!"

"Yes, well," Caylee said, not very apologetically, "the most important thing is that everyone gets here."

"Forty-two virtual meetings with Becky, Allie and Samantha," Meg reminded her. "One trip to Bridesmaid in Manhattan to choose four different styles of dresses that went together, and to finalize the color—"

"The love is the most important part," Caylee said, firmly.

"Who are you and what have you done with Caylee?" Meg asked dryly.

"I know! I was turning into an absolute bridezilla over everything. Why didn't you tell me?" This was said accusingly, and she didn't wait for Meg to answer. "Because you were three thousand miles away, that's why."

Caylee had not approved of Meg's move—or of her leaving Morgan. She had acted as if the move—and the end of her best friend's marriage—was a personal assault on her own hopes and dreams, never mind the wedding plans.

And yet, underneath that, always, the love was there.

The concern.

Meg had not confided the real reason, even to Caylee. It made the burden she carried feel really lonely. For the second time since she'd been here—less than twenty-four hours—she felt an urge to confess all!

"Let's forget about problems for now," Caylee said. She came and stood beside Meg and put her head on her shoulder.

"Can you believe it?" she whispered. "Look at us, two girls from East Vancouver, here."

She made a sweeping gesture with her arm, and Meg took it in. There was a huge turquoise pool with a bridge across it, and a waterfall cascading down at the far end of it, the lush tropical plants around it, the deck loungers under their white canopies.

Leading away from the pool was a wide path that opened onto a crescent of golden sand dotted with palm trees and outrigger canoes. The beach looked out onto a protected bay, the natural ombre effect, light blue deepening to navy by the time it reached the mouth, making Meg's artist's heart sigh.

As did all of it. The nearby mountains held the whole resort in a dramatic cup. Their sheer slopes were covered with lush rainforests and bisected by deep fissures and dramatic cliffs. From where the two friends stood, they could see a waterfall spilling down the side of the mountain, with rainbows dancing around it. The waterfall at the resort pool was obviously designed to look like a continuation of that spectacular natural feature.

"You see why I'm not worried about the dress?" Caylee said. "This. It makes me feel small in the best possible way. Like no matter how I try to create beauty, this will be the star of the show. It's a relief to just let go."

Meg could understand that. It had been months of organizing, worrying, ordering, perfecting details, ferreting out what could go wrong.

Everything Caylee could do had been done. It was good that she could let go.

"You're letting type A's everywhere down with this laid-back attitude," Meg teased her.

"You know, Jonathon and I got here three days ago, and I thought I'd get more and more wound up as the wedding approached. That hasn't happened at all. I mean, of course I'm worried about the plane delays, and missing parents and clothing, but in the end? There's absolutely nothing I can do about it."

"That's true," Meg conceded.

"I feel more and more relaxed, like the spirit of *aloha* is contagious."

"Keona mentioned the multiple meanings of *aloha* to me last night."

"It's not really a word," Caylee said, almost dreamily. "It's a feeling. A spirit of love and acceptance, compassion and forgiveness. It's kind of this lovely attitude that permeates *everything*. Like it's the life force and you feel it in every single thing here."

Meg knew artists, and plenty of them. She was used to this kind of talk. But from Caylee, her super-driven friend? It was ever so slightly distressing!

"Do you know what a *shaka* is?" Cay asked.

"A chakra?" Meg asked. Again, it was definitely artist talk. "You're making me nervous, Caylee. Very nervous."

"Not a chakra. A *shaka*. It's used here, almost in place of a wave."

Caylee demonstrated, thumb and pinky extended, remaining three fingers folded into the palm. "It means hang loose, take it easy, everything's fine."

While Caylee's new attitude was all well and good, Meg thought in her position, as maid of honor, she had to step up to the plate, and make some things happen! Somebody had to worry!

"Despite everything being goodness and light," she said carefully, "we still need a backup plan. In case the wedding wardrobe doesn't arrive."

"Of course! I've got it covered. I'm going to send you on a rescue mission today."

Meg pictured herself spending her first day in paradise making endless phone calls trying to track down the shipment of clothing and the missing parents. She actually liked the idea of having a job to do. It would keep her mind off Morgan. And besides, what was to say she couldn't do it from right here, beside the pool?

"Oh, look who's here," Caylee said in a conspiratorial whisper, as if they were still in high school and Bill Fletcher, captain of the football team, whom Meg had harbored a secret crush on, had just entered the room.

So, she knew before turning to see him, who it was. She was aware that Caylee was watching her face, and that she was smiling with satisfaction at whatever she saw there.

"I have to meet with the chef today," Caylee said. "We might have to do a menu change. Ingredients are not showing up."

This was said casually, as if a menu change for dozens and dozens of people was nothing.

"Can you go into town and find some dresses? Just in case?" Caylee said.

"What?"

"A backup plan, just like you said."

"I think a more sensible backup plan would be tracking down the shipment."

"Keona is working on that. Meanwhile, you know all our sizes."

"You want me to pick out a backup wedding gown for you?" Meg asked, horrified. "And bridesmaid dresses?"

"I'm sure we won't need them. Keona seems to be a bit of a miracle worker. But as you say, just in case. Something white for me. Flirty. Fun. Same for the bridesmaids. Not white, of course, but fun. I need your eye for color. Something that will look great in the photos. There're all kinds of cute shops in a little village not far from here. They'll have sundresses galore."

"Sundresses," Meg repeated sadly.

"Well, we'll have to wear something, and there's no way to replace a thirty-thousand-dollar Dianne Lawrence in three days."

"I can check if there's a bridal boutique," Meg said.

"I'll leave it in your capable hands," Caylee decided, way too lightly. "Take him with you. He can be in charge of the backup plan for the groomsmen."

Meg followed Caylee's gaze to where Morgan was helping himself at the buffet. How could guys do that? Load up on the waffles and smother them in syrup and whipped cream and never gain an ounce?

She looked back at her friend and narrowed her gaze. She actually wondered if the wedding wardrobe was really lost, or this was all an elaborate scheme by Caylee to throw her and Morgan together.

Meg had to nip such reconciliation efforts in the bud.

But suddenly she remembered Morgan warning her not to ruin this for Caylee and Jonathon. Caylee was obviously in the thrall of island enchantment at the moment, but that could change if things went sideways.

It was their wedding and if a backup plan—even a silly one—made the bride-to-be feel better, Meg was just going to have to suck it up.

Besides, maybe it could be an opportunity. To probe, just a little bit about the girlfriend, and find out if she was a suitable replacement.

"Morgan," Caylee called. "I have a job for you."

He ambled over with his carb-laden plate. "Yes?" He was scrupulously ignoring Meg.

"You know how the wedding clothes are lost? Meg had this excellent idea."

This was getting twisted somehow.

"You know how she always has such fun ideas?"

Morgan nodded reluctantly, his eyes on Caylee, sensing the trap.

"She thought she and you should go into town together and get some just-in-case backup clothes."

"Oh," he said. He shot Meg a dark look. He looked as if he was going to protest, and then he swallowed it.

She shook her head, letting him know it wasn't her idea. At all.

"Like what do you mean, backups?" he said.

"Probably something simple for the guys. White shirts? Black trousers? Well, maybe not black. We had gone with white for the custom suits and I don't want you to cook out there on the beach during the ceremony. Maybe shorts? Let Meg decide. She has an eye for these kinds of things."

"Meg has an eye for men in shorts?" he said, and lifted a dark slash of his brow. "Oh, all the things I didn't know."

Caylee laughed way too hard, evidently ignoring the faint bitterness of the final part of his sentence.

"Of course, we need the replacement items today. Because

you told us to set aside all day tomorrow for your surprise for the wedding party."

This was the first Meg had heard of Morgan planning a surprise. But then she was hardly in his inner circle anymore.

"Whatever you need, Caylee," he said smoothly.

Caylee beamed at him. It was a statement Meg was pretty sure Morgan was going to regret making, if he didn't already!

CHAPTER SIX

"DO YOU WANT to drive, or should I?" Morgan asked Meg. He was sorry they were being sent on this errand together, but he was determined to be civil.

They were standing at a selection of golf carts parked in the shade of a palm tree grove that was tucked away beside the front entrance of the resort. The golf carts were at the beginning of a paved path that would take them to an old sugar mill and plantation village. The buildings now housed boutiques and restaurants.

"I like it that you never assume you're going to drive, just because you're the guy," Meg told him.

The truth was, at this exact point in time, he didn't want Meg to like one single thing about him. It felt as if it wouldn't take much of a push to collapse his defenses completely.

He slid her a look. She was wearing cutoff shorts and a tied-up shirt that showed off the slender lines of both her long legs and flat tummy. She had her hair—each strand a different variation on blonde, from white to gold—scooped up in a clip. He'd always loved her hair, and he had particularly liked it when she wore it like that.

Had he ever told her that?

Would it have made a difference if he had?

Those were the kind of thoughts, Morgan knew, that could torment, if you allowed them to gain traction.

What had he done wrong? How could he have let Meg

know, any more than he had, that she was his world, that it felt as if he had needed her as much as air?

And yet, that was untrue, because without air you died, and without Meg? Here he was, surviving. A lesson life had already taught him.

You survived.

He reminded himself to replace all his *what-ifs* with *even-ifs*, a poignant lesson from a long-ago grief counsellor.

What if gave the illusion of control.

Even if acknowledged a kind of powerlessness, a lesson Morgan raged against, even as life showed him over and over—

"Would you drive?" Meg asked. "I just want to soak it all in. You've probably been here before? To Hawaii?"

"No," he said. "Never. Despite what you might think, rich people don't necessarily jet off to the tropics at every opportunity."

He saw she got his reference immediately. The center of his family for multiple generations had been a cottage on the shores of Okanagan Lake, outside of Kelowna, British Columbia. His great-grandfather had started a lumber company that, in the hands of his grandfather, father, and then him and his brother, had taken the Hart family into the ranks of the world's richest people.

It would have been easy for the Harts to become comfortable with elitist lifestyles: private jets, box seats, the best hotels and vacation spots in the world. It would have been easy to indulge in excess.

But the plain values of his hardworking great-grandfather and great-grandmother had stayed with the family, and grounded them.

And one place, more than any other, was responsible for that.

Named after his great-grandmother, the cottage—Sarah's

Reach—was a rambling log structure in British Columbia's interior, sitting on the edge of pristine forest and the immense shore of a deep, mystical lake.

The cottage had been a jumble of styles, a structure that had been added onto a million times, without once having had the benefit of an architectural design, so that it could accommodate an ever-growing family.

In complicated, busy-lives life, it had represented simplicity. It was icy water on summer afternoons, rickety boats with fishing lines dangling from them, the crisp smell of woodsmoke and toasted marshmallows hanging in the air.

Morgan could almost hear his brother laughing, the shrieks of his niece and nephew getting into the water of that lake for the first time in the season...

He realized Meg's hand was resting on his arm, drawing him back from the pain that crept up on him like this sometimes, when he had let his guard down, when he least expected it.

He looked deep into the unbelievable mossy green of those eyes and wanted to fall toward the understanding he saw there.

Instead, he shook off her touch, and swung away from her to the golf cart.

She slid into the seat beside him, and he embarrassed himself by jerking the golf cart violently as he reversed. He was unaccustomed to the pedals, which were touchy.

"It's not your sports car," she said, laughing.

Was that another dig about the lifestyle she had been unable to adjust to? Maybe it would be better not to run every single thing she said through that filter.

On the other hand, maybe that was exactly what he needed to do, because her laughter was like a drug to him, seeping past his defenses, erasing their painful history.

Thankfully, the golf cart required his full focus. With

Meg's propensity for disaster, he was glad she had not chosen to drive. The vehicle either responded too much to his foot on the pedal or not at all. The stop-and-go motion left Meg clinging to the support post beside her with both hands, as if her life depended on it, which maybe it did.

A few minutes in, Morgan felt like he might be getting the hang of it, but just when it looked as if maybe they could both relax, a chicken marched out on the path in front of them, forcing him to brake so heavily they both nearly hit their heads on the dashboard.

The chicken paused, did an annoyed tilt of its head and then strutted to the other side of the road.

"Why did the chicken cross the road?" she asked, deadpan.

Only the chicken was not crossing the road. Just as Morgan tried to slide by, it abruptly changed course and came back in front of them, causing him to slam on the brakes again.

"It's a good thing we don't have a windshield," he commented, "because I think both our heads would be through it."

"Surprising it didn't happen, given my curse," she said.

He couldn't argue with that! "The day is young," he said.

The chicken squawked its admonishment at him, fanned its wings, cocked its black silky head this way and that, and then tucked its wrinkled stick legs under and plunked itself down right in the center of the path, leaving no way to get around it.

"Is it laying an egg?" Meg asked, after a moment.

"How would I know what it's doing?"

"It's quite pretty, isn't it? Look at how the sun is bringing out a blue hue in the black of his feathers."

"I don't think boys lay eggs," he told her.

She ignored the lesson on the sexing of chickens. "I even see purple."

He remembered this so clearly: how Meg saw the world so differently than anyone he had ever met before. For her, an annoyance on the road became a moment to pause, to look at things more deeply, to notice something she had never noticed before.

"Do I see a chicken in a future art piece?" he asked.

"Possibly," Meg said agreeably.

Morgan found the horn on the cart and tapped it. It made a tiny beep-beep sound. He was not sure if chickens could yawn, but if they could, that one did. Annoyed, Morgan edged up on it.

"Don't run it over!" Meg cried.

"Actually, roast chicken for supper is sounding more appealing by the second."

"I don't think I could eat it now that I've met it."

"*Met* is a bit of a stretch," he noted, even though he was not sure he could eat it now either, having seen the colors of blue and purple sewn amongst its feathers.

"I'm not going to run it over. I'm just showing it it doesn't own the road."

"Showing it who's the boss," she agreed solemnly and then she giggled.

Morgan shot her a warning look.

The chicken apparently disagreed with his assessment of who owned the road, and hers of who the boss was. It tilted its head defiantly, decided he was not threatening and found something interesting to pluck at under its wing.

Morgan wondered if you could come up with an experience more humiliating than being bested by a chicken.

Meg snorted beside him.

He knew that sound well. It was her trying to hold back laughter. Once, they had attended the art show of an extremely well-known Canadian artist. It had been a mark of how well she was doing in the art world that she had been invited.

They had stood in front of the artist's newest painting, she doing her best to look reverent. She had not been succeeding very well.

Morgan had whispered in her ear, *It looks like a bag of trash a cat got into.*

She had made that exact snorting sound, and then, he'd had to take her out the side exit, and they had stood in the alley beside a bag of trash a cat had gotten into, howling with totally inappropriate laughter.

Small moments. Why were they always the best?

Morgan got out of the golf cart, partly to deal with the chicken, mostly because he did not want to share laughter with her.

He went around the front of the golf cart. He waved his hands at the chicken.

"Shoo," he said.

Nothing.

"Get lost," he said, a little more aggressively.

"Try it in Hawaiian," she called.

He glared at her. She was teasing him, and in some moment of terrible weakness, like remembering them laughing over that awful painting, he liked it.

She wagged her phone at him and made a great show of looking it up.

"Hele pela," she suggested, trying, without much luck, to swallow a snicker. "It means *get out.* Go away!"

Morgan glared at her, taking in her laughter-filled expression, her teasing tone. The most dangerous thing to do would be to play along.

So, naturally, he played along. He fanned his foot at the chicken, and yelled, *"Hele pela,"* and then the English translation.

The chicken gave him a baleful look, regained its feet with regal calm and strutted toward the edge of the road.

Meg could not hold it back any longer. She was full-out laughing now. He glanced back at her and she looked beautiful, the sun caressing flawless skin, her head thrown back showing him the delicate curve of her tender neck. Her hair was falling out of that clip.

Don't encourage her, he warned himself.

And then he encouraged her by flapping his arms and yelling *"hela pela."*

And then, helpless against it, he found himself laughing, too, as he returned to the cart.

How long since he had laughed? Nothing had seemed funny for a long, long time. And yet, less than ten minutes with his ex beside him, and there it was, a dangerous lightness of spirit.

With renewed concentration, he focused on the road. Meg, wisely, no longer trusted a smooth journey, and tightened her hold on the side posts, which, come to think of it, was a very good strategy for keeping her hands off of him!

Not that she had given any indication she was having trouble keeping her hands off of him.

Unless her cool, soothing touch on his wrist this morning counted.

"What's with the chickens?" she asked him when he had to swerve to miss another one that had darted out on the pathway in front of them.

He liked to think he was a quick learner. He didn't stop this time!

"I read that they've been here since the island was first inhabited, but they were contained. Tropical storms Inika and Iwa in the eighties and nineties destroyed the coops, and they were free to do as they pleased. Which is multiply, apparently. There're very few natural predators to contain them, and endless food sources."

"You always know *everything*," she said, pleased, and he remembered how much *this*—her approval, her admiration—had meant to him.

Just like her gift was seeing things through an artist's eye, this was what he did. He saw things from a business perspective. He enjoyed experiences more if he had the whole picture. He researched. He did his homework. He took in everything, because you could never be sure when knowledge of a certain obscure fact was going to be helpful in making good decisions. In business.

And in life.

Because suddenly obscure facts seemed like a good way to keep the barriers up between Morgan and his ex-wife.

"The sugar industry came here in the 1830s," he told her. "At its height, about a hundred thousand acres of this island were planted in sugar cane. But, just like with the pineapple plantations, successful unionization in the thirties drove industry to seek cheaper labor in other countries. The land value of the fields became greater than its value under cultivation. And then Hurricane Inika—"

"Freer of chickens!"

He smiled at her tone. "Came along and damaged major infrastructure and turned out to be the final blow for an industry already staggering under pressure."

"It's kind of sad that profits came before people just trying to have a better life," she mused.

"Ah, yes, the evil of business."

"Quit being so touchy!"

Tell that to a man who hadn't been left because he was too successful.

An uneasy silence fell between them.

"Oh!" Meg cried. "Stop!"

For a moment, Morgan thought maybe she had had enough of him and his corporate mentality. She could turn on a hair—as her abandonment of their marriage had proven—and maybe she had decided she was going to walk back to the resort rather than spend another minute with him.

But Meg scrambled off the golf cart and took a trail through jungle-like foliage. He saw that, as a passenger, she had seen an easily missed sign promising a waterfall.

It was wrong to feel relieved that she wasn't leaving. Tension between them would be the best possible strategy for getting through the next few days.

Knowing he shouldn't, he could not resist following her. The pathway led up a rise to a picnic shelter roofed in palm fronds. The open-air structure sat beside a tiny pool, with a tiny stream of water trickling over and between moss-covered rocks into it, and then exiting through lush growth out the other side.

"It's so beautiful," she whispered.

"Will you paint it?"

"It feels too big for me," she said, her voice soft.

"If anyone could do it justice, that person is you."

"Thank you for always believing in me," she whispered.

He changed the subject, rapidly!

"Parts of *Jurassic Park* were filmed here. I can see why. It's just a few steps from the paved pathway, but it feels primitive. Pristine. Untouched."

Somehow, trotting out that fact didn't help him keep his barriers up at all. Meg's face was radiant with wonder.

This is what had attracted him to her from the very first. Maybe because she was an artist, she saw beauty in a way others did not.

In fact, Meg did not seem to just *see* it, but to experience it with all her senses, as if she was pulling the beauty down deep inside herself, where she could find it and believe in it, even when life went terribly wrong.

Which hers had done.

And his had done.

The first time he saw her painting *Out of the Ashes*, it had been four years since his brother, his sister-in-law and his niece and nephew had all perished in the fire that had swept through Sarah's Reach on a cold autumn night.

He had known, looking at that painting, that Morgan would be the one who saved him.

But what had she saved him for?

Just to break him again?

Morgan suddenly regretted telling Caylee anything she needed from him he would give her. Because it was obvious that what Caylee thought she needed was for him and Meg to reunite and live happily ever after so that her own investment in love and the future seemed more certain.

That was why she had thrown them together on this errand.

She thought if she made the clumsy effort to reunite them, nature would take its course. There had always been strong—and very obvious—chemistry between Morgan and Meg.

Caylee would certainly take delight in their current accommodation dilemma, though hopefully that would be sorted out before she even found out about it. He could, unfortunately, see her having a whispered conversation with Keona to make sure that the estranged couple stayed together in Huipu as long as possible.

Morgan had to admit if he was correct that Caylee would like them back together, her strategy of forced proximity was a strong one.

CHAPTER SEVEN

MEG HAD SEEN every one of his losses flash through Morgan's eyes this morning when she had touched his arm. She had assumed he had been to Hawaii before, but she had known instantly that he had been swamped by memories of simpler times at his family's cottage, Sarah's Reach. Though the Hart family had the wealth of the world at their disposal, they had chosen that place over and over again.

He had shared so much about that amazing cottage with her, a story that ended in unthinkable tragedy.

It was one of the things that had drawn them together, initially.

They both understood, completely, what it was to lose a piece of your heart. They had both lost their brothers. But Morgan had lost even more.

In some ways he came from the opposite of her. Her family had been a small, desperate unit: a single mother, her and her brother, Bryan, who had a disability. She did not know who her father was, and had never met her grandparents.

Her memories of childhood were hellish. Poverty. Suffering. What little there was in the family for resources—including love—went to her brother. Meg had found refuge in art. And friendships, particularly her friendship with Caylee, who she had met in the first grade.

Morgan's family, on the other hand, had been prosperous.

Boisterous. Large. Tightly knit. They had a history that went back over generations.

It was from him sharing those many memories that Meg had longed for that thing she had never had, and also came to understand just how much family meant to him.

He had never been able to talk about his niece, Kendra, or his nephew, James, without his voice becoming hoarse with emotion.

And at the same time, he had known he honored them— and her—by entrusting her with the stories of his family's love.

If she knew one thing about Morgan, she knew this. The thing he wanted most was to be part of that again—that wonderful, messy, chaotic unit called family—that a freak fire had taken from his life.

In one night, his brother, Logan, gone. His sister-in-law, Amelia. His niece. His nephew. He was supposed to have been there at the family cottage that weekend. At the last minute he'd had to cancel.

And so he had lived. But his mother and father had never been the same. His mother had died—he said—of a broken heart within a year of the accident. His father, reeling from too many losses, had withered away, until he, too, was gone.

And so Morgan—terrified of love, and longing for it at the same time—had entrusted his battered heart to Meg.

And she had thought she would be worthy of it.

That they would build a family together.

That something beautiful could come out of the ashes, just as a painting she had done before her body knew him—but her spirit already did—had promised.

But then she had sat in the doctor's office and listened to his devastating words.

You won't ever be able to have a baby.

The one thing that Morgan needed, wanted, cried for in

his sleep, she could not give him. She could not give him the family, a baby, the final ingredient that she knew would fuse the broken pieces of his heart together, and make it even stronger than it had been before.

She had known she had to leave him, to give him the gift of the only destiny that would bring him back fully from the abyss.

In a life that had required both great love and great sacrifice from her—Bryan had always come first in the family dynamic—leaving Morgan had been the greatest act of love and sacrifice that had ever been asked of her.

But here she was, in this enchanted place, with Morgan beside her, walking the tightrope between loving him enough to let him go, and enjoying this time with him as if it was a gift from the universe.

It would be way too easy to lean into his words that she was worthy of painting this incredible landscape.

He had always believed in her so unconditionally.

In fact, she was pretty sure most of her success as an artist came when he had purchased *Out of the Ashes* and made it the official art of the foundation that honored that family he had lost to the fire.

She had never asked herself if she would have been as successful without his endorsement.

Without his love.

Because those things had always had a meant-to-be feeling to them, her destiny and his as intertwined as a braided rope of sweetgrass.

The only thing that didn't have a meant-to-be feeling was her decision to leave, to do what love did, and put his needs ahead of her own.

"Hey," Morgan said gently. "Come back."

His fingers were resting lightly on her cheek, and when

she looked up into his eyes, he was regarding her intensely, as if her thoughts were an open book to him.

He had always been able to read her way too accurately, and she ducked out from under his fingertips, even as she wanted to cover them with her own hand and draw them to her lips.

"Last one to the cart is a rotten egg," she called.

With a shout, he raced by her and slid into the driver's seat. "I win," he said when she joined him, breathless. "You know what I want for a prize?"

A kiss, her heart answered way too hopefully.

"No more chicken references."

She should have been relieved that his mind was not going down the same track as hers, but she felt anything but.

"I'm egg-static that I didn't agree to a prize," she said.

"Don't crow about it," he shot back.

"Ha. You're out of cluck."

"You're ruffling my feathers."

It had always been like this between them, these easy interchanges, feeding off similar senses of humor and each other's energy.

"Oh, cry me a cackle."

And then the worst possible thing—or maybe the best possible thing—happened. They were both laughing together as if eight months of pure torment were not sitting over them like dark storm clouds.

They pulled into the old plantation village, a small collection of lovely pastel-colored cottages with hip roofs, shady verandas, tidy yards. In one of those yards, a hammock swung gently between two palm trees. Meg was so taken with the serenity of it, she pulled out her phone and took a picture.

"Possible future painting?" Morgan asked.

"Yes." That feeling of being *known* filled Meg with a long-

ing she needed to quash. She focused instead on the enchantment of the commercial center.

There was actually a parking area designated for the golf
carts, and they left their vehicle there and walked the few
steps to the shopping area. It felt weird and wrong not to
be holding his hand, particularly after that feeling of being
known.

Morgan must have felt that, too, because he thrust his
hands into his shorts pockets, as if to avoid temptation.

Sitting in the shade of towering palms was a town-like
atmosphere, with shops lining both sides of a cobblestone
street that had long since been closed to vehicular traffic.
The stores, connected by a wooden boardwalk, were a delight of old clapboard storefronts, some with covered front
verandas. There were open-air cafés and coffee bars, and
the scent of coffee and fresh baking was in the air. Flowers spilled out of containers. The colorful chickens strutting
about only added to the ambience.

The shops were just opening, and people were putting out
sandwich boards and display racks. In front of the cafés and
coffee bars, tables and chairs were being arranged.

"Look." Meg pointed at where a woman was putting out
racks of women's clothing under a colorful sign that said
Wow-ee Wahine.

As they made their way toward the boutique, the cheerful
bustle of the morning was suddenly interrupted.

Protestors came, shoulder to shoulder, down the street,
caring flags and placards and shouting slogans.

Morgan pulled Meg behind him in an instinctive gesture
that was very protective. Meg felt extremely irritated that the
protestors were inserting themselves and their viewpoints
into such an idyllic setting.

She could tell, by glancing at the firm line of Morgan's
mouth, that he felt the same way.

The storekeeper who had been putting out the display racks paused and glanced at the protestors.

When she turned to Meg and Morgan, her expression was soft.

"So much anger," she said with a gentle shake of her head. "I hope they stay here awhile, so they can understand *aloha*."

Meg felt her irritation melt away, and looked at Morgan. She could tell the woman's words and her lovely, peaceful way of being had had the very same effect on him.

The woman now turned her full, beautiful energy on them.

"Oh!" she said. "I have exactly the right dress for you!"

"I'm not exactly shopping just for myself," Meg told her.

"On your honeymoon?" she asked.

Unfortunately, memories of her honeymoon blasted through her, and Meg could feel herself blushing. She glanced at Morgan. He was looking at his feet.

"Oh, no!" The woman moved toward her and lifted her hand. "You've lost your ring."

Meg was suddenly aware of the white band of skin on her finger where her ring had been. She had never taken it off until a few days ago.

Her eyes skittered to Morgan's ring finger. It, of course, did not have the telltale band of white of the freshly separated.

He was looking at her finger oddly.

She snatched her hand away and changed the subject.

"No," she said firmly, "we are not on a honeymoon."

The woman looked between them as if their whole history was laid bare to her soft brown eyes.

"We're visiting Kauai for the wedding of friends," Meg explained hastily, then outlined the dilemma of the missing wedding clothes.

"What a wonderful thing to help with!" the shop owner

exclaimed. "Come in. Come in. My name's Kamelei. Everything in my shop is designed and made in Hawaii."

Megan watched as Morgan took a glance inside the shop and tried not to look too horrified at the *all things feminine* theme. The crowded little store proudly displayed everything from bras and panties to negligees.

"I'll just go see what I can find for the groomsmen," he said.

"No," Kamelei ordered him. "Sit, sit. You can take the chair on the front lanai. She'll come show you. You'll need to send pictures to the bride. It's her choice."

Meg was glad Kamelei was there to help her stay focused, because she was distracted by one of the dresses on display.

"The print on this fabric!" she exclaimed, taking a closer look at an exquisite pattern of palm trees, chickens, mountains. "All of Kauai has been captured here."

"I work with local artists, and have their work printed onto fabric. Too busy for the bridesmaid dresses," Kamelei decided with a tilt of her head. She took Meg by the elbow and ushered her into a little curtained alcove at the back of the store, "I'll find everything I have in white."

Moments later, four white sundresses were slipped in through the curtain.

None of them was suited for a bra! Was she really going to model these for Morgan, braless?

Meg drew in a deep breath. This wasn't for her. And it wasn't for Morgan. It was for Caylee, and she needed to suck it up and do whatever needed to be done.

She put on the first dress.

It had been adorable on the hanger, and it was even more so on. The dress had a full skirt, puffy short sleeves and it left a whole lot of leg and cleavage on display.

She stepped self-consciously out of the change cubicle. "I don't think—"

"That's for your friend to decide," Kamelei said firmly, and shooed her out the door. "Show him. Send photos to the bride."

Meg trudged out the door.

"First one," she announced. Morgan was sitting in a deep wicker chair looking at his phone. It seemed unfair that he had the better of the two jobs.

He looked up.

Something so hot went through his eyes, she felt singed by it.

"Take a picture," she said through tight lips.

He raised his phone, then lowered it. "Do you have to look as if you're going to the gallows?"

She smiled. It felt as if her lips were stretching uncomfortably over her teeth.

"That's worse."

She tried widening the smile.

"Now you're trying too hard."

"Take the damn picture."

"You know, for the world's most gorgeous woman, you're amazingly unphotogenic when you want to be."

Her husband thought she was the world's most gorgeous woman. The longing to be what they had once been nearly swamped her. She needed to focus on the critical part.

"Thank you," she said sarcastically.

"Just try to make it about showing the dress off, not like you're a prisoner in a flour sack having your mug shot taken."

But a *gorgeous* one, she wanted to remind him. Instead, Meg glared at him. "You know I've always been awkward about having my picture taken."

He sighed. "I'm trying to get the dress to best advantage. Try resting your hand on your hip."

A bit reluctantly, she followed his suggestion.

"And maybe just put your other hand on that post, and put one leg down on the stairs."

"What are you? Mr. Professional Photographer?" she snapped.

"You never know what I might be called to do if planes don't start showing up," he told her mildly. He frowned. "Could you do something with your lips?"

"What does that have to do with showing Caylee the dress?"

He ignored that question. "You know, that thing girls do when they're taking selfies?"

"I don't know," she said stubbornly, even though that was a lie. Though she rarely took selfies of herself, she seemed to be about the only one in the world who did not.

It occurred to her Morgan was enjoying her discomfort very much!

"Do that little pursing thing with your lips, you know, like you're about to use a straw."

Since she didn't want to increase his enjoyment of her discomfort, she went along without complaint. She did as he asked, only she highly exaggerated the pucker of her lips, as if she was leaning forward to kiss a baby. Just as he went to take the picture, she crossed her eyes.

"Nice," he said, looking at the image he had captured with pretend annoyance. He snapped his fingers. "Think of your happiest moment."

That was easy. And also, heartbreakingly hard.

I do.

It had been the best moment of Meg's entire life, looking into Morgan's face, and being sure she saw forever.

Unless you counted what followed, his cool lips and her heated skin, the sense of owning each other in the most sacred of ways...

CHAPTER EIGHT

"There," Morgan said with satisfaction, clicking the picture. "Meg, you finally look like you."

"I don't see how looking like me has anything to do with showing Caylee the dress," Meg complained.

"You finally lowered your shoulders from around your ears, that's how. Why are you so self-conscious about having your picture taken?"

Even though she had said that herself, she didn't want to admit the truth. Maybe it wasn't about having her picture taken! Maybe it was about modeling for her husband. She turned to go try on the next dress.

"Don't go yet. I'll send this to Caylee. Hopefully, she loves it and…oh, that was fast," Morgan said when his phone pinged. For a moment he looked hopeful and then his face fell. So, despite tormenting Meg by making her pose for the camera, he wasn't loving this exercise any more than she was.

"She loves the dress, but it's a definite no."

Meg went back to the changeroom. The next white dress was a tube style, sleeveless and slinky. It required a great deal of wriggling to get into it. It was an obvious no, but when she slipped out of the change room with it on, Kamelei pinned a square of white lace to her hair and thrust a bouquet of flowers into her hands.

"There," she said with satisfaction, turning Meg toward the mirror.

The dress was way too revealing. It looked as if it was painted on. Meg did not want to model it for Morgan, but again, she sucked it up, telling herself it was for the greater good.

As she came out the door, she saw a little boy had appeared on the lanai. He was holding a chicken, and Morgan was leaning over in his chair, his hand out, making a clucking sound way in the back of his throat.

The little boy was laughing and so was Morgan. Probably because of his niece and nephew, Morgan had an ease around children that few men had.

When Meg saw the light in his face as he interacted with the little boy, it felt as if the wisdom of her decision was confirmed.

But she needed to quit being distracted and find out if Marjorie was going to be the one who would give Morgan the life he deserved.

"I can't believe this," Meg said, charmed despite herself. "I leave for one second, and you're romancing a chicken!"

"It's not any old chicken," he said. "It's Henry."

The little boy shouted with laughter. "I'm Henry," he said. "This is Clyde."

Meg saw that Morgan's mistake had been intentional to make the little boy laugh.

"Come meet him," he said, and she came over and shifted the flowers to one hand. But when she tentatively reached out, the chicken squawked, flapped its wings and ruffled its feathers.

She took a startled step back, and Morgan, by second nature, reached out and steadied her, his hand on her wrist.

Henry tucked Clyde under his arm and left the lanai on the run.

Morgan released her arm, almost as if he hadn't realized

he had taken it, and watched the child and the chicken depart with an unguarded smile.

"You can always tell," she told him softly.

"Tell what?" he asked gruffly, to hide the fact he was embarrassed she had witnessed his softer side. Not that his softer side was any mystery to her. On the other hand, in his mind, she had betrayed his trust. No wonder he wanted to hide the vulnerable parts of himself from her.

"If people like children."

"I guess you can," he said, but his tone suggested *who cares if they do or don't.*

Well, she didn't care if most people did or didn't. Only someone he was romantically involved with. And she didn't know how to probe that without seeming way too interested in his private life.

Meg became aware of something creeping through all her focus on Morgan. Seeing him with that little boy had brought back every feeling of that day she had been in the doctor's office and heard the news.

She thought she had dealt with her sense of loss and grief, but now, seeing that little boy, she felt it anew.

She would never have a chubby little boy calling her Mommy, looking at her with dancing, dark eyes like his father's, holding out a rock or a dandelion or a frog, inviting her to rediscover the entire world through his innocent eyes.

She would never have a little girl, with curly, sandy locks just like Morgan's, tongue caught between teeth as she labored over a drawing, or giggled and tossed handfuls of bubbles over her head at bath time.

Meg could feel herself being drawn further down the road of grief: no warm little bodies snuggled into her for stories before bed, no first day of kindergarten, no cold spring days at T-ball practice, no wiping away tears and dispensing of healing hugs and kisses—

"Meg?"

She started and looked at Morgan, who was frowning at her.

"Is something wrong?" he asked.

She jerked herself back to the here and now, and forced a smile. He did not look convinced, and so she did a little twirl in the dress. When she faced him again, she could see her distraction had worked.

Morgan was now intensely focused on the dress. His dark brown eyes darkened until they looked black. His mouth fell open.

"Holy," he croaked.

He quickly lifted his phone and hid behind it. He didn't give any instructions this time about Meg thinking happy thoughts.

Still, she left her sadness behind her and contemplated how evil it was that it was her turn to enjoy his discomfort, and she planned to play it to the absolute max!

Morgan really hoped Meg would go and take that dress off soon. It was crazy sexy, something suitable for a late night at a club, not for a wedding dress, not even as the emergency stand-in model. The little posy of flowers she was carrying, and the veil pinned in her hair, did nothing to water down the message of the dress.

"I'm pretty sure that veil has more fabric in it than the dress," he told her. He hoped the croak was gone from his voice, but he didn't think he was that good an actor.

Of course, *now* Meg found her inner model. She pulled the little scrap of lace in front of her face, and blinked at him from behind it. She walked across the lanai toward him. He wasn't sure if she was deliberately swishing her hips like that, or if the dress just made it seem that way. The hem was slithering up the length of her legs.

Once a man had known a woman as his wife, in every sense of that word, was it ever possible to put *that* behind you? He knew the tang of perspiration on her skin, and he knew the mole that was hidden where no one else had ever seen it, and he knew the location of a secret dimple...

"She says no," he cried when his phone pinged.

Meg gave him a knowing smile, before she turned and sashayed away. She threw a glance over her shoulder, her look filtered by the veil. He wished he would have been looking anywhere but at her butt, checking out if the clingy dress revealed the secret dimple. It did.

The next dress she came out in, thankfully, was demure. It was a simple white sleeveless knee-length sheath, overlaid with lace.

Morgan knew Caylee would say yes.

Meg looked like a bride.

So much so that he felt the sharp knife-edge of regret pierce him. Would things have gone differently if she had had *this*?

This moment in her white dress, with a veil in her hair, carrying flowers?

They hadn't been dating all that long before Morgan had known she was the one. He'd also known, shocked at his own old-fashionedness, that as glorious as their lovemaking was, he would never feel right about it until he married her.

Because she was that kind of girl. The forever kind.

And she drew out that kind of man in him.

The man who wanted to live up to what he saw shining in her eyes when she looked at him.

She believed in his decency. His honor.

Still, there had been no white dress, no cathedral filled with guests, no amazing dinner after, no first dance.

A man who had failed at his marriage wondered, endlessly, what could have fixed it.

Any of those things? The wedding of her dreams, like the one that Caylee and Jonathon were putting together on this enchanted isle?

But no, he'd been selfish. The last gathering of his family had been at the funeral—his brother, his sister-in-law, his niece, his nephew in polished caskets going up the aisle. His mother had collapsed, and his father had tried so heartbreakingly hard to be strong.

And Morgan could not do it.

He could not gather with family without those memories coming up. He could not have a traditional wedding without his brother at his side, without Kendra skipping down the aisle tossing flower petals, without James taking tiny steps, his tongue stuck out between his teeth, his eyes fastened, anxious, on the pillow that carried the ring he'd been entrusted with.

Meg didn't have any family to speak of. Her brother, like his, was dead. Her mother was a mess of addiction and treatment, and addiction again.

He thought that was why Meg had gotten his wish not to have a large celebration so completely. He thought it had suited her perfectly, too.

But had it really?

His phone pinged, and he glanced at it, relieved to take his eyes off Meg.

"Caylee says that's the one," he said with relief. He was not sure how many more wedding dresses he could stand having modeled by Meg, who had never had one. Should he ask her if she regretted that? Somehow it seemed like a topic he could not broach.

Once upon a time—back when he still believed in *once upon a time*—there was no topic he could not broach with Meg.

"I'm hungry," he announced, and he was. Hungry for the

way things used to be. No food could ever fill that—though he was willing to give it a try.

"You just had a huge breakfast."

He glanced at his watch. "Hours ago. The chicken turned my thoughts to food."

"That chicken was a pet!"

"I can't help myself."

"Well, then you'll be thinking of food a lot here on Kauai," she told him. "We're not done. Not even close. We have to choose bridesmaid dresses, and something for the grooms-men."

He talked her into eating something first. He gave Kamelei the mission of finding some suitable bridesmaid dresses for when they returned.

"If you want an authentic Hawaiian experience, get the *musubi* from the food truck on the corner," she called after them.

"I'm all for the authentic Hawaiian experience," Meg claimed, but she wasn't so sure when she stood in front of a dilapidated truck with a banner that proclaimed it Kauai's Purveyor of Fine Food.

She was stunned to see what the recommended *musubi* was made out of!

"How can Spam be Hawaiian?" she asked doubtfully. Since the purveyor himself—wearing a name tag that said Tim and a T-shirt that claimed Spam was not just something in your inbox—was leaning eagerly over his counter toward them, she didn't add what she was obviously thinking. As was Morgan.

How could highly processed ground pork that came in a tin with a peel-back lid be considered fine food?

"It came to the Hawaiian Islands during the Second World War," Tim told them. "We've been having a love affair with it ever since. You can even get Spam-flavored potato chips at the grocery store here."

"Oh," she said weakly.

"Can't wait to try those," Morgan said. She shot him a look. She was pretty sure he was serious!

"The *musubi* was recommended," Morgan said.

"Virgins?" their host asked them.

Morgan slid Meg a look. She was blushing.

"I mean *musubi* virgins," Tim clarified cheerfully. "I mean it's obvious you two are—"

Tim didn't finish the sentence, just wagged his eyebrows wickedly.

Geez. How annoying that something so untrue seemed obvious to complete strangers.

Meg giggled uneasily. "I think I'll have the fresh fruit platter."

"We'll take two *musubi*," Morgan said firmly.

He led her to a picnic table.

"I'm not eating pan-fried Spam—in oyster sauce—wrapped in roasted nori seaweed," she whispered to him.

"Don't forget the sushi rice," he reminded her.

Their host came and put the plates down in front of them. He'd either forgotten the fruit or didn't want it to dilute the full *musubi* experience. Tim waited, smiling. It became a contest of who could outwait whom.

Apparently the purveyor of Kauai's finest did not have the urgency of the fate of outfitting an entire wedding party in a few hours riding on his shoulders. Tim had all day.

Realizing she was not going to be able to outwait him, Meg reluctantly picked up the *musubi*, which looked like an extra fat sushi roll.

Morgan watched, amused as Meg closed her eyes, looked as if she was saying a prayer and then took a delicate bite. Her eyes opened. They widened.

"Morgan," she breathed, "you are not going to believe this."

Their host bowed and left them.

Morgan bit into pure ambrosia, and felt oddly grateful for one more moment like this with her.

The magic of pure discovery.

When they returned to Wow-ee Wahine, Kamelei had chosen a selection of sundresses she thought would be perfect for the bridal party. She had hung them outside in the window casings. Meg took pictures and sent them while chatting with Caylee.

"I think this one would be best in the photos," Meg advised her friend. "The deep burgundy won't compete with the backdrop, and there's no pattern."

"They have four, in the sizes we need?"

Kamelei nodded.

"Take them. Done and done," Caylee decided with obvious relief. Morgan was relieved, too, since she hadn't even asked Meg to try the dresses on. He wasn't sure he was up to another modeling session.

Since plastic bags were banned in Hawaii, Kamelei carefully wrapped the bridesmaid dresses together in brown paper and gave it to them with the other dress, which had already been wrapped.

"You can return them if you don't end up needing them," Kamelei said.

And there it was. *Aloha.* Concern for the wedding—and the well-being—of complete strangers overriding the sale.

She pointed them in the direction of the only men's store in the mall. It was called Surf Bums, and it had a selection of casual beachwear that lived up to its name. After endless going back and forth with Caylee, they finally had a backup plan for the guys' side of the wedding party.

Plain white T-shirts and the most subdued board shorts

in stock, which were black with a faint palm tree pattern on them.

It was now late afternoon and Meg and Morgan were hot, sticky and tired.

"Let's have a cold drink before we go back," he suggested.

They found a café and settled on the lanai at a wooden table under a bright awning. A man strummed a ukulele on a small stage. Morgan ordered a light beer, and Meg had a slushy made with Kauai's famous Sugarloaf White pineapple.

The drink had the unfortunate name of Pining For You.

"It's delicious," she said, and closed her cute little mouth over the straw, just like she'd done earlier for the pictures. "Want to try?"

No, he didn't want to try it! His lips closing over the same straw her lips had closed over seemed way too intimate. Which was ridiculous. If he refused, she would know he was being ridiculous.

"Sure," he said.

She passed him the drink and he took a sip. He'd been right. Way too intimate. He passed it back, irritated that the drink had an extra sweetness, as if the morning with Meg had made all of him come alive, even his taste buds. Even such a simple thing—sharing a drink on a beautiful afternoon—suddenly felt rife with complication.

Still, it was hard to remain irritated when it was idyllic sitting in the shade, watching the chickens and the tourists flock through the shops.

Then a man with a gourd drum joined the man with the ukulele, and a woman joined them. She was slender and golden-skinned, her shiny black hair—crowned with a leaf-and-flower headdress—cascaded down past the middle of her back. She had a lei around her neck, a chest covering that appeared to be made of coconut shells and a ti-leaf skirt.

As the man strummed the ukulele, the drum put out a pulsing beat. The dancer's graceful, sinuous movements were explained as she performed traditional hula, a storytelling dance of the Hawaiian Islands.

More and more people gathered to watch the performance. Morgan cast a glance at Meg. She was enchanted. The sense of discovering a new world with her intensified, though the world the hula dancer was opening up was soft and sensual, probably not the best thing to be experiencing with your nearly ex-wife.

He switched to water after the first beer. He did not want his guard coming down right now, but Meg ordered a second slushy.

She had nearly finished it when the dancer pointed at her. "Come try," she called.

Normally, Meg would not be the kind of person who was up for audience-participation invitations.

But she obviously could not think of a way to gracefully refuse. So, she lifted her eyebrows at him, left her chair and joined the dancer on the stage. She was asked to kick off her shoes.

"I'm going to teach you the very basic first step of hula," the dancer said. "It's called *kalakaua*. Mirror what I do."

The women faced each other. The dancer put her elbows up, hands pointed toward each other, fingertips just about touching at her chest level. Then she sank, slowly, bending her knees. To the exact beat of the drum, she turned to the audience and thrust one hip with a sinuous grace. She turned the other direction and thrust the other hip. She alternated her arms as she did this.

Meg gamely followed her lead, and they did the movement a dozen or so times.

The teacher nodded her approval. "All right, we are ready for double *kalakaua*."

The beat of the music intensified. Now, the women turned

to the audience and moved one hip forward, and then the other, before turning and doing it on the other side.

It was a simple movement, so stunningly sensual it took Morgan's breath away. He was entranced as Meg, normally somewhat inhibited, gave herself over to the impromptu dance lesson.

Meg was a little awkward, but only at first. Though she had never been any kind of athlete—he remembered trying to teach her how to throw a Frisbee—she soon caught on that she just needed to mirror what the other woman was doing.

He watched the exact moment that she let go, and gave herself over to the experience, her body surrendering to the music. He wasn't sure how much of the inhibition was a part of her he had never really seen before, and how much was the fault of the slushy.

As Meg mastered one step, the teacher would move on. "You're a natural," she said, and the audience applauded their agreement. Meg, normally on the shy side, was soaking it up.

Morgan looked around, feeling as if he might have to go to war if some lecherous old men were eyeing up his wife.

Nearly not his wife, he reminded himself sternly.

The two women looked absolutely stunning as they performed the dance in perfect sync, arms moving as gently as the breeze, bodies swaying, hips moving.

Meg's eyes locked with his. She moved her hips, her bare stomach swiveled, her arms floated out from her body. He had a sudden sense of being alone with her, as if she was dancing this dance only for him. As if it was an invitation.

To know her.

Of course, he already did know her in that way, but he was shocked by the erotic nature of this experience, and how he felt as much like Meg's husband as he ever had.

The drum beat died away. The women became still, and then the teacher hugged Meg.

"You were awesome," she told her, and the audience agreed with thunderous applause. Meg blushed and curtsied to the audience. She carried her shoes back to the table and sat down, her face alight, though she wouldn't meet his eyes as she finished the drink in one long slurp.

Another slushy appeared in front of her.

"Compliments of that gentleman over there," the waitress said.

Morgan glared *over there*. It wasn't even a lecherous old man. A lecherous young man, grinning cheekily at Meg. Handsome, too.

Good grief, was he jealous?

Of course he was jealous! He just couldn't ever let her— the woman who had dumped him—know that!

The dancer was joined by several other dancers onstage. They announced they would perform, as their last number, the Tahitian *ote'a*. The performance was quite incredible, the drumming fast-paced, the dancers keeping up with it with astonishing hip rotations. Meg was rapt.

"Wow," she breathed. "I'm glad I didn't get asked to do that one."

Me too, Morgan thought.

"Very common to have an afternoon sprinkle in the tropics," the ukulele player announced as the women finished their performance. "That's why it's so lush here. You might want an umbrella."

Morgan looked at the sky. There was no sign of rain.

Megan looked at her empty slushy glass, a bit bewildered.

"I think I'm tipsy," she whispered, mortified. "Did that have alcohol in it?"

"I thought you probably assumed that."

"I didn't! Why didn't you tell me?" she demanded.

"I thought you knew. Couldn't you taste it?"

"All I could taste was the pineapple. And maybe some coconut. Like a piña colada."

"An alcoholic drink," he pointed out.

She narrowed her eyes at him, as if he had known and she didn't.

She made her way back to the golf cart, her slight tipsiness made unfortunately hilarious by the fact she was trying to act as if she was completely sober. The graceful dancer of half an hour ago was completely vanquished, Morgan noted with relief.

He got her seated and the packages safely stowed behind them, and then took the driver's seat.

Halfway back, black clouds boiled up over the mountains. But if this was a "sprinkle," Morgan didn't want to see what a storm would look like. In the blink of an eye, a beautiful day turned into a tropical deluge.

Water fell from the sky in sheets. It sounded like drums as it pounded the foliage around them.

He was a Vancouver boy, born and raised. Morgan thought he knew every single thing there was to know about rain.

And he was wrong.

He was one hundred percent wrong.

CHAPTER NINE

"I'VE NEVER SEEN rain like this, ever," Meg said, her voice slightly slurred, but nevertheless awed.

Morgan hadn't either. The paved pathway was turning into a stream, the water pulling at the wheels of the cart.

The canvas roof of the cart began to sag, and then it dripped. Even without the failure of the roof, they would have been getting wet as the rain slashed into the cart sideways. They were completely soaked in seconds.

"The clothes are going to be ruined," Meg wailed, and then yanked the packages out of the back—nearly falling out of the cart to do so—before trying to fold her body over them to protect them.

Even for all the trouble they'd gone through to get those clothes, it was probably a measure of her altered state that Meg thought they should be a priority right now. He could barely see the track in front of them, and he was using all his strength to maintain control of the steering wheel. He was pretty sure their cart was about to turn into a boat, and he was not sure if it could float.

"Is everything okay?" Meg asked, her eyes suddenly fastened on his face.

The words *flash flood* were going through his brain, but he deliberately kept his tone calm.

"Oh, yeah," he said, "just a little tropical squall."

They might be barreling toward a divorce, but he felt one hundred percent like her husband in that moment.

This was what he had signed up for when he said *I do.*

This had felt like what he was born to do.

Protect her. Keep her safe.

In that moment, with the water beginning to boil under the cart, he was aware signing a piece of paper was never going to change that.

Meg gasped. "What is happening?"

We're getting swept away.

"The water was just pooling on that part of the road."

That was not exactly true. He glanced over his shoulder when he heard a roaring sound like a jet getting ready to take off. A torrent of water, just a few yards from where they had just been, rolled over the road, dark with mud and debris.

Meg turned back toward the roar and stared. When she looked back at him, she looked suddenly very sober.

What he saw in her eyes, though, was not terror. It was complete trust in him. Even as he vowed to be worthy of it, the earth seemed to be trembling under the cart. He saw the reason. Another torrent of water was racing toward the path in front of them.

To his enormous relief, Morgan realized they were at the picnic area they had visited briefly this morning. He remembered it was on a rise.

With all his strength he wrested the cart off the path. He got out. The water was swirling around his knees, the current unbelievable powerful.

Hanging on to the frame, he made his way around to her side.

"Leave the parcels," he ordered her.

She gave him a look as if he'd lost his mind, and hugged them tighter to herself. He yanked her out of the cart and tossed her over his shoulder. In a few steps, his feet mercifully found dry ground. Well, not dry, but not submerged in two feet of water, either.

Carefully, he set Meg down.

She was still clutching the packages. She turned back the way they had come and watched as the water scooped up the cart and it floated several feet before it lodged on high ground again.

She looked like a drowned rat. He hadn't realized she was wearing makeup until he saw it was smudged under her eyes. Her hair was plastered to her skull, and her clothes were plastered to her curves. Rain ran down her face in rivulets.

She had never looked quite so beautiful.

Or had the hula dancer just heightened his awareness of the sensual? The hula dancer, the unexpected storm, the close call with calamity.

"It's my curse," she wailed.

"That's ridiculous," he told her firmly. "No one's in the hospital."

"Yet," she said bleakly.

"Come on, the shelter is right over here."

She stumbled—way too much white pineapple slushy—and he grabbed her hand, and half pulled, half carried her toward the shelter.

It was open-air, but the picnic table in the middle of it was dry and protected. Three chickens were roosting underneath of it. The rain hammered on the palm-frond roof and the wind swept in.

Even though it was not cold at all, as he watched when Meg turned back and looked at the river now gushing down the paved trail, she began to shake.

Her soaked shorts and top were clinging to her, every bit as revealing as that second slinky dress had been. She looked as sensual as the hula dancer had been.

Morgan felt a tingling across the back of his neck, an awareness that one danger had been replaced with another.

Confirming this, Meg *finally* set down the packages, but only to press her soaked, trembling body against his own wetness.

Give me strength, Morgan thought, and tried to step away from her. Instead, her hands, frantic, wrapped around his neck. And then she was pulling his lips to her lips.

"Hey," he said gruffly, managing to get his lips away, though her hold around his neck tightened, "you've had a little too much to drink and—"

Her lips took his.

She's drunk, he told himself. *Don't do it.*

But she ran the tip of her tongue over the edge of his upper lip in that way that she knew drove him mad.

This had been brewing between them all day, an awareness growing, just out of sight, but as certainly as this invisible storm had been gathering strength in those high valleys hidden behind jagged mountain peaks.

Now, competing with all the sounds of the storm, was a voice, just as insistent, inside of Morgan.

And it said, *Why not?*

Why not give himself into the kind of forces of nature that swept things away without warning? Maybe especially a man's ability to say no. Wasn't a man's idea that he was in control the worst illusion of all?

They were still married. He had just figured out in some way, no matter if they made their divorce official or not, he was always going to feel married to Meg.

As if it was his job to protect her and keep her safe, forever.

Or maybe he was just making excuses for the fact he was already one hundred percent certain that he was not a big enough man to stand up to the temptation of what she was offering, no matter how dishonorable that might be.

And, come to that, where had being the decent, honorable guy gotten him last time?

And come to that, she was an adult woman, completely capable of making decisions without him. She'd proven that by leaving him, hadn't she?

Meg was not drunk. Not anymore. She hadn't been drunk, anyway. Tipsy at best. No, there was something else running through her.

Pure adrenaline.

And primal awareness that life was short.

That in a blink—*Mrs. Hart, I'm sorry to tell you this*—the whole life she had planned could be snatched away from her.

She had, somehow, evaded the curse, and a relieved euphoria was sweeping through her, obliterating her rational thought, just as the water and mud had obliterated the path behind them.

She could not keep her hands or her lips off her ex-husband. She never had been able to. Being with him all day, modeling for him, discovering new things, the drinks, the hula dancer, the storm—maybe even the chickens chortling away under the table—all seemed to be encouraging her to grab life while she could. Even the pungent smell rising from the earth seemed to call to her to explore the deep mysteries of primal urges, or creation itself.

Of course, she was going to regret this later.

Terribly.

All those months of making herself not call him, making herself not beg him, making herself not throw herself at his feet and explain it to him…all that agony of discipline out the window, those efforts as temporary and as insubstantial as the mist and mountain cloud that pressed in on them from all sides.

Right now, for Meg, later did not matter. In fact, it was incomprehensible.

All that mattered was the bliss of Morgan's arms around her, the heat of his wet, strong, familiar body pressed full along the length of hers. All that mattered was the familiar taste of his lips on her tongue. All that mattered was the moment when, with a strangled groan, he surrendered and wrapped his hands through the wet tangle of her hair and kissed her back.

Ferociously.

Hungrily.

Honestly.

They were in Hawaii. They were in a public place. How could something so wrong feel so right?

Even the chickens seemed to know that chances of anyone else being out in the storm were slender to none. Meg had watched the road close behind them. It was probably also now impassable in front of them.

They were utterly and completely alone in this place that paid complete homage to mystical forces that could not and would not be tamed by something so small, so fragile, as human will.

CHAPTER TEN

MEG WAS AWARE her hand—no, her entire body—was trembling, not from cold, but from white-hot desire. The shaking was so pronounced she was having trouble slipping the buttons free on Morgan's shirt. It felt like sweet torture, forcing them, one by one, through holes that seemed to have shrunk with the rain.

Once she had dispensed with the buttons, she worked on peeling the sodden fabric away from his belly and chest. Finally, she saw what she had longed for ever since she had glimpsed him lying in bed, naked, last night.

With hungry eyes, Meg took in the beautiful expanse of his flawless skin stretched over the broad plains of his chest and the taut drum of his belly.

She touched it. She thought, because he was so wet, Morgan's skin would be cold. But it wasn't. It radiated heat and felt like silk. Letting her fingertips explore him made her so aware of how acutely incomplete she had felt without *this* in her life.

But soon, touching him with her fingertips was not enough to quell the need, a tiny flame within her that demanded to be fed. Meg kissed his chest. She flicked the hard pebble of his nipple with the tip of her tongue.

Combustion. The spark flickered stronger, took hold, licked heat into parts of her that had been cold for way too long.

The growing flame fanned between them, touching, drawing back, touching again, stronger, hotter.

Morgan's groan was raw and his fingers found her blouse. He undid the knot at her waist with an easy flick of his wrist, dispensed with the buttons, drew the fabric over her shoulders and off her arms with the ease with which one might peel a banana.

And then he shrugged off his own wet shirt, and the sodden clothing lay in a puddle at their feet.

Only the filmy fabric of her bra was preventing them being skin on skin, and with his eyes never leaving her face, Morgan dispensed with that, too.

And then lowered his head over what had been revealed.

"You are so beautiful," he whispered, his voice raw, and then his lips, hot, found her breast, and she drew his head closer against her, reveling in the sweet torment of sensation.

He dropped his head lower, trailing his tongue down the center line of her body, flicking it in and out of her belly button.

Her shorts—and then his—joined the clothes at their feet. The moist, warm air embraced them, their skin pebbled with droplets of humidity, perspiration, need.

There hadn't been a volcanic eruption on Kauai for four hundred thousand years, but it felt as if the rain all around them had turned to fire as he poured his white-hot kisses down on her, slowly anointing every inch of her skin, cherishing every single thing about her that made her a woman.

She gasped and tangled her hands in his hair when Morgan dropped on his knees before her and wrapped his arms around the small of her back, taking her as a willing captive.

He dropped a trail of fire—exquisitely possessive, tender—as he moved downward. Without a trace of self-consciousness, he tasted her most secret of places, then kissed her inner thighs with deep reverence.

When he released her, and stood up, Meg was quivering with sensation, and the same need to *know* him that he had just shown to her.

She worshipped the strong lines of his magnificent male body with her eyes, and then with her lips, and then with her tongue.

There was not one part of him that was not entirely beautiful, there was not one part of him that she did not come to know completely. She *loved* his need of her, his trembling, the sounds that came from him as he exercised exquisite discipline, waiting for her to feel complete in her exploration of him.

She rose, once again, and pressed against him, swaying and sliding, until he uttered a muted groan of complete surrender.

She whispered *yes* to that, marveled at the powerful beauty of a man and a woman coming to this complete understanding of what it was for the masculine and the feminine to dance together.

With gentle, exquisite strength, Morgan turned her, then lifted her onto the edge of the picnic table. He scanned her face, a question in his eyes. Her truth met that question, and her legs wrapped around the small of his back.

His lips took hers, not with gentle welcome now, but fiercely, possessively, urgently. The firestorm was not just outside of them, but infusing every cell of their beings, burning hotter and hotter, until they melted together.

Lava.

Fused.

Flowing into each other.

Becoming one.

As the world erupted around them.

After, they rested in the deliciously sharp contrasts of making love—fury and delicacy, tenderness and force, hunger and satiation—all living in complete harmony within the same exquisite moments.

Meg touched Morgan's face with the pure wonder of one who had thought they would never be whole again, a half-living person who had been restored to life.

She contemplated the fact that they had made love in some of the most luxurious places in the world. They had made love on silk sheets with rose petals being crushed around them.

But nothing matched the intensity of the experience they had just shared. In an open-air shelter with rain sluicing off the roof, on a picnic table with chickens roosting under it. It had felt bold and yet also vulnerable. And Meg thought that perhaps it was the very vulnerability—physical, emotional, spiritual—that had made the lovemaking so exquisite.

Gently, gently, gently, Morgan gathered her. He lifted her nakedness to his own, cradled her against him, walked out into the rain, and held her up to it, as if she was a virgin being sacrificed on the altar of desire.

The warm rain on her skin, his touch, sang across her heightened awareness, a bow to taut strings, turning her to music.

Finally, he set her down and they raced, hand in hand, down the bank into the pool. Just this morning, a trickle had gurgled over those rocks, but now it was a torrent.

Nonetheless, they stood beneath it, letting the natural forces that had brought them together scrub them clean.

At first, the heat of their experience kept them warm, but then that dwindled, and Meg felt suddenly cold. She shivered, and Morgan took her hand and led her back to the picnic shelter.

Quickly, he began opening the clothing packages.

"Hey," she protested, through chattering teeth, "those are for the wedding."

He took one of the white T-shirts and came and stood before her. He began, methodically, tenderly to dry her.

"White T-shirts are a dime a dozen," he assured her. "We'll replace them."

And so she surrendered to his ministrations, to his wringing water from her hair, and tousling it dry, journeying downward over her body. Morgan's touch was efficient, and yet there was an element of reverence to it, as if she was an altar he worshiped at.

And when he was done, she took the T-shirt from him, and dried him off, glorying in the look and feel of his flawless skin, his beautiful body, the wonderful familiarity of it all.

When she was finished, Morgan turned again to the open packages, dropped a dry T-shirt over her head. It came to her thigh, like a minidress. He pulled on a pair of the black shorts.

And then they lay down on top of the picnic table, side by side, she nestled under the shelter of his arm. Considering how hard that surface was, it felt to her like a feather bed. Because he was there. Because she could feel the beat of his heart, and the heat of his skin, and in this moment, everything felt so incredibly right in her world.

They listened to the steady drum of the rain on the shelter roof, and his breathing was so steady and strong. She thought he might have gone to sleep.

But, he hadn't.

"I wonder what you're going to tell Marjorie," she said.

He let out a huff of annoyance. "There is no Marjorie. Really, Meg? You don't know me any better than that? You think I'd cheat on someone?"

"I'm sorry. She wasn't right for you, anyway."

"How would you know?"

"She didn't like children."

"How would you know she didn't like children?"

"Because I asked you, and you didn't know. You always know if people like children."

"This may strike you as odd, but we hardly went to the playground on our dates."

"You don't have to go to a playground," she said. "It's in the way they cock their head when they hear a child's laughter, or the little smile on their face when they see a child on a bicycle with training wheels."

The way they look when a little boy shows them his pet chicken.

His fingers came to life, played sweetly with a tangle in her damp hair.

"Why wouldn't you even talk to me, Meg?" he finally asked gruffly, and yet she heard the pain in his voice, and felt the sting of how she had behaved. She knew it could be perceived as cruel.

There was no point in telling him she had suffered, too. None.

Talk to him? How could she? The sound of his voice would have weakened her resolve at a time when she most needed to be strong.

For him.

There was an expression—maybe part of a song—*cruel to be kind.*

"I couldn't," she said, and that was the truth.

His chest heaved under where her cheek was laid against it.

"There's things we need to talk about," he said. "Logistical things."

If her refuge was art, this was his. Logistics. The science of making things work.

"Such as?"

"Have you looked at the separation agreement?"

He took her silence as an answer. He sighed. "Have you even got a lawyer?"

A lawyer? To deal with Morgan? It made sense, of course. It would be a good way to keep her distance while the *logistics* were looked after. And yet, the very thought of using a lawyer to communicate with Morgan turned her stomach.

She considered the possibility that legal representation, advice, paper, documents, made everything permanent and irrevocable.

But isn't that what needed to happen? Exactly?

Was she not taking the next steps because she hoped she would weaken? That this would all be a nightmare that she could put behind her?

Wasn't this, after all, enough? To be together? To live in the ecstasy that came from being in one another's arms?

No! Nature had assigned a purpose to what had just transpired between them! The purpose was the children she could not give him. That he needed, desperately, to make his life what it had once been.

Whole. Happy.

"You're entitled to half," he said. His fingers had stopped playing in her hair.

"I don't want half, Morgan."

"Oh, right," he said, and the faintest bitterness closed in around the edges of the beautiful afterglow. "You can't handle the lifestyle. Still, in our province, there's a legal requirement. You get half. I don't care what you do with it. Give it to a charity if you can't handle it."

That's what she would do, she decided. She would give it to a charity. His charity.

"How is everything at Out of the Ashes?" she asked him.

Her question made Morgan contemplate the twists and turns of life. Once, his life had seemed entirely predictable.

And then the fire had come, torn through the beloved family cottage and taken his brother, his sister-in-law and his niece and nephew, a harsh reminder that chaos waited at the gates of the most ordered of lives. A man thinking life was predictable was the grandest of illusions.

He'd met Meg at her first art show, in an upscale gallery in Vancouver. He'd stood before her painting *Out of the Ashes*, and he had felt the most dangerous thing of all.

Hope.

The painting depicted a burned-out hull of a building with one tender sapling growing out of the rubble. Against that grim backdrop, the new tree was reaching its tender, brilliant green leaves toward a bright sun.

He had been shocked at the coincidence that the painting bore the same name as the charity he had just started to honor his lost family members.

He had purchased the painting with a sense of urgency, needing to have it before someone else snapped it up. He knew that this work of art would become the official image of his fledgling charity.

"Would you like to meet the artist?" the gallery owner had asked him.

And then she was there. Shy. Blond hair swept up around an exquisite, delicate face. Green eyes huge, promising incredible depth of spirit. She'd been wearing a simple black dress, no jewelry and hardly any makeup. She kept tugging at the hem of that dress, self-consciously, as if she didn't have the most beautiful legs in the room.

Possibly in all of Vancouver.

Meg Lawson had been extraordinarily beautiful, and totally unaware of her beauty. From the moment his eyes had connected with hers, he had felt it. Her incredible intensity.

The earth moving under his feet.

That sapling within him, pushing relentlessly through the

rubble that was his heart. He had allowed himself—foolishly, it seemed now—to hope.

He had allowed himself to believe he and Meg could rebuild. Not replace what he had lost but honor it.

As it turned out, she had losses, too.

The loss of her brother, just like him.

They understood each other in ways that no other person could. She alleviated the deep loneliness his walk with sorrow had caused him.

They had slowly uncovered each other's stories. Hers was filled with tragedy. The brother with a disability, the single mom, spirit-numbing poverty and challenges, the death of the brother, and her mom's slide into despair and addiction.

He understood that kind of despair that her mother suffered, and at the same time, Meg allowed him to see how much he had to be grateful for.

He had known the security of love and family, he had been so sure in his knowledge of it that he had taken it for granted.

When he shared stories of his family with her, he saw her deep longing for what he had always had.

And he thought he could give it to her. They longed, after all, for exactly the same thing, though they came at that longing from different directions.

He wanted what he once had with a desperation that frightened him.

She longed for what she had never had with equal desperation.

They both wanted a family.

That place to call home, the destination the heart longed for, where you were secure in your place, where you felt safe, protected, accepted, valued.

But then Meg, the one he was counting on to be his partner as he reengaged in the journey of life, had just become another bitter reminder of how unpredictable that life was, and what a terrible force hope could be, like a fickle woman, teasing, promising, then withdrawing.

He'd just made love to his wife in the fury of a storm. A case in point about life's unpredictability. Because he could not have predicted this moment, and if he had been able to, he would have predicted that he had the strength to resist it.

"How is everything at Out of the Ashes?" she asked, again.

"We're going to build a children's camp on part of the land around Sarah's Reach," he told her. "That's what should be there. When I think of the sound of children's laughter over that lake again, it makes me feel—"

How much was he willing to reveal to her? It made him feel less wounded. It made him feel as if good could come from bad. It made him feel as if he wasn't completely powerless in the face of tragedy. That he could do something.

"Good." He finished his sentence abruptly.

Her hand squeezed his. He wanted to jerk it away, at the same time he wanted this moment with her.

Maybe even needed it.

A beggar satisfied with any kind of crumb.

"What's going on with your art?" he asked her, sliding his hand from hers.

If only it was so easy to pull his heart away.

Meg felt him pull his hand away.

She contemplated what Morgan had just told her. It emphasized, really, how important and how correct her decision had been.

She knew when he had hesitated over finishing that line about how he felt. He had almost said *happy*.

And then he had deliberately watered it down.

Still, she knew the truth. When Morgan thought of happiness, whether he was aware of it or not, he thought of children.

What she could not give him.

And the subject that haunted her paintings, now. The gallery she was working with in Ottawa was begging for new things.

But she could not part with her most recent work. Not yet.

They were of families, mostly beach scenes. Children, focused intently on buckets and shovels, a baby under an umbrella with mom and dad, she reading a book while he kept an eye on the kids.

Her favorite was one of two young boys on a wooden platform-style float, out in a lake, pushing each other into the water, one captured forever, head thrown back in laughter, arms flailing, midair, about to hit the water.

Meg was aware she had never experienced anything like that.

Morgan's longing was her longing, too. She was painting not what she knew, but what she had hoped for.

What he knew.

And what he would have again if she could just be strong enough.

Without warning, a chicken, with a great flapping of wings, got itself up on the table with them.

It settled in the middle of Morgan's naked belly.

It broke, thankfully, whatever intensity had been building between them, and he sat up, laughing. Meg sat up beside him.

The chicken slid away, but sat beside him, and then cocked its head, regarded him, and jumped right onto his lap, settling itself again.

His hands closed around it, stroking it.

Meg looked at his face, and the small smile that played across the curve of the lips that had just possessed her.

In his unguarded expression, she could see every single thing the chicken, by instinct, sensed.

Such a good man. Strong, gentle, caring.

Her heart felt as if it would break when she thought of how he would have looked holding their baby.

Could she paint that? A father looking down at the miracle of the child he had helped create, the child he had made a decision to bring into the world?

She didn't think she could paint that. And on the other hand, is that not what painting was about?

Capturing the essential moments of life?

Watching him with that chicken just confirmed what she already knew. There were things that were essential to Morgan's life that she could not give him.

And then, as abruptly as it had begun, the rain stopped.

The sun came out, and rainbows danced at the edges of that waterfall they had stood naked beneath. Birds called out, and the chicken in Morgan's lap stretched out its wings, clucked fondly, and then leaped from his lap. The water dripped—*plop, plop, plop*—off the edges of the roof, and the soaked leathery leaves of the jungle-like foliage around them.

And then, Morgan cocked his head. "Someone's coming."

She sensed a change in his whole demeanor, his armor sliding back into place. At first she didn't hear anything, but then she heard voices coming from the direction of the resort.

He reached into the open packet of clothes, and handed her a pair of shorts, and he pulled on one of the white T-shirts.

They were dressed just in the nick of time, too.

A small army of golf carts, led by Keona, came around a twist in the trail. Jonathon was driving another one, all the groomsmen riding with him.

They stopped at the first washout, and the men, armed with shovels, all hopped out of the golf carts and cleared the mud and debris within seconds.

This was one of the most admirable things about Jonathon and Morgan and the group of guys they hung out with.

Despite being amongst the wealthiest people in the world, they all carried an air of humility about them. They were hardworking, willing to do what it took to get the job done.

As the rescue team got back on their golf carts, Morgan turned to her.

"I'm sorry," he said, his voice a low growl. "That was a new low. Taking advantage of a woman after she's had a couple drinks."

Meg felt as if he had slapped her. What had happened between them was a new low? What had happened between them needed an apology?

"I was not—am not—drunk," she snapped, but the little army of golf carts arrived before she could pursue it further.

Jonathon and the others came toward them. Jon was a good-looking man, tall and well-built, his coloring dark like Caylee's.

They were going to make beautiful, curly-haired babies with enormous brown eyes.

Babies.

Again she thought of that. The gift she could not ever give Morgan. It should have given her an imperative reason to resist all her impulses.

Morgan had been right. She may not have been drunk, but certainly her inhibitions had fled her. Participating in that dance hadn't helped. It had put her in touch with her sensual side, unleashed her desires, made her eager to embrace everything it meant to be a woman.

As if just being with him wasn't enough to do that.

Jonathon took them in with a quick glance.

"Matching outfits," he said with a raise of his eyebrow. "Cute. Like the von Trapp family singers wearing their matching curtains."

"We were soaked. We changed." Morgan's tone did not invite more questioning.

Meg was sure what had just transpired between her and Morgan was written all over their faces—like guilty children with the chocolate from the stolen cookies smeared around their lips—but all she saw in Jonathon's face, underlying his teasing tone, was relief that they were safe.

And if he suspected something had transpired between them, their friend was likely nothing but happy about it.

"Beginning to think the wedding is cursed," Jonathon said good-naturedly, clapping Morgan on the shoulder and wrapping her in a quick, hard hug.

"It's me," she said. "I'm cursed. Whenever I travel to a new place you can count on bad things happening."

Jonathon gave her a bemused look. "Really? All the events of the world fall on your shoulders?"

When he put it like that, it did seem ridiculous.

"Flash flood warnings started coming on our phones and we realized you two were unaccounted for."

The guys quickly enveloped them, joking about them being pranked for a survival show. Apparently, they had hoped to find Morgan in a loin cloth, and Meg roasting a freshly caught chicken over a spit.

She *loved* the camaraderie Morgan had with his friends. It was one of the ways she had managed to stop herself from going back to him.

Knowing he was surrounded with *this*.

Back-clapping, and boisterous laughter, and teasing, and underneath all that, running so deep, the strength of men's friendships.

"Have Caylee's parents arrived?" Meg asked Jonathon when the noise had settled down a bit.

"No parents, no wedding regalia."

"At least we have a backup plan for that," Meg said.

"Caylee showed me the pictures. You missed your calling,

Meggie, you could be one of those bloggers or influencers or whatever they're called this week."

He put his hands on his hips, leaned toward her and did the pursing thing with his lips.

She laughed, but she noticed Morgan didn't.

"Mr. and Mrs. Hart," Keona said, pulling up to them.

Jonathon raised an eyebrow when neither of them corrected him, but Morgan deflected. "Please. Just Morgan."

"And Meg," she agreed quickly.

Was she blushing? Was what had transpired between them obvious to a casual observer? Would Morgan think it was amusing, like two high school kids caught necking behind the athletics storage shed?

She glanced at his face and swallowed.

He had not laughed at Jonathon's lighthearted imitation of her, and did not seem to think this was funny, at all.

In fact, as the passion that had caught like fire between them was doused, Morgan's expression was distinctly grim.

"Thank goodness you're all right," Keona said. "We've been trying to text you."

The last thing either of them had been doing was checking their phones over the last hour or so!

"Is everyone else accounted for?" Morgan asked, always *that* guy, who understood priorities, who was genuinely concerned about others.

"We have one other couple trapped on the other side of that," Keona nodded toward where mud clogged the road behind them. "But they've been texting us."

"You guys can head back," Jonathon said. "I'll help dig out."

They said nothing as they gathered their packages and then followed Keona to where a large group of men were muscling their golf cart off the rock it had lodged on. Once successful, one of them took it for a quick spin to make sure it was still in working order.

Meg hated it that Morgan wouldn't look at her.

As if they were Adam and Eve in the garden, and they had just tasted the forbidden fruit.

And he was ashamed of the weakness that had driven him to it.

"Can you drive the cart back yourself?" Morgan asked her. "I'd like to help dig out, too."

"Of course," she said. But she read in between the lines.

He probably did want to help out. He and Jonathon would always be those two guys you could rely on to be decent. But Meg suspected Morgan's desire to help out was not nearly as strong as his desire to get away from her.

Well, she'd show him she wanted to get away from him, too!

She stepped on the accelerator of the golf cart. Rather than making a graceful exit, it jerked unbecomingly for several feet, stalled, jerked again, and then, rather than sweeping away, she trundled off to the snickers of the road crew behind her.

Meg drove herself back to the resort, marveling at how the sun was shining again. Except for the occasional palm frond lying across the path, Kauai was once more a tropical paradise, as if nothing had happened.

Meg was well aware it wasn't going to be as easy for her and Morgan to pretend their private storm had not happened.

She parked the golf cart and gathered the packages.

Caylee practically fell on her as she made her way down the path.

"I've been so worried."

Her friend held her back and looked at her appraisingly. "Have you been drinking?"

Oh, geez. "A bit. By accident. I didn't know it had so much alcohol in it."

Caylee cocked her head. "I'm not sure that's what's causing that look."

"What look?"

"You look—" Caylee paused, searching for the right word.

"What?" she snapped.

"Radiant!"

"Snatching your life back from the jaws of death will do that for you."

"Was it terrifying?"

She thought of Morgan's lips on her, of the passion between them, of how she was going to keep that at bay for another few days.

"Terrifying," she agreed.

"When that rain started to come down, the first thing I wondered was where you and Morgan were. The box with the wedding clothes in it was found. It nearly got here, but then the plane had to divert because of the storm. Our wedding clothes are sitting on the Big Island at the moment."

"Oh, dear."

"And Mom and Dad are getting closer! San Francisco, at the moment. The storm here is what has delayed them now."

"They have to get here!"

Caylee flapped a hand languidly, again astonishing Meg with her laid-back attitude. "What will be will be. That's *aloha* apparently. Go have a shower and then come to my cottage and let me look at what you got. And then let's hook up with the rest of my entourage—"

They both giggled at the fact a girl from their neighborhood had an entourage!

"—and then go to the spa. We're glamming up for the wedding. The whole deal—manicures, pedicures and facials!"

And then they giggled again, because they both came from a neighborhood where people not only did not have entourages, but they didn't even work at the spa. They worked at big-box stores, and in housekeeping at care homes. The spa? They sneered at those high-and-mighty snobby, pampered types, while maybe harboring a secret envy.

Caylee looped her arm through Meg's and it felt, impossibly and deliciously, as if everything was okay in the world.

CHAPTER ELEVEN

AN HOUR OR so later, the five women of the wedding party—the entourage, as Caylee was now calling them—had all gathered in Caylee's cottage. One thing that Meg had never expected when she had packed her bag and moved across the country was how much she would miss her friends.

Most of these women had been her circle—just as Morgan had his circle—since she had still been in her teens.

Meg and Caylee had known each other since first grade. They had met Samantha at a throw-together beach volleyball game when they were all just out of high school. The boys they had been trying to impress that day were but a memory, but the friendship had stood the test of time.

A year or so later, Allie had joined them after a hysterical night at a karaoke bar. Her rendition of "My Heart Is a Stone" could set cats within a one-mile radius into a caterwauling competition with her. After three glasses of wine, it still didn't take any coaxing at all to get her to sing it.

Becky, the quietest of them, was a writer whom Meg had met through artsy circles. The five of them had an unbreakable bond. They had each other's backs through it all, and there had been so much that had happened to them all in the seven or so years they had hung out together.

A lot of it involved men, of course: hookups, breakups, makeups.

But a lot of it didn't. Becky had her first children's book

published. Meg had done the illustrations for it. What a celebration that had been! And for at least a year after, every member of that group was selling copies to strangers on the subway out of their purses.

Samantha graduated from university and was working for the best law firm in the city.

Allie had started the most amazing cosmetics company. It had flopped spectacularly, but still, it had been amazing! She was doing something with interior design now.

Caylee got her dream job with an event planning company, and had been able to put all her skills to use on her own wedding.

For a long time, Meg had worked as a cashier at a grocery store. Besides having illustrated Becky's book, she didn't do very well with her dream, which was pursuing a career in art. But then, she sold a few pieces. And then a few more. When a gallery took some of her things on commission, this group of women had made sure that gallery was swarmed.

A year later, she'd had her own show.

And been introduced to Morgan Hart, who wanted one of her paintings to become the official symbol for his charity Out of the Ashes.

Meg shook off that memory, and replaced it with precious ones with girlfriends. Caylee had instigated Adventure Club and they'd taken turns coming up with ideas. Rock climbing, white water rafting, a cattle drive, skydiving.

And yet it was the most simple moments of friendship that shone: admiring somebody's new kitten or kitchen set, watching movies, conducting a book club, grabbing lunch downtown, spending nights at home with a few bottles of wine and guaranteed laughter.

And those friends had meant there was always someone to catch the tears.

Allie had had an accidental pregnancy, as a result of a

one-night stand. The guy had been a jerk about it, and all of them had sworn they would be that baby's family. They had talked and dreamed and bought adorable clothes and planned a nursery. And all of them had been equally heartbroken when she miscarried.

Becky had lost her mother after a long battle with cancer. Samantha had found out her fiancé of four years was a serial cheater.

They had all been a bit shocked that it was Meg who had been the first to get married. And oh, the catch that Morgan Hart was! They had *all* loved him. After the awful experiences Samantha and Allie had had, it had restored some hope to them.

Love was out there!

Then Jonathon had taken up with Caylee and they—independent, career-oriented, adventurous women that they were—had been in absolute delirious fits of joy that happily-ever-after really happened to ordinary women like them.

Meg had not been aware how much she needed these women, her friends, until she had made the choice to leave the warmth of that circle behind her when she left her marriage.

Really, when she needed them most, she had chosen to go alone.

She had chosen a terrible, lonely route for herself.

And her friends had been hurt and angry—not because she had destroyed their newly nurtured hopes in fairy tales—but because they had needed to be there for her.

But how, with all that love around her, could she have kept the secret of *why*? How long before, in a moment of weakness, she confided in one of them?

She trusted them completely. Almost.

Each one, in their own way, would think they knew what

was best for her. Which one of them would have felt compelled to share her secret with Morgan?

Maybe none of them would have.

But it was a chance Meg had not been prepared to take.

Instead, she had deliberately moved away from the temptation of being loved by them. She had nursed her broken heart alone. No one to knock on her door and say—steaming hot lasagna from Pargarios in hand—"Have you eaten?"

No one to bring over a bottle of wine. Or two. Or three.

No one to say "How about bull riding for our next adventure? Or an electric-bike tour of Napa?"

No one to suggest a marathon of sad movies to let the dam of tears burst. Was there anything better, in the whole world, than five women bawling their eyes out at the end of *The Other Side of the Mountain*?

Well, maybe one thing better.

And Meg had just done that one thing with Morgan.

She wondered if these sisters of her heart knew. Or suspected. She felt as if the passionate encounter she had just had with her ex was written all over her.

But they, thankfully, were preoccupied with all things wedding. The topic of Morgan and her failed marriage—and the awkwardness of Meg's reunion with Morgan—were carefully avoided. This led Meg to suspect they might have discussed their strategy in dealing with her beforehand.

Today, only fun, lighthearted wedding stuff was allowed. Caylee tried on the backup bridal dress, and the rest of them all tried on their wine-colored sundresses. They took turns at the mirror and took pictures of each other and oohed and aahed. The focus, interestingly, was not really on the bride nor on the replacement dresses. Instead, each of her friends made it all about Meg and her great taste and her artist's eye, and now much they all missed her.

Their love and acceptance was like water to a person who

had crawled across the desert, sunlight to a person who had been locked away in darkness.

By the time they all linked arms and headed to the spa, Meg told herself she had put the romantic afternoon interlude with Morgan behind her.

"Meg has highly recommended a drink called Pining for You," Caylee told the person taking their drink orders. "One for everybody."

As they lay there on white-sheeted beds, open to the ocean, avocado masks on their faces, Meg was so aware of one thing.

She and Morgan would be together again tonight. Unless, finally, flights were leaving Kauai? Shouldn't she really be checking the availability of a different room instead of lying here, relishing her state of absolute decadence and wallowing in the love of friends she had missed so much?

Aloha, Caylee had said with a wave of her hand. *What will be will be.*

Meg had never been much of a *what will be will be* kind of a person. She liked control. On the other hand, Caylee had never been that person, either, and look at her now after just a few days here.

Kamelei had suggested if you stayed here long enough, you could understand the concept.

So for now, Meg was just going to give herself over to enjoying the experience, even as she acknowledged at least part of her enjoyment was not because of being surrounded by the love of her friends.

It was because Morgan had coaxed a part of her back to life.

The most dangerous part.

The spark was glowing.

Waiting. An ember that could flicker, then sputter, then

gain strength and then roar. A little tiny spark, and a whisper of a breath on it, was all it took to burn a whole world down.

So easy to dismiss that with the turquoise water in the distance, the sounds of waves and chickens and birds, lulling her.

Into a sense that everything could be okay.

She did not touch the slushy drink beside her.

Because if things did unfold, again, between them, she was not going to give Morgan the opportunity to blame it on a Sugarloaf White pineapple slushy.

Though, ironically, the blame could be laid squarely at the feet of one thing.

For eight long months she had been pining for Morgan.

Ridiculous to believe everything would be okay, for even one second, in the face of all the evidence of how wrong things could go. Look how her world had collapsed beyond repair the day that doctor had given her the news.

And yet, lying there on that massage bed, naively, stupidly, happily, believe it she did.

She was not unaware that the fact she had made love with her husband had a great deal to do with this rosy feeling of well-being.

She could let the fact that this was only the briefest respite in her dark journey overshadow that.

Or she could surrender to *aloha*.

And just let whatever happened, happen.

And Meg hoped that involved Morgan's arms wrapping around her—and quite a bit more—again.

Morgan came back to the resort with his friends. They were all tired and dirty, and somehow it felt as if clearing that pathway of storm debris had turned into the best prelude to a bachelor party ever.

It also meant he did not have to encounter Meg. Tonight,

Caylee had scheduled the guys and girls in separate camps.
Girls were at the spa, prepping fingers and toes and faces
for the big day. Then they were planning dinner together and
having a kind of bachelorette party.

So the guys ended up roughhousing by the pool. A couple of them had too much to drink, and the party moved
to Ralph's bungalow. They ordered pizza from the resort's
wood-fired oven, and found a football game to watch on
pay-per-view TV.

Which Morgan was fine with, because once he went back
to that bungalow, how the hell was he going to act normal
around Meg?

He wasn't entirely sure what happened at a bachelorette
party, and he hoped it didn't involve male dancers. Because
if Meg was building on those pineapple slushies of earlier,
that could lead to trouble. She had no idea how beautiful she
was, but guys got it. Look at that drink that had been sent
her way by a complete stranger.

She wasn't, Morgan told himself firmly, *that kind of girl.*

Of course, her abandonment had left him with the distressing knowledge he didn't know her nearly as well as he
thought he did. And that dance she had done seemed as if it
had revealed all her secrets.

How she behaved with male dancers was none of his business, Morgan told himself sternly. The fact that just thinking
about it made him feel faintly angry and faintly protective
meant he was already in big trouble.

Hadn't he proven this afternoon that what she most needed
protecting from was probably him? One thing he knew for
sure, *that* was not happening again.

His phone rang partway through the game. Caylee. He
answered way too fast.

"Thank you for shopping today. Spectacular choices."

"I hope we don't need the backup plan," he said. "Any sign

of the real deal?" He listened for sounds of music. Rowdiness. *Male dancers.*

"On the Big Island. Supposed to be here tomorrow."

"That's cutting it close. Your parents?" He heard women laughing.

"San Francisco at the moment. Fingers crossed they'll be here tomorrow night."

"You must be a nervous wreck."

"Oddly enough, not. Maybe because Meg has introduced us all to the most amazing concoction." She giggled. "Pineappling for You."

That was all he needed to know!

CHAPTER TWELVE

IF THE LADIES were imbibing the pineapple slushies, Morgan knew he had to stay away from Huipu—and Meg—tonight.

Despite telling himself it was none of his business, he heard himself asking what they were planning next for the evening ahead.

"Oh, I'm dragging the ladies away from the slushies now. Nobody's allowed to stumble around and wreck their newly polished toes! Besides, everyone's tired, and you said your plan for tomorrow starts early."

"Sunrise," Morgan reminded her. "Meet on the beach. Don't eat first."

"Sunrise breakfast on the beach!" Caylee said, delighted. "Morgan, you're just the best guy."

"Well, that's why I'm called the best man," he said dryly.

He could hear giggling behind Caylee.

She lowered her voice. "I meant you're the best guy as in *how could anyone let you get away*?"

Meg hadn't let him get away. She'd thrown him back.

But there was absolutely no point arguing semantics with anyone who had indulged in an unknown number of Sugarloaf White pineapple libations.

"Bring a bathing suit," he said, ignoring her invitation to commiserate with her over the unfairness of his wife abandoning him when he was clearly perfect.

"Ladies," Caylee called, "the dress of the day for tomorrow is bikinis. Morgan says the teenier the better."

"I did not say that!" he called, hopefully loud enough for all of them to hear him. Sheesh.

"Ha ha," one of women yelled out. He thought he recognized Becky's voice. She was generally shy which, unfortunately, underscored the inhibition-releasing powers of Pining for You.

"I bet Meg doesn't even own a bikini." This caused raucous laughter and more rowdiness.

"It's just the women there, right?" Morgan asked, against his own orders to himself not to.

"Who else would be here?" Caylee responded, startled.

"I don't know. Sometimes you hear of things getting a little wild and crazy at the bachelorette party."

Silence. "In what way?"

Stop, he ordered himself. "Like in the Mad Mike way."

"Mad Mike?"

He should leave it. He still had a chance to save his dignity. On the other hand, what if Meg needed saving?

"Those guys," he said tersely, "that take their shirts off. And more. While dancing."

"I think you mean Magic," she said dryly. "Are you asking if I have male strippers lined up for my bachelorette party?"

She said that way too loud, and behind her he could hear squeals of what could only be interpreted as excitement.

"Sorry, ladies," she called, "I'm afraid the craziest thing here was avocado masks."

He didn't want to admit, even to himself, how relieved he was.

"Let's stream *that* movie next!" Was that Becky again? Who knew about her secret side?

On that note, Morgan disconnected and put away his phone.

His relief was short lived. What was he going to do about tonight? He'd had enough danger for one day. He was not going back to Huipu to deal with Meg pining for him. But only when her guard was down. Or maybe watched a sexy movie.

The rest of the time, it was *so long, Morgan, have a nice life*.

He ended up sleeping on Ralph's couch. Not because he was drunk, though if people wanted to think that, they could.

He lay awake staring at the ceiling, thinking of her soaked hair, and the feel of her skin and the way her eyes had looked.

She loved him.

But he'd always known that. It only deepened the torment to wonder why—when it was so evident how she felt—she had left him?

It seemed to Morgan he had just gone to sleep when those damn chickens started crowing. He got up feeling not as if there was a great day ahead for him to anticipate, but as if he was a warrior strapping on his armor for battle.

And somehow he wasn't ready for the first battle being going over there to find something to wear, to face Meg in the intimacy of that cottage, sharing the bathroom, going into a shower that still smelled of her.

He stepped over Keith, who was on the floor, and went down to the beach in the predawn darkness. He'd heard the ocean was full of sharks at this time of day. He could only hope!

Fighting off sharks seemed preferable—not to mention easier—than fighting off his attraction to the wife who'd abandoned him.

He stripped off his rumpled shirt and dived into the waves. Swimming in the salty water, with the stars evaporating from the sky above him, Morgan felt as if his strength was restored to him. He felt his resolve hardening.

He wasn't going to beg Meg for an answer as to how she could love him and leave him. What if she denied loving him? Wasn't he in enough pain already?

He wasn't going to fall under her spell again, either. Nothing good lay that way. He had only one mission. He was the best man. It was his job to make sure this wedding went off without a hitch, which included tension, in any variety, particularly between he and Meg.

He only had to get through today. His surprise. And then tomorrow, the wedding. Caylee and Jonathon would be off to the most secluded seaside bungalow Hale Iwa Kai had. But they had invited their guests to enjoy the resort for three more days after the wedding.

Still, nothing said Morgan had to stay. His best man duties would be officially ended. He could make his excuses and leave.

So, two more days of Meg.

Anybody could swear off anything for two days. In the span of the cosmos that was nothing. A speck of dust.

After his swim, he sat on the beach, his arms folded around his knees, and watched as the world around him came to light. It was beautiful and for a moment his troubles and torments seemed as miniscule as that cosmic speck of dust that was time.

One by one, the other members of the group joined him. He was so aware when Meg came, in an oversize sun hat, dark glasses and a swim cover-up.

If anybody thought it was unusual that he was wet and shirtless, they didn't comment. He suspected, like him, they were caught in the complete enchantment of a new day beginning in this mystical land.

Only Meg would know the shirt lying beside him in the sand was the same one he had worn yesterday, familiar with it because she had peeled it from him. Meg noticed details, regardless. It was part of her artistic nature.

In fact, when he slid her a glance, Meg did seem to be taking in the details of his naked chest with way too much interest! He picked up the shirt—crumpled as it was—and put it on. He should have shaken it first. It was full of sand. She raised an eyebrow at him.

"Where's the promised feast?" Jonathon growled. "We're starving."

"I don't see anything to eat," Caylee said, looking up and down the empty beach, her hands on her hips. "We've been summoned here under false pretenses. Let's throw Morgan into the ocean."

"He's already been in. It's not as if we're throwing him off an ice floe in Antarctica," Ralph pointed out.

But why let the facts spoil a good dunking? It was too late. His buddies grabbed him, two on his arms and two on his legs and splashed out into the surf with him to give him the old heave-ho. Everybody was laughing. He found himself laughing, too.

How long since he had laughed?

Allowed himself to feel like a part of something?

It felt more than good. It felt wonderful.

And despite all his guards, and all his best efforts, did he link this ability to laugh, to feel wonderful, to yesterday and to the part of him Meg had unleashed?

The part of him that wanted to live?

"What is that?" Becky asked before the count to three was completed.

The guys released him without tossing him to the sea, and everyone turned toward a sailboat coming into the cove.

"That," Morgan said, "is breakfast. In fact, we're going to spend the whole day on the MeloMelo."

His surprise for the wedding party was a private charter of

a sixty-five-foot powered catamaran that also worked under sail, if the winds were right. Booking the super luxury yacht had, admittedly, been a bit of a dig at Meg. *You think can't handle the lifestyle?*

Check this out.

Okay, maybe he even hoped to make her sorry for everything she had left behind.

Though his motives weren't all tainted by Meg.

"Apparently the only way to experience the true majesty of the Napali Coast is from the ocean," he explained to the group. "The MeloMelo will give us the best vantage point, plus there's planned stops at famous snorkeling spots, including Lehua Crater, and one off the Forbidden Island of Niihau."

"Why's it called forbidden?" Caylee asked.

Good question. Did forbidden things happen there? His mind drifted to the forbidden thing he'd indulged in yesterday. He deferred to his phone. Meg was watching him closely, as if she knew where his mind had gone.

"'It was closed to visitors during a polio epidemic to safeguard the residents, and that's when it became known as the Forbidden Island,'" he read, "'but even before that the family that bought it from King Kamehameha in the 1800s promised to preserve Hawaiian culture and language, so development and visitors have always been limited.'"

"Oh," Caylee cried, as the vessel launched boats to come and get them. "Morgan! It couldn't be more perfect. What a wonderful foil to all the frazzle of the last few days."

See? It was that easy to be the best man. He had made the bride happy and that was all that counted. Wasn't it?

CHAPTER THIRTEEN

MEG HAD TROUBLE keeping her eyes off her shirtless ex-husband. That interlude yesterday had made her feel as if she was starving—and not for breakfast, either.

She had lain awake waiting for him to come back to their suite. She had deliberately refused drinks at the spa. She was determined Morgan wasn't going to regret their lovemaking this time. He wasn't going to blame it on her being under the influence.

She knew she was playing with fire.

But she couldn't stop herself. What if she never saw him again after this wedding? What if they signed those papers and went their separate ways?

Oh, sure, they'd probably meet at weddings. And anniversaries. Birthday parties.

Showers, baptisms, those events that celebrated what she couldn't give him.

But life might never hand them this again: this opportunity to be so intensely together. She knew it was wrong to want him so badly. She knew it was wrong to give in to the temptation to touch him, to taste him, to possess him.

To have him possess her.

But she was like an addict who had been promised one more spectacular fix before heading into a life of abstinence.

She was an addict who wanted one more chance not to feel pain.

She wanted just one more memory to carry into a bleak, lonely, future with her.

But looking at Morgan, in the same shorts he had worn yesterday, his rumpled shirt, also from yesterday, she recognized they were at cross-purposes. He had obviously slept on someone's couch to avoid her.

And of course, he was right.

Of course that was the reasonable thing to do.

And yet, watching that sailboat pull into the cove, the wind filling the vibrant colors of its billowing sails, Meg surrendered to the sensation of being in a place of pure magic.

Where anything could—and would—happen. *Had* happened.

Consequences be damned. Consequences belonged in that world she would go back to. And she would be there for a very long time.

Here? Here she had—she counted them on her fingers— five more days. Today, the wedding tomorrow, and three days following that. She felt like someone who had been given a life sentence ordering their last meal, being given one more chance to experience the fullness and the vibrancy of life itself.

She was suddenly glad that, underneath her very modest swim cover, was the bathing suit Caylee had talked her into borrowing.

Becky had been quite right last night. Meg did not own a bikini. She owned practical one-piece bathing suits with racing backs that were made for swimming.

Caylee had opened her closet to an assortment of bathing suits, most purchased just for her Hawaiian honeymoon. None of them had been worn, and in fact, most of them still had the price tags on them.

Her circle of friends had insisted Meg try on half a dozen of the skimpiest numbers.

The try-ons had stopped when she had put on the one she now had on underneath her swim cover.

It was black. It was tiny. It was the kind of swimsuit that was featured in that famous February issue of the sports magazine.

When she had looked at herself in it, she had expected to feel utterly ridiculous. Instead, Meg had felt, fully, her own power.

She had known Morgan didn't have a chance.

And yet, standing here on the beach, watching boats come in to pick them up and ferry them out to the MeloMelo, she felt a sudden flagging—not her mission, but her courage to accomplish it.

The dilemma: she couldn't have him if she'd been drinking. He'd made that clear.

And yet she wasn't sure how she'd find the nerve to get out of the swimsuit cover without a little liquid encouragement.

In fact, she needn't have worried. She was soon totally immersed in exactly the lifestyle she had told Morgan she couldn't handle.

What was to handle? Meg mused. There were more staff members than guests on the incredible yacht, catering to their every whim. The excursion Morgan was treating the wedding party to seemed to be designed around one goal and one goal only, and that was to give the clients an experience of pure bliss.

Breakfast on the deck of the MeloMelo consisted of an amazing selection of rare cheeses, local fruits, freshly baked croissants and just-squeezed orange juice, with or without a splash of champagne.

The delectable feast was served on fine china with real silverware. As they enjoyed breakfast, they passed the longest stretch of beach in Hawaii, Polihale. Then they began to see the wonders of the Napali coastline, which cruise leader Leilani referred to as *sacred*.

Indeed, Meg had a deep sense of the sacred all around her as she listened to Leilani explain how this geographical marvel had been created by five million years of volcanic activity and erosion.

Five million years. It gave Meg a sense of her own struggles—and even her own existence—being put in perspective.

They cruised by four-thousand-foot cliffs, hidden beaches, deep sea caves and breathtaking lava arches. Because of yesterday's rainfall, the waterfalls that cascaded down the face of those sheer drops were abundant and spectacular.

Meg felt inconsequential and it made her troubles and challenges fade into the background.

In the shadow of the sacred, she made a vow to not let *thoughts*—especially thoughts about Morgan—bother her, to intrude on this experience.

She vowed the rest of her time here in paradise would just be about full immersion in the sensations that enveloped her.

There would be plenty of time to think after the wedding, once she left Hawaii and *aloha* behind her. For now, she recognized this was the most exquisite gift she could have been given, and she was being asked to embrace it all.

With that vow, she took in the sights and sounds and scents of her friends, the yacht, the ocean and the Napali Coast with an overwhelming sense of delight. She thought the coast and those incredible mountains should be one of the Seven Wonders of the World. It was so stunningly beautiful.

Everyone on board, including the crew, seemed to understand they had been invited to an experience that was rare and compelling.

A kind of quiet reverence—like the deepest of prayers— seemed to infuse everyone on board that vessel.

Midmorning they paused in a beautiful cove and the passengers were invited to swim. There was even a slide from the top deck down into the water!

The quietness they had all experienced seemed to give birth to a kind of exuberance, especially for the men. The guys needed no encouragement, unselfconsciously tossing off their shirts and lining up at the top of the slide, pushing and shoving playfully.

Morgan took his turn. Hands up, head thrown back in laughter, he catapulted down the slide. Maybe she had not even realized how the shadows had become so much a part of him, until that moment when they were completely erased.

Meg felt her love for him, in the joy his happiness made her feel. There was no need to think about tomorrow, she could just relish in his happiness for today.

And her own. She contemplated the delicious feeling inside of her and scrambled up the stairs to the top of the slide.

"It looks like a death spiral," Becky said pensively. She had never been fond of heights. She was the only one who had opted out of the skydiving adventure.

Becky also brought up the possibility of sharks.

There was a delay as Caylee pointed out no one was to get sunburns or strap lines that would spoil the wedding pictures. Sunscreen—provided by a crew that anticipated their every need—had to be applied.

Meg didn't even hesitate to peel off the swim cover and stand there in her bathing suit. If anything, the skimpiness of it made her feel *more* immersed in the experience. She *wanted* the sun and the water to kiss the very same skin Morgan had kissed yesterday. She wanted her body to be baptized by the mountains and the ocean and the very air.

She felt exquisitely, wonderfully, joyously sensual.

So even the potential of sharks and sunburn—and all the other unknown dangers that lurked—could not take that feeling away from Meg. Of being fully alive. Of being determined to delight in whatever gifts were given to her today.

"I'll go first," she said, and stepped up to the top of the slide. Before the other part of her—cautious, adverse to risk—could take over, she plunked herself down and launched.

Becky had been right! It was a death spiral! She was going way too fast, but there was no way to slow herself down.

And so she surrendered, and felt the pure exhilaration of it. She flew off the end of that slide feeling not as if she'd been shot from a cannon, but as though she was able to fly.

The water was gorgeous. Pure and refreshing. It closed over her head. She went down and down and down. And then felt the ocean lifting her back up, as if she was an offering it was spitting out.

When her head popped above the water, she lifted her arms in triumph to the cheering of her friends.

And then the cheering stopped abruptly.

She lowered her arms and scanned the water. Had the dreaded shark been spotted?

Then she saw the item everyone suddenly seemed fixated on.

She squinted at it. What? A jellyfish?

Fear tried to penetrate her sense of euphoria, but it couldn't. Then she saw that tiny, floating black object was even worse than a shark. Or a jellyfish.

Moving on the playful swirl of current created by her splash—and moving right toward Morgan—was her tiny black bikini top.

The strangest thing happened.

She didn't feel embarrassed. At all. In fact, she shouted with laughter.

And then Meg was in very real danger of drowning as she used her hands and arms to cover herself, instead of to keep her head above water. She went under and breathed some water in. She rose, coughing and flailing but still laughing.

And then Morgan was there.

"Hey," he said, getting one shoulder under her arm, and treading water.

Here she was topless in the South Pacific, with all her friends looking on, and her nearly ex-husband rescuing her. It should have been one of the most embarrassing moments of her life.

But it wasn't.

"Hey," she said back, and it felt as if it was just the two of them. And then he was laughing, too.

"Do you have my top?"

He held it up to her like a kid who had captured the flag. And then he wedged his body between her and everyone else. Her exposed breasts were nearly touching him. Of course, she couldn't press against him in front of people!

But he was being so effective in blocking them!

He was just as effective at blocking her, somehow keeping an arm's length between them as he slipped the loop of the bikini strap over her head and behind her neck.

She tugged it into place. When he swam behind her and did up the string knot at the back, the brief touch of his hands was exquisite and intimate, blending beautifully with Meg's decision to enjoy everything.

"I'm doing it up nice and tight."

"Thank you," she said.

"But I'm not sure this *thing* can withstand the slide again. It wasn't exactly made for it."

She glanced over her shoulder, met his eyes, and grinned. She could feel the invitation to be playful—something she had rarely been in her whole life, let alone in the last few months—sparking in the air around them.

"Let's find out," she said. She splashed him in the face, then raced back to the ladder of the yacht. "Last one back down is a rotten egg."

She was only partway up the ladder when his hands circled her waist and he pulled her down and tossed her back into the ocean. He scrambled up the ladder. He was on the second rung when she regained herself and went after him. She got her hands on the waist band of his shorts and pulled.

Hard.

"Hey!" he said, indignant. He reached back with one hand, the other still firmly on the ladder. He tried to yank the fabric from her hands. She held on tight.

"No sense just one of us being exposed," she cackled with delight.

"Full moon on the MeloMelo," Jonathon yelled.

Morgan twisted hard, broke free, but lost his balance and tumbled back into the water. Chortling gleefully, she hefted herself up the ladder and ran across the deck. She raced up the stairs of the yacht, but by the time she was back at the slide, he was right behind her.

She launched herself, arms thrown wide. He hit the water right behind her.

"Best out of three," he called, already nearly to the ladder. Jonathon was part way up it, and turned and gave him a hand. Then shouting like schoolboys, Morgan and Jonathon ran up the sets of steps to the ladder, and came down the slide nearly together.

Everybody was soon infected with the joyous abandon of a game that really didn't have a purpose or a winner or loser. It was just a wild ride to see who could get down the slide and back up to the top of it the fastest. And then come down it the most creatively. People came down the slide in twos, and they came down backwards, they lay flat and they slid on their bellies.

The air rang with squeals and shouts and laughter.

Caught up in it, still in some kind of race with Morgan, though she was pretty sure he had lapped her twice, Meg was at the top of the slide again.

She dived onto it, on her belly, hands extended in front of her. She felt like superwoman flying down that wet, slippery slide.

When she hit the water, she suddenly lost her superpowers. In fact, Meg felt her right arm fold behind her at a strange angle. The pain was instant and immense.

There was an exuberant shout behind her. Meg looked over her shoulder Morgan was flying down it. He was going to land right on top of her!

She was going to die, her pain-filled mind informed her dutifully.

But the part of her that was not dutiful at all, the renegade who had just been released, thought, right through the pain, *But what a way to go.*

CHAPTER FOURTEEN

"MOVE!" MORGAN YELLED at Meg. But, defiantly she didn't. Somehow he managed to grab the sides of the slide just enough to slow himself down. By some miracle, he managed to twist in midair at the last moment so that he didn't crash into Meg.

When he surfaced, he was laughing, but he felt the laughter die when he looked at her face, which was now white with pain. It wasn't playful defiance after all. He swam over to her in two quick strokes.

"What happened?" He wanted to kiss the pain off her face!

"I hit the water wrong," she managed to croak, "I've hurt my shoulder. I can't move my arm."

"Which one?"

"Right."

He looked at her submersed shoulder and felt his heart sink as he peered through the water and saw the weird angle of skin and bone. It was evident to him it was dislocated.

"Your damned curse," he said, softly. "You know there's a sign right at the top of the slide that warns about going down headfirst?"

He used his stern voice to distract her—or maybe himself—as he went over to her uninjured side, getting his shoulder under her arm for the second time today.

"Look, if there's any more rescues, I'll have to start charging you," he said. "I'm not a fireman."

"Oh," she teased, "firemen."

How he missed *this*. Being teased by her.

"What would you charge me?" she said huskily. Even with her in pain *that* was leaping and sizzling in the air between them.

"I'll think about it."

"Okay," she said, a little dreamily. He was pretty sure she was going into shock.

He felt her arm curl around him, the full length of very wet, slippery, nearly naked self press up against his side. But she groaned with pain every single time he moved.

Somehow, inch by torturous inch, he managed to get her to the side of the boat, and then scoop her into his arms and get her up the ladder and on board.

The joyous shouts evaporated as the group realized there had been an accident. Morgan deposited Meg in a lounge chair, and then quickly—like a jealous lover—found a towel to flick over her while the member of the crew who did first aid raced up with the kit and dropped to his knees beside her.

The man looked vaguely familiar.

"Your shoulder is dislocated." He confirmed Morgan's suspicion in an Aussie accent. "I can try and put it back in. It'll hurt like hell, but then the relief will be almost instant."

"Leave it," Morgan said, at the same time Meg said, "Yes, please."

Morgan raced up the deck looking for his clothes, retrieved his cellphone. He was sure he could have a helicopter here in a few minutes. He didn't care what it cost, he was getting her to the hospital.

Then he heard her scream.

He dropped the phone and raced back across the deck.

Meg had her head buried in Caylee's shoulder, sobbing.

"I told you not to," he snapped at the crew member.

"She looked as if she was old enough to make her own

decision," he snapped back. Morgan felt an unreasonable desire to punch him in the nose.

"Morgan," Meg told him, backing away from Caylee, "it's good. It's such a relief." Meg lifted her head, smiling through the tears at the first aid guy. "Thank you. I don't know how you knew what to do, Andy."

Andy? When had they come to be on a first-name basis?

"I'm Australian."

Like we couldn't tell from the accent, Morgan thought, but the thought gave him pause. Why, exactly, was he so hostile?

"I worked as a lifeguard at Bondi Beach," Andy said. "Dislocations are one of the most common injuries there."

He seemed to be speaking to Meg alone. She, naturally, beamed at him.

Honestly? An Australian lifeguard? Who had just rescued her from an afternoon of intolerable pain? It was worse than a fireman.

In fact, Andy seemed worse than Magic Mike! And not that he knew anything about those performances, but they did play on women's weaknesses for things like firemen and lifeguards.

Morgan realized, shocked at himself, he was jealous. Well, of course he was jealous! Meg was his wife. She looked unbelievable in that black bathing suit. Okay, the suit was covered with the towel.

But she still looked unbelievable, her wet hair tangled around her face, her green eyes huge, her lips faintly puffy.

Plus, Andy had probably seen her running by at least half a dozen times to get back to the slide.

It occurred to Morgan, current suspicions about Andy having designs on his wife, aside, that he and Meg had been having fun together.

Which he had thought would never happen again.

This hope stirring in him was the worst possible thing!

Look at how it was making him react to Andy. As if Meg was *his*.

She lifted her arm experimentally. "It feels tender, but better."

"I think maybe we should turn back," Caylee suggested, but reluctantly. "We'll cut the trip short, and have you checked out by a doctor."

"No! I'm fine now. I wouldn't dream of spoiling the day for everyone else."

"The worst of it is over," Andy said. He went into his first aid kit and pulled out a packet. He took a pen out of his pocket and wrote something on it. He grinned at Meg and handed her the packet. "In Australia, on Bondi, you would have got the famous green whistle to alleviate the pain. The best I can do here is this."

She took the packet. "What is it?"

"Just over-the-counter painkillers and anti-inflammatories. What's that famous line? Take two aspirin and call me."

The saying was actually *Take two aspirin and call me in the morning*, Morgan thought suspiciously. He glanced at the packet and realized those weren't instructions Andy had written on it. It was his phone number!

"Hey," he growled at Andy, suddenly knowing why he looked familiar, "were you at the shopping village yesterday? During the hula show?"

Andy gave him a baffled look.

Which meant men who found her attractive were coming out of the woodwork! And they all looked the same.

"Right then," Andy said, "I'm going to immobilize it, anyway."

Morgan thought it was very unfair that Australian men just needed to open their mouths and women seemed to find them sexy. He knew that was immature, and he didn't care.

"I'll look after the sling," Morgan said firmly. "I've had first aid training."

Andy stood back and looked at him, and then looked at Meg. Understanding dawned in his eyes.

Morgan wanted to thump on his chest and say *Mr. Hart* and point at her and say *Mrs. Hart*, just so that there were no further misunderstandings on Andy's part.

But Andy seemed to get it completely. He slipped back into purely professional mode as he addressed Meg. "You should take it easy for the rest of the day. If it gives you any trouble, go to the hospital when we dock again."

He searched through his kit and handed Morgan a square of rough white cotton and some safety pins.

Morgan carefully folded the cloth into a triangle, sat on the edge of Meg's chair and gently secured her arm, way too aware of every single thing about her: the droplets of water in her hair, the beads of it on her eyelashes, the salty smell of her skin, the rise and fall of her chest beneath the towel.

He had to resist the impulse to kiss her on the forehead when he was finished. He stood up quickly. Caylee slipped into the place he had been sitting.

She kissed Meg on the cheek. "Maid of honor in a sling. I should have guessed, and adjusted your dress accordingly."

"Well," Meg said, "it might not have been a sling. It might have been crutches. Or a cast on my foot. There's no predicting the direction the curse will take. Or the future."

Caylee's gaze slid to him, and then back to Meg.

"That's true," she said with soft hopefulness. "There's no predicting what will happen next."

"I'll make a prediction," Andy said.

Morgan turned and looked at him. He thought he had gone.

"There won't be any ill effects," Andy said.

"Your accent is making me swoon," Becky said.

Aha! Just as Morgan thought.

Andy grinned cheekily. "By tomorrow, she'll be right as rain. I mean, I wouldn't go zip lining, or outrigger paddling, but she'll be fine for a walk down the aisle holding a posy.

"And another prediction—lunch and then snorkeling at the crater. Except for you, young lady."

He leaned in as if he was going to pat Meg on her naked knee. Morgan wasn't sure if he made a sound like a growl in his throat, or if his look was enough, but Andy managed to resist the touch to the leg, grabbed his kit by the handle and sauntered off whistling.

Lunch, of course, was exquisite, and the mishap didn't seem to change the dynamic of the day. If anything, it seemed to bring the bonds of the groups' friendship into even sharper focus.

After lunch, the boat anchored off Lehua Crater. Morgan didn't want to enjoy the snorkeling when Meg was sidelined, but she insisted he go.

Reluctantly, he listened to the brief lesson on how to use the snorkel, took the camera that was offered him and went into the water with the others.

His sense of astonishment and wonder was instantaneous. The scene just under the surface of the sea was beyond amazing. Colorful fish—some in huge groups like the yellow ones, and some solitary—swam in and out of a world of coral formations that mirrored the mountain formations above the water.

He took a few pictures, then swam to the ladder, climbed back on the yacht and crouched beside Meg.

"Look at this," he said, scrolling through.

One of the deckhands brought them a laminated card with images of fish on it. Together, Morgan and Meg identified the large school as yellow tangs, a smaller one as convict tangs.

A yellow-and-white-and-black fish with a spectacular fin was a Moorish idol.

Morgan looked at the delight on her face, and had a sudden realization. All this time, had his love for his wife had strings attached?

Unspoken rules?

You must love me back.

You must meet my needs.

He wondered, suddenly, if that was love at all. Wouldn't true love look at the beloved and just genuinely want what was best for them?

Well, maybe not if it involved Andy.

But real love would hold an intention, wouldn't it? That you would always want the best for the other person.

Happiness.

Prosperity.

Peace.

Wouldn't true love require you want that for them, with or without you? Morgan suddenly felt as if he truly understood *aloha*, the spirit of the islands.

It wasn't about getting through the next day and a half with his pride—and his heart—intact. It wasn't about showing her, with a display of wealth like chartering the MeloMelo for a day, what she was missing.

It was about loving her, without strings. Without expectations. Without needing something in return.

Morgan, in that instant, made a vow that he would set aside his personal hurt, pride and feelings and make sure Meg had the best time possible. A gift of pure love to her.

With that in mind, he left her studying the card, jumped back in the water and took more pictures to delight her with. Looking at some extraordinary underwater creature with an eye to sharing his experience with Meg made it, oddly, even more pleasurable.

He loved coming back on deck, sitting beside her on the lounger, water from his hair dripping on her, her uninjured shoulder touching his, as she pored over the photos and then, together they looked them up on the card.

"Look at this one. It's the official state fish of Hawaii," she said, tapping his camera, her eyes round. Then she squinted at the card. "Morgan, look at its name."

He followed her finger to where it was tapping the card. *Humuhumunukunukuapua'a.*

"Say it," she demanded. "Look, the pronunciation is spelled out."

"Hoo-moo-hoo-moo-noo-koo-noo-koo-ah-poo-ah-ah."

She giggled, and then she tried to say it. And then he tried again. And then that damned Andy came along to check on her, glanced at the card, and rattled off the difficult name with annoying ease.

The afternoon melted away as he climbed on and off the boat. And even though sharing with her in this way was fun, Morgan knew if he had to move heaven and earth, he was going to make sure Meg had the real experience some-day, too.

The snorkeling portion of the trip came to an end, and the sailboat was moving on. Morgan pulled a deck chair up next to Meg, and let the sun dry the water off his skin.

Though the rest of the group was there, of course, it felt somehow as if he and Meg had formed a unit, with an invis-ible wall around them.

Connected in a way the others were not. He was aware some tension between them had dissipated.

And been replaced with something even more danger-ous. Morgan felt a way with Meg that he had never felt with anyone else on earth.

A deep sense of comfort. Of belonging. Of being at home with her. Of giving her the uncomplicated gift of loving her.

He could not let himself think about where was all that going to go after tomorrow.

He couldn't even let himself think about what it would mean tonight, after they were off the MeloMelo. Would he go back to the bungalow with her?

Good grief, Morgan couldn't believe he was entertaining these kinds of thoughts about Meg. She was wounded! The very thoughts made him aware of how nearly every aspect of his relationship with her was tinged with self-interest.

If he did go back to the bungalow with her, he swore it would be more of *this*. Giving, not receiving. Love without strings attached.

That vow was strangely freeing. It made him feel intensely and purely focused on this moment, as if it was all they had, and all they needed, and nothing—not even tonight and tomorrow—existed outside of this little cocoon of sanctuary they found themselves in.

CHAPTER FIFTEEN

MEG WATCHED AS the sunset stained the sky the most vibrant orange she had ever witnessed. As the MeloMelo pulled back into the bay in front of the Hale Iwa Kai Resort, the ocean, incredibly and impossibly, seemed to be glowing pink.

The group had been served an incredible catch-of-the-day dinner aboard the yacht. By then it had been under sail, instead of using its motor, and the experience of a silent sea and the power in the wind had been as exhilarating as the rest of the day.

In fact, when Meg contemplated her day she was aware of feeling pure bliss. How odd it could feel so perfect, even with her arm in a sling and her shoulder throbbing.

She realized that though the backdrop had been nothing short of spectacular, she could be feeling this same way if she was walking through a dumpster-filled back alley.

It was Morgan at her side that made the world magic.

Something had subtly shifted in him today. She had felt the most exquisite tenderness radiating off of him.

Though it wasn't exactly a new experience—she had felt the same with him before when her curse had played out on their trips together, one of those trips being their honeymoon in Paris.

Morgan just stepped in, did what needed to be done. But he didn't just make things okay, he infused them with his light.

Perhaps it had felt so special today because she had resigned herself to never having that feeling again.

If only, Meg wished wistfully, she had been able to make his world *okay* too. If only she would have been able to infuse his world with the element he most needed: children. Family, and all that meant. Water balloon fights by the lake, little fingers getting burned on marshmallows, the new puppy coming home…all things she had never experienced.

But he had, and he had shared those experiences and memories with her, the longing so strong in his voice it had made her want to give that to him as she had never wanted to give anything to anybody before.

Meg made herself stop this runaway train of thoughts. She would ruin what was left of this perfect day if she indulged in a journey down the road of what she had wanted and could not have.

Instead, she made a conscious effort to just breathe it all in. Her friends were all trying to decide the best way to get her off the sailboat and into the rowboat that would bring them to shore.

"I'm fine," she laughed. "I can do it."

"Let's not risk that, given how I need you slingless tomorrow," Caylee said. Instead of feeling guilty, as if she was a burden, Meg let herself just enjoy *this*.

Her friends caring about her.

Morgan leading the team that was working to tackle the obstacles the world gave them.

Somehow, amid shouts of laughter, Meg found herself in a hammock, being passed carefully from the MeloMelo to the rowboat.

How was she going to live without this? Not just without Morgan, but without all them around her, knowing someone who had your back was always just a breath away?

They let her out of the hammock when she was safely in

the rowboat, but they were all there to help her again as they reached shore.

"I can get my feet wet," she protested as Morgan and Jonathon crossed their arms and linked them to make a seat to get her the last few feet to the beach.

It was now nearly completely dark.

Though the shadows, she saw a couple standing there, hand in hand, and she knew who they were even before Caylee squealed.

"Mom, Dad!"

And the perfect day became even more perfect as Caylee's mom hugged Caylee first and then took Meg in her arms, carefully embracing her around the sling.

"My little muffin, what mess have you gotten yourself into now?" she asked, but didn't wait for an answer. "I have missed you so much."

It was homecoming.

This woman, Caylee's mother, had always so generously been her mother, too. It was a sharp and poignant reminder of just how much she had left, how much she had sacrificed, so that Morgan could have the perfect life she dreamed for him.

Mrs. Van Houtte put Meg away from her, and looked at Morgan. "It's good to see you, too, Morgan." And then her gaze went back and forth between the two of them, bewildered and sad, and Meg was afraid she was going to burst into tears or ask, out loud, what every single person had been thinking.

How could this happen to you two when it is apparent you love each other so much?

But she didn't ask it. She bit her lip and returned her attention to Meg.

"Do you want me to look at that? What is it? A dislocation?" Mrs. Van Houtte was a retired nurse.

"No, that's okay," Meg said at the same time Morgan said, "I've got it."

The look Mrs. Van Houtte gave the two of them turned from bewildered to hopeful. She turned to her daughter.

"Caylee," she said. "You're coming with your dad and I. Don't even think you're going to spend the night with Jonathon before your wedding."

"Mom! That's silly, we've been—"

Mrs. Van Houtte held up her hand. "That's between you and your priest, dear. I have only one night left with my little girl before I am the mother of a married woman."

Meg watched them go, and felt that touch of wistfulness she had always felt when she saw how most mothers and daughters were together.

"How's your mom doing?" Morgan asked quietly, watching them go.

He was so in tune with her, and despite the sadness his question made her feel, it intensified her feeling of connection with him.

"She's going through another bad spell. She had been doing pretty good. For a while, I actually thought she might make the wedding."

She laughed—how silly to count on her mother—but heard the undertone of disappointment.

Morgan heard it, too. He put his arm gently around her good shoulder. "I'm sorry, Meggie," he said. "I really am."

"I know," she whispered. He had never, ever acted as if her mother was an embarrassment to him, to a family that had been unsullied by the rollercoaster ride of addiction.

Even though he had never made a judgment, she had probably made enough judgments for both of them.

"Come on," Morgan said, "I'll look after you."

"I can look after myself." That felt like such a lie.

But he gave her the dignity of not challenging it.

Instead, he said mildly, "Well, now that I've promised Mrs. Van Houtte that I'll make sure you're okay tonight. I'm a man of my word, after all."

That was part of the problem.

He was a man of his word, so much so that he would have stayed, even when he knew she couldn't have babies.

Because he was so honorable. But as their friends started having families, would he have regretted his sacrifice? It seemed like it was one of those things that was best not to know.

They walked together back to Huipu. All day, Meg had felt such awareness for Morgan, and of Morgan.

That awareness led her to this realization: it wasn't just about the sex, as incredible as that was between them. It wasn't just about how over-the-top attractive he was.

His masculinity had this other side to it that she could take deep comfort in. Morgan could be counted on, always, to do the right thing.

And tonight, that was just looking after her.

He helped her out of the sling, and then ever so gently, out of the swim cover. He reached around her and undid the knot on the back of her bathing suit, all with about as much feeling as you might expect from a nurse. Then he adjusted the shower, put a towel within her reach, and slid out the door, calling over his shoulder, "Shout if you need help."

Exhaustion from the injury and the active day in the sun was setting in.

She let the warm water from the shower sluice over her, rinsing away the salt water. She stepped out, and grabbed the towel and dried off as best she could one-handed. Then she took another one and tucked it awkwardly around herself.

She padded through to the bedroom. He was in the bed, on top of the covers, pillows propped up behind his shoulders. He looked up from his tablet and leaped from the bed.

"The valet forgot to lay out my pajamas," she teased him.

Teasing Morgan shouldn't feel nearly as good as it did. Homecoming, just like seeing Mrs. Van Houtte had been.

"Failure of duties," he said, with fake contriteness. "What do you want to put on? Pajamas? A T-shirt?"

Both seemed equally unmanageable.

She went over to the bed, pulled back the sheet and slid in between them in the towel. He left the room and came back a few minutes later with water and painkillers.

"Here, take these."

She realized he was as sticky with salt as she had been. Plus, he hadn't changed clothes since yesterday.

"Go shower, Morgan," she said, and he nodded, and went into the closet where his things were and got fresh clothes. Well, that was just as well. There was no telling what would happen if they were both wearing only towels.

Still, it was sweetest torment listening to that water, imagining it sluicing over the hard lines of his body.

By the time he emerged, whatever he had given her for pain was kicking in. She gave him a smile, but she could tell it was distinctly crooked.

He came and sat down on the bed beside her.

"Would you kiss me?" she whispered.

He did. He leaned over and kissed her with exquisite tenderness on her cheek. It wasn't what she expected, and yet, it felt so right.

"How's the pain?" he asked.

"Fading." She actually felt relieved about that platonic kiss, the fact that she could trust him to know what was right in the moment. Somehow, this was just as nice, him beside her, looking at her with tender concern.

"I can tell," he said. "Your eyes are crossing."

"Oh, no!"

"It's kind of cute, like a Siamese cat. Do you want the sling back on?"

"No."

"How are you going to stop yourself from rolling on it in your sleep? We've got you this far. Don't ruin the wedding now."

He was teasing her, and yet, she felt the sting.

"I always ruin everything," she said. "And you always seem to end up like this. Looking after me."

He cocked his head at her, as if she was talking complete nonsense.

"Remember Paris?" she asked.

"I'll never forget Paris," he said softly. "We might not have had the wedding of your dreams, but we had that."

"What do you mean about the wedding of my dreams?"

"It wasn't like this," he said quietly. "A beautiful location. A wedding party. A gown. A special day for you to feel like a princess."

"We agreed about the wedding," she said, puzzled. "It was what suited both of us."

"So you say," he said dubiously. "Aren't you sorry we didn't have this? Just a little bit?"

"No," she said. "We had Paris to make up for it."

"See?" he said triumphantly. "There was something you lacked, that you needed making up for."

"Morgan! That's not true."

He looked so unconvinced, that Meg wanted to remind him of that special, special time.

"What was your favorite thing?" she asked.

Despite how brotherly he was being at the moment, the look he gave her was white-hot.

She gulped and felt heat rising in her cheeks. "Besides that?"

He didn't even hesitate. He didn't say the Louvre or the Eiffel Tower or the Arc de Triomphe.

"We'd been walking all day and into the night. We'd squeezed so much sightseeing into our first two days. Then, we stopped at that little café overlooking the Seine as the sun was setting. It was on a cobblestone street and we sat outside under a pink awning."

"We ordered hot chocolate," she remembered, "and they brought us heated milk with pots of chocolate on the side."

"And the waiter brought us an éclair, on the house, to share. It felt as if the whole world knew we were madly in love and everyone was celebrating with us."

"Everything seemed to shine," she recalled softly, "as if it was lit from within."

They were silent for a moment.

"And then I ruined it all. Just like I said. I always ruin everything."

He looked genuinely surprised. "Is that how you see it?"

"Of course. That's how it was. Five minutes after we finished that hot chocolate and the éclair, I tripped on that loose cobblestone. Snap. The romance of Paris traded for a ride in an ambulance and the bright lights and chaos of an emergency room." Meg sighed heavily, remembering. "Honestly? I didn't expect to test for better or worse quite so soon."

"I never saw it like that," he said quietly.

"How else was there to see it?"

"I felt as if we saw a side of Paris others don't get to see."

"The inside of an emergency room?"

"The old grandma, in her lovely pink beret, and her jewels, with her family surrounding her. Even though I don't speak French, you could tell every word they said to her was loving her into the next life. They cherished her, and she knew it."

Meg's eyes sparked with tears. A man who saw *this*.

"That little boy," he continued softly, "clutching the teddy bear, his mother soothing him. Again, you didn't have to speak French to know the universal language."

Of course, he would see the little boy. With longing for a little boy of his own one day, no doubt.

Still…

"I never knew you saw it like that," Meg whispered.

"When I was with you, I saw the best in everything, I guess, even in what you saw as the worst."

She felt as if she was holding back tears.

"I liked looking after you, Meg," he told her softly. "It never felt like it was a burden. I should have made sure you knew that sooner."

The tears were still threatening. She tried to hold them off with good, healthy skepticism.

"Even when I got food poisoning in Thailand? I was in the bathroom for three days. Our whole holiday, practically. And you barely left my side. Just to go in search of ginger ale."

"Not an easy item to find in Thailand," he agreed, but with astounding affection. "I had to go to a bar in a hotel where Canadians hung out. Three blocks, in that grueling heat, at a dead run."

"At least a dozen times," she reminded him.

"At least," he said with a fond smile.

"Switzerland," she reminded him, "We went out on that boat on Lake Geneva. And I just wanted to look gorgeous for you, and I didn't dress warm enough, and the next thing you knew…"

"The best part," he said. "Crawling into the hospital bed beside you, your ice-cold body next to mine, under the sheets with a heating pad, feeling you coming back to life."

The love she felt for him was suddenly so intense, more intense, even, than after they had made love.

The pills seemed to be working.

"Meg," Morgan said, "even though it never bothered me, what do you think it was about? The curse?"

"Bryan." She shocked herself by saying it. What part of her subconscious were the drugs unleashing?

"What? Your brother?"

"I loved him," she said. "I loved him madly."

"Of course you did."

"But—"

She fell silent. She had never said this to a living soul.

"But?" Morgan's voice was so soft. She looked deeply at him. The man she could say anything to. And yet she had never said this.

"Everything was about him, Morgan. I remember once Mrs. Van Houtte and Caylee asked me to go to a movie with them. You know what I did? I asked if I could have the money instead. I'm embarrassed thinking about it, but Bryan needed a new wheelchair. Of course, Mrs. Van Houtte gave me the money, and then some.

"I remember my mom kissing me and calling me a saint when I gave her that money. I felt so approved of. Sometimes I feel like the only time my mom acknowledged I existed was when I did something for Bryan.

"I babysat all summer and gave the money to Mom? That was wonderful! I didn't join school clubs, because that cost money? What a beautiful soul I had. I didn't need a new winter jacket this year? What a trooper! Bryan got a new winter jacket, of course, because we wouldn't want Bryan to catch a cold."

Meg heard Morgan's sharp intake of breath, and felt guilty for saying these things. But she'd started and now it felt as if she was compelled to finish.

"And then I got the scholarship for art camp! I was going away, I was going to the one place where I could lose myself, where I could be free of all the reoccurring drama and trauma at home. Art! The one place I got recognized for me, where it wasn't all about my brother. And what happens when I did something for myself? The hammer of fate dropped on my head. Bryan died while I was away."

"Meg, I'm so sorry," Morgan said gruffly.

She sighed. "And did my mom turn all that love and affection she'd lavished on Bryan onto me, her grieving daughter? No, she did not. It became all about her. Maybe it always had been. I think soaking up all that attention and sympathy made her feel special in ways I could not.

"I think my mom was totally addicted to Bryan and when he was gone, she turned that addictive personality on to something else.

"That's why I have the curse," she finished, with a dangerous hiccup. "I'm scared to have fun. No, I punish myself for having fun."

"You never said any of this before," Morgan said, drawing her head onto his chest.

She let the tears flow. "Because I never wanted you to know what kind of person I really am. Resentful of my brother and my mom."

"Oh, Meggie," he said softly, and she wept at the acceptance she heard in his voice. It occurred to her she might tell him. Her deepest secret. About the one thing she could not give him.

But then, instead, with his hand in hers, her eyes shut and she floated off feeling safe and loved and protected in a way she had not in eight months.

When she woke up in the morning, Morgan was gone. Meg waited for a feeling of guilt about revealing the things she had to hit her, but it did not. Instead the sensation was one of bliss—of being loved by a man like Morgan even when he knew everything there was to know about her.

Well, almost everything.

There was a note next to the bed.

Not a love note. A stern warning to use the sling. She remembered today was the day Caylee and Jonathon were getting married.

For Meg, that feeling that had begun on the boat—of being part of something bigger, of being accepted into the tribe, of being loved—only intensified as the day unfolded.

Her right shoulder was quite a bit better. Tender, and bruised, but it was in no way debilitating. Still, she put on the sling, just to make sure she was at her best for the ceremony.

For some reason—maybe it was the crate of wedding clothes that had been delivered while they were on the yacht, maybe they all carried the beauty of the day on the MeloMelo inside of them, maybe it was *aloha*—but the feeling of bliss grew and grew and grew as the ceremony drew closer.

No one was frazzled.

There were no arguments.

There were no upsets about last-minute details.

Even the unpredictable Kauai weather seemed intent on cooperating.

The day started with the women gathered under a shade shelter, with a palm-frond roof. Tables were laden with flowers and leaves.

Local women had come to show them how to make leis for the guests and the bridal party. The first leis were made with the gloriously scented purple-and-white plumeria. The scent of the flowers intermingled with a smell of burning wood drifting up from the beach.

At Mrs. Van Houtte's insistence, Meg's arm was still in a sling.

"Right up until the ceremony," Mrs. Van Houtte told her with a stern shake of her finger. It felt good to be mothered.

At first, Meg didn't know if she would be of any help, but

a job was found for her—sorting through the huge baskets of flowers and choosing only the perfect, unflawed blossoms.

As she sorted, one of the local women began to speak. "The wedding luau feast is being prepared. That's the burning smell. The resort has a permanent pit for events like this, so it didn't have to be dug.

"The wood and rocks were put in it early, early this morning. When the wood has burned down, it will be removed, and a whole pig will be put on top of the hot rocks, then wrapped in banana leaves. It will slowly cook and steam all day. The first slow cooker!"

A bridal lei of orchids was made for Caylee to wear around her neck. After that, satisfied perhaps that the visitors to the island had a basic grasp of the work, they were shown how to make the white *haku lei*—the Hawaiian flower crown—that Caylee would wear.

For the men, they made ti leaf maile-style leis. Rather than a circle, it was a long line of leaves with a few flowers braided into it that the groom and his groomsmen would wear over their shoulders, a bit like the vestments of a priest.

For Meg, the beauty of working with the women was astonishing. The tropical breezes embraced them, and the view of a turquoise ocean was stunning.

But it was being with this circle of women that made her heart feel as if it was glowing like the warm rocks that were now cooking the pig, the scents of the meat beginning to hang tantalizingly in the air.

The shelter was filled with the murmur of quiet voices, the occasional laugh or giggle, the fragrance of the flowers.

Stories were told. And songs were hummed. Chants were taught. Prayers were murmured.

Meg realized she loved the traditional feel of the women gathering in the shaded structure. It felt as if there were no differences between them. The barriers of different ages, cultures, physical appearances, faded away as they worked together toward doing what women do, creating. They became one, weaving the ancient secrets of feminine energy into these wedding adornments.

As their fingers moved, it felt as if blessings were being sewn in: the celebration of love, the age-old dreams that could be fulfilled when a couple chose to walk through life together, how their choice to join brought the future into sharp focus.

As the morning progressed, Meg was aware of a kind of bittersweetness overcoming her.

Because, at its very heart, a wedding was a vow to the future.

I will send my children and my grandchildren forward to a time I will never see.

So, while it was a wonder to be included in this women's day, Meg also acutely felt her lack. Her barrenness. The fact that she could not fulfill what her wedding had promised.

All through the morning, Meg was aware of the men working toward the same goal, the making of a perfect celebration of love, but separately from them.

She strained to catch glimpses of Morgan. Every time she saw him, or heard him, her heart did this trill of recognition, like a bird singing.

She longed to be with him, but was so aware it was the longing of the damned. A kind of desperate need to see Morgan, to fill her senses with him, before she found the courage to say goodbye to him once again.

So that he could someday realize everything that a day like this stood for.

The continuation of the life cycle, the perpetuation of the generations.

After they had finished with the leis, they went to the spa to have their hair and makeup done.

And then, finally, they slipped into their dresses. Caylee looked so stunningly beautiful that they all wept and then had to have their makeup repaired.

Meg was finally allowed to remove her sling. She needed help getting dressed. The bruise around her shoulder was spectacular and they were all thankful that her dress had a short cap sleeve on it that hid the worst of that discoloration.

It felt like a dream as Meg waited for her turn to walk down the aisle that had been created on the beach.

Chairs with tropical flowers on the backs of them had been set up on a newly constructed wooden platform. The seating faced the ocean and a shade arbor, the side and top of which were woven with more beautiful flowers.

The guests, each who had been greeted with a lei, were now seated.

The groom and his groomsmen waited under the arbor, the ti leaf maile leis dark against the whiteness of their shirts and suits.

Morgan was standing at Jonathon's shoulder. Meg had waited all day to fill her senses with him, and the moment did not disappoint.

Looking at Morgan filled her with a poignant delight. He looked tanned and relaxed, and so, so handsome it took Meg's breath away. When he looked at her, she saw a look on his face that every single woman lives to see.

That he cherished her.

That he would protect her with his own life if needs be.

She would not spoil one second of what was left of this day by thinking of tomorrow. Not one. Instead, she would give herself over to the magic that was unfolding around them.

A single ukulele began to strum, not the traditional wedding march, but instead "It's A Wonderful World."

Samantha went first, then Becky, then Allie.

And then Meg was walking down the aisle, and it felt as

if this was only about her and Morgan, her walking toward him, as his eyes fastened on her, wistful and reverent as any groom.

When Caylee came on her father's arm, Meg was finally able to drag her eyes from Morgan's.

The bride was stunning, but even the glory of that dress paled in comparison to the look on Caylee's face, a radiance spun out of pure love. She reached Jonathon, and Meg took her bouquet.

The bride and the groom exchanged those age-old vows.

For better or for worse.

In sickness and in health.

Meg had said those words. Hearing them again, for the first time since she had left Morgan, she allowed herself the luxury of doubt.

She had made that vow to him. He had made his to her.

And she had broken hers.

For the best possible reason, and yet…

She couldn't. Not today, she couldn't doubt herself. She would just give herself over to what time she had left.

Doubts were for after.

Doubts, regrets, were for the rest of her life.

Not for this magical day.

At the end of the ceremony, Jonathon slipped the ti leaf maile lei from around his neck, and placed it on Caylee's. She took off her orchid lei and put it around his neck.

And then, they kissed.

And it was so much more than a kiss. A fusion. A bond. A promise.

The future shimmering between them like an enchantment.

After the wedding party signed the register, Caylee and Jonathon went down the aisle, and the spectators showered them in flower petals.

Meg and Morgan joined hands and followed. The walk through the rain of petals, with his hand warm in hers, invited her to journey into the world of enchantment that the kiss between the bride and groom had begun.

"How's your shoulder?" Morgan asked, quietly.

Always *this*. The tenderness, the concern, the sense he gave her of being protected and cherished.

Loved.

Just the way she loved him.

Meg considered this: Had she broken her vow to him when she left him, or had she kept it? Had she been true to it, by putting his needs ahead of her own?

He touched her forehead.

"Not today," he said gently. "Let's not worry today."

"Okay," she agreed, and smiled up at him. That felt like a vow.

And she gave herself over to that vow completely. She left her worries behind and immersed herself in the activities of the day, beginning with the photo session.

There were traditional photos, with the spectacular backdrop of the ocean and the mountains.

The photographer was wonderful, giving them tips on how to look natural, but to Meg, it felt as if it was Morgan who coaxed the best out of her. Teasing her, cajoling her, reaching over to rearrange a single strand of hair, removing an imaginary smudge from her lip with his thumb.

After the more traditional shots, the photographer encouraged the men to take off the jackets and to let loose, so there were playful photos, too. Jonathon shinnying up a palm tree and dropping a coconut to his bride; Morgan and Meg running along the edge of the sand, barefoot, shrieking with laughter; the women wading out into the white froth of the surf, holding up their dresses and bouquets.

The entire day was simply infused with that energy of

enchantment. All things were touched by it, from the preparations that morning to the ceremony, to the photos to the unearthing of the pig and now the luau in full swing.

Besides her own wedding day, and despite her shoulder trying to remind her she really was cursed, Meg decided this was easily the best day of her life.

She refused to look at the goodbye looming like storm clouds on the horizon.

CHAPTER SIXTEEN

MORGAN HAD NEVER been to a wedding quite like this one. As well as the unbridled joy, there was an unexpected sensuality shimmering in the air around the entire day.

But, of course, it was Hawaii, that deeply ancient, mysterious and sensual land.

And of course it was in the looks and touches that passed between Caylee and Jonathon, so unconsciously loaded with passion and intimacy that surely it was creating this sense of deep longing in everyone, not just him?

But, perhaps most of all, it was in just being with Meg.

It was remembering all they had been to each other, but experiencing her anew, also. It felt as if some part of him that was essential had been restored to him, some part broken was repaired.

And the feeling just built as the day went on.

Of a connection so strong it felt sacred and unbreakable. It felt as if no man—and no woman—could possibly stop it, not any more than they could have stopped that storm that had literally swept them back into each other's arms.

The dancing had begun and now, under a dark tropical sky, with the lap of the waves a backdrop to the music, they were in each other's arms. Well, arm. Because Meg had her sling back on, and her one arm was sandwiched between them as they swayed together and he gazed into her eyes, thinking, *It will never be enough.*

Even a lifetime with her, and it will not feel like I've had enough of her.

Her scent filled him, her body felt exquisitely right against his, the look in her eyes was something every man lived for.

The stars had long since come out. Even the chickens had gone to bed. And yet no one wanted to say goodbye to this day.

The dancing continued until well past one in the morning. It might have gone on until dawn, except that Kauai decided to show them who was in charge, and it was not mere mortals.

It began to rain, gently at first, and then harder. When it began to pelt down, the band gave up and hastily packed up their equipment. The staff scurried to get food off the table that had been set up for snacks hours ago.

And then, without any discussion, he had Meg's good hand in his, and they were running, laughing, along one of the paved paths.

At the last minute, though, he did not turn toward Huipu.

Morgan wanted to show her what he had found on his first day here, before she had arrived.

He took her down a paved path, the torches sputtering in the pouring rain. They came to a subtle signpost. An arrow pointed toward Lover's Grove.

On that sign was a placard that read Unoccupied.

He turned it over. *Occupied.* A simple system, a guarantee of privacy for lovers who came here.

The path wound through a jungle of lush thick greenery into a little grotto. A turquoise pool, lit so that the water danced as if it was living, was surrounded by growth, leathery green leaves, flowers, delicate ferns. At one end of it, a man-made waterfall cascaded down. Under that tumbling water was a cave.

From the first moment he had seen this place, Morgan had been stunned at how clearly he could see himself here.

With the woman who had abandoned him.

And broken his heart.

Even when he had woken, that first night, to find Meg standing beside the bed, this is where he had pictured her.

The next morning, he had felt as if it was his mission—if he wanted to protect himself—to keep her away from this place.

But all his efforts now felt ridiculously puny in the face of what was between them. He had been clearly shown that when the flash flood had driven them into that shelter.

That at close proximity he was powerless against her.

Now, this place, Lover's Grove, felt as if it had been a premonition. As if he had known, all along, they would end up here.

And that somehow, what happened between them here would make everything that had gone wrong between them right again.

Tenderly, he reached for her.

Tenderly, he took her in his arms.

Tenderly, he removed her sodden dress, kissed the raindrops from her lifted face, and then from the other soaked, perfect surfaces of her skin.

And then his own clothes followed hers to that heap of sopping cloth as their feet.

Morgan took Meg in his arms, and did what this entire day, this entire time here in Hawaii, had been calling him to do.

He claimed his wife back. He laid his poor battered, bruised, damaged heart at her feet. He told her with his lips and his touch, and his tongue and with his gaze, the truth that laid him bare to her, that opened his chest to her sword, should she choose to use it.

He told her, without words, but with every other tool at his disposal, that he loved her.

And that he always would.

To his dying breath.

* * *

This had been building between them, Meg thought with wonder, as surely as the storm that had let loose all around them.

She had never seen a place like this secret little grotto. She had never been in a place that felt so perfect.

To answer the calling of her body to his.

Her lips to his.

To answer the calling to be Morgan's wife. One more time.

On the last occasion that they had made love, there had been an undeniable fury to it, a repressed urgency, a pent-up need that had to be satiated *right then*.

This time was totally different.

Maybe partly because the recent injury to her shoulder, though that just felt, to her, like part of it.

The injury was the world giving them the *shaka*: telling them to slow down, hang loose, take it easy, everything's fine.

Oh, no, so much more than fine, Meg thought, as Morgan lifted the hem of her sodden dress, and she raised her arms to help him. Even the pain of that effort on her injured shoulder felt oddly delicious as he dropped the dress away, helped her lower her arm, placed kisses that felt as if they had the power to heal any wound all over that bruise.

Just like her, he seemed to feel the whispering—*Slow down. You have all the time in the world.*

He explored her with heart-melting tenderness. She felt the wonder that she had chosen this man to be her husband, the only person in the world who knew her in this way.

The only person in the world who would ever know her in this way.

Of course, she knew what was not true was that they had all the time in the world. That knowledge, tucked away in some dark corner of her mind, made *this* even more exquisite, achingly poignant, terrifyingly tender. Because she knew she could never give herself in this way to another person. Not ever. Not if she lived to be in her hundreds.

So, this was it for her, before she entered a world of self-imposed chastity, a world that would not have Morgan coaxing a side of her to the surface that she had never known before him.

And would never know again, after.

She slipped his clothes from him with all the exquisite tenderness that he had shown her. She drew him into the turquoise water, and then into the waterfall.

With the warm water tumbling around them, joining the rain, wet on wet, she tilted her head and he dropped his mouth over hers.

His kiss was lingering and sweet, as was her answer. She explored the jagged edge of his front teeth with her tongue, the swell of his top lip.

They moved past the tumble of water into the cave behind it. It felt like a secret place, entirely removed from all the world. The walls reflected dancing light from the water, and that light danced off their faces, too.

She explored his face, and then every silky inch of him with excruciating slowness. First, she let her fingertips commit his body to her memory, and then she made sure to burn it in, forever, by following that trail laid by her fingertips with her tongue.

And then Morgan stilled her quest, and their positions reversed. He became the explorer as he kissed droplets of water off her lashes, nibbled her earlobes, claimed her mouth, trailed fire down her water-slick body.

She noticed he was trembling with leashed desire. She realized she was, too. And still, by some silent agreement, it was a slow cherishing.

His lips returned to her mouth, and he tasted, and tasted

and tasted, as if her mouth was a delicacy he could never get enough of. His tongue ran over her lips, already puffy from kissing, then darting into the hollow of her mouth and back out. He nibbled her lips with his teeth, drew them into his mouth, sucked on them gently, plundered her mouth with his tongue again.

And all the while that his mouth held hers captive, his hands roamed her with the same slow tenderness.

Morgan did what he had always done to her.

In this secret place, he brought her to her secret place. He exposed things about her that only Morgan knew. What he knew was that Meg, just below the surface, was erotic and sensual. Her secret was that she was hungry. Her secret was that she was desperate for every stroke of his hands laying claim to her.

His touch awakened her. Her breasts, her belly, between her legs, her very skin screamed its wanting of him, its insatiable need for him.

And yet, still, as the water cascaded down around them, he held back, stoking the fire, hotter and hotter, pulling back and letting it cool, only to stoke again.

His lips and his hands were the fuel to her flame. He knew it. He played it. Only when she was sobbing with wanting and need did he back her up against the wall of the cave. He lifted her with such easy strength, lifted her to him, guided her legs to wrap around the power of his torso.

It was, to this point, as if they had been swimming against a current, and suddenly let go.

To the bliss of pure surrender.

His eyes never leaving hers, he claimed her, the bliss building and building and building until it was something else entirely, until it felt as if they stood on the edge of a cliff ready to plummet to their deaths.

A scream formed on her lips when they fell toward their

destiny, but he covered her mouth with his, and took the scream from her.

And they did not plummet.

They flew.

They joined the pounding of the rain and of the waterfall, they joined the blackness of the sky, and the cry of the wind.

In that explosive crescendo they became everything.

And everything became them.

This moment, this mystical moment between a man and his wife, had been written long before they were born.

It was what the mountains around them bore silent witness to, what the women had woven into the leis, what had underscored the humming and the chants.

This was a land of ancient knowledge.

And it called for them to know.

To know each other completely.

To become a part of all of it.

To embrace the darkest unknown secrets a heart could hold, until they were the secret, to sink into the great mystery until they were the mystery, to honor the forces of creation until they became creation itself.

Complete, with the stars and the water and the mountains swirling around them and in them, Morgan lifted her.

He walked out of the pool. Now she noticed there were two deep lounge chairs here and there were stacks of white towels on a rack. It was a bit jarring to realize that they were not really in a secret grotto.

Morgan, ever so tenderly, set her on her feet, and tucked a towel around her, and then one around himself.

With the rain still pouring down around them, they gathered up the soaked piles of clothes, and ran, clad only in their towels, barefoot and laughing back to Huipu.

He laid her across the bed and came on top of her, traced the line of her lips with his thumb.

And then he said it.

"I love you."

She knew she should not say it. That it would only make the farewell worse when that time came, and that time was coming soon.

But she could no more have stopped the words from coming out than she could stop the rain from falling down.

"I love you," she whispered in return.

And in the half light, she traced the line of his nose and his lips with her fingertips, drank in his moonlight-drenched face, memorizing every glorious detail of him.

"Don't ever leave me again, Meg." His voice was hoarse with pain, his need laid unvarnished before her.

She saw her silence register in his eyes. She saw he was stunned by it, and then he pushed himself off the bed, gave her one look of betrayed astonishment and was gone into the night.

Meg wept.

CHAPTER SEVENTEEN

MORGAN STEPPED BACK out into the night and felt a war of conflicting emotions. The rain had stopped, though he could hear water dripping off the nearby foliage.

He felt the fullness in his heart. Tenderness.

Love.

He loved Meg. He was never going to stop. And yet, nothing was resolved between them.

He had done tonight what he did not want to do.

He had begged her. *Don't ever leave me again, Meg.*

Had Meg rewarded his vulnerability with an assurance? A promise? A commitment?

No, she had not.

Her silence had spoken for her.

For all that they had given in to the enchantment around them today, for all that the love in the air—*aloha*—had melted every one of their barriers, now Morgan felt unsettled and uncertain.

How could it have been a good thing to let Meg back in, when they had not discussed where were they going next? In three more days, would she simply go back to the life she had found?

Without him?

He was tempted to go back and demand answers, and yet he was not sure he could handle what those answers were.

He had seen something terrifying in her expression when he had begged her not to leave him.

Begged.

In his defense, it had come on the heels of an entire day that could only be called blissful. He glanced at his watch.

It was nearly 3:00 a.m.

The perfect day was over. The new one was already unfolding. Soon, the damned chickens would be cheering on the sunrise.

Restlessly, he walked down the dark pathway through the quiet resort to the ocean. It was gorgeous in the moonlight, and without hesitation he went into the water and swam.

He told himself he was giving in to the water, but he knew the residue of uncertainty remained.

When he stepped back onto the sand, he was no longer alone on the beach.

Caylee was sitting there, still in her wedding dress, looking like a dream of a princess out of a fairy tale. If he had his phone with him, he would be tempted to snap a picture. If he shared it with Meg, she might paint it.

But again, everything was so nebulous between them. How much would they be sharing?

He walked over to Caylee, and she patted the sand beside her. He sank into it.

"The bride alone on her wedding night?" he asked.

"Not in a bad way," she said. "Jonathon's fast asleep. I somehow can't let go of it. The day. The vows. The perfection. The joy. It's singing inside of me, and it's not ready to stop yet."

"Every single person felt that, Caylee. Your wedding was a gift from you and Jonathon to each of us who shared the day with you."

It was true. Morgan was not sure he had ever experienced

a more wonderful and amazing day. The wedding had been exactly what every bride dreams of, perfect, blissful, magical.

That enchantment had gotten all over everyone. *That* was how he was going to explain what had happened between him and Meg, again. A spell they were under.

And underneath that, awareness of the enormity of it all.

"We're going to have babies together," Caylee whispered, her arms wrapped around her knees as she gazed out at the ocean.

He slid her a look. "You're pregnant?"

She gave him a playful slug on his shoulder, a lovely little familiarity, the kind close friends enjoy.

"Morgan! I meant *someday* Jonathon and I will have children. We're going to be adults."

He and Meg had shared that dream. But he realized adults didn't get to claim they had been under a spell rather than taking responsibility for their actions.

It also occurred to him he had not given a single thought to taking precautions with Meg, which also seemed irresponsible given how up in the air things were between them. On the other hand, he felt this sense of delicious wonder when he thought of Meg having their baby.

"Things seem good between you and Meg," Caylee offered, as if she knew his thoughts had turned to Meg. Her voice was soft with hope.

He sighed, took up a fistful of sand and then let it sift out between his fingertips.

"*Are* things going to be okay between you?" Caylee pressed.

He looked at her and then looked away. "I'd be able to answer that better if I understood what had happened the first time. When she left. Did she tell you? Did she confide in you? Anything beyond what she told me? That she couldn't handle the lifestyle?"

"That's exactly what she told me. I never believed her, though."

"Me either."

"I never pressed her, Morgan. I've known Meg so long. I've known her since we were little kids. I trusted whatever reasons she had, they came from that good, good heart of hers."

"Sure," he said cynically.

"It's true."

"Meg seemed so happy married to me," Morgan said pensively. "But last night she told me some things that made me realize she's wary of happiness."

He realized, just saying that, it was a failing on his part that Meg had not told him those things sooner.

Caylee drew in a long breath and slid him a look.

"It's not just happiness," she said pensively, after a long silence. "You know, us girls have our crazy adventure club. We've been rock climbing and white water rafting and horseback riding. Not a single scratch on her. Not one visit to the hospital. No famous travel curse when she was with us. But even yesterday, there it was. Like she was just having way too much fun *with you*."

Morgan drew in a breath. "What are you saying?"

"It's love," Caylee said quietly. "I think Meg is manifesting her deepest belief. That love is gonna hurt. That she doesn't deserve it. That she'll be punished for every moment of happiness that she steals from the jaws of fate."

Caylee was silent again. She wouldn't look at him.

He felt as if he was going to stop breathing as he realized the truth.

"You know," he whispered. "You know why she left me."

"I'm only guessing."

"Please tell me what you think."

Caylee wrapped her arms tighter around her knees, drew them in closer to her chest.

"She left all of us," she confided softly. "You know what that made me think, when she cut herself off from everybody? That she had a secret she didn't want to tell, that she was going to carry all by herself, that good little soldier she was raised to be. She didn't want to be around us because we would have loved her secret out of her, and she knew it."

"What secret?" he asked, hoarsely. "Was there someone else?"

Caylee shot him a look loaded with scorn. "Do you know her at all?"

"I thought so," he said defensively.

The awful thought that maybe she was sick crossed his mind. It was everything he could do not to leap up right this second, go to her and look at her for signs. She did look like she'd lost weight, those new hollows under her cheekbones, the jut of her shoulders...

"She never told me," Caylee said, drawing patterns in the sand with her hand, letting her hair fall in front of her face so he couldn't read her expression.

He wasn't having it. He nudged her with his shoulder and when she looked up he saw the sorrow in her eyes.

"Tell me what you think," he said.

He'd never, ever been a pushy kind of guy, but he heard the demand in his voice.

Caylee nodded.

"I think she thought she could have a baby like Bryan. That it was genetic. I always wondered if she'd been tested. You know, they can discover all kinds of things with genetic testing these days."

Morgan went very still. Meg had, after all, just revealed to him how her whole life had revolved around her brother.

Was it possible that she was terrified of her life revolving around a child with disabilities?

They'd been trying so hard to have a baby. They'd been just like Jonathon and Caylee, so ready for the next step in their lives. But when he thought back on it, Meg had been way more invested in it than him. He'd just thought it would happen when the time was right.

And then, one day, he recalled, she seemed to lose interest.

And not long after that, he had found the note.

He wished he felt compassion for her as he got up off the sand. He didn't even say goodbye to Caylee. He strode back toward their bungalow.

But he didn't feel compassion at all.

He felt fury. Because they would have weathered anything they faced together. But he had not even been consulted. Or trusted. The fact was, Meg had not thought he would honor those words he had spoken to her on their wedding day.

Meg wiped away the tears. She knew she had to leave and she had to leave right now. It didn't matter that it was the middle of the night.

She had been greedy. She had stolen more time with him.

Ultimately, she had been so selfish. Because she had hurt Morgan even more. She couldn't be here when he got back.

She couldn't.

Because if he asked her that one more time—*Don't ever leave me again, Meg*—she would not be able to do it. She would not be able to do what she knew he needed her to do to have the life he so desperately wanted and that he so deserved to have.

She tumbled from the bed, found her suitcase, began to throw things in it, her movements fraught with a sense of urgency.

But she was not quick enough. She heard the door open

and she whirled to face Morgan, steeling herself to be stronger than she had ever been before.

Meg stared at her husband. He'd been in the ocean. He was shirtless, his skin had the faint sheen of salt on it. His hair was curly and damp. His beautiful, perfect male body was illuminated in moonlight.

And yet, he looked like a stranger. She had never seen that expression on his face before. She had never seen him angry before. Oh, sure. Irritated. Annoyed. Frustrated.

But nothing like this. His eyes were snapping with fury, his expression was grim, his mouth was a slashing frown.

He was not the same man who had held her so tenderly not even an hour ago. He was not the man who had left here. He was not a man about to beg her to change her mind.

CHAPTER EIGHTEEN

"I'T'S FOR BETTER or worse," Morgan said, his voice harsh.

"Wh-wh-what?" Meg stammered.

"I know why you really left," he told her, and she felt everything in her go cold.

"I don't know what you mean."

"Can't handle the lifestyle, my ass."

"Okay," she said. She stopped putting things in the suitcase. She went and sat on the edge of the bed. She braced herself for the fact that somehow he had found out the truth. She braced herself against the rage pouring off of him.

"Tell me why I really left," she whispered.

"You had some kind of test done. You thought you carried the gene. For what Bryan had. And you didn't trust me with it. You didn't trust me to be man enough to live up to those words, for better or worse."

"You're wrong," she said quietly. "It didn't have anything to do with Bryan."

The wind went out of his sails. He collapsed, then sat on the edge of the bed beside her, but not touching her.

"Just tell me the damned reason, Meg. Tell me! You're killing me, do you get that? Especially after the last few days. If you leave me again, I won't make it."

"But you will," she said softly. "We both know that. That people can survive what seems unsurvivable."

"But you're not dead," he spat at her. "You're alive. I can't function on this planet knowing you're alive somewhere and you don't want to be with me."

The torment on his face collapsed every wall she had built against this very moment.

She moved beside him, guided his head to her shoulder, ran her fingertips through his beautiful, damp, salty sand-colored curls.

"I can't have babies," she whispered. "That's why I left."

For a moment, he froze, and then he leaped away from her touch and off of the bed. He turned back to her, looking down at her, his fists clenching and unclenching.

"That's why you left?" There was something dangerous in his tone.

"Yes," she said.

He stared at her, his eyebrows arrowed down, his eyes flashing with disdain.

"That's even *worse*," he told her, the quietness of his tone accentuating his fury, rather than dissipating it. "You couldn't trust me with that? As if you're the only adult in the room? You're the only one who can handle it?"

She took a deep breath, and closed her eyes.

"I've seen how you pined for your family, Morgan," she finally said, when she felt she was composed enough to say it without crying. "For your brother and your sister-in-law, but especially for the children, for Kendra and James.

"I've seen how your eyes follow children playing with this world-weary sorrow in them. I knew what it would take to make your heart whole again, and when I found out I couldn't give it to you, I backed away. So that you could find what you needed with someone else."

His mouth fell open. The fury didn't lessen in his eyes. It deepened. "That's why you fixated on Marjorie and what you perceived as her lack of interest in children."

"Yes," she confessed, her voice a whisper.

"Thank you, Saint Meg," he said, his tone so caustic it felt as if it could flay the skin off her bones. "Thank you for knowing the miracle I needed, and even the kind of woman I needed to achieve it. I'm surprised you didn't set up interviews for your replacement! Maybe she could have provided a doctor's certificate proving fertility.

"Thank you for knowing everything I needed in life before I knew it myself.

"Thank you for breaking my heart, for nearly killing me with grief and self-doubt, but all for my own good, of course."

"Morgan, please don't make what I did ugly."

"I don't have to make it ugly," he said. "You did that. I'm just naming it."

She wanted to get up and run from the disdain pouring off of him, but she made herself sit still.

"Thank you for not looking at a single option," Morgan spat out. "Are there medical things we could have done? What about adoption? For God's sake, lots of people our age just get dogs."

"Right," she said, holding her hands together so he could not see the shaking. "You would have been happy with puppies instead of children."

"I would have been happy with *you*. I would have been happy if you were my whole life and my whole reason for being, forever and forever.

"That's the slap in the face, Meg. That you didn't trust my love for you."

His tone and his look were ferocious, but in a way he had just confirmed what she had believed all along. Because his first reaction to her telling him that she couldn't have babies?

He went right to it's for better or worse.

And not the better part.

"We both know for you, not having kids is the worst possible scenario," she said, keeping her composure as best she could. "How could I claim to love someone and set them up for their worst possible scenario?"

"You just won't let it go," he snapped, raking a hand through his hair. "Saint Meg, in charge of the world, in charge of my happiness, whether I like it or not. If I'd known this about you—this supercharged control freak side—I would have never married you in the first place. Because now I'm sorry I did."

He turned and left the room.

The brutality of his words hit her like axe blows, made even more painful because she could see an awful truth in there.

He was right.

In a trance, Meg finished packing her clothes. She walked the path to the still and empty front lobby. The chickens were just starting to crow, promising there was going to be a new day even if she did not want there to be.

She checked her phone. On an impulse, she checked the rideshare app that she used in Ottawa. Imagine that. It had transferred over. Given the earliness of the hour, the sleepiness of Kauai, she was astonished to see a car in the vicinity.

As she clicked on that car, she could not help but think how awful it was that leaving Morgan, again, had a terrible meant-to-be feeling to it.

When he returned to Vancouver, his anger carried Morgan through several weeks. The truth was, he fueled it. He *liked* being angry. It felt powerful. It felt as if his fury kept barriers up where they needed to be.

But in those moments when his guard came down, just before he slept at night, a little girl would come to him.

It wasn't his niece, Kendra.

No, it was a little girl who couldn't accept one good thing for herself, not even a movie with a friend.

Despite his trying to keep the message at bay with anger, Morgan in those sleepless moments at night, the full truth about his wife crept in.

She hadn't run away from him because she couldn't have a baby.

That was just a symptom.

She had run away because she didn't believe she deserved anything for herself. So part of what she had said was true— she could not adjust to the lifestyle. But it wasn't just the wealth and all the things that came with it.

No, what she couldn't adjust to was being loved. What Meg couldn't adjust to was coming first.

Understanding began to dull the sharp edges of Morgan's fury. He stood in the dilemma of the vulnerability that arose to take anger's place.

Did he protect himself?

Or did he summon some remnant of courage that remained in him, that was willing to risk it all, one last time, to rescue the woman he loved?

Meg was an absolute mess. She couldn't paint. She couldn't eat. She couldn't sleep. She was pretty sure the rent was due and she hadn't paid it. It was so much worse than the first time she had left Morgan.

She had seen the look of utter contempt on his face. She had destroyed the most precious thing she had ever had.

She had destroyed Morgan's love for her.

There was a loud knocking on the door. From somewhere in her haze of despair, she thought it was probably the landlord.

She wanted to ignore it, but what could possibly be made better by an eviction?

"Just a sec," she called. She got out of the rumple of sheets she was tangled in. She knew she looked like hell. Tangled hair, shadowed eyes, in her pajamas at three o'clock in the afternoon.

She went out of the bedroom. Her place was a mess. There were canvasses and easels everywhere. It was the beach series, the paintings she had not worked on since her return but that she hadn't been able to part with, either, despite rent being due and the gallery clamoring for more.

But also displayed on easels, around the living area of the small apartment, were the magical photos from Caylee and Jonathon's wedding.

She had one or two of the bride and groom displayed, but mostly she had photos of her and Morgan. His head bent over hers, smiling down at her, him chasing her playfully through the surf while she held up her dress. Him kissing her injured shoulder.

The photos were both a torment and a comfort.

But at the moment they added to the cluttered chaos in her apartment that Meg did not want the landlord to see.

"Mr. Jones?" she called through the door. "I'm e-transferring you right now."

No answer.

She opened her banking app, tapped furiously for a second. "There," she called. "It's done."

"Meg, open the door right now."

Everything in her went still. It wasn't her landlord on the other side of that door. It was Morgan.

And now, because she had spoken, mistaking him for the landlord, she could not pretend she wasn't here.

If she opened that door, he would know how she was suffering. He would see that she wasn't coping without him.

He would see the wedding photos and the beach paintings, her every longing on display for him.

Maybe he would understand how deep the well of her love

was, that she was willing to give up her own hope for him to have what he deserved.

What good could come from this?

She closed her eyes. She drew in a deep, shuddering breath. He did not need to know she was suffering.

"Now's not a good time," she called.

"You open this door, or I'm going to break it down."

If she was going to open the door, she needed to run a brush through her hair, maybe try to do something about the shadows under her eyes. She needed not to be in her pajamas looking defeated. She needed to hide the paintings. And especially the wedding photos.

"I'm counting to three."

Suddenly, pretending she was okay felt like way too much effort.

"One."

The back exit out the kitchen window seemed cowardly and pathetic.

"Two."

She was too weak not to open the door for him, too weak to deny herself seeing him again.

"Three."

She opened the door and stood before him, defeated, cowardly, pathetic and weak. The sight of her, and the mess behind her should make him do what everything else had not: turn tail and run. Save himself.

But he didn't turn tail and run.

He looked gorgeous, casual in faded jeans, a white T-shirt, a leather jacket. Some men, dressed like that, would look as if they didn't care about their appearance. Morgan looked ready for a front cover photo shoot for a men's magazine.

He stepped in and took in her place, his eyes resting on each of the photos and paintings, oddly not with surprise, but with a deep *knowing*.

"Caylee asked me to pick the best of the wedding photos for her," she said defensively, when his eyes lingered on the one of him kissing her shoulder.

"There doesn't seem to be that many of Caylee and Jonathon here," he pointed out.

She could feel her face turning crimson, just as he turned his full attention back and took her in. She realized Morgan looked as though he had been suffering as much as her.

His face was gaunt. There were dark circles under his eyes. He had cut off his beautiful curls, as if he was a soldier going into battle, as if caring for his hair was too much. She felt an absurd desire to touch his shorn head, and maybe she would have but Morgan did not look pathetic or weak.

He looked very, very strong, and his eyes were dark with resolve as they swept over her, missing nothing, taking in all the suffering she could not hide from him.

"Oh, Meggie," he said.

It felt as if she could defend herself against his fury. But that? His fury was, after all, about him. But this empathy was about her.

Morgan was reaching past his anger and caring about her, the one who had caused his anger in the first place.

She could feel some tenderness rising in her that she knew she did not have the strength to hold down. Again, she had to tuck her hands behind her so that she didn't give in to the temptation to touch his hair.

"Come in," she whispered, which was silly, because he was already in. She shut the door behind him.

He strode across her tiny living room, moved a heap of clothes off the sofa and sat down. As his dark eyes swept over her, it felt as if he knew every single secret about her.

She went over and sank into the chair across from him.

"You shouldn't have come," she said, but the way she drank him in gave lie to those words.

He lifted a broad shoulder. "I needed to come. You needed for me to come."

If she had the energy, she would argue that he had no right to tell her what she needed, but she didn't have the energy.

While she'd been sulking, and not eating, and not sleeping, she really should have been preparing herself for this final battle.

Of course, she had not foreseen it coming, and now she was in no kind of shape to fight all the feelings rising in her.

"I get it now," Morgan told her softly.

"Do you?"

"It was never about not giving me a baby. It was never about not being able to give me back a family."

Her mouth dropped open. "That is not true!"

"Oh, yes it is," he continued with soft determination.

"It was all about that," Meg said fiercely. "It was all about loving you enough to do what needed to be done."

He actually had the nerve to throw back his head and laugh. Then he stopped and took her in with a shake of his head.

"I almost fell for your lies," Morgan told her quietly.

"I've never lied to you."

"Couldn't handle the lifestyle?" he reminded her.

"Okay," she conceded, "that."

"But that lie was okay, wasn't it, because that was for my own good?"

"Correct," she said stiffly.

"It was never about the baby, Meg."

"It was. That's all it was about."

"You know who you're lying to?" he said, his voice so soft, barely a whisper. "Yourself."

She was silent, but she could feel fear pounding inside her chest. Fear, and maybe just a little tiny bit, hope.

"You didn't know what to do with someone putting you

first," he said, his voice still soft, caressing, like a touch. "You didn't know how to be the one who got the attention. You didn't know how to be the center of my universe. You didn't know how to accept pampering and gifts and someone genuinely cherishing you. You didn't know how to *accept* love. Only how to give it.

"What you couldn't handle was being with someone who didn't need you to make sacrifices. What a sense of emptiness that must have caused in you. How could it be love when it wasn't causing you pain, when you weren't scrambling to fix things and giving up every single thing that gave you pleasure?"

Meg's mouth fell open as his arrows of truth hit her heart.

"It must have felt so familiar, so comforting, so satisfying," he continued softly, his eyes never leaving her face, "when you found you couldn't have a baby."

"It was the most devastating moment of my whole life," she said hoarsely.

"No, it wasn't," he challenged her. "It was like coming home. You could give it all up for someone else, the way you've done your entire life. You could be the martyr."

She stared at him. She took in the look in his eyes. There was truth there. And so much love. She began to cry.

"If I let you," he said softly. "You could throw it all away in a misguided sacrifice intended to give me a better life. But, Meg, I'm not letting you. You saved me when I was trying to deal with the loss of my family."

"No," she said through her tears, "you saved me."

"Don't you see? That's what people do. They save each other. You don't overcome those kinds of things alone. That's what we promised when we said *I do*. That we would have each other's backs, that we would heal each other and save each other."

The truth of what Morgan was saying pierced the darkness around Meg like a shard of sunlight finding its way through dark clouds.

She understood, suddenly, the gift she was being given.

Someone who *saw* her completely.

Who saw her flaws and her secrets and was willing to love her anyway. Who had found the bravery to come here, to face, once again, the possibility of her rejection, so that she *knew*.

She was loved exactly as she was.

She did not have to be alone.

That this man would have her back, no matter what.

She could not walk away from what Morgan was offering her. Not this time. She'd been granted a reprieve from the life she had sentenced herself to and she opened to it like a parched flower opening to life-giving rain.

She got up from her chair, crossed the floor to him, lowered herself onto his lap and finally, finally, touched his hair.

She had thought it might feel bristly, like the new growth of whiskers. But it didn't. His short, short hair felt glorious and soft under her fingertips. She curled her arms around his neck.

She knew it didn't matter to him that she was a mess. In fact, Morgan knew she was a mess, in every possible sense, and he had come anyway.

"Is that yes?" he asked gruffly. "To trying again?"

"Absolutely," she whispered. Her lips found his, and she allowed herself to revel in a sweet sensation she had thought she might never have, ever again.

He kissed her back with tender welcome at first, but the pent-up passion erupted between them.

He held her to him, stood, found his way to the bedroom and put her down on the bed.

"Mrs. Hart," he whispered.

"Mr. Hart," she said, and it felt like a vow. She opened her arms to him, and he came into them.

They were home.

A long time later, nestled in each other's arms, she reveled in the simple rise and fall of his naked chest under her cheek.

"I think we should go to Hawaii and renew our vows," he said sleepily.

"Isn't that what we just did?"

He stroked her hair. "I want to do it again. We'll do it the right way this time."

"It was right last time," she said.

"I want to celebrate it with the world, the way Jonathon and Caylee did."

She could tell it meant the world to him, and she did love the idea of including all their friends in this: the hope and the healing of love.

"Is your shoulder completely better?"

Meg giggled. "You couldn't tell?"

"Okay, because I'm not going back to Kauai until you can snorkel."

"I could be ready for tomorrow," she said huskily.

"No! I'm sure it will take some time to make all the arrangements."

"It won't really. We have wedding-in-a-box. We could probably have all those clothes that Caylee ended up not using."

"I loved you in that dress," he agreed. "Still, accommodations, invitations—"

"Should we say we'll return to Kauai to renew our vows with all our friends as soon as it's humanly possible?"

"Finally," Morgan said tenderly, "we're on the same page."

"Forever," she agreed softly.

EPILOGUE

Three years later

IT WAS AN absolutely perfect summer day. A sun-on-pine-scented breeze drifted through Morgan's open office window, and he looked out at Okanagan Lake. The surface of its navy blue water was sprinkled with thousands of glinting sunshine stars.

He was getting some last-minute paperwork done before company started arriving at Sarah's Reach for the weekend.

He heard the shriek of a child, followed by a splash, gales of laughter and then Meg's quiet voice in the background.

Morgan got up from his desk and took the adjoining door out onto the deeply shaded deck that wrapped around the whole cottage.

It was a better vantage point to see them.

His family.

They were out there on the float, the four children, the boys shoving at each other, while Ophelia ran joyous circles around them, squealing. Meg sat cross-legged at the center of it all with Marie, thumb in mouth, fighting a losing battle to keep her eyes open. Meg looked, in the middle of that happy summer chaos, calm and light-filled.

Meg's beach series—those whimsical paintings of families enjoying the sand and water on perfect summer days—had become her bestselling work ever.

Looking at this scene before him, Morgan couldn't help but wonder: How had she been able to paint the future? Had it been a premonition? Or had she literally been *drawing* this scene, playing out before him now, into reality?

Of course, as was the way with the world, this was not the life he and Meg had planned. Not even close.

They had investigated every option that would bring them a baby. They had looked at everything from in vitro to surrogacy. They had been approved by a global adoption agency. Unlike many in their position, Morgan and Meg Hart had unlimited resources.

Ironically, it was not their resources, in the end, that brought them to family. It was that worst of human travesties.

War.

A friend had told them, almost in passing, about a story she had heard. A bombed building collapsing, a mother and father killed, three children and a baby pulled, unharmed, protected by the bodies of their parents, from the rubble.

Though, of course, unharmed was a relative term.

He often thought—especially now—of those protestors he and Meg had seen in Hawaii, waving their signs and chanting their slogans against war, oblivious to the fact that their anger was the very thing war sprang from.

And then there had been Kamelei, keeping the values of her culture safe in the face of an ironic assault against it by people who claimed to be against the importation of values from other cultures.

His and Meg's relationship with the shop owner had deepened over the years. Meg had done some artwork for her that had ended up being printed onto fabric for her clothing line.

Morgan hoped he carried some of the things Kamelei continued to teach them about *aloha* within him.

Problems could not be solved from the same place they had sprung.

Love was the only force that changed things.

And love in action took on a force and power like nothing else that existed.

Life had taught Morgan the hardest of lessons. All his wealth and all his power and all his success had not been able to hold back calamity.

He was a man painfully aware he could not save the world.

And yet, that didn't mean he couldn't try. That didn't mean he couldn't save some.

Morgan was not sure his resources had ever been put to a better use than finding those children. He had been pushed by a force so compelling he could, to this day, not explain it.

He and Megan had known what they would do even before they met those children. Max, eight, Stefan, six, Ophelia, three, and Marie, at that time just turned a year.

Those children. Max, radiating anger and lashing out. Stefan, hostile to the world, cold and withdrawn. Ophelia, completely shut down, a zombie child. And Marie, a baby who could not sleep more than fifteen minutes without waking up screaming and terrified.

He and Meg had known, without a single word passing between them, that they had not, after all, been broken by their losses. Their losses had prepared them. For this.

They were possibly the two people most qualified to love children that some might say—and did say—were damaged beyond repair by the horrific harms they had survived.

But in that moment, meeting those children for the first time, this is what Morgan and Meg knew. They had been made for this challenge.

They had also felt loss so crushing it felt as if you could not breathe, let alone rise from it.

But both of them also knew this: beneath all that blackness, beneath the char of a life destroyed, a spark of spirit remained, a spark that could not, ever, be extinguished.

It was a tiny ember that love slowly fanned back to life.

Love took so many different forms, and he had seen this firsthand when he had watched Meg thrown into the arena of parenting four damaged children. It was the job she'd been born to do, her calling.

And in those first days and months, her love might not have looked like love at all. By instinct, she had been strict, firm, disciplined, unflagging.

"We are raising people to be responsible," she told him, after she'd put Max in his room for beheading a teddy bear. "We can't get there if we teach them it's okay to be mean, self-pitying, entitled, pampered.

"We can't get there if we give them the message *Oh, poor you, look what the world has done. Let's make up for it every day for the rest of our lives forever.*"

Having had a brother with a disability, Meg was uniquely placed. She knew it was too easy to let sympathy dissolve boundaries, to let pity accept the unacceptable.

"People," she told him, "do not have a ticket to be obnoxious because they've been victims."

As it turned out, what those children needed most, particularly at first, was not hugs and cuddles. What they needed was structure. Bedtime. Bath time. Storytime. Chores. A meal on the table every single day at the very same time.

They needed a sense that they were part of something bigger, necessary to something bigger.

That was how love had come to them.

And made them a family.

Love whispered of all their tragedies. *It's true. You will never be the same.*

But you will find reason in your suffering.

You will be led to your purpose.

You will be more than you were before: more compassionate, more intuitive, more humble, more able to surrender to a life path you have realized you cannot always control.

This, really, was what it was to be human. It was to suffer, and to rise from the suffering, not healed, but changed, altered in fundamental ways.

It was exactly the promise Morgan had seen in Meg's painting all those years ago. On the wings of love, you will rise out of the ashes.

His and Meg's life experiences had made them the perfect parents to these grieving children.

Sarah's Reach had also risen from the ashes. The cabin rebuilt, but just like Meg and Morgan, she would be more than she was before.

Sometimes, late at night, Morgan, who had always considered himself the most pragmatic of men, thought he heard the giggles of Kendra and James in the hallways of the new house, sometimes he thought he heard the rumble of his brother's laugh. Sometimes, he thought he heard a wheelchair on the wooden floors, and caught a shadowy glimpse of a boy he had never met. Sometimes, he felt as if his sister-in-law looked at Max and Stefan, at Ophelia and Marie, and touched his shoulder.

Whispered an approving, grateful *yes*.

Whether they were really there or whether they were a figment of his imagination, Morgan knew he and Meg were using their lives to honor the love that they grew out of.

On the other side of the bluff, he could hear hammers hitting wood, the voices of men calling to each other.

It was the first phase. Someday, a camp would be here, in this place where his family had known so much joy.

Hart's Reach would gather the children of trauma, and give them a respite from whatever horrors the world had brought them.

It would give them a small window of hope. It would show

them there were safe places in the world. It would show them there would be laughter again.

It would just be that little breath of love that would fan to life that flicker of hope that lived, unquenchable, in each human heart.

As he watched, Stefan, who had been pushed off the float, hoisted himself back on it. He chased his bigger brother, and they wrestled playfully until Max pretended he had been overwhelmed, and they both fell in the water.

Right now, it felt as if every single thing they had been through had led to this moment. From the other direction, Morgan heard a car door slam, and Caylee's voice, calling to her and Jonathon's twins.

"Joseph, Jolie, do not go that way, do not—"

Morgan could imagine Jonathon chasing after those rambunctious children, tucking one under each arm.

Caylee's voice came again, "It's like herding cats…"

In the last three years, almost every single member of that wedding party had gotten married.

Part of it, Morgan knew, was because they were just at that stage of life where people began to settle.

But he also wondered how much of those beautiful, blissful times they had all spent together on the island of Kauai had influenced this.

He and Meg had renewed their vows there six months after their reconciliation. The same group of people had come back.

Meg laughingly called it wedding-in-a-box since they had used all those items of clothing that had been the backup plan for Caylee.

So, her dress did not equal the budget of a small country for a year, and yet as Meg had walked across the sand toward him, Morgan had been aware that there had never been a more beautiful bride than her.

The sound of a door opening jarred him out of that memory. "Hello?" Jonathon called.

And then he heard little feet running, and Jolie calling out, "Unkie? Unkie? Unkie?"

A shiver went up and down his spine, because it was so like moments he'd had with his niece, Kendra.

He and Meg had lost family, and that grief was always there. And yet, so was an understanding that family was bigger than blood bonds, and that everything you lost would come back to you, maybe in a different form, but it would come back to you nonetheless.

Came back to you, multiplied.

Look at those children out on the dock right now.

Their friends who had married were all starting to have children. Again, it was that time of life, though Meg liked to claim it was because she had touched the Hawaiian fertility god, Lono. She said that what you wished for yourself blessed your friends, as well.

Sarah's Reach was filling up with families again. Laughter. Skinned knees and kisses, the smell of marshmallows, the shriek of warm bodies hitting cold water.

This is what he and Meg had said when they got married.

And then Jonathon and Caylee.

And then their other friends.

This is what they said when they had babies and sheltered children in need, and created families in an uncertain and an unpredictable world where there were no guarantees.

These were acts of pure hope.

These were the arrows manifested by faith. They carried a belief in the goodness of life, and the truth of love. Tentatively, they were removed from the quiver, set against a taut string, that bow stretched back and back and back.

And when it could be pulled no farther, when the arm that held it was trembling with effort, then the arrow was released.

Shooting forward in a beautiful, powerful arc.

Soaring, unstoppable, toward its destination. This was pure faith in the power of love, to send this arrow to a place only partially visible to the archer, to a place he would never be able to explore completely.

Love sent its arrows, strong and true, toward the greatest of all mysteries.

The future.

* * * * *

If you enjoyed this story,
check out these other great reads
from Cara Colter

The Billionaire's Festive Reunion
Accidentally Engaged to the Billionaire
Winning Over the Brooding Billionaire
Hawaiian Nights with the Best Man

All available now!

MILLS & BOON ®

Coming next month

FAKING IT WITH THE BOSS
Michele Renae

'It's late, but do you have time for the entrance interviews?' the receptionist asked. 'They take about fifteen minutes and will help us to fine-tune your schedule for the week.'

Asher glanced at her and shrugged.

Maeve grabbed his hand. 'Just a second. I need to talk to my boss—er...boyfriend.' With a forced smile to the receptionist, she then tugged Asher aside near the fountain bubbling in the center of the pristine Prussian-blue-tiled lobby.

'What's up, sweetie? Sorry. Maeve.'

A momentary thrill of hearing him say her name swept through her like a cyclone, only to be followed by an even bigger, and more harrowing, disaster. 'It's this.' She waved the flyer between them. 'This is not just a couples' spa vacation.'

'What? The signs say Reconnecting Romance. Kind of cute.'

'Right, it is a spa, and about romance, but it's also focused on this.' She turned the flyer toward him and tapped the top line.

Asher read, 'Relationship *rehab*?'

Maeve swore under her breath. 'I'm so sorry, I didn't notice this when signing up. I can't believe I let that slip by me.'

'What does it mean exactly?'

'It means that not only are we faking being a couple, now we're going to have to fake relationship issues. We're here to *fix* our relationship, not relax and rejuvenate.'

Asher winked at her. 'Guess I'm calling you sweetie after all.'

He turned and told the receptionist they could do their interviews now.

Continue reading

FAKING IT WITH THE BOSS
Michele Renae

Available next month
millsandboon.co.uk

COMING SOON!

We really hope you enjoyed reading this book.
If you're looking for more romance
be sure to head to the shops when
new books are available on

Thursday 27th February

To see which titles are coming soon, please visit
millsandboon.co.uk/nextmonth

MILLS & BOON

FOUR BRAND NEW BOOKS FROM
MILLS & BOON MODERN

The same great stories you love, a stylish new look!

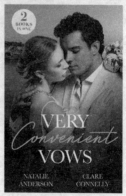

OUT NOW

Eight Modern stories published every month, find them all at:

millsandboon.co.uk

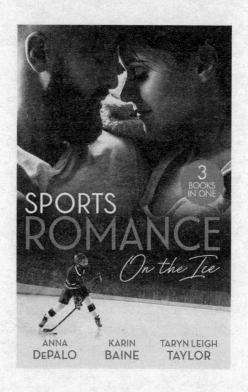

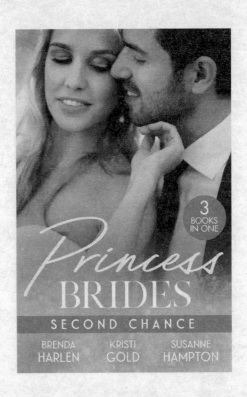

LET'S TALK
Romance

For exclusive extracts, competitions
and special offers, find us online:

- MillsandBoon
- @MillsandBoon
- @MillsandBoonUK
- @MillsandBoonUK

Get in touch on 01413 063 232